CAPTIVE SECRETS

CAPTIVE SECRETS

Fern Michaels

This title first published in Great Britain 1996 by
SEVERN HOUSE PUBLISHERS LTD of
9–15 High Street, Sutton, Surrey SM1 1DF.
First published in hardcover format in the USA 1996 by
SEVERN HOUSE PUBLISHERS INC. of
595 Madison Avenue, New York, NY 10022,
by arrangement with Ballantine Books,
a division of Random House, Inc.

British Library Cataloguing in Publication Data

Michaels, Fern
  Captive secrets
  1. American fiction – 20th century
  I. Title
  813.5'4 [F]

  ISBN 0-7278-4939-5

Typeset by Palimpsest Book Production Limited,
Polmont, Stirlingshire, Scotland.
Printed and bound in Great Britain by
Hartnolls Ltd, Bodmin, Cornwall.

For Chelly Kitzmiller, Dorsey Adams, and Jill Landis

Author's Note

There are many species of hawks to be studied. For this novel I chose the goshawk because I fell in love with the winged creature's capabilities. I was astounded to find that a hawk, if hand-raised, could become a loyal pet capable of deep affection, anger, and jealousy. They're also generous, offering tidbits of their food to those they like. They love to tease and provoke for a gentle caress. They adore sparkly stones and bright colors. Often they "borrow" items and return them days later. Their prowess in the air is nothing short of incredible. They can fly a mile high in the air and rocket downward almost as fast as a speeding bullet and can literally stop in midair, work the wind, and continue downward or onward. They're loyal to their owner, mate, and young, and will kill any attacker with their talons, their only weapon, if they feel threatened. They're also known for their long-distance flying, sometimes six to eight hours at a time and often through the entire night.

I ask your indulgence and to believe, as I do, that there really could have been a Gaspar and Pilar in 1665.

F.M.

Prologue

Java, 1665

The old salt smacked his lips over toothless gums, relishing the moment the stranger standing before him would hand over the jug of rum.

The stranger was tall, muscular, with the torso of a tree trunk, arms full of hard muscle that rippled beneath the fine lawn shirt he wore open to his belt buckle. He was bronzed by the sun, a seaman by the look of him. The old man narrowed his eyes, trying to see around the cataracts that filmed them. Handsome, he thought. Hair as black as a raven's wing and eyes the color of . . . He searched for a word from his past to describe the stranger's eyes. Coal-black, like pitch. He'd never seen such black eyes before, and these held something else he'd never seen: contempt. Oh, he'd seen his share of emotions over his eighty-six years, but always love, hate, anger, or vengeance. He blinked his bleary eyes for a better look, but the film blotted out the fine details of the man's features.

"I would hear your tale, old man, and for the pleasure of your company the jug is yours." The stranger spoke quietly, his voice deep and . . . educated, the old man decided.

"And what name do you go by?" he asked, eyeing the jug greedily.

1

"Is it important?" the man asked blandly.

"A man needs a name when he drinks with another man. Every mother gives her babe a name. Mine is Jacobus."

The stranger debated a second before replying. The old lush would finish off his jug and not remember a thing. Lies always come back to slap one in the face.

"Luis Domingo," he said at last, and smiled—a flash of white teeth in the hazy lamplight that reminded Jacobus of a shark at feeding time.

Luis Domingo . . . The old man rolled the strange-sounding name over his toothless gums and thick tongue. He'd never heard it before, but then, his memory wasn't what it used to be. "You smell of the sea. I like that. Sit down and I'll begin my tale if you'll pass that jug along." When the stranger slid the bottle across the table, Jacobus snatched it and brought it to his lips. After a hearty pull, he wiped his mouth with the palm of his hand and sat back with a contented sigh.

"She had the face of an angel, the Sea Siren did. She was so beautiful, even her enemies fell about her feet. Her heart was pure, and she always spared the unfortunate souls who sought to attack her. Mind you, she fought fair. Oftentimes she would switch from a cutlass to a rapier without a misstep. Razor-sharp they were. Shiny like a hawk's eye and just as deadly. I seen her myself, hundreds of times, as she danced across that black ship like the sea sprite she was." He paused to take several long swallows of the fiery liquid in the jug, then picked up on his words immediately.

"There wasn't a man at sea that didn't hunger for the Sea Siren. Her eyes saw everything at a glance. Like emeralds they were. Her hair was black as yours, and it rode her head like a raven's wings. Her skin was like cream in a crock. She carried a wicked scar on her arm that men would have died from, but not the Sea Siren. There wasn't a man that could best her in a duel. Not a single man.''

Jacobus's voice became dreamlike as his memories took him back in time. ''The black ship she sailed was like a ghost. One minute it was there and the next minute it would disappear. Into nothing. She had this laugh that carried across the water. Made many a man's blood run cold,'' he said in awe.

''They could never catch her, and hundreds tried. She ruined the man who was the head of the Dutch East India Company. Sank his ships because his men raped and killed her sister. She swore revenge on the bastards and killed every single one of them—fair and square.

''The Dutch East India Company put a price on her head, and handsome it was, but to naught.''

''You make her sound like a saint in a costume,'' Domingo said coldly. ''She was a pirate and she pillaged and plundered ships, so how can you say she—''

''If you know all about her, then why are you asking me to tell you what I know?'' Jacobus said, bristling at the stranger's words. ''I seen her hundreds of times. Once she smiled at me, and it was like the Madonna herself gazing on me. She never hurt those who didn't deserve to be hurt. She never kept a thing from the ships she boarded but let her crew have it. Rights of salvage.''

The old man swigged again from the bottle, and then continued, his words slurring slightly. ''I think she came down from heaven. That's my own opinion, because she . . . she would just disappear in a cloud of fog. You could hear her laugh ringing across the water when she was victorious. My hair stood on end. Such strength she had, it wasn't human, I can tell you that. I seen her the day she dueled with Blackheart. He was twice her size and twice her weight, and she cut him down. 'Course he was maimed from his first encounter with her, so he wasn't starting even with her. That blade danced in the sun, I can tell you that. Blood rivered the decks of that frigate.'' Jacobus lowered his voice to a hushed whisper. ''That black ship was . . . magic. She sailed high on the water with a speed I've never seen. Never!'' The old man sat back once more and gulped from the bottle.

Domingo leaned forward on his chair, his dark eyes piercing the old man like twin daggers. ''Do you expect me to believe this garbage that a woman, even a beautiful woman sailing a black ship, is something mythical?''

The anger in his voice jolted Jacobus, who looked up groggily. ''Real or magic, I don't know. I told you what I seen,'' he said fearfully, suddenly aware that the stranger's eyes were angry and calculating. All sign of contempt was gone.

''Where is this infamous black ship now, and where is the Sea Siren?'' Domingo asked harshly.

The fine hairs on the back of Jacobus's neck prickled. He'd said too much. He had to hold his tongue now and not give away the fact that he'd been a member of the Sea Siren's crew. The rum jug beckoned, but he set it on the table. If this stranger had a mind to, he could rip out his tongue and . . . ''Only God knows,'' he blustered.

Domingo laughed, a chilling sound in the sudden hush that had descended over the tavern. ''Does this Sea Siren's god allow her to kill and maim and . . . disappear into thin air? A fine story from a drunken sot.''

Jacobus did his best to meet Domingo's dark gaze. ''It's not a story, it's true. There is a Sea Siren, and there is a black ship. I don't know where they are. No one has seen either for over twenty years.''

Domingo's eyes turned to slits as he leaned across the table. ''Is she dead, old man? Is the Sea Siren and that black ship at the bottom of the sea? Tell me the truth, or

I'll wring that stringy neck of yours. Or is this a fairy tale?''

Jacobus shook the man's hands off his shoulders. "It's no fairy tale. Go to the offices of the Dutch East India Company and see for yourself. A wanted poster has been hanging there for twenty-five years. And when the Sea Siren is needed, her ship will sail again. You mark my words.''

Domingo stomped from the room, the laughter of the tavern's patrons ringing in his ears. Were they laughing at him? Was it all a trick of the old sot's? Tomorrow at first light he'd go to the Dutch East India offices and see for himself. This was the closest he'd come to actual proof that the legendary Sea Siren really existed and wasn't a figment of his father's imagination. The Sea Siren and the deadly black ship she'd captained had ruined his father.

Domingo's head reared back as he bellowed into the night. "If you're alive, I'll kill you for what you did to my father! No quarter given!''

Chapter One

Cadiz, Spain, 1665

Furana van der Rhys fingered the costly material of her ball gown, a gown of her mother's choosing, with deep sadness. She would wear it this once, and then it would be packed away with all her other worldly possessions. The sadness in her indigo eyes deepened as she gazed around her bedroom. For many years she'd slept in this room, cried in this room, fought and played with her brothers in this same room . . . and always at the end of the day she prayed.

For days now she'd kept herself busy packing up her things in huge brass-bound trunks that would be carried to the attic when she left this house, this room, for the last time. There was very little left now to prove she'd inhabited it all these years, save her comb and brush and the jewelry she would wear for her birthday ball. When the clock struck midnight she'd be twenty-one years old. Parents and old friends would toast her and say good-bye. Only then would she smile.

At noon the next day she would leave for the convent, where she would lead a cloistered life until her death. It was the only thing she'd ever wanted. For years her parents had denied her entrance into the convent, saying she was too young and didn't know her mind. Finally they'd agreed that she could follow her vocation when she was twenty-one and of age. Just a few more hours. . . .

Fury, as her parents called her, walked away from the elaborate ball gown to stare out at the bright sunshine she loved. She'd been so happy here, growing up with teasing, boisterous brothers, climbing trees, sliding down trellises, and chasing after her siblings as they played game after game.

Doubts assailed her, and immediately she started to finger her rosary. She was doing the right thing, the right thing for her. Only once had she questioned her vocation—when her four brothers were lost at sea aboard the *Rana*. After their deaths, she was all that was left to her parents; only she could provide grandchildren to carry on the ancient lineage. But the thought of herself with a man—and a child of that union—brought a rush of color to her cheeks. A man, a strange man who would covet her . . . want to make love to her . . . Her lips moved faster, fingers furiously working the beads in her hand.

A fluffy cloud sailed overhead and dimmed the sun for a moment. Fury blinked to ward off tears. Of course she would miss the sun and the bright blue sky. She would miss a lot of things, at first. But she would adapt to the cloistered life, learn to sleep on a straw pallet, adjust to the perpetual gloom of the convent. The vow of silence would be hardest to accept, but that was years away, not until her novitiate was over. She would be ready then.

The rosary at an end, Fury pocketed the beads. If she hurried, she could say another in the chapel before lunch, this one for her parents. It was going to be so hard for them when their only remaining child stepped aboard the ship that would take her back to Java. Will I have the strength to leave, Fury wondered, to say good-bye to those I love with all my heart? She had to trust in God that her leavetaking would be bearable for all of them.

The chapel was small, intimate, built for her mother by her father, who was not of his wife's faith. It had been a labor of love, and any who entered to worship thought it a beautiful place, peaceful and holy. Fury herself had from her early years kept fresh flowers on the small altar—mostly jasmine, her mother's favorite. The rosary found its way to her hand, familiar prayers tumbling from her lips. *"I believe in God the Father . . ."*

Sirena van der Rhys crept close to the chapel, her emerald eyes full of unshed tears. She knew Fury would be inside, but she could not bring herself to cross the threshold. Her daughter, the most precious jewel in her crown, would soon be lost to her forever.

Sirena swallowed past the lump in her throat. Fury was so beautiful. Long-limbed like herself, and with the same tawny skin, but with her father's indigo eyes and square jaw. She had Sirena's hair, but Fury's was thick and curly, cascading down to the small of her back. As a child she had changed her hairstyle seven times a day, delighting in using all manner of jeweled combs and sparkling hairpins. Once she entered the convent, they'd shave her head and make a pillow of her hair.

Sirena raised her eyes heavenward. "Why?" she whispered. "Why are you doing this to me? You've taken everything from me—my parents, my firstborn, Miguel. Wasn't that enough? Five sons I've given up to you, and now you're taking my only daughter. You're punishing me, aren't you? For all those years I sailed the seas to avenge my sister and uncle. I renounced you as my God, and now you're claiming what is yours. What kind of God are you, that you leave me with nothing? Miracles are for other people, not the likes of the Sea Siren, is that it?"

Sirena's knees buckled and she would have slipped to the floor but for her husband, who had come up silently behind her and now caught her in his arms. "I have no God anymore, Regan," Sirena whispered to him. "He has forsaken me. I will never say another prayer. Never!" she cried against his shoulder as he carried her away from the chapel entrance to their bedroom at the far end of the casa.

Regan felt his throat constrict as he gently lowered his wife to the bed. Memories of Fury, their beloved little girl, washed over him in wave after wave of anguish. He remembered her birth—during the eye of the worst storm ever to attack Java. It had been a difficult labor, but he had seen Sirena through it. The child had squalled furiously at the first smack to her bottom. Regan recalled his words from that long-ago time: "This one is a fury, Sirena!" he'd said proudly as the storm descended on Java. When they christened the tiny bundle a month later, it was he who said she was to be called Furana. "So you'll never forget the *Rana*," he'd murmured to his wife. Now he struggled in his mind for the right words to tell her that things would be all right. But he knew they wouldn't be. He knew this beautiful woman so well, knew her better than he knew himself. The moment Fury left their lives, Sirena would climb into the same shell she'd closed about herself when their other children died. She would be lost to him. And when that happened, his own will to live would shrivel and die.

Sirena met her husband's anxious gaze with shimmering, tear-filled eyes. She knew him so well, knew exactly what he was thinking, and she wanted so much to say the words he needed to hear. She loved this man with every breath in her body. He was so handsome, with his fair hair and bronze skin. Her Dutchman. They'd gone to hell and back and survived, but this . . . At last she shook her head and smiled at him.

"I'm all right now, darling," she said, brushing away her tears. "And I promise that I won't put you through any more misery. In the past my grief consumed me, but I won't let it happen again. When we sail for the Americas tomorrow at sundown, this life will be behind us. You have my word. Come, now we must get ready for dinner. Fury will be waiting for us.''

Regan was almost dizzy with relief at his wife's words. And when Sirena reached up and kissed him full on the lips—a long, lingering kiss—his pain melted away, and he forgot everything but the love he bore for this, the most beautiful woman in the world.

While the house buzzed and seethed with preparations for her birthday ball, Fury perched on the wide windowsill of the secluded breakfast nook at the back of the house. She loved this sunny spot and her feathered friends waiting outside the window. Fury's eyes scanned the birds, looking for Gaspar, the wide-winged goshawk she'd found as a wounded nestling and raised with care. Gaspar was always the last to arrive, and he did so with silent fanfare, his wings flapping with authority. The smaller birds, Gaspar's offspring, took wing and circled overhead until his perch was steady. Fury giggled as they flew down to take positions to the left and right of their impressive sire. She was reminded of a row of soldiers awaiting orders, she the general in command. She clapped her hands and watched in amusement as twenty pairs of eyes turned to watch her expectantly.

· ''Ladies first.'' She smiled as she held out a handful of meat scraps flavored with congealed bacon fat. One by one the birds ate their fill, pecking daintily from the palm of her hand. When they finished she said, ''Shoo,'' and as one they flew to separate perches in the trees.

Gaspar waited patiently for the words that would signal it was his turn. And as always, it was her scarred arm, thonged with leather, that he perched on—the right one, scored deeply in several places from a long-ago battle to save him from the talons of a huge marauding kite. "For you, my darling," Fury crooned. "Eat like a gentleman." And he did, allowing her at the same time to tweak his long beak with her soft touch.

"I'm going to miss you, Gaspar, and all the others, too, but I have to go," Fury murmured. "I'll never forget you." Gaspar cocked his dark head and stared at her with his shiny eyes. "I know you understand everything I say. From the day I saved you, we . . . it must be like that special feeling a mother has when her baby recovers from a sickness after she nurses it through the night. You'll always belong to me, Gaspar. And you'll be well taken care of when I've gone, that's a promise. Now it's time for you to get out of this hot sun. Go, and later I'll have a special treat for your little ones. Take this to Pilar for now," she said, holding out two small chunks of bacon fat. Gaspar took both pieces in his talons and flew high into the trees, where Pilar sat with her fresh crop of nestlings. Fury had christened the two tiny birds the moment they'd emerged from their protective shells: Sato and Lago. She had no way of knowing from the vantage point at her bedroom window if the birds were male or female. And she'd never see the little ones take wing for the first time. A single tear dropped to her hand. She would miss them terribly. Another tear fell on her hand as two pairs of dark eyes watched from the branches overhead. Wings flapped and leaves rustled as the young woman wiped away her tears with a lace-edged handkerchief.

"Fury," Sirena called from beyond the closed bedroom door, "is it safe to come in?"

Fury smiled and opened the door to her mother. "Yes, they're gone, Mother, dinner is over. I think Gaspar knows I'm leaving. Pilar, too. It makes me very sad."

It was on the tip of Sirena's tongue to beg her daughter

one more time to change her mind, but she resisted the impulse. Fury loved Gaspar and Pilar as much as she loved her family—in a way, they were *part* of her family—but she was willing to leave them behind. "The cook will take good care of them, darling."

"I know, Mother, it's just that Gaspar is like a child to me. I will worry about him and Pilar, I can't help it." She shook her head and sighed. "I'm not very hungry. Would you mind if I walked through the garden for a while?"

"Of course not, go along. But I'd like you to take a nap before the ball. Will you do that for me?"

"Of course, Mother, but only if you promise to take one, too."

Sirena nodded, not trusting her voice, and gave her daughter a kiss as she left the room.

"She has so many good-byes," Regan said hoarsely. "Every bird, every animal in the garden, will get a pat and a few words of loving remembrance. My God, Sirena, what did we do wrong to make our daughter want to leave us like this?"

Sirena toyed with the food on her plate and tried to speak past the lump in her throat. "Is it possible we loved her too much? . . . Oh, Regan, we can't talk about this again, it's killing me." Sirena's eyes flew to the wall above the sideboard in the dining room. Crossed rapiers, hers and Regan's, gleamed in the filtered sunlight. "He's punishing me, Regan, you, too. I know you don't believe in Fury's God, but this time you must believe me. We're being punished."

Regan's clenched fist pounded the table, causing china and silver to dance in front of their eyes. "I refuse to believe that! I won't believe some . . . spirit controls our lives, our daughter's life. I never understood all those holy words you say over wooden beads. It's demented. If there is a God, why did he allow your sister to be raped and killed? And our sons. What kind of God would allow our flesh and blood to be lost at sea? Why did he allow you to suffer so, and why is he taking Fury from us? How many times you called me a heathen, Sirena, because I don't believe. Twice now you have renounced this God of yours. Is it going to help matters? Is Fury going to stay with us? The answer is no."

Sirena lifted her head, her green eyes sparkling dangerously. How many times they'd had this same conversation, and always it ended in anger, with each of them going for their rapiers and threatening the other with death. "Damn you, Regan, not today! I refuse to fence with you."

"And I have no time to fence with the winner," came a soft voice from the dining room threshold.

Regan and Sirena whirled about, surprised. Then Sirena laughed, the tense moment between her husband and herself broken . . . which had been Fury's intention. Always before when husband and wife worked out their hostilities with the rapier, it was the daughter who fenced with the winner. Every bit as artful as Sirena, she also had the stamina and hard-driving determination of Regan. She'd lost only one match, and that had been several years before. Now she was better than ever with a rapier. The cutlass was another story altogether. Her father had worked with her for hours at a time, strengthening her weakened right arm until even he had admitted they were evenly matched.

Fencing was an art, a sport, and Fury excelled at it just as she did at everything. She knew she brought tears to her mother's eyes when she plucked the strings of her guitar and again when her nimble fingers slid over the spinet that sat in the drawing room. Her voice was trained, thanks to her mother, and she often sang for guests.

They'd given her everything, these wonderful parents, big strapping brothers to love, a fine education, their love, this beautiful casa to live in . . . everything parents gave a child, and now she was casting it all aside.

Sirena gazed warmly into Regan's eyes. "She's right, darling, today is not the day to vent our hostilities." She rose to embrace her husband.

Watching them, Fury smiled. Now she knew *exactly* what her parents would be doing later instead of fighting.

"I think that I will check on the progress in the ballroom," she drawled. "Guests should be arriving in a few hours. I want to make sure there are enough fresh flowers." Sirena winked roguishly at her daughter as she and her husband glided from the room.

As Fury walked through the halls, she thought about her parents and their wonderful life. They loved passionately, quarreled just as passionately, and nothing would ever separate them. They lived and loved for each other. She thought it miraculous the way their love had survived all these years. "There are other kinds of love," she muttered to herself as she picked a wilted leaf from a flower arrangement. Love *had* to be more than just physical—passion-bruised lips, sweaty bodies, touching and caressing . . . When she was fifteen her mother had tried to explain about that side of it, but she'd felt too much shame to listen. *That* had been a mistake. She should have tried to understand instead of harboring such wicked imaginings. Right now, this very second, her parents were probably . . . touching, feeling, kissing . . . Swallowing hard, she ran down the corridor like a wild boy past her parents' bedroom. Face flaming, she made her way to the pond in the garden, where she dropped to her knees and splashed cool water on her burning cheeks.

The air around her churned as Gaspar and Pilar, their huge wings creating an umbrella over her, finally settled on her shoulders. Fury sighed. "You always know when something is troubling me, don't you, Gaspar? Pilar, you get back to those babies right now, do you hear me? I'm fine. Gaspar, make her go back, the babies might tumble from the nest."

Gaspar daintily moved on her shoulder until one large wing nudged Pilar. Pilar tucked her head down and pecked Fury's cheek before she took wing.

"You have to be stern with her, Gaspar, she's a mother now. You must make sure nothing happens to the little ones. It's your responsibility to care for them until they can fly themselves. Look at me. Tomorrow I leave this nest and head for Java. It's time for me to leave and be on my own, to find my destiny. It's been so wonderful, but all things must come to an end. Come here, Gaspar, I need to hold you, to feel the beat of your heart, to know I'm the one who has saved you so that you could find Pilar and . . . and . . . make . . . babies like Sato and Lago. It's natural that this should happen for you, for others, but not for me. I promised myself to God, so these worldly emotions are not for me. You can go now," Fury cooed. "Go ahead, I'm fine now. Pilar will peck your eyes out if you don't behave yourself."

"Haw!" the huge bird squawked. Fury laughed as Gaspar flew toward the trees. "Haw!" his mate answered. Everyone, even the birds, had someone.

Fury flirted with her image in the mirror, twirling this way and that way to assess the effects of the costly gown on her lithe figure. Miss Antonia was to be congratulated: with this particular dress, the seamstress had achieved perfection. Her mother had chosen the design, but she had picked the color, a deep azure blue that complemented her indigo eyes and honey coloring. She loved the deep cleavage and the way the dress fell away from her tiny waist in deep swirls. Miniature seed pearls and sparkling gemstones were randomly sewn over the gown and along the length of the hem and sleeves, winking and shimmering every time she moved. Her mother would be delighted.

She'd dressed her own hair, piling it high on top of her head with ebony ringlets curling and feathering about her ears and neck. A veritable waterfall of diamonds graced her ears and slender throat. She would be the belle of this particular ball—her parting gift to her mother and father. They expected her to enjoy herself, to dance with all the eligible gentlemen and to flirt shamelessly. And she would; it wasn't too much to ask, and she was more than willing to create one last memory for her parents.

She was ready with minutes to spare, enough time to add just a smidgin of color to her lips and cheeks. Next she eyed the sparkling diamond garter her mother had given her when she was seventeen. It was decadently wicked, but as long as she was going through all the motions, she might as well put it on.

She braced one long, tawny leg on the dressing table bench and secured the garter a few inches above her knee. It fit as perfectly as it had the day of her seventeenth birthday. Cheeks awash with color, she walked to the mirror, skirts in hand, and stared at the precious gems adorning her thigh and felt a rush of heat through her body. She turned from the mirror in time to see Gaspar land daintily on the window ledge, his talons securing his position. "Haw."

"My sentiments exactly," Fury said, quietly letting her skirts drop. "I don't like the way this makes me feel, Gaspar. It . . . it makes me feel . . . so . . . sinful.

"I can't wear this," she muttered. "I don't know what Mother was thinking of when she gave it to me." In a frenzy she released the catch of the garter and threw it on the bed, where it shimmered like a snakeskin. Her color still high, she ran to the basin of water on her nightstand to wash her hands.

"Lord, forgive my sinful thoughts. I'm trying to do . . . to act . . . I'll never think such thoughts again," she gasped.

"Gaspar, Gaspar," she said, an hour later tripping over to the huge bird. "You've never seen me looking like this, have you? At first I felt rather silly, as though I were dressing up in Mother's clothes, but now . . . I rather like the way I look. It's just for this one night," she said, stroking the bird's velvety feathers.

His perch secure, the bird dipped its head and pecked at the dangling diamonds in her ear. Fury smiled. "I saw your babies fly. You should have warned me somehow, Gaspar. They were wobbly, but Pilar was right behind them. It was wonderful. Tomorrow they will fly farther and the day after still farther. The basket was a good idea, one of my better ones," Fury cooed to the hawk. "They all told me Pilar wouldn't make her nest in it because I touched it, but I knew better because you carried it to the trees for her. I feel like crying, Gaspar, and I don't know why. I'm going to miss you and this house and everyone. Part of me doesn't want to leave, that little part of me I'm selfishly withholding from God. That small part that is me, Furana. I want to give entirely of myself, but—" One large wing fluttered and opened to spread over Fury's dark head. For a moment she allowed herself to lean against the bird's hard chest. "Don't forget about me, Gaspar," she choked. "I must go now. I'm going to be late."

The hawk's eyes never left the girl until the door closed behind her. "Haw, haw, haw!" he screeched. An answering sound echoed down from the basket perched high in the breadfruit tree. The bird's talons dug deep into the chair back as his huge wings lifted outward. He swooped about the room, heading straight for Fury's bed. His talons dug into the coverlet until his grasp on the diamond garter was secure. His surge through the open window was swift and sure as he soared upward to his mate. "Haw, haw!"

"My God, Regan, she's a vision of beauty," Sirena whispered as Fury entered the ballroom.

Speechless, Regan stared at his daughter. She looked exactly like her mother. He wanted to say something, to compliment this child of his, but as always at moments like this, his tongue stuck to the roof of his mouth.

Fury assumed her position in the receiving line, and the formality of her birthday ball began. She smiled charmingly, every inch her mother's daughter as she greeted the guests who'd come to wish her well. When the last guest sailed through the flowered archway, Regan raised his hand to the musicians, their signal to start the music. Instantly a handsome young man claimed Fury and whisked her onto the dance floor.

"She's more graceful when she fences, don't you think?" Regan observed to Sirena as he saw his daughter stumble over her partner's foot.

"She gets her clumsiness from you," Sirena muttered. "We Spanish are light of foot, graceful, and demure." Regan chuckled as his wife glided away to mingle with her guests.

"Sirena, my dear, however did you manage all this?" Doña Louisa asked as she waved her arms about the flower-decked ballroom.

Sirena smiled and squeezed her friend's arm. "With a great deal of patience, Louisa," she said. "The flowers were brought in this afternoon from the greenhouses. I wanted to make sure they didn't wilt. Darling, you must try some of the rum punch we've laid out; it's a family recipe— Oh, there's Don Carlos. I must speak to him, Louisa. We'll talk more later, I promise.'' With that, Sirena hurried off into the crowd.

She had to admit that the great ballroom did look like something out of a fairy tale, with the monstrous crystal chandeliers and matching sconces that winked and twinkled with the dancers' movements. The musicians were dressed in impeccable white with crimson cravats and cummerbunds that set off the scarlet blooms surrounding the dais where they strummed their guitars. They were playing a lovely ballad, and more couples swirled onto the dance floor in time to the music.

Sirena moved to the rear of the room to check the serving tables. Her practiced eye told her everything was in order. The Spanish lace that had been in her family for ages was pressed and draped to perfection on the long tables, and she knew the linen skirts under the fine lace held no wrinkles either. Satisfied that the dining room and buffet tables could not be improved upon, she turned and peered over the heads of a young couple ready to move onto the dance floor. Fury whirled by in the arms of a dashing young man who devoured her with the eyes of a puppy, warm and adoring.

Catching sight of her mother, Fury grimaced, either at her own clumsiness on the dance floor or at her partner's obvious devotion. Sirena winked at her daughter to show she understood perfectly and then lost sight of her as the crush of dancing couples swallowed them up. Suddenly, Sirena found herself blinking back tears, and she hurried away.

When Fury lost sight of her mother, she returned her attention to the engaging young man in her arms. Ramon was everything a girl could wish for—charming, well brought up, and classically handsome, with olive-toned skin and ink-black eyes. He was also sweating profusely, and at last Fury took pity on him. "It's beastly hot in here, Ramon, would you like a breath of air? I know I would."

"Yes, yes, I would," he replied eagerly, his heart beginning to pound as she linked her arm in his to lead him off the dance floor and through the wide double doors to the veranda. If only he could kiss her, hold her face in his hands and kiss her until . . . He stumbled, and Fury's tinkling laugh made him bolt for the open door.

"What is it, Ramon, do you feel faint?" Fury asked as she noticed the young man's trembling shoulders.

He hated Fury's sisterly tone. "No, it's just that I—I had this sudden urge to . . . kiss you in there," he said, waving toward the ballroom. "You look so beautiful, *carida*. Everyone always said your mother was the most beautiful woman in Cadiz," he blurted out, "but they're wrong, you are."

Fury stepped backward, aware suddenly that the air about them was no longer still. Trees rustled overhead, a familiar sound. Gaspar was close, probably perched on the veranda roof observing her. She craned her neck to peer past the lanterns that were strung along the sloping roof.

"What is it?" Ramon asked, looking about uneasily.

"Nothing, why do you ask?" she replied, her eyes searching past the lantern light for some sign of the hawk. "You said you wanted to kiss me; well, here I am." At twenty-one, Fury had yet to be kissed. Now she decided it was time. She moved closer to her young man, holding up her head, eyes closed, and puckering her lips in a classic pose of breathless anticipation.

Ramon swallowed, his Adam's apple bobbing in excitement as he licked at his dry lips nervously. He reached out and grasped Fury's shoulders with both hands.

How long did it take to kiss someone? Fury wondered

peevishly—and then a sudden rush of air in the warm evening startled her. She knew it was not Ramon.

Her eyes snapped open the next moment as she heard the sound of wings. Gaspar and Pilar swooped down from the veranda roof, and there was nothing playful about their descent. In the lantern light she could see the birds' glittering eyes as the tips of their huge wings bombarded Ramon, knocking him over the veranda railing. Fury knew instantly that the birds were merely warning the young man: their talons were curled; otherwise they would have ripped Ramon to shreds. But *he* knew nothing of the kind.

Forgetting herself, Fury hiked up her skirts and leapt over the railing. "No!" she shouted sternly. "Gaspar, no! Pilar, no! Now look what you've done!" She tried to stifle her laughter at Ramon's ungainly position in the oleander bush. "He's fainted. No doubt from fright."

Gaspar circled overhead, his eyes intent on the figure on the ground. "He wasn't going to hurt me," she called softly. "Kisses don't hurt. I . . . wanted to see what it felt like."

Pilar's wings flapped twice before she headed back to her perch in the trees. Gaspar circled the couple several times, his wings flapping angrily before he headed back to the veranda roof.

Fury knelt over the prostrate young man. "I'm so sorry, Ramon . . . Ramon, wake up. It's all right." Fury leaned down and kissed him lightly on the lips. She blinked and then kissed him again, just as lightly, savoring the feel of his lips beneath hers. She wondered then what it would feel like if he were awake and responding. She sat down amid the oleander leaves, her elbows propped on her knees.

"Fury, what in the world . . . ?"

Fury looked up into Sirena's emerald eyes . . . and

sighed. "It's a long story, Mother, and I don't think you'd believe it. It's not what you think."

Sirena dropped to her knees to peer at Ramon. "He looks like he was attacked. Darling, did he fight over you?"

"What's going on?" Regan demanded, hurrying down to join his wife.

Fury laughed then, a delightful tinkle that wafted through the garden as she tried to explain what happened. "He's not dead, is he, Father?" she asked anxiously.

Regan felt for a pulse, then shook his head. "I doubt it, but he looks as if he was damn near frightened to death."

"My God, Regan, what will we tell his parents?" Sirena asked anxiously.

"Nothing, Mother. Go back with Father, and I'll . . . I'll think of something to say when he wakes up. He's going to be embarrassed when he comes around, and doubly so if you're here."

Sirena nodded. "She's right. Come along, darling, and let's leave these two . . . lovebirds to their explaining."

Regan shivered when her laughter, so like Fury's, rippled about him. How was it possible they could be alike in so many ways and yet so opposite in others? Could two predatory hawks truly be emotionally tied to his daughter? If one of his men had told him such a story, he'd never have believed it.

"I'll be damned," he muttered as he suffered through a second dance with his nimble-footed wife.

"Damn you, Fury, if you didn't want to kiss me, all you had to do was say so instead of knocking me over the railing!" Ramon grumbled as he got to his feet.

"It wasn't me," Fury said, stifling a giggle at the look on his face.

"What do you mean, it wasn't you? There wasn't a soul out here but us." His voice carried the full weight of his indignation and bruised pride as he swiped at the crushed petals and leaves on his clothing.

"It was Gaspar. He's on the roof. I guess he thought you were going . . . to hurt me," Fury explained. "You're lucky, Ramon, he and Pilar could have torn you to pieces. He was playing." She smiled indulgently.

"Playing!" Ramon cried. He eyed the huge bird uneasily, afraid to move toward the veranda. Fury linked her arm through his and led him around the garden to the wide, white steps.

"They kill, and you keep them as pets. It's insane," Ramon sputtered. "Their wings alone could crush a person to death and those feet . . . My God, Fury, they'll turn wild when you leave!"

Fury sobered instantly. She'd thought the same thing more than once. "They have their little ones now to protect; they'll miss me for a while, but I don't think they'll . . . You're wrong, Ramon. If the servants continue to leave food for them, they'll stay here. They're the way they are because I saved Gaspar once from the talons of a kite. It's his way of repaying me."

"And you're scarred for life. Your mother told my mother you almost lost your arm," Ramon said heatedly.

"Well, I didn't, and that's behind us. You're not hurt, only your dignity is wounded. No one knows but us, and I won't mention it."

"Well, I certainly don't intend to stay *here* any longer, not with that . . . that *vulture* guarding your every move! Good night, Fury," Ramon muttered, and marched toward his parents' waiting carriage.

Fury sat down on one of the veranda's wicker chairs. She supposed she should be upset, but she wasn't. Ramon was such a . . . boy, even if he was her age. Kissing him would have been like kissing one of her brothers.

The shadow was ominous as it sailed gracefully into the lantern light to perch on the veranda railing. The bird's glittering eyes stared at the girl, and one wing lifted slightly in apology. Fury inclined her head and smiled.

"Apology accepted," she said softly.

The bird soared upward, the white tips of his wings eerie-looking in the yellow light.

Inside, the musicians were readying the guests for the quadrille. It was her party, and she'd been outside far too long. Fixing a smile on her face, she sailed through the door to join in the dance.

Regan stood on the sidelines and watched his wife and daughter on the dance floor. His eyes sparked dangerously as he noticed Sirena's partner—a slick, overdressed dandy twenty years younger than his wife—blatantly attempting to seduce her. His wife, he noticed, was flirting outrageously.

Suddenly he laughed. There was a time when he would have hauled the younger man out to the veranda and whipped him soundly for such behavior, but he'd mellowed over the years. She was his, she always was and always would be. He was the one who sat across the table from her, and it was his arms that enfolded her at evening's end—he who made wild, passionate love to her until break of day. While he may have mellowed, his passions had not. She still excited him beyond comprehension. All she had to do was look at him, smile or wink, and he wanted to snatch her by the hair and drag her off to his lair.

He could watch her now and feel sympathy for the man twirling her around the dance floor. No one but Regan van der Rhys would ever taste Sirena's charms.

Sirena whirled by again, her tinkling laughter swirling about him like a soft caress. He played the game and scowled, to his wife's delight. Then he looked around, and noticed that the eyes of all his guests were on Sirena. She was easily the most beautiful, the best-dressed woman in the room, or perhaps the second best. It was hard for him to make that particular decision when he compared her with Fury.

The dance ended with a loud fanfare. Sirena smiled at her partner and placed her hand on his arm as he escorted her to Regan, who was still scowling. Sirena lowered her lashes and then inclined her head slightly. Regan blinked at the searing passion he saw in her eyes. Involuntarily, his loins twitched. Sirena laughed, her gaze now bold and openly seductive. "Later," she cooed as she was whisked away in the arms of another guest.

"Jesus Christ," Regan muttered under his breath. Later was still hours away. She always did this to him, and he always reacted in the same way. Just as she was his, he was hers, and she was letting him know it. He inched forward, and as Sirena danced by, he mouthed, "I love you." She smiled radiantly and blew him a kiss. He was the envy of every man in the room, and he loved the feeling.

Watching them, Fury flushed at her mother's open display of love for her father. Then she laughed—to her partner's delight. Unlike her mother, she'd never flirted or pretended to like men much. It might be fun to try. She smiled and stared into her partner's warm gaze.

"You look especially handsome this evening, Diego," she purred, her hand on his arm tightening imperceptibly.

Diego stiffened and then relaxed. This wasn't the Fury he'd grown up with. And what about Ramon? he wondered. Wasn't he her favorite? He'd seen Fury go out to the veranda with him, yet she'd returned alone. "Did you kiss him?" he blurted out.

Fury laughed gaily. "But of course, and if you draw me closer to you, I'll kiss you too . . . on the cheek," she murmured, and slipped from his arms to those of another as the dance ended and another began.

Suddenly Fury realized she was having a wonderful time, something she'd thought impossible, as she flitted from one partner to another like a bird. Out of the corner of her eye she became aware of a tall, handsome stranger, a guest of the Parish family. In another second her partner would swoop her by the Parishes, and if she so desired, she could smile at him the way her mother did. Without a second thought she turned her head and stared directly into the eyes of Doña Louisa's guest. What would it be like to kiss *him*? she wondered. She laughed, a gay, throaty chuckle—much to the surprise of her partner, who wondered what it was he'd said to make her laugh.

Breathless from her dancing, Fury walked over to her parents. When she turned back to give the handsome stranger a demure smile, she saw that he was not even aware of her! No, he was too busy bowing low over her friend Daniella's hand and ogling her low-cut gown. Daniella was blushing and making cow eyes at him in return. Annoyed with herself, Fury turned to meet her mother's gaze.

"He didn't come through the receiving line, so he must have arrived late," Sirena said softly. "I'm surprised that Doña Louisa hasn't brought him over to be introduced. Handsome devil, almost as good-looking as your father."

"No one is as handsome as Father," Fury said loyally. She wondered if he would ask her to dance; good manners dictated it, but this man, Fury decided as yet another man led her out onto the floor, this man did not abide by rules of any kind. She flushed again, wondering where and how she'd come by such a thought.

"You look angry, Fury," her partner observed quietly.

"Angry? Me? How absurd!" No, she wasn't angry, Fury told herself. She was . . . *jealous*—jealous of Daniella, an emotion she'd never felt before. She hated it. "Ruiz, I really could use a breath of air if you wouldn't mind." Cheeks burning, she almost ran from the ballroom to the coolness of the veranda.

"It's such a beautiful evening, isn't it? I love the darkness with the stars and moon for light. Look how silvery everything looks. It's so . . . so romantic, don't you think?" She didn't wait for Ruiz's reply but rushed on. "I wonder how many lovers have kissed and embraced under the stars. Thousands, probably. Even the animals like darkness, it protects them, but there's no one to protect lovers except . . . Why aren't you saying anything, Ruiz?"

Ruiz smiled wryly. "Because you haven't given me a chance. Fury, we've known each other since you came to Spain at the age of eight. In all those years I've never seen you act this way. Is it because you're leaving tomorrow for . . . your holy life, or is it that you're beginning to realize you're making a mistake? I—I couldn't help but notice the way you looked at Don Parish's guest. We've been friends a long time, Fury, and if you want to talk about this, I'm willing to listen. You have my word that it will go no further."

"Even to Daniella's ears?" Fury teased. "Were you jealous when she danced with . . . him?"

"Yes, very. Daniella told me she wants a man who makes her blood sing. I don't think I'm that man," Ruiz said ruefully.

"How is that possible, to make your blood sing?"

Ruiz shrugged. "I have no idea, but Daniella said that's what every woman wants from a man. If I knew how to accomplish that, I'd probably be the most sought-after man in all of Spain."

Fury contemplated him with thoughtful eyes. "I think Daniella was teasing you, Ruiz."

"No, she means it. I would marry her in a minute, but she won't have me."

"Because . . ."

"I don't make her blood sing." Ruiz threw up his hands in disgust.

They stood together for several moments in silence, staring out across the manicured gardens. At last Fury turned to Ruiz and placed a gentle hand on his arm. "Come, let's go in, Ruiz. I have to speak to my mother, and it's almost time for the food to be served. Father plans on making a toast or two. . . . And I wouldn't worry about Daniella. She'll soon see what a wonderful person you are. I believe that, I truly do."

He drew her arm through his and began to escort her back inside the ballroom. "You'll never know, will you? You'll be off praying for all of us, and we'll never see you again. You'll never know who will marry whom and who will have children." He stared down at her with wide, troubled eyes. "Oh, damn you, Fury, why are you going off to some damn-fool convent never to be seen again? It's not natural!"

Fury stopped in her tracks. It was true, everything Ruiz said. Soon all her friends would be just a memory.

"And another thing," he continued bitterly, "don't go praying for me. Pray for yourself. . . . Oh, never mind," he muttered. "Happy birthday!" And with that, he stomped off in Daniella's direction, leaving an astonished Fury to return unescorted to her parents.

"Mother, can I ask you something?" she said as Sirena took her arm and drew her in beside her. "It's . . . what I mean is . . . Ruiz said something to me out on the veranda just now that . . . Well, it seems impossible, but he did say it, and I was wondering . . . Does Father . . . does he make your blood sing?''

Sirena laughed. "Twenty-four hours a day, my sweet. From the first moment I saw him. Come, let's ask your father the same question." She turned to her husband, who was several feet away chatting with an elderly gentleman. Catching his eye, she beckoned discreetly.

Regan excused himself and joined his wife, giving Fury an affectionate smile. "Yes, my dear?"

"Regan, Fury has a question for you. Do I make your blood sing?"

Regan stared first at his wife and then at his daughter. He fought the laughter bubbling in his throat when he saw from his daughter's face that she was quite serious. "Yes, my darling daughter, she does. The moment I laid eyes on her, she captivated me. My blood has never been still. It's called love, Furana." Regan held her chin in his hand and stared into her eyes. "I truly regret that you will never experience this particular emotion."

"I, too, regret it," Fury said, so softly her parents had to strain to hear the words.

Suddenly, to break the moment, Regan clapped his hands and announced a toast. "Well wishes for our daughter's birthday!" Waiters appeared as if by magic with elaborate trays full of crystal goblets filled to the brim with sparkling champagne. A chorus of Happy Birthdays reverberated throughout the ballroom. Regan raised his hand, and once again the musicians took their places. He bowed low. "Señorita, I believe this dance is mine," he said gallantly.

Tears streaming down her cheeks, Sirena watched her husband and daughter trample upon each other's feet as they whirled and twirled about the room to uproarious applause. When at last the music stopped, the dancers limped off the floor to another round of applause.

"I think our guests are getting impatient," Regan said, beaming down upon his lovely daughter, "so let me get your dinner partner and we'll get things under way. I hope you don't mind, sweetheart, but so many of your young men clamored for the honor of escorting you in that we thought it most politic to accept the invitation of Don Parish, who has volunteered his guest to do the honors. Stay right here and I'll be back in a moment."

Sirena heard her daughter's gasp and smiled. So, she mused, her daughter's blood *was* capable of singing.

Luis Domingo was as tall as Regan, broad-chested with narrow hips and well-muscled legs that strained slightly against his immaculate white linen trousers. His eyes were dark and as inky black as his hair, a lock of which tumbled over his forehead. *Handsome* was the only word Fury could think of as her father introduced him.

"Furana, may I present Luis Domingo, Don Parish's house guest. Señor Domingo, my daughter, Furana."

"Señorita, it is my pleasure," said Luis, bowing low over her hand.

Fury was unprepared for the timbre of his voice, deep and oddly compelling. Unaccountably, she blushed and withdrew her hand, averting her eyes demurely. "Bewitching," he murmured.

"What—I beg your pardon?" Fury stammered.

"He said you were bewitching," Regan said sourly.

White teeth flashed in amusement as Luis held out his arms. Fury's heart skipped a beat at the feel of her escort's hard, sinewy arm. This was no boy like all the others. She wondered what Gaspar would do to *this* man if he kissed her.

Domingo gazed about him at the lavish banquet tables

with their rainbow-hued waterfalls. His dark eyes took in the fine crystal and silver and lace. This ball had to cost a fortune, he reflected, probably more than he earned in a year. But that would all change . . . soon. He smiled at Fury. "Forgive me for staring like a field hand, but I've never seen anything to equal this," he said with a wave of his hand. He took a plate and began to fill it from among the countless delicacies spread out before them.

"It's my birthday." There was a note of apology in her voice. "My parents wanted this to be an elaborate affair since it will be the last . . . what I mean is . . ."

"You're leaving to enter the convent tomorrow." He nodded. "Doña Louisa explained it all to me. There's no need for apologies—unless you're uncertain of your vocation."

She flushed. "I guess I was apologizing, and no, I'm not uncertain. It's just that we Spanish tend to do things in a grand way." She was babbling, she knew, but she couldn't help herself.

Again Luis smiled at her. "But you're half Dutch," aren't you?"

Fury stared at her escort with unabashed admiration. His was a beautiful smile, endearing somehow, she thought. "Yes—I—I am half Dutch," she roused herself to reply. "But my upbringing has been Spanish. My mother is Spanish, my father Dutch. . . ."

White teeth flashed. "Yes, I know," he said. With a flourish, he offered her a plate piled high with pink shrimp, squab, and lobster on a bed of rice.

Fury stared at it with bewildered eyes. "I can't possibly eat—"

"I'll help you finish it," Luis assured her. "Doña Louisa insists that one never go to the table twice—in public. I would prefer to eat on the veranda, if it's agreeable."

Obediently, Fury followed alongside him, praying Gaspar would just this once leave her alone to enjoy the attentions of such a fascinating man.

As the couple ate, they talked of inconsequential things, the weather, the beautiful casa she lived in, the tropical flowers that scented the air, her parents.

"I think I've been doing most of the talking," Fury said at last, folding her napkin neatly beside her plate.

Luis laughed. "It's your birthday. I understand that once you enter your order you will take a vow of silence. This is something I cannot comprehend."

"You are not a religious man, then?"

"I believe in God, if that's what you mean, but I don't spend all my time in church praying. Goodness must come from here." He touched his chest.

Fury remained silent, her eyes drawn to his hands. They were the largest she'd ever seen; she wondered if they were rough and callused. Then she looked up and found him staring at her intently, so intently that she flushed. Obviously, he was waiting for a response. "I—I believe that most people believe in God, some more than others," she said hesitantly. "There are those who call on Him when they need something and forget about Him the rest of the time. I've known I was meant for the convent since I was ten or so, but I waited until now for my parents' sake. . . . But enough about me," she said, clapping her hands to dismiss the subject. "What do you do . . . Luis?"

As he gazed into the depths of her blue eyes, Luis suddenly found himself wanting to tell this lovely creature everything about him . . . every secret he'd ever held close to his heart. But did he dare? And, even more to the point, would she understand? "What do I do?" he said lightly. "I turn up in unlikely places and escort beautiful ladies to dinner. . . . No, actually, I spend most of my time looking for the marauder who ruined my father's small company—which certainly isn't proper dinner conversation at a birthday ball."

Fury blinked at Luis's startling response. She was utterly mesmerized and wanted to hear more, but . . . "I think Doña Louisa is trying to attract your attention," she said reluctantly. "She's usually the first to leave a party. I—I would like to thank you for your kind gesture this evening. . . ."

Dark eyes scalded her. "You were a damsel in distress, it was my duty." His voice was suddenly as mocking as his countenance.

Fury's eyes sparked. "I didn't realize it was such a chore—or is it that I'm going into the convent and you feel you can't waste your time with someone who . . ."

"Yes?" he prodded.

"Nothing, señor," she said stiffly. "Thank you again. I enjoyed our talk . . . for a little while."

Luis bowed low and then brought her hand to his lips. His dark eyes caught and held hers. "Might I ask a favor?"

Blood rushed to Fury's cheeks, and her heart started to pound. He was going to ask if he could kiss her. Not trusting herself to speak, she nodded.

"Pray for me that I find the marauder who ruined and killed my father." An instant later he was gone, weaving his way through the clusters of people in the ballroom.

Fury turned and ran down the veranda steps into the darkest part of the garden. She knew her cheeks were flaming; even her ears felt hot. She clutched her chest as though the movement would still her heart.

The handsome Spaniard hadn't wanted to kiss her. No, *she* had wanted him to kiss her. Now she felt shame and wished for her rosary. She would pray through the dawn, begging God's forgiveness for her wicked thoughts, and then she would pray for Luis Domingo—not for the vengeance he sought, but for his immortal soul.

The moment the last coach clattered down the cobblestone drive, Fury embraced her parents. "It was a wonderful party! I think everyone had a wonderful time; I know I did. Thank you so much. I'll never forget it. Never!"

Sirena hugged her, then pulled back to smile into her daughter's eyes. "It's almost dawn, darling. Why don't you try to sleep for a little while. Your father and I are exhausted. Shall we have breakfast around nine o'clock?"

Fury nodded. "That sounds wonderful, Mother." She kissed both her parents and hurried off.

In the privacy of her own room, she removed the confining gown and petticoats and laid them over the back of a chair with a weary sigh. Her jewelry was placed in a velvet-lined jewel cask, to be turned over to her mother before she left. Then, clad in a soft silken wrapper, rosary in hand, she dropped to her knees at the side of the bed and bowed her head. Her lips moved soundlessly. When, hours later, she raised her head and opened her eyes, it was full light.

She looked around, disconcerted for a moment. A shaft of sunlight speared across the room, bathing the clock on her night table in its bright light. Fury peered at the numerals and realized she had less than thirty minutes to dress for breakfast.

Breakfast was a tense affair: Sirena on the verge of tears; Regan grim and tight-lipped, staring at his plate.

"It's a beautiful day," Fury said brightly.

"Good headwinds. The *Java Queen* will get off to a good start," Regan agreed soberly. "Your mother and I made the decision for the *Queen* to sail with an empty hold. She'll ride high in the water, proof that she carries no cargo. Any marauding pirates will think twice about attacking a ship without cargo. It's for your safety, Fury. Ronrico Diaz is the best seafaring captain, next to myself, that I would trust with you and the *Queen*.

"I don't like it one damn bit that you made us both promise not to take on passengers. I know what you said, that you wanted to pray and be alone with your thoughts," he said when he saw that his daughter was about to protest. "You'll have the rest of your life to pray. You should have company, people to talk to, to dine with. I don't like it one damn bit, and neither does your mother." Frustrated, Regan banged his fist on the table, and Fury flinched.

"I don't give a damn about the revenues," he continued. "I do give a damn about your sailing alone with a crew and no passengers to keep you company. It doesn't matter if the crew is loyal and hand-picked or not. We're giving in to your wishes because you begged us, and indulgent parents that we are, we can deny you nothing. In our hearts we know Captain Diaz will protect you with his life."

Fury thanked both her parents with her eyes. She smiled. "I have as much faith and trust in Captain Diaz as you do, Father. I've known the crew of the *Queen* for years. They won't let me fall in harm's way. I need this time alone. Please, you must tell me that you understand. Mother?"

Sirena smiled at her daughter, tears shimmering in her eyes. "No, there's no one better than Diaz," she echoed.

"Sixteen weeks will see you in Java. We've arranged for you to go to our house and rest before . . . Father Miguel will be waiting to personally escort you to the convent doors. It's all been arranged. You must promise

me, Fury, that you won't deviate. . . . What I mean to say
is . . .''

Fury leaned across the table, her voice earnest yet quiet.
''Mother, I'm twenty-one years old. I've sailed with both
you and Father since I was five. I can take care of myself.
Please don't worry about me. If I remember correctly, you
yourself were quite notorious at my age. And as for you,
Father,'' she added impishly, ''what would the world think
if they knew the governor of the Netherlands was married
to the infamous Sea Siren?''

''They would think I'm a very lucky man.'' Regan
grinned. ''As far as the world knows, the Sea Siren retired
long ago and was never heard of again. Sometimes I think
she was a myth myself, the way she disappeared into the
mist. Someday, Sirena, I want to hear how you pulled that
little trick. And don't tell me it was black magic, either.''

Mother and daughter smiled at each other. Clearly there
were some things this husband-father didn't need to know.
Theirs was a secret Fury would carry with her to her new
world of silence. Sirena winked roguishly at her husband
and laughed when he scowled.

''What time will you and Father leave for the harbor?''
Fury asked, watching them with affection and delight.

''The *Java Star* sets sail at six o'clock. You'll be six
hours at sea by the time we get under way,'' Sirena said
quietly. If it weren't for the anguish she felt over Fury,
she'd be looking forward to visiting Caleb, Regan's son by
a previous marriage, along with his wife and Regan's
grandchildren. But she had little heart for the journey now.

''Be sure to give Caleb a big kiss for me and tell Wren
my prayers are with her and her brood,'' Fury said
brightly. ''It's going to be wonderful for you to see the
children. How long will you stay?''

Regan sent Sirena a pointed glance. ''As long as your
mother wants. We have no itinerary. I've resigned my post

as governor and am now fully retired. Perhaps we'll end up in Java at some point in the future. If we do, we'll leave word at the convent.''

Fury stirred spoon after spoon of honey into her coffee. They'd gone over all of this before, at least a dozen times, she thought sadly. Another hour and she would walk out the door for the last time. She dreaded the last good-bye, imagining her mother clinging to her, crying, while her father stood by, stone-faced, angry that she was deserting them. But she couldn't help it—at last the future was hers. She would be doing what she was meant to do: serve God for the rest of her life.

"Do you have the bishop's letter, Fury?'' Sirena asked suddenly. How many times she'd wanted to kick herself for giving her daughter that damned acceptance letter. Had she kept it, Fury would not be leaving them now.

"Yes, Mother, and also the letter from Father Sebastian. You mustn't worry.''

With a bittersweet ache in her heart, Fury gazed around the breakfast room, memorizing it with her eyes. She'd always thought it the homiest of all the rooms in the casa, and it was her favorite, even over her pretty bedroom. Potted blooms in clay pots graced every boundary of the red-tiled floor. Wispy ferns hung from straw baskets near the multipaned windows, all favorites of her mother. The table and chairs, whitewashed iron with persimmon-colored cushions, were also made by her mother. She particularly loved the ancient chestnut tree, outside the wide triple window, that held Gaspar's nest high at the top. He always knew when she was at the table and would come to perch on the sill . . . until today.

"Mother, has Gaspar been at the window?'' she asked suddenly.

"No, he hasn't. Perhaps the party kept him awake and

he's sleeping." Sirena smiled wanly. It was so easy to indulge this child, she thought.

"I don't think Gaspar ever sleeps," Fury said fretfully. "I think he understands that I'm leaving." She leaned across the window seat and whistled to the huge hawk. The leaves remained quiet.

"Maybe he's fishing." Regan grinned. "Don't worry, sweetheart, he never goes far."

Fury smiled at her father's small joke. She knew he was trying to keep the moment light for all their sakes, and she appreciated it. Now that she was within minutes of departing, she felt strangely at odds with herself. Knowing she might never see these beloved parents of hers again . . . Then she straightened her shoulders and willed her eyes to remain dry. This was what she wanted, had begged and pleaded to be allowed to do. She wouldn't back down now. "I'll just run upstairs and get my things. I heard the carriage arrive a few minutes ago. I'll be down in a moment."

Fury fled the room, afraid the tears she felt burning her eyes would overflow. Upstairs, she bolted into her room and ran to the window, her handkerchief clasped to her mouth with a trembling hand. Again and again she called to the birds, but there was no response. Tears slipped down her cheeks as she craned her neck to peer high into the trees. All she could see was the umbrellalike leaves, and none of them stirred in the soft, warm morning air. "Oh, my fledglings," she whispered, "not even to say good-bye?"

Slowly Fury gathered her traveling cloak and vanity case. This awful feeling of suddenly being alone, deserted by the winged creatures she loved . . . she hated it. She was half-way down the long, winding staircase when she stopped, eyes wide with sudden understanding. What she was feeling her parents were feeling, only more so. She was their flesh and blood, created from love. Their hearts must truly be shattering. She'd been only a temporary guardian to Gaspar and Pilar. The knowledge nearly undid her. Fighting the sob in her throat, she continued down the stairs to join her parents.

"Let me lean on you," Sirena whispered to her husband, devouring Fury with her eyes.

"Only if you let me lean on you, too," Regan whispered back.

"Well, I'm ready," Fury said when she reached them. "I couldn't see Gaspar or Pilar. I guess they're out . . . with the little ones."

Sirena bit down on her lower lip and was rewarded with the salty taste of her own blood. She'd promised herself she wouldn't cry, and by all that was holy, she wouldn't. She didn't want her daughter to remember her as a sniveling, cowardly weakling.

Outside in the bright sunshine, their good-byes were brief, almost aloof. As the carriage rumbled away, Fury moaned and gave way at last to her tears, eyes fixed sightlessly on the road ahead of her. If she had been able to look back, she would have seen her mother crumple against her father's unsteady form. But she would not have noticed Gaspar and Pilar, whose glittering eyes charted her course down the road.

Once the carriage was out of sight, Pilar immediately took wing and headed for the basket in the chestnut tree. When Gaspar was satisfied that she was safe in the top of the tree, he spread his wings and soared high overhead.

Tears streaming down her cheeks, Sirena pointed to the large hawk circling overhead. "He's going to follow her, Regan. Mark my words."

Regan gathered his wife in his arms and stroked her dark head, his eyes on the huge bird. "How do you know this?" he asked in a shaky voice.

"Because he loves her. She saved his life and provided for him all these years. I also have this feeling that he will not . . . let her know he's near. I feel he's going to take our place and . . . protect her."

Regan laughed. "Protect her from whom, God?" The moment the words were out of his mouth, he wished he could take them back.

Sirena stared into her husband's eyes. "There's a special affinity between that hawk and our daughter, and if there's one thing I know, it's that he will protect her with his life. By the time the *Java Queen* reaches Java, those two fledglings in that nest up there will be fully grown. And I like those odds, Regan, I like them very much. I feel much better now, knowing that Fury sails with an escort of four. And as for God, He will have to take His chances the way the rest of us do."

Regan nuzzled his cheek against his wife's glossy black hair, knowing better than to debate the matter further. "Let's walk through the garden, Sirena, before it gets too hot. We are creatures of leisure today. A cooling bath, a short nap, and if you feel in the right frame of mind, a little lovemaking before we sail."

Sirena laughed, the sound tinkling about the garden. She was more than pleased that her husband of so many years still found her desirable at the oddest times.

Overhead, Pilar's wings flapped once at the sound of Sirena's laughter and then stilled. Her diamond-bright eyes never left the strolling couple.

Chapter Two

The justice was old, his footsteps heavy and un-sure as he climbed from the carriage. He cursed his age, the dry, dusty road, and the fact that he was here at all. He'd wanted nothing more than to disregard Amalie Suub's petition, but honest man that he was, he knew he had to at least consider her request.

Sudam Muab looked up at the three-tiered house that had once been Chaezar Alvarez's castle—or kingdom, as Alvarez preferred to call it—before his untimely demise years ago. He'd never forget that day as long as he lived. The servants had carried in the self-appointed king's body, his manhood carved from his loins by a wicked-looking woman wielding a rapier and cutlass—or so said the wide-eyed servants.

The small town had buried the body at sea, but he couldn't remember why. Along with everything else these days, his memory was failing him. This would be his last major de-cision before turning the reins over to a younger man.

Rotted jungle vegetation all but obscured the fairy-tale house that was once a kingdom for the crafty Spaniard who had built it to his specifications. Muab supposed that if someone had enough money and the inclination, the jungle could be hacked away and the house restored. He'd been

41

the one who had insisted on having the property posted, believing that at some point in the future, Alvarez's heirs would arrive to claim it. But they hadn't. From time to time he'd come out to check on the place, never sure why.

He remembered the day Amalie Suub had walked into his cramped offices, one year ago. She'd said she was daughter and legal heir to Chaezar Alvarez and that she wanted to claim what was hers by the time she reached her twenty-first birthday, which was now a few days away. To support her allegation, she'd presented a marriage contract legalizing Alvarez's union with Amalie's mother. Muab suspected it was a forgery. In any case, he wasn't sure it mattered anymore. The house and holdings, which consisted of furnishings that were full of mildew and rot and two ships that should have been sunk years before, along with a small grove of nutmeg trees, were all that Alvarez had left behind.

Muab mopped his perspiring brow. No one would chastise him if he made a decision in favor of Amalie. If there was a way for her to restore the house to its original splendor, she would make a fitting queen.

The old justice laughed. Amalie Suub, daughter of a king and a slave woman. His rheumy gaze fell on a round shield dangling haphazardly from a tree. It was rusted and pitted from the elements, but the old man knew that if he were to throw a rock at it, it would clang, and the sound would reverberate for miles. He'd heard stories that the shield was always hung to herald a guest's arrival.

Well, he'd come here for a reason, and he'd best get to it so he could return to the relative comfort of his offices. All he needed was one thing, one piece of paper with Chaezar Alvarez's signature. Amalie had suggested he look here. There was no reason in the world to suspect he would find anything in the house after all these years; on the other hand, there just might be something . . . courtesy of Amalie Suub. For example, there would undoubtedly be something in the house to verify Amalie's copy of her mother's marriage contract. The girl was no fool; that much he'd decided after their first meeting.

The justice cleared the sweat from his eyes as he tramped through the choking vines and flowers that obscured what was once a decorative stone walkway. The huge teakwood door was closed tight, possibly locked, and he could not budge it.

"Warped," he mumbled as he picked his way through the rotting vegetation to the back of the house. This door yielded to his touch. He entered a huge, sunny kitchen with an open fireplace that took up one entire wall. Huge chopping blocks and tables were scattered about, testament that at one time there were many guests to cook for. But even here the jungle had crept in. Vines twisted up the walls near the windows. Bright red and purple flowers hung from shelves as though designed that way. Reedy shoots, various forms of underbrush, forced their way up through cracks in the tile floor, and he thought he saw a snake slither away.

Farther into the house, rotting vegetation made him gasp for breath. He tried to breathe through his mouth, walking from room to room until he came to Alvarez's study.

It was once an impressive compartment, the private sanctuary of a successful man. Now it was full of worms and rotting leaves and flowers. The books lining the shelves would probably crumble to the touch. Everywhere he looked there were thick black patches of mildew. His eyes strayed to the desk and the six long drawers that Amalie told him held Alvarez's papers. One paper with one signature was all he needed. Just one paper. . . .

The moment he found it, he backed out of the room. It had been far too easy, but he didn't care. The law was the law; if the signatures matched, then this property and any-

thing else Alvarez owned would go to Amalie, his legal
daughter.

Muab matched up the signatures in the murky light that
struggled through the stained-glass windows Alvarez had
brought all the way from Spain. Satisfied, the old justice
deposited both pieces of parchment into the cloth bag he
carried. All that remained was to affix his signature to
several documents and write a letter to Alvarez's superiors
in Spain, which they would probably ignore the way they'd
ignored his other three letters asking them to forward the
Spaniard's belongings. As he made his way to the carriage, Muab had already determined that the beautiful Ma-
layan was now the owner of all that Alvarez possessed. In
the Spaniard's life it had been a kingdom of untold riches.
In death it was nothing but rotting timbers and stone. What
Alvarez's daughter would do with it he had no idea, and
he didn't care. All he cared about right now was returning
to his cool offices by the harbor.

Amalie Suub stepped onto the same trampled vines and
flowers Justice Muab had trampled. It was all hers now,
she thought happily. Not that it was much, but it was better than the shack she'd lived in with her mother until her
death.

She walked around the estate, her eyes calculating the
cost of refurbishing the mansion her father had lived in
with her mother, who had been little more than a slave to
his whims. All she needed was money, lots of it. And
short of selling her body, there was little chance of laying
her hands on the kind of money she would need to restore
this magnificent house and grounds. The ships, of course,
would require even more to make them seaworthy.

Amalie sat down on the steps leading to the wide double
teak doors, her long, tawny legs stretched in front of her.
She hiked up her thin, worn dress well above her knees.

Men liked her legs, white men especially. Some had even fought over her charms, and she'd been elated, knowing she was desired in their eyes. One of her favorite pastimes was dreaming about the day she would own a pair of shoes with heels so she could walk in front of a man the way the grand ladies did who attended her father's fancy balls.

It was beastly hot now. She knew she could go inside where it was cool, but the house wasn't really hers yet. Oh, yes, she'd sneaked inside after her mother's death just to look around. She'd found her father's journal the first time, but it had meant nothing to her then because she couldn't read or write. Thanks to the missionary who'd taken her under his wing, she could now do both. In fact, she was so adept, she helped the missionary with the younger children.

Father Renaldo was the reason she was sitting here now, the reason she'd had the nerve to appeal to the justice for aid. And thanks to him, she owned something at last—and that's what she had to remember. No slave owned anything, even the clothes on his back. She alone was the exception.

From the moment she'd created the forged marriage contract she'd stolen from Father Renaldo, she'd never thought about the deed again, only its outcome. True, she was Chaezar Alvarez's daughter, but only an illegitimate one with no rights at all. Her expert forgery had changed everything; now she was respectable, not that it was going to do her any good. Unless . . . She laughed, an eerie sound that echoed in the jungle surrounding her. She looked up as the birds in the branches took wing at the sound. Cat's eyes, yellow in the golden sun, watched them circle higher overhead, then lowered to stare sightlessly at the foliage.

Over the past years, before Father Renaldo's tutelage, she'd been an expert thief. Twice she'd been hauled before the burgher, only to be let go when her eyes promised things old men only dreamed of. The day Father Renaldo rescued her, at the age of seventeen, he'd made her promise not to steal again. And, as a show of good faith, she'd turned over the six diamonds she'd found in her mother's possession at her death—jewels stolen from her father at his death. Perhaps it was time to reclaim those diamonds as her rightful inheritance.

Amalie smiled. The world, she reflected lazily, was made up mostly of the weak and downtrodden, people like Father Renaldo and her mother. And then there were the others, greedy people like herself who dared to take a chance.

Amalie's eyes sparkled dangerously. She needed money, more than even the town burghers had, and the only way she could get it was to steal from those who had it. But how?

She brushed impatiently at the long black hair falling over her eyes. One thing she'd learned: When you stole from someone you had to be quick and fast. Proof of that simple fact was in her father's journal, written in his own hand. A master thief himself, he'd met his match, according to several entries, in a scantily clad, long-legged woman who roamed the seas pillaging and plundering any ship that crossed her path. Amalie had devoured the words until she knew the entire journal by heart. And at the back she'd found a dozen drawings of the long-legged woman, all done in fine detail. While knowing little of art in any form, she'd realized the sketches had been done by a man obsessed. Every conceivable pose the artist could imagine had been rendered in fine India ink, right down to a wicked scar on the woman's arm.

It was this same woman, named the Sea Siren in the journals, who, according to her mother, had carved the manhood from her father's body. A witness to the event, her mother had regaled her with tales of how she and the other servants had silently applauded the deed. And the moment she'd known Alvarez was dead, her mother had raced to his room to steal those few small diamonds.

Amalie herself knew little of jewels, but there was no reason to suspect her father would have anything less than flawless stones. If Father Renaldo could be persuaded that they really belonged to her after all . . . and if she could convince him to sell them to the right person, she might have enough money to either refurbish the plantation or have one of the ships restored. She promised herself that she would decide later in the day when the evening meal at the mission was over and her time was her own.

Amalie Suub was beautiful, and more than one head turned as she picked her way through the small mission. She was as tall as most men, with a long, loose-legged stride, and her thin chemise did little to hide her shapely body. Perhaps her most startling features were her wide, white smile and her cat's eyes, a yellowish-brown that seemed to see everything at a glance. She knew the others envied her light skin and that if she lived in a different place, she could pass as a Spaniard. It was a fact that pleased her to no end—more so once she'd read her father's journal.

Father Renaldo watched Amalie as she ladled out dinner to the children. His spectacles were almost useless these days now that the white film had started to grow over his eyes. He could barely make out her features, but he could certainly smell her sharp, earthy scent. God, he told himself, had chosen to strengthen his sense of smell when He took his eyesight. Give and take.

He was worried about Amalie, afraid she would do something . . . terrible. The justice had been to see him three days in a row in his efforts to come to a decision. Renaldo had known for some time that his wayward charge had stolen a marriage contract from his satchel. But he'd said nothing. He understood how important it was for her to be more than just a slave's illegitimate daughter. When the justice had examined the marriage contract, he'd held his breath and waited . . . God forgive him. Then he'd heard the man's sigh of resignation, and at that moment he'd known that the plantation, as well as the name Alvarez, would be bequeathed to Amalie.

He could smell her now as she swished back and forth among the plank tables. For the first time he realized that he didn't like the smell, that he didn't really like Amalie. He felt sinful and bowed his head at his wicked acknowledgment. Amalie was a child of God, as were all children. *No, not this one,* whispered a voice deep inside him. *This one is a child of . . . the devil.* The old priest started to shake and tremble as his fingers fumbled for the rosary tied around his waist.

Amalie came up behind him, her bare feet soundless in the loamy earth. "Would you like me to read to you for a little while, Father?" she asked quietly.

The old priest felt his neck and face grow hot. "Not this evening, Amalie. I want to say my rosary."

"Father, I've been meaning to ask you . . . Can I have those stones I gave you?"

"Why?" he asked sharply.

"Well, they did belong to my father—and now, like everything else of his, they're mine. Or they should be. I was going to ask you to sell them for me, but I think the trip into town might be too much for you. I'm going to need the money to . . . for whatever I decide to do. Of course I will give some of it to you for the children. God would want me to be generous."

The priest flinched as though she'd struck a blow to his body. "Your mother stole the stones, Amalie. They won't bring you any peace. Still," he mumbled, more to himself than to Amalie, "I suppose the diamonds do belong to you. In the morning will be soon enough. Go along, child, read the Bible until it's time for sleep."

Amalie laughed, a deep, sensuous sound, and slipped away silently. Renaldo breathed deeply and almost choked on her animal scent. He heard her laugh again as she moved off, this time to her pallet. Involuntarily, he shivered and crossed himself.

Amalie Suub Alvarez was evil; he could feel it in every pore of his body. The old priest's hands worked feverishly on the beads in his hands. Over and over he said the familiar prayers. Always before they had comforted him, but not this evening—and perhaps never again.

Amalie awoke to a slow, sleepy dawn. As yet the birds were still cradled in their nests, their shrill early-morning cries minutes away. The others were asleep, the mission quiet and peaceful. Soon she wouldn't have to sleep under the stars with hundreds of others pressed close for warmth during the chilly nights. Soon she would be free of this damnable mission.

She closed her eyes and tried to picture the plantation alive with people and music. Her father had wanted to be a king, to live in grand splendor with the infamous Sea Siren as his queen. Instead, she'd killed him and sailed away, probably to her own death. If she, Amalie, were careful and planned every single detail, she could become a queen and resurrect the Sea Siren from her watery grave. It was an exciting thought. There would be obstacles, many of them, and primary among them was that she knew nothing about ships and had never been on one in her entire life.

Amalie sat up and hugged her knees. There were hundreds of books in her father's office, most of them about sailing. She'd looked through some of them, but they were full of rot and mildew, their pages either sticking together or crumbling in her fingers. At least her father's navigational charts were intact in their oilskin pouches, that much she knew.

A bright beam of sun shafted downward through the glossy leaves overhead, bathing Amalie in an eerie yellow glow. She moved out of the sun, muttering to herself as she left the room to prepare the morning meal.

First there would be the endless prayers, then breakfast, then cleaning up, then lessons. She hated it, but she'd gone on pretending because she needed this place and what it offered. After today, however, she wouldn't need this mission or Father Renaldo. Oh, she would stay on for a while longer—but only long enough to learn what was needed and to put her plan into operation.

Amalie's eyes flew to the priest's quarters as she padded down the hallway. It was possible the old man would die in the meantime. If he didn't . . . such things were simple to arrange. She smiled. At last her life was on a steady course.

After breakfast, Father Renaldo announced his intention to accompany Amalie into town. Instantly her suspicions were aroused; fear tightened like a vise in her chest as she scrutinized the old man. Why did he want to come with her? What was in his mind? Did he intend to thwart her plans somehow—perhaps even refuse to give her the diamonds?

Her yellow eyes narrowed. She didn't want him with her, but she had no choice. If he tried to get in her way, she would simply have to cut him down. They were adversaries now.

The moment breakfast was over, the old priest hobbled to the schoolroom, the children in tow. "Today," he said in a reed-thin voice, "there will be no lessons. Tomorrow is All Saints' Day, so you will fashion garlands of flowers for the chapel, and I want to see the biggest, the prettiest blooms in crocks at the foot of Our Lady. Saria will be in charge of the garlands, and Celeste will oversee the chapel arrangements. I'm going into town with Amalie and should return by sundown, but in case we are delayed, Rita is in charge of supper. Hurry now, for it will take many hours to do the flowers. And remember, they must be perfect.''

Amalie cursed under her breath, words she'd heard in town, words no lady would ever allow to pass her lips. Her best course of action, she decided, was to act as if nothing were amiss. She waited until they were alone and then approached the priest, forcing a note of cheerfulness into her voice. ''Do you have the stones, Father?''

''Yes, Amalie, I do. If you will prepare the horse and wagon, we can leave immediately.''

He listened as Amalie went off to hitch the old bay to the mission supply cart. He should have told her of his intentions. His conscience demanded she be told. Perhaps on the ride into town, he decided. All night he'd prayed for God to tell him what to do. He'd been a foolish old man, succumbing to the caress in a girl's voice—a foolish old man who'd thought he was doing the right thing by remaining silent in the face of deception. But she was Alvarez's daughter, although illegitimate, and nothing could change that.

The old priest sighed. Perhaps while he was in town he could go to confession. Father Juan would hear his sins and they'd talk afterward. It would ease his mind considerably. And tomorrow was All Saints' Day—God's way of giving him a chance to atone. He'd spend the entire day in prayer and fasting.

''Father, the wagon's ready,'' Amalie said, startling him from his sober thoughts. ''Please, allow me to help you.''

Father Renaldo suffered her touch as she helped him onto the hard, high seat. Before she snapped the reins she leaned over and said, "Father, I—I would like to see the diamonds before we start out."

Father Renaldo debated a moment, but only because he didn't want to touch the hard, bright stones. In his eyes they represented death. In the end he handed over the pouch, crossing himself imperceptibly. He wished he could see the girl's expression as she shook the glittering stones from their cloth bag into the palm of her hand.

"I hope they fetch a good price," Amalie muttered as she dropped them, one by one, back into the little pouch and tucked them away. "Thank you, Father."

The old man shook his head wearily. "I deserve no thanks for surrendering you to the forces of evil. Come, child, let us be on our way. I have no desire to travel during the hottest hours of the day."

An hour into their journey Amalie noticed that the priest was deep in prayer, his hands telling the rosary with an almost frantic intensity. He's afraid, she thought with sudden realization. He's afraid of me. We're bound together in this deception, and it's tearing him apart.

"Father, forgive me for asking, but why are you making this trip?" she asked, breaking the hour-long silence. "I appreciate your company, but the heat will shortly be unbearable, and we still have a long way to go."

The priest did not answer her; his lips moved silently in prayer. Amalie didn't repeat her question; she knew the answer. Father Renaldo intended to reveal the truth to Justice Muab. When she spoke again a little while later, her tone was light, conversational. "The sun today is particularly brutal, Father. And you're not well. Perhaps we should turn back," she said softly.

"No, no, I must get into town." He turned to her then, his rheumy eyes striving to pierce their prison of shadow. "Amalie, I cannot allow the justice to believe the lie I told him. I was blinded with what I felt was your need.

That house, child, will not make you happy. It's all based on lies, and I compounded those lies. Please . . . I want you to stay at the mission and help with the children. It's a good, honest life, and you are well suited to it. Forget that grand house and those rotting ships in the harbor. The diamonds are yours, although I feel in my heart they will only bring you misery and heartache. But as for the rest . . . Please tell me you understand,'' the old priest pleaded.

Amalie contemplated him coldly. "Of course I understand. Because I do not embrace your faith does not mean I am incapable of understanding. I simply disagree, which is my right. My father was a disgusting, treacherous, lustful man. He used my mother in ways that aren't fit for your ears to hear. I have a right to avenge her—and to see to it that I do not fall prey to the same fate. I refuse to die a slave, at the mercy of some man's whims of kindness or cruelty. This is my chance to live the life I want for myself—and neither you nor anyone else will stop me! Now, Father, I suggest you climb down from this wagon and return to the mission. Now. I'll go into town alone." Amalie reined in the horse and turned to the old priest with glittering eyes.

Father Renaldo heard the threat in her voice. Evil . . . He gripped his cane tighter in his gnarled old hand as he struggled down from the wagon. Walking back to the mission was better than forcing the issue now, here. He was no match for this one. Some way, somehow, he'd get word to the justice. His rosary in his hands, he began to trudge along the road, head bowed in prayer.

Amalie never looked back as she urged the old bay onward, to town.

Amalie arrived in town during the hottest part of the day without a drop of perspiration on her brow or a hair out of place. For the first time since starting out, she allowed her gaze to stray to the right and to the left as she observed the stately town houses of the rich traders and politicians. She particularly liked the grilled gates, manicured shrubbery, and long, circling drives. One day she, too, would have a town house here, she vowed.

One day she would ride into this town in a shiny black carriage, and every head in town would turn—the men's eyes full of desire, the women's full of envy. One day everyone would know and respect Amalie Suub Alvarez.

As the wagon clattered down the street, Amalie stared straight ahead; she was in the business district now, and she knew the shops were open, their proprietors lazing behind drawn shades. At the end of the street she tethered the old horse and ramshackle wagon and strode up the south walkway with her head held high. She was Amalie Alvarez—or she would be soon—and the sooner the people in town became aware of her, the better she would feel.

Her bare feet made slapping sounds on the wooden planks. Soon, she promised herself, she would have shoes to adorn her feet, as did all proper ladies. A splinter gouged her toe, but she kept on walking, her eyes searching for the gilt lettering that represented the jeweler's establishment. When she found it, she approached the entrance, heart pounding.

A cluster of bells tinkled as Amalie opened and closed the shop door. Sun ribboned through the windows, bathing her in a golden glow, shining through her thin chemise and outlining every limb and curve of her body. Grasping the small pouch, she walked up to the counter and shook the stones into the palm of her hand. She waited, her beautiful face impassive, for the arrogant-looking proprietor to get up from his chair and walk to the long counter that separated his offices from the entry area.

The jeweler's eyes widened at the sight of the girl in her

faded, worn dress. He almost ordered her out of his shop—until he saw the stones in her hand. Greedily, he made a move to pluck them from her palm, but the moment he did she closed her hand into a fist.

"I want to sell these. I know they're worth a lot; how much will you give me?" Amalie said, fixing him with her cat's eyes.

"Where did you get these?" the jeweler demanded. "I don't buy stolen goods."

"I didn't steal them; they're mine. Do you wish to buy them or not?"

"I need to examine them first," the jeweler said, clearing his throat.

Amalie opened her hand and gave the jeweler one large sparkling diamond at a time. She smirked as he licked his lips, eyes aglitter. Obviously he hadn't seen many diamonds of this quality.

The man held the jeweler's glass close as he examined each stone carefully. Amalie waited until he had replaced the last diamond in the pouch. From underneath the counter he withdrew a cash box. The small mound of guilders he counted out shocked her. She hadn't been prepared for this. Was it enough or not? She didn't know. Taking a gamble, she shook her head.

"I want gold sovereigns, and this is not enough," she said coldly, and waited, hardly daring to breathe. The man replaced the guilders and withdrew another box. Again he laid out a small mound, and again Amalie shook her head. The man added two more sovereigns to the small pile of gold. Again and again she shook her head, until she sensed that the man was nearing his last offer. Should she take it or not? Instinct warned her not to accept. "Add *all* of the guilders, and I will sell the diamonds," she told him.

The jeweler snorted. "Ridiculous! They aren't worth

that much. I have to be able to sell these at a profit. This is my last offer.''

''What would you offer for me?'' Amalie asked quietly.

''Why, I . . . I'm a respectable man and run a respectable business. I—''

''Have a wife.'' Amalie's yellow eyes flashed. ''But would she do the things to you I would do, Mynheer Jeweler?''

The jeweler licked his lips again. ''What . . . what kind of things?'' he asked in a quivering voice.

She smiled. ''Things to remember . . . things you'll take to your . . . grave.''

Slowly, seductively, Amalie leaned across the wooden counter, her cat's eyes dark brown now and moist with heat. The jeweler tore his hungry gaze from hers and looked down the front of her dress. He nearly choked at the sight. Amalie's smile promised untold delights as her tongue snaked out from between her teeth. She allowed it to caress first her top lip, then her lower lip. The jeweler moaned.

''All of the guilders, Mynheer. A larger pouch. Now . . . before—''

''Lock the door,'' the jeweler said hoarsely as he stuffed the gold into her pouch.

''No,'' Amalie said, walking around the counter. ''You will find what I do to you much more exciting if you fear . . . the unknown.''

''Yes, yes, hurry. This is unbearable,'' he said, unfastening his trousers. He was suddenly shy, muttering under his breath, ''I'm . . . I'm not very . . .'' His face reddened miserably.

''I can see what you mean, Mynheer. I know how to remedy your problem,'' Amalie said with a hint of sardonic laughter in her voice. ''Trust me, Mynheer, you will never want to bed your sensible wife in her sensible bloomers and corsets again.'' A deep growl of pleasure ripped from her mouth as she lifted the chemise over her head and stood before him naked in her splendor. The jeweler's eyes rolled back in his head as Amalie pulled him to the floor.

Several minutes later, sweat dripping from every pore in his body, the jeweler squealed like a pig going to market. ''What . . . wha . . . *oh!*''

''Shhh, I am about to remedy . . . your problem, Mynheer.''

Amalie's touch was light, almost playful as she caressed, tickled, and prodded, her strong, muscular thighs contracting against the jeweler's flabby limbs. Her face, however, was impassive as she recalled other times when she had been used and abused by some of the white plantation owners. Because she was tall and long-limbed, those men had thought her impervious to pain and had not been gentle. She'd promised herself that someday she would be as cold and brutal with fat Dutchmen and foppish Spaniards.

Barely audible moans and squeals of delight from the man beneath her brought her back to the job at hand. Her fingers stiffened as they moved downward to the patch of fair hair, and then lower still. With a lithe movement she slid between the man's spread legs, her knees closing and then widening against his manhood. When he yelped with pleasure, she intensified the pressure.

Long, velvety hair fell over her face, a veil to hide from the jeweler the contempt she bore him. She crooned soft words, words pleasing and sensual to the prone man beneath her.

''You're hurting me!'' the jeweler gasped.

''But it feels good, doesn't it?'' Amalie cooed as she pressed her knees against his throbbing testicles. When she released the pressure, the man sighed, and Amalie almost laughed. She waited a moment and then brought her knees together with such force, the jeweler's head jerked backward in pain. The palm of her hand shot forward and upward against his chin in a single, savage thrust. His eyes widened in disbelief, then glazed over as his life drained quickly out of him.

When Amalie had slid the chemise over her shoulders, she returned to the man lying on the floor. Working quickly, she pulled up his underdrawers and trousers, then dragged his body over to the chair he'd been sitting in. She continued to struggle with the man's enormous weight until she had him propped in the chair. Next, she scattered all his books and papers about the floor. Finally she came to his cash box. Without a qualm, she emptied it of all but a few gold coins, then jammed the lid so that it looked as though someone had tampered with it. She savored the feel of the pouch in her hand. Weight meant money, power, and leverage.

Without a backward glance at the jeweler, she let herself out the rear door of the shop into a deserted alley full of refuse and empty barrels. No eyes looked on her as she walked through the alley, her head high, her back ramrod stiff. She started to sing under her breath, a silly little tune the old priest had taught the children. She felt victorious. She had all but a few guilders of the jeweler's money, and she still had the diamonds.

Her next stop was the justice's office, where she stood waiting in respectful silence until he raised his head from the papers on his desk.

"I can see why you would be impatient after all these years," Muab said, nodding. "I affixed my seal to this proclamation earlier today, thinking you would soon come into town. As of now all of your . . . father's property and possessions, those that remain, are yours." He handed over a packet of papers and wasn't surprised to see the beautiful girl's hands tremble as she accepted it.

"Thank you, sir, for your time and trouble," she said quietly.

"Hrumph, yes, yes. You are now Amalie Alvarez. I've sent a letter off to the . . . to your father's superiors, informing them of this action. It is entirely possible they will respond, but unlikely. Give my regards to Father Renaldo," the justice said, dismissing her.

"I will tell him you send your regards."

The justice watched the tall girl walk through the door, wondering what she would do now. His stomach churned. It was wrong, he knew it was wrong, but . . . he no longer cared. He'd gone by the evidence, and in the end that's all that mattered. He wished the girl well.

The blazing sun boiled downward, but Amalie paid it no mind as she walked toward the harbor, shoulders drooping and head down in a subservient manner. For once she desired anonymity and knew full well that in her present posture the scurvy few at the harbor would virtually ignore her until she raised her head and challenged them with her yellow eyes.

The harbormaster was no stranger to Amalie. He'd always been civil when she appeared and asked to see the ships that belonged to Chaezar Alvarez. She also knew that he was a friend of the justice's and would now know that she was entitled to her father's property.

A monstrous banyan tree surrounded by thick greenery at the side of the road beckoned with promise of shade, and Amalie was drawn toward it. She needed time to think, to rest a moment, time to massage her aching, callused feet.

As she lowered herself onto a mossy patch beneath the old tree, she was suddenly assailed by doubt. Perhaps she should wait to visit the harbormaster, buy some clothes and shoes and come back another day. Those she would deal with now would regard her as a slab of meat, a slave's bastard child dressed in a worn, thin chemise that left nothing to the imagination. Would the gold in the pouch she held in her hand garner respect?

Her head snapped upward as another thought struck her. What would be the outcome in regard to the jeweler's death? Was there anyone who knew how much money he kept in his cash box—his wife, some family member, a shop owner? Had she left enough coins there to satisfy the authorities that burglary had not been the motive for his death? It had taken all her strength to snap the man's fat neck, something some men wouldn't be able to do. Certainly no one would suspect a woman. No, a simple crime of passion, a murder—probably at the hands of one bent on vengeance—would be the verdict rendered by the . . . justice, the same justice responsible for giving her her new life.

Satisfied that her interpretation of the incident would be shared by the authorities, Amalie rose to her feet in one effortless movement. She'd had all the rest she could afford, and as inviting as the tree looked, she had to move on. She straightened her shoulders and headed for the harbormaster's quarters.

Hans Wilhelm was a crusty old man with twinkling eyes and a hatred for soap and water. On his desk were two guns and a saber that he used or threatened to use on a daily basis. He was so fat he was grotesque, and his twinkling eyes were merely a trick of the light filtering through the wooden shutters. He was a hard man to deal with, and his only priority in life was to gouge as much money as he could from the owners of the trading vessels he dealt with.

Wilhelm leaned back in his chair, his belly jiggling with

his effort. His coarse shirt was stained with weeks of sweat, and he reeked of himself. Amalie breathed through her mouth as she entered his office and waited for him to speak. He knew why she was there; she could see it in his beady eyes. His voice, when he spoke, came from deep in his belly, gruff yet hollow-sounding.

"I've been waiting for you, Amalie, my dear."

"I want to know if you'll take the brigantine, the galleon, and the sloop and trade me a frigate." Amalie forced herself to sound casual, indifferent, as though she really didn't care one way or another what the harbormaster's answer would be.

Wilhelm's nostrils quivered. He smelled money. "Now, why would I want those rotten ships? And why would the likes of you be wanting a frigate?"

Staring at him, Amalie was reminded of a mound of dough with finger indentations. "I asked you a question, Mr. Wilhelm. If you can't give me an answer, I'll go to the Dutch East India Company. Or I can make inquiries elsewhere."

Wilhelm sighed wearily. "It would cost a fortune to have those ships careened, and they're rotted with teredo worm," he lied. "That will have to be taken care of before we can begin to discuss the possibilities you mentioned," the harbormaster said craftily. He wondered uneasily if this was some kind of trick to trap him. His fat stomach lurched when he remembered how he'd spent the money that came from Spain for repairs and harbor fees. Long ago he'd made up his mind to lie if any of the Spaniards' superiors ever came to claim the ships left in his care. He'd never been able to bring himself to the point where he would sell off or dispose of the ships out of fear that perhaps one day some fool would arrive with the proper credentials and claim the ships.

"I'm prepared to pay the bill . . . in full. But don't try

to cheat me, Mr. Wilhelm," Amalie said quietly. "I know how much upkeep costs per year. My father kept a ledger with all his debts."

"Yes, your . . . Mr. Alvarez was a crafty bastard." And so are you, he added silently.

They haggled for well over an hour until Amalie suddenly turned to leave. "We're getting nowhere, Mr. Wilhelm. Either you're interested or you aren't. I wish to settle this now. As to the frigate, I know there is one in the harbor that has been there for two years. Set your price . . . now!"

"All right, all right." Wilhelm waved a hand in the air as if tired of debate. "If you have a mind to, we can walk out to the wharf and see just how rotten those ships are."

"Both of us already know how rotten they are. They can, however, be salvaged, so why not finalize our business now? I'll return tomorrow, and you can have the papers ready for me to sign. I want the justice to oversee this transaction. I'm sure he'll want to send off another letter to my father's government, apprising them of the fact that I'm selling the ships to you. Is that satisfactory?"

After another twenty minutes of haggling, the final price was agreed upon. "I want the frigate careened and then taken to the cove at Saianha," Amalie said. "How long will that take?"

"A month, possibly less," the harbormaster said, rubbing his jowls thoughtfully.

"Good. Then it's a bargain?"

"Yes, a bargain." Wilhelm's eyes gleamed at the thought of how full his cash box would be.

Amalie nodded. "I'll return at eight o'clock in the morning. Will that be satisfactory?" Again Wilhelm bobbed his head.

Smiling, Amalie strode down the plank walkway to the harbor and stared at the row of ships in their berths. She knew immediately which ones were her father's, and she also knew where the frigate was. She shaded her eyes from the burning sun for a better look. To her, the frigate looked in worse condition than her father's ships. When she'd had enough of the brutal sun and the sailors' leering eyes, she retraced her steps and headed down a well-trod path to the town's only brothel.

Amalie hated the place and all that went on behind the curtains on the second floor, hated it because the women were used and paid a pittance for their bodies. Three girls from the mission were here simply because there was nowhere else for them to go.

At the back door of Christabel's establishment she called out and announced herself. Anyone who knew her would have been astounded at the look of compassion in her eyes as several young girls ran to her. How old and weary they looked, and none of them was as old as she. She stared into the eyes of the old hag who owned the brothel. "I've come to tell you that these *children* won't be returning to this . . . place," she said coldly, defying the hag to question her further.

Outside in the sultry late afternoon, Amalie explained to her charges that she was taking them back to her plantation, where they would live and work. "All I ask is your loyalty; if you can pledge that to me, then I will take care of you." The girls nodded, their eyes alive for the first time in months. "Then it's settled. I must stay in town this evening so I can be at the harbormaster's office at eight o'clock. We'll have to sleep in the wagon this evening, and we'll need food. One of you can go to the shop for it. I also need to know where I can hire some able-bodied men to crew my frigate once it reaches Saianha."

The girls giggled. The oldest, at fourteen, pointed to the path behind her. "All you have to do is waylay them on their way back from Christabel's parlor. Or we can do it for you, they know us.'' Three pairs of grateful eyes waited for Amalie's response. After a tense moment, she nodded.

''Waylay them, then—but that's all. Believe me when I tell you you'll never suffer at a man's hands again. It's getting late now, and I have no desire to be on this street once darkness falls. We'll come back after midnight.''

The children, as Amalie thought of them, huddled close together in the wagon, a huge banyan tree shielding them from the late-afternoon sun. For a while they whispered and giggled; then, eventually, they slept, sweet smiles on their faces.

Amalie sat on the ground with her back against the age-less tree, her long, honey-colored legs stretched out in front of her and her future secure in the pouch around her neck. Her head buzzed with the day's activities and the knowledge that by tomorrow she would have a frigate and a crew to man it. She would also have her father's mansion. The girls would clean it and keep house, but would there be enough money left to initiate the necessary repairs to make the place livable? There would have to be; she'd see to it.

A much more serious problem was what to do about the old priest and the dangerous knowledge he possessed. He alone could ruin her scheme. If walking back to the mission in the heat hadn't killed him, then she would be forced to deal with Father Renaldo more directly. It would be at least a year before another missionary would arrive, possibly longer.

She could move the rickety mission to her plantation. The children could live in the old slave quarters, and their first major task would be to clear away the jungle from the main house. She knew that the fussy, flighty town women would cluck their tongues at first, but in the end they would approve as long as the quarters held beds and were clean.

Amalie Suub Alvarez . . . protector of small children. Who would ever fault her?

Amalie's yellow eyes calmed, and as she relaxed she gave the appearance of a sleepy cat. Her plan, as she thought of it, had many parts. The children were the first part; she needed them to work for her. The frigate was the second part of the plan, and securing a good crew was the third part. The last part of her plan, the grand finale, hinged on the first three parts.

Excitement coursed through Amalie. It would be dangerous, deadly even, but if she didn't make any mistakes, she was sure she could assume the identity of the woman her father called the Sea Siren. An able crew would help her plunder the seas. Riches beyond her dreams would be hers. Her father's kingdom would be restored. She would be a queen and the children her loyal subjects. It was a perfect plan. The only flaw—if it could be called a flaw—was that her kingdom wouldn't have a king. Perhaps a prince or two, but never a king.

Amalie chuckled deep in her throat and dug her toes into the soft dark earth. Father Renaldo had always said one must anticipate problems and work them out before they became major concerns. There would be problems. She had no wicked scar on her arm, for one thing. The pictures in back of her father's journal denoted a terrible scar that ran the length of the sea witch's arm. Yes, the scar was going to be a problem, but it could be dealt with if she was willing to endure pain and disfigurement.

But how would she explain her sudden wealth? The thought had been in the back of her mind for days now. Anticipate, anticipate . . .

Amalie bolted upward, her cat's eyes lighting with sudden inspiration. The justice had said he was sending a second letter to her father's superiors in Spain informing them of his decision. Months from now she could say her father's holdings in Cadiz and Seville had been transferred over to her. The yellow eyes gleamed. The only person who could dispute her was the justice, but he would have given over his post by then. And he was a very tired, very old man, looking forward to his retirement.

Her plan, Amalie decided, would have no flaws, none at all.

A long time later, when the slice of moon rode high in the heavens, Amalie stirred. It was cool now, with a light caressing breeze. Overhead, stars sprinkled the sky in the velvety night. The birds had been silent for hours, and not a sound crept to her ears. It was time.

She walked on callused feet to the wagon, betraying her uncertainty as she roused the girls and asked, "How do we do this? Should we walk through town or . . . ?"

One of the girls giggled and said, "No self-respecting lady walks about after dark unless she's escorted by a man. Christabel's place is past the harbor. I know another way to get there, but it is longer."

"Show me the way," Amalie ordered, relieved. She wanted no encounters with any of the townspeople.

In the following hours, Amalie made many promises. Some she would keep; others were mere words. There was no honor in what she was planning, and the only reason she knew she would keep some of the pledges was to stay alive herself.

Shortly before dawn she issued her last order to a swarthy seaman with a stubble of beard and a nose that had been broken in too many places to count. "One month from today you will sail my ship to the cove at Saianha. Once the ship is berthed there, you will live aboard until I am ready to set sail. You will have a home with me for as long as you need one, providing you do not betray me or cross me in any way. You will be well paid, and you will be richer than you ever dreamed. I demand only one thing of you, and that is loyalty. Do you agree to my terms?''

The seaman looked Amalie over from the top of her head to the tips of her toes. His eyes strayed to the little girls, all of whom he'd had over the past months. Mellow now with rum in his gut and his loins sated, he nodded agreeably, but his eyes were those of a shark in open water.

''Aye, one month from today I will be in Saianha,'' he replied.

Amalie watched as he stumbled down the road to town. She nodded to the girls. ''It seems I have the scurviest, deadliest crew imaginable. For the right price one can get *anything*.''

''Cutthroats,'' one of the girls whispered.

''Devils,'' said the second little girl.

''Vermin,'' said the third.

''Yes, all those things, but they will make us rich. They are men—stupid creatures who understand greed because money can buy them women and rum. But they don't think beyond that. I, on the other hand, am a woman, and there are no limits to what a woman can do, especially one who understands her adversaries.''

Amalie's plan was under way.

That morning, Amalie's business with the harbormaster was completed in less than an hour, and she was on her way back to the mission by nine o'clock, a satisfied smile on her face. The smile lasted for several hours—until she and the girls discovered Father Renaldo's body alongside the road. Amalie leapt from the wagon and cried real tears . . . of relief.

Chapter Three

The trees overhead were silent in the soft, warm breeze, an indication that Pilar was calm . . . for the moment. Jet eyes watched, their field of vision almost limitless as her young sailed up and then down, testing their newfound freedom.

Pilar's killing talons were tucked beneath her long, fluffy belly feathers and had been in that position for some time. Slowly, calmly, she ruffled her feathers, taking on the appearance of a dry pine cone, and then shook them free a second later. Shiny emerald leaves moved in the dry breeze as the huge bird was transformed suddenly into something swift and deadly. The houseboy standing under the tree dropped the pail of raw meat and ran as fast as his bare feet would carry him. Safely inside, he peered through the breakfast room windows, his eyes searching fearfully for Gaspar.

The hawks were his responsibility, the housekeeper had told him, and he had given his word to the van der Rhys that he would care for the winged devils until they were ready to move on. He hated and feared them and their deadly sounds.

The evil-looking male, Gaspar, had been gone for almost two days, something that had happened twice before since Miss Fury's departure. The female was not her usual calm self. "Devil birds," he spat out, and blessed himself before returning to his other duties.

Outside, the branches of the chestnut tree dipped and

swayed as Sato and Lago frantically sought purchase with their talons. Satisfied that her offspring were secure, Pilar soared to the ground, her talons digging into the wooden pail. She waited, wings tucked close against her chest, for her young to descend. The moment they left their perch she sailed upward. She watched as the young ate their fill and then returned to their perch beneath Pilar to wait for Gaspar.

The huge hawk returned as the sun was setting. Pilar fanned her wing and lowered it delicately over his tired body. He slept, his shiny eyes at rest, with Pilar next to him.

Six weeks to the day of Fury's departure, Sato and Lago were able to fend for themselves. Their glittering eyes watched as Gaspar and Pilar emptied the basket in the chestnut tree.

Gaspar ruffled his feathers before he soared straight up, Pilar in his wake. They circled overhead several times before they started their journey.

"Kukukukuku." Good-byegood-byegood-byegood-bye. For one startling second Pilar faltered, her huge wings dipping in the soft breeze. Then Gaspar tapped her wings with his own, his signal not to look back.

Their journey was just beginning.

Ronrico Diaz, the captain of the *Java Queen*, was a religious man, and he found himself looking forward to the late afternoons when Fury would walk about the deck and talk with him about her beliefs and her decision to enter the convent. He himself had two daughters who were nuns and one son who was a priest, and he constantly spoke of his family. Every night he prayed for this girl because he wasn't sure she was ready for God. So many rosaries, so many prayers tumbling from her lips, so many questions in her eyes.

"Miss Fury, do you think you will recognize Java once

we dock? It's been many years since you were there," he said gruffly.

"I think so. I was ten when we left, and my parents talked about Java constantly so that I would remember. I'm looking forward to seeing my old home again. You seem pensive this afternoon, Captain Diaz. Is something troubling you?"

"Yes and no. We're due for some bad weather shortly, I can feel it in my bones, and we sail with an empty hold. Cargo makes it easier to ride out a storm."

"I have every faith in you and the crew. And to add to that faith, I will say some extra prayers. I thought . . . what I mean to say is, I was concerned that you might be worried about pirates. We're approaching dangerous waters, are we not?"

He patted her arm. "The *Java Queen* is a fortress, your father saw to that. There's no need for you to worry about pirates. They won't waste time attacking a ship that carries no cargo. In ten weeks you'll be safe and sound in your old home. I made that promise to your parents."

"God sees to our safety, Captain Diaz. I myself have no fear. Long ago I placed my hand in His, and He will protect me, and you, and this crew. But I must admit I'm so bored, I would almost relish some excitement," she blurted out.

"What kind of excitement?" the captain asked uneasily, wishing Regan van der Rhys had allowed him to take on at least a few passengers. But the governor had been adamant about the empty hold and not taking on passengers.

"Anything!" Fury cried. "Captain, do you think the men would allow me to join in some of their games, the ones they play with cards and dice?"

"Your father would have me drawn and quartered!" the captain exploded.

"My father isn't here. And I don't see what harm it can

do. Not every day, of course, just once in a while," she coaxed.

"They're a motley crew, and they swear and cheat," the captain told her. "And they play for money. It's no place for a woman promised to God."

"Would they swear and cheat with a woman promised to God? I think not. And I have money to play with. I see no problem, Captain."

"They drink and tell bawdy stories," the captain said desperately.

"Captain Diaz, I was not raised in cotton bunting. I grew up with four brothers who were all hellions. I've heard all the bawdy stories. I'm an adult, Captain, and just because I'm entering a convent doesn't mean I don't know what goes on in the world." To drive her point home, she added, "Don't forget how my father took us all to sea every year. He told me I needed a well-rounded education. I even know how to swear, what do you think of that?"

"I think it's a sin," Captain Diaz groaned.

"We're all sinners in one way or another. Captain, I wish to play," she said firmly. "And tomorrow I would like to take the wheel for a little while if you have no objection."

The captain had plenty of objections, but he wasn't about to voice them now. "I'll speak to the men. If they say nay, there isn't much I can do about it. If they agree, then you . . . may participate. Now, isn't it time for your evening prayers?" he asked sourly.

"So it is. I'll pray that you tell me during the evening meal that it's agreeable. Adios, Captain." Fury laughed all the way to her cabin.

Alone in her cabin, Fury realized she was more than just bored: she was lonely. She'd been at sea for a little over six weeks and still had ten more weeks to go before she set foot on dry land. Her rosary, always a source of comfort, found its way to her hand. She fingered the beads, but she didn't pray. The holy ritual did not comfort her; she felt angry and didn't know why. She made a tight fist of the prayer beads before she placed them under her pillow to gaze around her with somber eyes.

Her quarters were rough yet comfortable, with a few of her more treasured possessions scattered about. The cubicle was small, but she knew her room at the convent would be smaller still. She would have a candle, a pallet to sleep on, her prayer beads, and possibly a prayer stool.

In a way, Fury thought morosely, this long sea journey was to prepare her for her lonely life. The first day she'd rejoiced to be truly alone with God and her prayers. After several hours of repeating them, she'd tired of prayers, and her thoughts had strayed to her parents and her beloved brothers, to Gaspar and Pilar . . . and to Luis Domingo. She'd daydreamed of excitement and adventure and indulged in one satisfying reverie after another. The first time it happened she had wanted to pray, needed to pray, but the familiar, comforting words wouldn't come. And today she'd spent four hours on her knees willing the prayers to pass her lips, but to no avail.

"This *is* what I want," Fury whispered fiercely. "It's what I prayed for all my life, and now that it's almost in my grasp, it's slipping away from me—and it's my own fault. My thoughts are no longer pure. I've become selfish in my boredom." The realization that she'd cajoled the captain into helping her relieve her boredom sent scorching color to her cheeks.

"What kind of person does that make me?" she asked herself, mortified. Her conscience answered: *Human, normal . . . mortal.* "Yes, but my life has been promised to God," she protested. "I want everything. I don't want rules and taboos. I want . . . I want. It's that simple."

Fury stretched out on her bunk, hands reaching beneath the pillow for her prayer beads. They were her lifeline to God, a now tenuous bond that was slowly being severed by . . . herself. She wept tears of anger and humiliation that the life she'd planned so carefully was eluding her through self-indulgence and cant. At last, exhausted by her inner struggle, she slept.

Up on deck, the captain—an honorable man, for the most part—was attempting to persuade his crew to Fury's request. "It is a small favor I'm asking of you. Think of the girl and not yourselves for a change. What harm will it do to give up your grog for an hour or two? What harm is there in letting her win once or twice? And, it wouldn't hurt you to spruce up a little for the lady," he added meaningfully. "Now, I'm not asking you, I'm *ordering* you to do me this *one* favor!"

Tobias, the first mate, grinned crookedly at Diaz. "No need to shout, Cap'n. The men will act accordingly. When she loses all her money, the jig's up. She can't play without it—those are the rules. It'll be fair and square, Cap'n, you have my word."

The captain gave his first mate a gruff smile. To his surprise, he found he was looking forward to the confrontation between his salty crew of sea dogs and the little lady of God. It would do the scurvy lot good to act like gentlemen for a little while. And he seemed to recall Regan van der Rhys telling him that his daughter was a fair hand with the dice and the cards. "A female gambling shark" he'd called her.

The laughter rumbling in the captain's belly as he strode away made the back of Tobias's neck prickle. He stared after the old sea goat with suspicious eyes.

When Fury woke an hour later she was drenched with perspiration. She brushed at the fluffy tendrils of hair that clung to her cheeks and knew a quick wash and powder were in order before she dined with the captain in his quarters.

Normally, after a nap, she would rise and then drop to her knees and pray. Now she squeezed her eyes shut and willed a prayer to her lips.

Hail Holy Queen . . . Merciful Father, I implore you . . . What was *wrong* with her? Where was her God? Why wasn't He there to comfort her?

"You're testing me!" she cried, anguished. "And I'm failing miserably. I can't remember my prayers, my knees are sore, and my thoughts are far from pure. I'm contemplating a diversion to drive away my boredom. Why are You letting me do this? I don't understand!"

In desperation she dropped to her knees and reached for the wooden cross on her pillow. "Oh, my God, I am heartily sorry . . ."

For what? a niggling voice inquired.

"For failing my God," Fury murmured, weeping.

You cannot fail God unless He allows it, the tiny voice responded. *Perhaps He isn't ready for you yet.*

Fury shook her head. "I must be stronger. I know that. And I try to be . . . but it's the dreams, the terrible, sinful dreams. I cannot make them go away. I have no control over them!"

Your secret desires, the voice tormented her. *Women of God hold no secret desires. In your heart you aren't ready to embrace God.*

"*No!* No, that's not true! I love God more than life itself." But no matter how hard she tried, Fury could not deny the words. She *was* having sinful dreams, and she *was* dwelling on them, trying to decipher them, willing them in her mind to mean nothing.

Defeated by the knowledge of her own unworthiness, she rose from the bed to splash cold water over her face and rub her fiery cheeks with a towel. When she'd changed her dress and run a brush through her hair, she again sat down on the bed, reaching automatically for her crucifix. As her fingers caressed the figure on the cross, her eyes filled with tears. This wasn't supposed to happen. She was supposed to be happy, and she was more miserable than she'd ever been in her life.

The dreams were part of it—dreams of Luis Domingo and the hawks. Dreams could be explained away, even squelched if one had enough willpower. But the picture flashes she experienced when she was calm, her mind at peace—those truly bothered her.

Premonitions? Daydreams? Her head felt like a beehive, all jumbled sound and mindless fury. She had to think, and she had to think *now* about what she'd seen before she drifted into sleep . . . Gaspar and Pilar flying in a tight formation to reach her, their eyes seeking out the *Java Queen*. She shivered in the warm cabin. They were searching for her now, pursuing the ship. Soon she would know if these pictures were real or the devil's work.

The devil's work . . . She rubbed her knuckles against her eyes. That's why she couldn't remember her prayers: she'd allowed the devil inside her mind, and now she was no longer holy.

"Begone, Satan!" she shouted. "I renounce you in the name of Jesus Christ!" She waited, holding her breath, for the imagined holocaust.

The supper bell rang. Shoulders slumping, Fury slammed the door behind her as she fled, heart pounding, up the ladder to the captain's quarters. One picture pursued her as she ran—that of Luis Domingo wrapping his strong arms about her naked body. Shuddering, squeezing her eyes tight against the image, she careened into the captain's quarters, flustered and breathless, an apology on her lips for her unladylike behavior.

It wasn't until the galley cook served up a dessert of thick-crusted, greasy apple pie that the captain spoke about Fury's request. "They agreed," he said gruffly.

"When?" Fury asked, suddenly nervous.

"They're waiting topside for you now. Mind you they play for blood; it's more than sport with them."

"Thank you, Captain, I know it wasn't easy for you to . . . coerce the crew."

Diaz leaned back on his chair, a cigar clamped firmly between his teeth, watching as his slim young charge left the table to do battle with his band of sea serpents. He wasn't sure whom he pitied more—the girl or the men.

A purse of coins in her hand, Fury tripped over to the sterncastle and motioned to the men that she was ready to play. She fought the laughter bubbling in her throat at the sight of them. Their hair was combed but still wet, their beards trimmed, and they wore clean shirts. To a man, they looked embarrassed and uncomfortable.

Fury gathered up her skirts before she settled on her haunches the way the men did. She folded her hands primly in front of her. "Gentlemen, if you will explain the fine points of this game to me, I think we can be under way," she said, eyes twinkling.

Two hours later Fury looked down at the pile of coins next to her. Clearly she was the evening's winner. "However did this happen?" she asked innocently.

"I thought you said you never did this before," grumbled Basil, the second mate.

"Makes no difference, mate," Tobias said gruffly. "She won it fair and square and wiped us out."

"And to show you that I am fair and a good sport, I'm going to give you all a chance to win it back." Fury smiled sweetly. "Now, I'm going to divide this money into even stacks, and I'll cut the cards with each of you, winner takes the pile. Is that agreeable with you?" Slowly, reluctantly, the men nodded and gathered around her. "Good. All right, then"—she held out the pack of cards—"who wants to go first?"

Suddenly a brisk wind whipped across the deck, and a clap of thunder rumbled ominously in the distance.

"Let's make short work of this, mates," Tobias said, rising and brushing off his leggings. "We're going to have a downpour any second now."

Four minutes later Fury walked away with her three original coins in her hand. "Weather permitting, I'd be more than pleased to join you tomorrow," she called over her shoulder. "Thank you all for being so kind to me."

The crew stared at one another, their mouths hanging open. "She's better than any of us," growled Esteban, the cook.

"I never saw a lady spit on the dice before. In fact, I never saw a lady *roll* dice before," Basil said in awe.

"She didn't cheat, either. I watched her like a hawk," Javier, the bosun, said sourly.

Tobias grinned. "At least she gave us a chance to win our money back. I for one like the lady, and I think we all enjoyed the evening whether we admit it or not. C'mon, now, lads. It's time to secure the ship for the squall."

The storm, when it finally hit, lasted a full five hours. Not until the sea was calm again, lapping against the sides of the ship with rhythmic familiarity, did Fury relax enough to fall into an uneasy sleep punctuated by vague images of two black shapes riding a tall man's shoulders.

The following morning, when Fury knelt by her bunk, the prayers she couldn't remember came easily to her lips. She prayed aloud until her voice grew hoarse and her knees protested. She had so much to make up for, so many prayers to be said. Unbidden, a prayer for Luis Domingo tumbled from her lips. Heat spiraled up from the core of her being and settled on her cheeks. She said a rosary and then another for her wicked thoughts, and still they stayed with her.

She was angry now, with herself and with her God, who kept testing her over and over. Well, she'd had enough!

Fury washed and dressed and realized that she'd had nothing to eat, but she wasn't hungry. She'd walk along the deck and soak up the warm sun. Perhaps she'd read or write a little in the journal she'd kept since childhood. When her mother had given it to her many years before she'd whispered, "For your secret thoughts, darling." She'd been afraid to write down her secret thoughts, though, for fear her inquisitive brothers would somehow find the journal and mock her.

The crew nodded to her amiably as she strolled along the deck. Fury sighed as she settled herself on a caned lounge with her book. Today was going to be like all the other days—slow-moving and boring.

The following days crept by on tortoise legs and then swept into weeks, and Fury's routine was always the same: she ate, she slept, and she prayed—or tried to pray—and at night she gambled with the crew. At best it was a monotonous and predictable business, and she realized she hated it. Her devotions were more sporadic now, less intense, and she constantly questioned her God. Daily she prayed for a sign that she was doing the right thing. At first she felt dismayed when her prayers went unanswered, and then she grew angry and demanding, even to the point of threatening to abandon her vocation altogether.

At some point—she wasn't sure exactly when—the notion struck her that she was being tested not by God, but by herself. The realization left her so unnerved that she forced herself one morning to sit down with her journal and make two lists—one of everything she loved and was giving up and a second of everything she would gain once she entered the convent. Even after several hours' concentration, her second list was pitifully short; still she clung stubbornly to the conviction that, despite her threats, she was meant for a life devoted to God. "I'm going into the convent," she declared fiercely, "and that's all there is to it!"

Suddenly the sun was blotted out overhead. Fury raised her eyes, and for a moment her heart stopped when she realized what she was seeing. She ran to the rail and shouted, "Here! *Here!*" Her arms flailed in the air as she cried out, bringing Tobias running to her side. "It's Gaspar and Pilar! I can't believe it! They've found me!"

The weary hawks worked the wind, racing down, then up, literally hanging in the warm breeze. Fury's heart pounded in her chest as the majestic birds made one final circle and then sailed gracefully to the deck.

Tears streamed down Fury's cheeks as she reached out to stroke "her beauties," as she called them. Pilar lifted one huge wing in greeting. Gaspar, his glittering eyes triumphant, leaned toward his mistress and laid his head against her cheek.

"I knew you would come, I felt it in my heart," she whispered. "Oh, I'm so glad you're here—I've missed you terribly!"

She turned to Tobias, smiling at him through her tears. "They're exhausted, and probably haven't eaten for ever so long. They need food and a basket—wide, but not deep. Please fetch them for me," she said.

Warily the captain came up behind her. "I see it, but I don't believe it. Your father told me about these birds—killers, aren't they?"

Fury laughed. "Nonsense. Wild hawks, perhaps, but not killers, these two. I raised both of them from the time they were mere fledglings. They're completely loyal to me. As long as I'm not threatened in any way, they'll remain quite calm. Can you imagine, flying all this way! You look surprised, Captain Diaz." Fury laughed. "I can tell you exactly how they got here. They can fly six to eight hours straight. They roosted in ships, and when possible they probably flew along the coast, stopping in ports like . . . like people!'' She gurgled with laughter. ''Who cares how they did it? They did it, and they're here safe and sound. Not to mention exhausted.'' She crooned softly to the weary birds, stroking their sleek backs. She swallowed against the lump in her throat when she noticed how many feathers both hawks had lost. She thought her heart would burst with love for the birds.

Diaz watched as Fury stroked the hawks' silky backs, her delight and pleasure in them evident on her face. It was the happiest he'd seen her since she boarded the *Queen.* But he didn't care what reassurances she made; these were hawks, and hawks were killers. He wanted no part of them.

''I cannot conceive how you flew all this way and actually found me,'' Fury whispered to the exhausted birds. ''I know I'll never understand, but I thank you for coming.'' Tears blurred her vision as Gaspar and Pilar leaned forward to touch her cheeks with their beaks. She yowled her pleasure then, sobs racking her body. The hawks looked at each other. They'd never heard these sounds before. They rustled their wings, stretching them to cover the girl's head and shoulders.

Tobias, on his way back with the basket in hand, stopped dead in his tracks at this display of devotion from two birds of prey. He inched forward cautiously, then set down the basket and slid it with his foot toward the rail. In his other hand he held a bucket of salt pork. With the hawks' glittering eyes on him every second, he lowered it to the deck, and then without a word withdrew as quickly as he could, heading for the crew's quarters and the keg of rum the men had stowed away there.

Fury dried her eyes and reached for the basket. When

she spoke, her voice was soft, a comforting caress. "We have only two more weeks before we reach land. Until then you can rest, both of you." She pointed to the mizzenmast and held out the basket to Pilar, who clasped it with her talons.

Pilar turned into the breeze and with barely a ruffle of her wings, the stately bird sailed upward on the gentle breeze. Gaspar and Fury watched until the basket was secure in the rigging. The moment Pilar's head disappeared, Gaspar swooped downward and with one talon lifted the bucket of meat. His wings fanned as he, too, caught the breeze, and he swooped upward. Fury clapped her hands in delight. "Rest, you've earned it," she called up to them in a lilting voice.

Fury's faith, which had slowly been deserting her since her journey began, was now restored. She clasped her hands reverently and murmured, "You sent them, I know You did. Forgive me, God, for doubting. Forgive my doubts."

She gave no thought to the fact that when she entered the convent, the hawks would have to leave her . . . once and for all.

The *Java Queen* was three days away from the Port of Java when a storm lashed across the ocean. It was the worst of his career, Captain Diaz declared worriedly as he ordered Fury below decks until the faltering storm had subsided. "If it ever does," he added mournfully.

"I have to get Gaspar and Pilar," Fury cried, running forward to the rail. "They'll die up there with no protection!"

Diaz grabbed her arm. "I'm *ordering* you below, Miss Fury. *Now!*" He spun around and bellowed for his second mate. "Basil, take this girl below decks and lock her door!"

The moment Basil reached out for Fury's arms, two

black shapes swooped across the quarterdeck, screeching their disapproval. Fury wrenched free of Basil's hold and fell to her knees in the driving rain. "Go below!" she screamed to the birds. "I'll try to follow you."

Gaspar flew ahead of her, Pilar at her back, her powerful wings urging the frightened girl on toward safety. At the top of the ladder Fury turned to look behind her, but all she could see was the blackness of Pilar's outfanned wings. Gaspar was above her, she could sense his presence. Choking and sputtering, she slid down the ladder and landed flat on her back. Gaspar fluttered down the hold to her side, and Pilar, talons curled beneath her, joined him.

Amid the muted howl of wind and water, Fury struggled to a half-sitting position, her eyes on Gaspar. Twice she tried to get on her feet, but Pilar's wing tips held her down. "Hawhawhaw," she screeched.

Suddenly the deafening sounds of the storm above decks lessened and Gaspar was alongside Pilar. Fury watched as Pilar dropped her wings to wipe the rain from Gaspar's drenched feathers.

On her hands and knees Fury crawled to her cabin, the hawks urging her forward.

Safe in her cabin, she sat on the edge of her bunk, the hawks perched on the mahogany footboard, their gleaming eyes finally at rest.

Above decks the sea boiled and the heavens split as Captain Diaz steered the galleon under her close-reefed sails. He kept her bow pointed as near into the wind as possible, but never dead into the eye of the storm. Gigantic waves, whipped by the gale into curly white combers, rolled continuously from the west. Spindrift lashed out with unrelenting fury, stinging his face as he fought the wheel.

The maelstrom demanded his full concentration. Powerful seafaring hands, rough and callused, gripped the stout wheel. Lightning flashed, illuminating the dark, spectral shapes of clouds scudding across the sky. This rain could kill him, he knew, drive him overboard, beat the strength from his body. He'd once heard Regan van der Rhys liken the rain to a vampire draining a man's vitality bit by bit until he could no longer stand erect. Already the savage torrent was whipping up his nostrils and down his throat, choking off his air supply, pounding him to nothingness. The bastard wind was going to drive the *Queen* to destruction if he didn't regain his strength and do something.

Diaz realized something in that moment of fear. It wasn't the storm that frightened him out of his wits, but the thought of what Regan van der Rhys would do to him if anything happened to his daughter.

Fearing the worst, Diaz grappled with a length of sailcloth to lash himself to the wheel, but it was ripped from his numb hands by a violent breaker.

Minutes seemed hours and hours seemed eternities as the storm raged. Diaz was blinded by the brutal downpour but kept to his heading by sheer instinct. Suddenly a crashing breaker and a yowling cannon of wind exploded behind him. He had no time to think or pray as he was carried away, crashing and sliding in the unholy cataclysm. No man heard his screams as he was swept over the side.

Fury knew the moment they lost course. The huge galleon listed, righted, then rolled almost on her side. She was thrown from the bunk, her body crashing against the wall. Dazed, she struggled to her knees.

"The captain's lost control of the wheel," she moaned to the glowering hawks. "This storm will carry us off our course, back out to sea!"

The galleon's hold on the monstrous roiling ocean was weak—she was in dire need of ballast. Fury rolled from one end of her cabin to the other as the *Queen* fought to remain upright under the first mate's hands.

She was beneath the hawks now at the foot of the bunk, her fear-filled eyes on their gigantic talons. Deadly talons. They could grasp hundreds of pounds and lift it straight into the air and still fly as though unencumbered. There was no other word to describe the hawks except to say they were powerful.

She cried out in despair, knowing full well there was nothing she could do to fight the battering storm and keep the galleon on her course. She'd manned the wheel on her father's ships hundreds of times, but always in calm waters. She was strong, but no match for this.

Her stomach heaved sickeningly. She'd never before given thought to her own mortality. If she died now at the hands of the storm and sea, she would never enter the convent, never, ever see . . . neverneverneverever.

She wished she knew more about eternity, that nebulous place after death. Her final accounting in the eyes of God. Was she clean and pure enough to enter the gates of heaven?

With one mighty shove she was on her feet. "Oh, God, I don't want to die, not yet. Please!" she shrieked.

The hawks' feathers rustled, the sound vying with the storm, their jet eyes on the girl.

She was upright now, holding to the bunk with a vise-like grip. "I must ask the impossible of you," she told the two hawks, whose eyes were fixed on her with uncanny comprehension. "Of you . . . and of myself."

When she made her way, weaving and stumbling, out of the cabin and down the passageway, they followed. Twice she was thrown against the wall with the violent pitching of the boat. At the ladder, she paused. She knew the hawks couldn't help her open the hatch to the deck; there was nothing for their talons to grasp. She swore then, words she didn't know she knew, words she'd heard her brothers hiss at one another when they were angry, words her father had muttered under his breath. With a strength born of desperation, she threw herself against the hatch door again and again, but each time the battering wind slammed it shut, her shoulder taking the brunt of the blow. She waited, counting seconds before she gave one last heave. A flurry of angry sound roared past her ears as Gaspar soared through the tumultuous wind, his talons securing a hold on the stout wood support. A second later Pilar was at his side.

Fury stumbled up and out, then fell to her hands and knees, fighting the wind and blinding water. She saw no one, but could hear the crew cursing and shouting as they struggled with the sail and rigging.

Her nails were broken to the quick, her hands and knees full of splinters as she crawled a few steps and then was driven backward by the ravaging wind. She had no idea how long it took her, but at last she reached the wheelhouse and pulled herself upright with the wheel for support.

Everywhere was black as India ink; the lanterns had all gone out. Fury's hands moved on the wheel and touched something cold and hard. Gaspar's talons. She moved her hand to the right: Pilar's talons. *How did they know this was what she wanted them to do?* An eerie feeling swept through her as she realized that her life depended on these hawks that were so tuned to her feelings. She would have cried for joy but she was too frightened. In the very core of her soul she knew no force on earth could make them relinquish their hold on the wheel.

Fury felt silly and ridiculous when she shouted, "Steady on, mates, a true course to Java or dry land, whichever comes first!" The crew couldn't hear her, and if they did, she didn't care.

For hours the *Java Queen* heaved with the force of the surf, the masts groaning with the weight of the saturated rigging. The battered ship rose and fell in the angry, swelling sea. Fury steered her course straight and true—frightened, yes, but exhilarated and buoyed by the unshakable conviction that Gaspar and Pilar would see the *Java Queen* home safely.

The relentless wind and surging sea left with the last of the black night, and dawn appeared, gray and misty. Fury's shoulders slumped as a weary sigh escaped her. Gradually her ears picked up the jabbering sounds of the men as they emerged one by one from their posts onto the now gently rolling deck. They'd all survived, she thought in relief. The disbelief she read on their faces at the picture of herself and the hawks at the wheel made her smile wanly.

"Where's the captain?" Tobias asked uneasily, his eyes still on the hawks.

"I don't know." She shook her head. "I took the wheel from Eduardo."

"He ordered us to take cover when the storm was at its worst. There was nothing we could do but go over the side. We did our best, miss, so did the captain." He blessed himself to make his point. "Spread out, mates," he ordered the others, "and see what you can find."

Tobias turned back to Fury. "These birds steered this ship through the storm?"

Fury smiled. "I helped a little, but, yes, they did exactly that. And the three of us will be more than happy to turn the wheel over to you, Tobias. I have no idea where we are or how far off course."

Pilar's wings rustled slightly, and in the blink of an eye she and Gaspar were sailing upward toward the mizzenmast.

"Devil birds," Tobias muttered as he took the wheel.

"Would devil birds save your life and mine? We'd all be dead now without them. Remember that," she called over her shoulder as she stumbled out on deck.

Seven days later the *Java Queen* sailed proudly into the Port of Java. No one noticed the huge black birds at the top of the mizzenmast, their glittering eyes raking the harbor of their new home.

There was a tension about the crew that troubled Fury as she prepared to go ashore. Obviously they were uncertain of their future, which was understandable. They were without direction for the first time in many weeks. Without Captain Diaz they might find themselves stranded with no hope of returning or even of signing on to another voyage.

Fury stared at the pouch in her hands—it contained all the money she'd won from the crew over the long voyage. Coming to a decision, she sought out Tobias and handed him the velvet purse. "I'll have no use for this where I'm going," she told the first mate. "Please . . . divide it among the men. In the absence of my father and Captain Diaz, I urge you to stay aboard until matters can be arranged regarding your welfare. I myself will see to it tomorrow." She turned to those of the crew who had gathered near. "Adios, my friends." They nodded, their eyes full of relief as they prepared to carry her trunks to shore.

Fury's eyes roamed the dock until they rested on the familiar face of Father Sebastian. He was older than she remembered, his round hat sitting on his head like a fat pancake. She watched as he waddled to the gangboards leading to the wharf, his round, pigeon's body shaking with each step he took. "Welcome to Java, Miss Fury," he called. "You're as beautiful as your mother, and I would have known you anywhere."

Fury hurried down to meet him. "Thank you, Father Sebastian. I was hoping someone would be here to greet me. I'm most eager to reach my parents' home, but first I must go to the Dutch East India offices. Our captain was . . . lost at sea during a murderous storm. His family must be notified and provisions made for them and the crew."

Father Sebastian blessed himself as he escorted Fury to

his flat wagon. "Yes, of course. It's what your father would want. I never met a fairer man than Mynheer van der Rhys. In his last letter to me he said he was sailing to the Americas to see his son, Caleb. Did your mother accompany him?"

Fury nodded. "When their visit is over they will come here, or at least that was their plan. Circumstances . . . I've found lately that one cannot count on anything fully."

The priest favored her with a gentle smile. "It's about to rain, so I suggest we hurry. You remember the rains, don't you, my dear?"

"Yes, Father. There is very little about Java that I don't remember." She gazed about her fondly. "I loved it here, and that's why I chose to enter the convent here. . . . Is Juli still at the house?"

"Yes, and she's looking forward to serving you as she did your mother."

Fury smiled. "She'll have exactly one week to fuss over me. I hope you told her it would just be temporary."

"I told her," Father Sebastian said quietly. The priest's eyes were fretful as he snapped the reins and urged the horse forward.

"The Dutch East India offices are just up the street here. And afterward I'll drive you to the house." He gazed up at the darkening sky. "I think," he said, reining his horse to a halt, "that we did beat the rain by a scant second or two. Step down, child, and run into the offices. My hat will protect me. I know how fussy you ladies are about your hair." Fury raced for her father's old offices just as fat raindrops began to splatter.

The man behind the desk stood up in greeting, his hands outstretched. "It's uncanny," he said, a look of awe on his face. "I don't know who you resemble more, your mother or your father. The best of both, I suppose."

"Captain Dykstra, it's nice to see you again. I have a

letter for you from my father. Will tomorrow be soon enough to deliver it?''

"Tomorrow will be fine." He searched her troubled eyes for a moment, then escorted her to the chair beside his desk. "Please sit down for a moment. The rains will let up shortly. And I can see by your expression that all is not well. Tell me what's wrong."

Dykstra rubbed his chin thoughtfully as Fury spoke. At least the girl was safe, but that wouldn't stop Regan from flying into a rage when he heard this particular piece of news.

"Ronrico Diaz was an able-bodied seaman, one of the best. Your father and I both sailed with him on many occasions. His family will be well taken care of, I assure you. I myself will arrange a service with Father Sebastian. The crew's wages will be paid, of course. In the meantime they can stay aboard until a decision is made regarding the *Java Queen*'s next voyage. If they have a mind to, they can sign on with another ship."

"And a bonus, Captain Dykstra. They've earned it," Fury told him.

Dykstra laughed. "Ah, your mother's daughter through and through! That's exactly what she would have said. Your father, on the other hand, would have offered extra rations of rum and ale."

"Both, then," Fury said firmly.

"Done!" Dykstra boomed.

She clapped her hands in delight. "My father said you were one of the fairest, most honest men he'd ever met . . . after himself."

"I always say that myself," Dykstra agreed, nodding pleasantly. "Tell me, who brought the *Queen* into the harbor?"

"I did . . . in a manner of speaking. But I had a little help."

"Well done, my dear. Your parents will be proud of you." He turned to peer out the window behind him. "Ah, the rain is letting up. You'll want to be on your way to a nice long bath and a hair wash, no doubt. Well, the house is ready for you. We'll talk later, and you can tell me tall tales of that rascal father of yours."

Fury grinned. "Only if you tell me of some of your escapades."

"I'll walk you to the wagon; I want a word with the good Father," Dykstra said, offering her his arm.

Midway to the door, Fury's eyes fell on the cork board attached to the wall. "Is that what I think it is?"

"The infamous sea witch? Yes, it's been hanging there for twenty-some years now. I think every man on Java was in love with her. She's become a legend. She nearly destroyed the Dutch East India Company, something your father did not take lightly. He didn't have a peaceful day until the witch retired from her plundering ways. I met her once," he murmured, his eyes fixed on some long-ago memory. "She was the most beautiful, most magnificent woman I've ever seen."

"Were you in love with her, too?" Fury asked quietly.

"Yes, unfortunately."

"Do you think she'll ever roam the sea again?" Fury asked.

He glanced at her. "It's strange you should ask me that. A few weeks ago a bark sailed in for repairs, and there was talk of a black ship off the coast of Africa. The men aboard swore it was captained by a woman. Every so often such tales are whispered about. That's why the legend of the Sea Siren will never die. I live in dread of the day she might return to the sea. Of course, if she just did away with the bloody pirates and left my fleet alone, I wouldn't mind."

Fury smiled. "A fairy tale, Captain Dykstra."

"No, my dear, the Sea Siren was no fairy tale. She was a live, flesh-and-blood woman with vengeance in her heart. And the black ship was indeed seen—the fear I saw in those men's eyes convinced me of that. As to the Sea Siren, I don't know," he said nervously. "Only time will tell."

Impossible, Fury thought as she settled herself in the wagon while the priest and Dykstra conversed in low tones. Her mother was the Sea Siren, and she was in the Americas. A rumor started by a drunken sailor—that's all it was. But the first moment she had to herself, she would visit the bend in the river where the *Rana* was hidden. The black paint had been stripped away long ago; she was just another frigate now and probably rotting away to nothing.

The knot of anxiety that formed in her stomach at Dykstra's words remained with her until the wagon neared the front entrance of the van der Rhys mansion. At first sight of the two story, white-pillared veranda and the massive, intricately carved mahogany double doors, Fury forgot everything but her delight in being back home. As always, the grounds around the estate were meticulously kept. Even now several gardeners went about their chores of pruning and weeding the brightly colored flower beds. The scent of spices and flowers permeated the air, and exotic wild birds called raucously to one another. The house, the grounds, everything reflected her parents' pride. Many years and much labor had gone into the completion of this manor house. The front steps had been chiseled out of the precious "pink marble" from the foothills of the China mountains. In Europe, her mother told her, craftsmen carved jewelry and statues from the deep red stone. Here on Java, a wily agent for the Dutch East India Company— her father—had used it for his front steps.

"Is it as you remembered, child?" Father Sebastian asked softly.

"Oh, yes, Father. Look, the servants are coming out to greet me. Let's see if I can remember them. Ling Fu, of course, Juli, Marion—and there's Valie!" Fury leapt from the wagon and ran up the cobblestone path, her eyes shining as she embraced those she'd known since childhood.

Impertinently Juli held her nose as Fury approached her. "Miss Fury, you are in need of a nice hot bath and clean clothes. Come inside with me."

Fury smiled fondly at the motherly housekeeper. "In a minute, Juli. I must talk to Father Sebastian before he leaves." She beckoned to the old priest and drew him to one side.

"Father, you said you had a letter for me from the Mother Prioress. May I have it?"

"Tomorrow is time enough for such things, my daughter. Go along now to your bath and a nice bed with clean sheets. We'll talk over breakfast."

"Very well, tomorrow it is," Fury called gaily as she ran up the steps to her old bedroom.

Tomorrow . . . tomorrows always come, the priest thought sadly, watching her. The child was so happy, and tomorrow he would destroy that happiness. Sighing, he settled himself in the wagon and was about to drive away when suddenly his horse shied and snorted, nostrils flaring. Two monstrous birds sailed directly overhead, momentarily casting great shadows across the sun. The priest had never seen such huge, black-winged creatures. He watched them for a moment as they hung suspended in the light breeze. It was an omen, some kind of omen. He blessed himself and began to pray.

From her position in the high bed, propped up by frilly pillows, Fury stared through the open windows into the soft dark night. The heavens and the stars looked different here, on land. *Everything* felt and looked different here.

This was her home, and she was happy to be back at last, but it didn't feel right somehow.

Her girlhood room was offering no comfort this night, exhausted as she was. A thousand thoughts, doubts, questions, assailed her—questing demons that tormented her and destroyed her peace of mind. At last, realizing that sleep was out of the question, Fury swung her legs over the side of the bed, threw on her wrapper, and padded to the door. Maybe if she slept in her mother's bed . . .

Inside her parents' room, she gazed around her in admiration. Everything was exactly the way she remembered it. The beautiful, high-ceilinged compartment; the full-length windows that opened onto a terrace abloom with potted flowers of every shape and color; the furniture, dark and heavy, with colorful draperies and pillows in perfect complement. How often she'd run to this room crying over something or other! It had been a sanctuary in so many ways.

It was out these very windows, Fury recalled, caressing the polished teak frame, that her mother had escaped—sliding down the trellis into the bushes below to slip off to sea in her identity as the infamous Sea Siren. And when she'd returned it was Juli who'd helped her undress, Juli who had secretly washed the Sea Siren's costume and polished the slippery black boots. Juli, her father said, was the only person in the house, aside from Frau Holz, in Sirena's confidence.

This room was full of ghosts, memories of another time, yet Fury didn't feel as though she was trespassing. How wonderful and exciting it must have been for her mother to wield such power, to have big, strong, able-bodied men bow to her as their superior.

Fury stood in front of the full-length mirror at the far corner of the room and struck a pose, one her mother had taught her that had given her a slight edge during her fenc-

ing lessons. "En garde!" she called, hiking up her skirts
to show an alluring length of leg. Laughing, she brandished a make-believe rapier in the direction of the open
windows. Suddenly, Luis Domingo appeared in her make-
believe drama.

"You're mine!" he declared, approaching her, his eyes
mocking and murderous at the same time. "To the victor
go the spoils, Siren!"

"Never! I'm promised to God!" Fury cried as she
backed up one step at a time, her hands grasping a cut-
glass perfume decanter from her mother's dressing table.
"One more step, you detestable swine, and I'll cut you to
the quick!"

The Luis Domingo of her fantasy roared with mocking
laughter. "Forgive me, señorita, I see now that you are
not the Siren I seek. My apologies for thinking you were
that lustful, vengeful, beautiful woman. Go to your convent—that is where you belong!"

"You lie! You know you can't best the Sea Siren! You
aren't man enough! Only one man can tame the Siren—
and it isn't you, you insufferable toad!"

Domingo laughed, a deep, sensuous sound that set Fury's nerves to tingling. "I'm man enough. The problem is
you, señorita. You aren't woman enough, and you'll never
know if I'm lying or telling the truth because you belong
to God . . . and God doesn't permit such things." His
eyes raked her body with a boldness that both shocked
and titillated her.

"A pity, señorita."

In a fit of pique Fury threw the decanter, which shattered against the wall behind her phantom tormenter.
"Now you'll carry my scent forever. You'll never forget
me! Never! Roam the seas in search of me until you die,
and *you'll* never know if I'm real or not!" Domingo's
laughter rang in her ears, so real that she almost swooned.

"Miss Fury, are you all right?" Juli called from the doorway.

Fury spun about, her cheeks crimson. "I'm fine, Juli. I—I was talking to myself. I always do that when I'm—"

"Upset." Juli smiled. "Your mother used to do the same thing, but her words were . . . more colorful. You've grown to look just like her except for your blue eyes. Will you be staying in this room, Miss Fury?"

"Why do you call me Miss Fury and my mother *juff-rouw*?" Fury asked lightly, hoping to draw the housekeeper's attention from the embarrassing pantomime she'd just witnessed.

"Your mother disliked the Dutch language; she said it was harsh and guttural-sounding. When you were little she instructed me to call you Miss Fury or señorita. The word *señorita* does not come easy to my lips, but if you would prefer it . . ."

Fury smiled. "Miss Fury will do nicely. I won't be here long enough for your tongue to get tangled up in words." She sank down onto her mother's bed with a sigh. "I feel so strange, Juli. Not like myself at all. At first I thought it was the anticipation of my return. But here, in this room, it's even worse." She lowered her voice, and Juli had to strain to hear the words. "One second I feel like a stranger, and the next moment I feel like I'm . . . my mother."

"That's only natural, Miss Fury. You are among your mother's things. When I come here to clean this room, I, too, feel her . . . spirit. Sometimes my memory takes me back, and my eyes fill with tears. When they spoke of the Sea Siren in town and the havoc she wreaked, I think every woman secretly cheered her. I know I did. Our lives have been dull and boring these past years."

"It must have been exciting," Fury said, eyes sparkling at the thought of such adventure.

Juli nodded. "Doubly exciting because your father lived

under this roof. Do you have any idea how we plotted and schemed and then worried and watched until she returned safely? I would give anything to have those days back again.''

Burning with curiosity, Fury beckoned Juli to her side. ''I've heard so many stories about my father. He says he knew all along, but my mother denies this. Do you think he did?''

''In the beginning, never,'' Juli declared firmly, sitting beside her young charge. ''Later he may have suspected, but he wasn't sure. You see, we all heard him storm about the house and curse the Siren every time she sank one of his ships. All he did was dream of ways to vanquish her. She made a fool of every man in Java; she brought the Dutch East India Company to its knees, and when she found what she was seeking, she . . . retired.''

Fury sighed. ''She's truly a legend. It's so hard for me to think of my mother as a bloodthirsty pirate. She's so gentle and caring. When I was ill she used to sing to me or sit by my bed for hours and tell me stories. And I know she loves my father more than life itself. I've never understood . . . what I mean is, there has been so much tragedy in her life. She suffered unbearable agonies aboard the *Rana* on her trips to Java from Spain. Her sister . . . her uncle, and then Miguel, her first child, and then my four brothers lost at sea . . . and still she's managed to survive and be happy with my father.'' Fury's voice trembled, and her eyes filled with tears. ''I don't believe I have that inner core of strength.''

''After death there is nothing,'' Juli said, smoothing back a lock of Fury's hair with tender fingers. ''Life is sunshine, warm breezes, and the hope that a new day will make things better. Isn't hope better than the blackness of nothing? I myself cannot imagine life without the sounds of the birds in the morning, the stars at night, and the beauty of the flowers that are all about us. One must make the best of one's life. Your mother had choices, and she chose to live each day to the fullest. You are most fortunate to have her.''

Fury smiled. ''You really love her, don't you?''

''As much as you, and I was only her servant. She taught me to read and write. Once a year I receive a letter from her and a box of wonderful presents. When she appointed me housekeeper to this grand estate, I wept.'' Juli patted her hand and stood up. ''Come with me, Miss Fury, there's something I want to show you.''

''What?'' Fury asked, curious.

''Shhh,'' Juli said with a finger to her lips. ''The walls have ears.''

In the housekeeper's room off the monstrous kitchen, Fury watched as Juli opened a huge brass-bound trunk at the foot of her bed. Inside was an overwhelming array of fine laces and silks and small wooden boxes, obviously all gifts from Sirena.

''Your mother has been most generous over the years,'' Juli said softly, rummaging through the trunk. ''She said I should consider these things as part of my dowry. What she didn't tell me was where I was to find the man to give them to. . . . Ah, here it is!''

Eyes wide, Fury watched as the older woman untied the string from a roll of goatskin. ''I wrapped all of it in this oiled skin to protect it,'' she explained, working carefully to separate the skin from the treasure it concealed. When she had succeeded, she held out her arms to Fury, who accepted the bundle reverently.

How shiny the black boots were, she marveled. She could see her reflection in them. The shirt was blindingly white, tattered in places but neatly mended, as was the abbreviated skirt, which had been stitched together in the middle the way a man's drawers were. The red-and-black bandanna was folded neatly.

"They still smell of the sea," Juli whispered. "They smell of . . . *her.*"

Fury nodded, unable to speak, her eyes on the cutlass. "How many men did . . . do you suppose . . . ?"

"Only those who deserved her hand, Miss Fury, no others."

"My mother once made a costume and tried it on, but it didn't make me feel like this. These things are . . . so real."

"I didn't know what to do with them," Juli told her. "When she gave them to me she said they belonged here because it all started here and there was no place for them where she was going. She said the Sea Siren was dead. Perhaps I should have destroyed them, but I could not bring myself to do it, and I was glad I hadn't when I heard of your brothers. I thought for certain your mother would return and search the seas for them. I waited and waited, and she didn't come, so I put them away, but I never forgot they were here."

Fury itched to try on the neatly folded clothes, but it was to the cutlass that her eyes kept returning. At last she reached for it and picked it up. "Dear God, this is heavy!" she gasped.

"Be careful, Miss Fury, it's razor-sharp," Juli cautioned. "I stone it down from time to time."

"A rapier is very different from this," Fury said as she did her best to brandish the wicked-looking blade. "My father had one of these, but he's very strong. This is a man's weapon. Where did she get the strength to use this?"

Juli smiled. "Your mother told me once that everyone has a hidden source of strength that rises to the fore when needed. She wasn't dealing with swooning women, she was fighting to survive the only way she knew how. She drew on that strength. That's why she's alive today. You have that same strength, Miss Fury, inherited from both your mother and father."

Fury groaned as she rent the air with the cutlass. "I feel like my shoulder is being pulled from its socket," she said wryly.

Juli began to laugh, but the sound died in her throat as two black shapes flew into the room with a wild rush of feathers. Crossing her arms over her ample breasts, she backed against the wall.

"Merciful God, what . . . !"

Fury giggled. "They won't hurt you, Juli. Believe it or not, they followed me all the way from Spain. This is Gaspar and this is Pilar. I raised them from fledglings, and now they're my friends." She rolled up the sleeves of her wrapper to show Juli the scar on her arm. "When Gaspar was still a nestling, he was attacked by a full-grown kite. I saved him, but was badly scored in the process. It's turned out rather like my mother's scar, don't you think?"

Juli nodded, her eyes full of fear. "It's an omen. A bad omen," she said.

Fury laughed. "No, no, it's simply a bad wound that healed. There's nothing about it that can be construed as an omen."

The hawks were on the floor now, their talons gripping the carpet as they minced their way to the goatskin packet. Pilar's wing tips rustled as she flicked out at the shiny black boots, her eyes glittering at her reflection. Gaspar, more intent on the cutlass, moved closer. He circled Pilar and the packet twice before he was satisfied that nothing was amiss. Then, with a wild flutter of his wings, he swooped up and out of the French doors, Pilar following in the wake of the breeze he created.

Juli's hand flew to her throat. "What . . . ?"

"They're curious," Fury said lightly, trying not to show her own unease. "Perhaps they picked up my mother's scent."

"They—they look like devils straight out of hell!" Juli cried, crossing herself. "You aren't going to leave them here when you go to . . . Not here!"

Fury sighed and crossed to the window, peering out. "I tamed them, Juli. I truthfully don't know what they'll do when I leave. They've never had to forage for food, and they'll die if they aren't fed."

"Please, Miss Fury, don't ask me to feed them," Juli pleaded. "Ask anything else of me, but not that!"

"Once they get to know you, they won't hurt you," Fury said reassuringly. "All you have to do is put their meat in a pail and leave it for them. Let's do it together while I'm here. Later, if you're still afraid, have one of the djongos do it." She turned away from the window. "Come, let's put these things back."

From their perch on the low stone walls outside Juli's room, Gaspar and Pilar watched as Fury helped the housekeeper replace the costume and cutlass within the protective goatskin. Gaspar's eyes glittered as the lid of the trunk was raised and then slammed shut. Pilar's eyes were on the brass handles at each end of the heavy trunk.

Fury slept fitfully in her mother's high, wide bed, her dreams invaded by demons with talons, disguised as mortals. When she struggled awake, darkness was still caressing the dawn, loath to unleash the soft lavender that would herald a new day.

Minutes later she entered the kitchen, washed and dressed in a gay cherry-red day gown, and found Juli at the table sipping coffee. "I gather you, too, didn't sleep well," Fury said bluntly.

When she'd seated herself, Juli rose and stood next to

the chopping block, her cup of coffee in her hands. It would never do for her to forget her place. Her tongue, however, was something else.

"Why are you up so early?" Fury asked. "You needn't worry about making breakfast for me. All I really want is coffee."

"I'm baking for Father Sebastian," Juli explained. "He has a ferocious appetite in the morning, and then I make up a basket for him to take back to his parish. Your mother always had us do that."

Fury smiled. "It would seem that little has changed here; why is that, do you suppose?"

"People change, not places," Juli said, shrugging. "If this house changed, you would be unhappy. You have wonderful memories of it. Your parents knew you would return from time to time, and really, what is there to change? The herbs on the windowsill grow and are cut and grow again. The floor and walls will last hundreds of years. My chopping block has a few more cuts and nicks, but otherwise it, too, will last a lifetime."

"I guess what I remember most is the smell of nutmeg and cinnamon and the little frosted cakes," Fury murmured. "Once I asked my mother if a person could get drunk on the smell of spices and flowers, and she said yes. Do you know, Juli," she said suddenly, "that a man can make a woman's blood sing?"

Juli's round, dark eyes widened. "Now, where did you hear such a thing?" she gasped.

"From my mother. She said my father has always made her blood sing, and that's how you know you're in love." Fury propped her chin in both hands and gazed dreamily at the housekeeper. "I wonder how that feels."

"I don't think either one of us has to worry about that," Juli said grumpily as she punched down a mound of dough on the floured board. "You're going to the convent next week, and I'm here in this house with no men about."

Fury laughed. "Speaking of men, I think I'd like to take a walk in the gardens before Father Sebastian arrives," she said. She kicked off her slippers and hiked up her skirts. "Would it be too much trouble to serve him outside?"

"Of course not, and you will be served, too," Juli said bossily. "Once you leave here you will be fasting and eating rotted fish and God knows what else. You will eat breakfast with Father Sebastian."

Fury grinned. "Now I understand why you and my mother got along so well; she can be just as bossy. Well, I humored her, and I will humor you, too. Pink ham and golden eggs on a fluffy cloud." She laughed as she raced out to the garden.

Out of Juli's sight and hearing, however, the laughter died in her throat. There must be something wrong with her, she thought. She'd never felt this way before—uneasy, on the verge of tears all the time, achy and . . . lonely. The bad dreams were with her all the time now; no wonder she had shadows under her eyes. And her appetite was completely gone. In fact, she didn't care if she never ate again. What was wrong with her?

"Dear God," she cried suddenly, "I didn't say my morning prayers!" In the whole of her life she'd never forgotten the important ritual. "Now, *that's* an omen," she said sourly.

But she didn't rush to clasp her hands in prayer. Didn't raise her eyes heavenward to beg forgiveness. Instead, she walked around the gardens to the long drive in front of the house to wait for Father Sebastian.

An hour later, when the priest clattered up the driveway in his wagon, Fury was the picture of misery and dejection. The elderly cleric noted the shadows under her eyes and sighed. He'd intended simply to hand over the letter he'd brought and leave, without having to witness its effect on this beautiful girl. But seeing her here, looking so wistful, so alone, he changed his mind.

"Good morning, Father," Fury called, running over to meet him. "It's a lovely day, isn't it? Juli is going to serve us breakfast in the garden."

"Good morning, my child. Yes, I think I would enjoy a light repast on this beautiful morning. . . . Furana, I've brought the letter as promised. But I'm afraid the news it contains may not be to your liking."

"Thank you, Father," she said, frowning as she accepted the heavy vellum envelope the priest was holding out to her.

Father Sebastian watched as Fury read the letter from beginning to end several times and tried to digest its contents. He'd been expecting outrage, tears, a fit of temper, and was almost disappointed when she looked up at him, dry-eyed, and said, "I don't understand."

The priest fanned himself with his pancake hat. "The bishop himself ordered the nuns to Surabaja, where a deadly fever has broken out," he explained gently. "They've been gone for over three months and aren't expected to return until next year. There is also a possibility they may not return to Cirebon at all. Much depends on the sisters' stamina and endurance. Several weeks ago the bishop told me three of the sisters had fallen prey to the fever. For now, Furana, I'm afraid you must remain here."

"Is the convent closed?" Fury demanded.

The priest frowned, puzzled. Was he hearing relief in the girl's voice? "No, it isn't closed. There are three old nuns who were not well enough to make the journey. The bishop gave them a special dispensation. But the gates are locked and chained, and no one is to be admitted. I take in a wagonload of food once a month; I ring the bell to let them know it's there, and then I leave. Those were my orders from the bishop. If you wish, you may make the next journey with me, but you cannot speak to the nuns. Nor will they let you see them.''

Fury's eyes filled with tears and her voice trembled. ''What am I to do, Father? What if they never return? What will become of me?''

The elderly priest regarded her compassionately. ''Child, God works in mysterious ways, and we must not doubt His wisdom. Perhaps you were not meant to enter the order.''

Fury gazed off into the distance, her eyes narrowed against the glare of the early-morning sun. At last she sighed and turned back to Father Sebastian.

''I think, Father, that you may be right. God has chosen this way to tell me that for now, at least, I am not meant to join the Holy Order. I must accept it. I have no other choice.''

Father Sebastian nodded. ''Those are my thoughts exactly, Furana. We both must accept God's decision.''

''I suppose that means I am now mistress of this house— and my first duty in that position is to escort you to breakfast. Your arm, Father,'' Fury said, and gave him a tremulous smile.

Chapter Four

The tall, lean, bare-chested man standing so easily on the bow of the *Silver Lady* bore little resemblance to the distinguished gentleman who had attended Fury van der Rhys's birthday celebration in Cadiz. His dark eyes took on a brooding quality as he stared out at the sparkling blue of the ocean. He'd felt out of his element at that party in his crisp linen suit and neat cravat; generally he preferred the casual dress he affected on shipboard: a loose flowing shirt and dark trousers tucked into soft leather boots that were kept polished every day.

Absentmindedly, he massaged his month-old beard with one sun-bronzed hand. It itched like hell, but he scarcely noticed; his thoughts were far away, back at the grand casa in Cadiz. "Too ornate," he muttered. The young women attending the birthday celebration had been silly creatures . . . with the exception of Fury van der Rhys. The food had been too rich, the musicians and decorations too costly—all memories of a life he himself had been obliged to give up many years before, thanks to the witch they called the Sea Siren.

Luis Domingo lifted his spyglass to search the sea for any sign of other ships. He'd worked too hard over the past fifteen years trying to rebuild his father's shipping company to let this first commission fall into the hands of bloodthirsty pirates. Someday when he was as rich as Regan van der Rhys he would count the cost of all the sleepless nights and missed meals and paid-off debts. Someday . . .

Luis allowed his thoughts to carry him away as the *Silver Lady* sliced through the water, her Spanish colors billowing in the light breeze. This was a lazy time of day for him, the winds calming, the air still, the smell of the sea teasing his nostrils. He was relaxed now, so relaxed that he found himself drifting back in time, back to the single moment that had changed his life forever. At the age of eight he'd had no idea what death meant, but he remembered how it felt when one of his father's friends had told him that his father would never be returning to their fine house.

Domingo snorted. Fine house indeed! His mother had been forced to sell that house as well as the furnishings and hire out as a domestic to some of the richer families in Cadiz. She'd been only fifty years of age when she died, but she'd looked twice that, bent and crippled from hard work and not enough nourishing foods. Domingo's eyes narrowed against the pain of that memory.

All that was changed now, thanks to his diligence and hard work. He'd worked like a slave, day after day, just to pay off his father's debts. Fifteen long years of blood, sweat, and even tears that none had witnessed save his sweet, gentle mother. A pity she wasn't alive to see the results.

Once he'd paid off the debts, it had taken him two more years to earn the money to outfit the two remaining ships that belonged to his father. He'd had small consignments, but none like this one, and none that yielded enough profit for anything but the barest necessities. This particular commission was a lifelong dream of his father's and one the man would have accomplished if it hadn't been for the sea witch.

For the thousandth time, Luis ran the route over in his mind—he'd memorized the navigational charts. Cadiz to the Canary Islands and on to Cape Verde, and from there to Gabon, where he would weigh anchor, seek any needed repairs, and lay in fresh supplies. Three days at the most in port and then on to Cape Town, where he would lay in his most precious cargo, ivory. Then northeast to Madagascar and from there to the Sunda Strait and his last port of call, Java.

He closed his eyes as he envisioned his full hold, bales of shimmering silks, ivory, and spices. Coffers full of pearls, barrels of tobacco and molasses that would fetch a king's ransom—providing he wasn't accosted by pirates. There was no doubt in his mind that he would be a rich man when he returned to Spain, rich enough to set up a household and think about marrying . . . someone as beautiful as Furana van der Rhys.

A light breeze tickled the sails of the *Silver Lady* as she skimmed among the small breakers. "Tighten sail," he called as his eyes searched the vast ocean.

"Aye, Cap'n," came the reply.

Soon he would sail into Cape Town with the mysterious cargo that he kept in his quarters. He had no idea what he carried in the enormous brass-bound trunk that had been delivered to the harbor just as he was about to sail. The royal communiqué the imposing man offered identified him simply as an emissary of the Spanish Crown and ordered the captain of the *Silver Lady* to keep the trunk sealed and secure in his quarters at all times. Upon arrival in Capetown, it was to be delivered to one Amalie Suub Alvarez, who would then sign a letter of acceptance that was to be delivered to the Crown on the return journey. Finally, and most impressive, he'd been paid in advance for this service, something unheard of in the shipping business.

Luis found himself staring up into the rigging, his eyes searching for flaws or weaknesses. In an instant he was scaling the intricate maze of ropes with ease, while his crew watched him warily. None of them relished the tongue-lashing they would receive if the rigging proved unsatisfactory.

Out of the entire crew only Julian Castillo, the first mate, had sailed with Domingo's father. He'd been a boy not yet out of his teens when he'd signed on with the elder Domingo and frightened out of his wits the day the Siren had cut down his captain's ship. Pressed for details by the authorities, Julian could only say that the Siren was as deadly as she was beautiful. Over the years his boyhood memory turned fanciful, and he began to embroider his stories with more detail: "The Sea Siren is stronger than any man, with a laugh that tinkles off the waters like an eerie sound from hell before she disappears into a black mist!" In truth he remembered very little, what with fear of going over the side and the possibility of becoming shark fodder; but he did remember the terror he felt when he first saw the black ship approach the *Spanish Princess*.

Julian frowned, heavy brows drawing together across his forehead. His head pounded fiercely, as it always did when he tried to remember a detail, something that was said as he cowered in fear. Always it was the same when he fought the mists of memory: his head would pound so unbearably, he couldn't think. He wanted to remember, for Luis Domingo's sake. Perhaps someday . . .

Luis slid down the rigging, his movements agile as he landed gracefully on his feet. He nodded to his crew, who relaxed perceptibly. Whatever he'd imagined he saw was fine, and no new orders were given. Once again he picked up the glass, but this time, as he returned it to its case, a vague feeling of apprehension settled over him.

"Cap'n, I'd like a word with you," Julian called.

Luis shook off his uneasiness and grinned at the first mate. "My ears are yours, Julian."

"If you've a mind to, Cap'n, I think you could pick up some sandalwood at our next port of call. I know several merchants who have storehouses full of the wood and are just waiting for the right moment to strike a business deal. There's still some room in the hold. I don't pretend to be up on the latest female trends, but I did hear that the ladies of Seville have been begging for treasure boxes made from the fragrant wood. I'd say they'd fetch a pretty penny if the right craftsman was commissioned. Tack a fancy price on one of those little boxes and every lady'll want one.''

"That means an extra day in port," Luis said thoughtfully, stroking his bearded chin. "What the hell, a man can't have too many sidelines now, can he?" He clapped Julian on the back. "If the price is right, we'll take on as much as we can carry. Advise the crew we'll be making port at this time tomorrow."

"Aye, Cap'n."

As Julian strode down the deck, Luis stood alone, measuring the sea. In the last hour the wind had increased steadily, and before long the waves would be churning furiously. Another hour and they'd be in for a stiff storm. He'd be fighting a southerly wind, where his course now lay, and he might have to veer off to the west if the gale increased.

Hours later, with the storm behind them and a mug of freshly brewed coffee in his hand, Luis congratulated his crew. "Well done, men. In a few hours we'll make port, and the drinks are on me. It's up to you to find your own women, though," he added, chuckling.

To a man, the crew saluted their captain. They would eat, drink, and bed as many wenches as possible in the time allotted, and while Domingo had said the drinks were on him, they knew he wouldn't join them. It was an arrangement agreeable to all.

The *Silver Lady*'s arrival in the Sandalwood Islands was as smooth as silk, each member of the crew doing his job to perfection—their reward, ten hours on land to do whatever they wanted. Once Luis had agreed on a price for the sandalwood, Julian stayed long enough to supervise the loading and then departed to enjoy a few hours of freedom with the pouch of coins Luis handed over.

"We sail with the tide, Julian," Luis said, his eye on the fragrant wood being loaded into the hold. Julian was right; it would fetch a tidy price, more if he could find a suitable craftsman with whom to share the profits.

A little before dawn the next day, much to Luis's delight, a staggering Julian led the brigade of drunken boisterous sailors to the *Silver Lady*. They saluted their captain, vapid smirks on their faces. "Hell of a night, Cap'n," Julian said, his words slurred. He threw an arm over Luis's shoulder in a sweeping gesture that almost knocked them both off balance.

Luis grinned and helped his first mate stand upright. "So it would seem. All right, look sharp now, men, this berth isn't what the *Silver Lady* is used to."

The crew fell into step, all signs of drunkenness gone as if by magic. Luis watched in amazement as sail after sail was loosened or tightened, the grips on the rigging as expert as always. He nodded and took his place in the wheelhouse. Later, when the ship was in calm waters, he knew the men would groan and moan and hold their heads and retch over the railing, the cook standing by with pails of strong black coffee laced with mint for their sour stomachs. But for now they would work like dogs to do his bidding—because they respected him. He never asked them to do anything he wouldn't do himself. He was a fair man, as fair as his father before him. Over all, he was proud and pleased—proud of them, and pleased with himself.

As his hands manipulated the wheel, he noticed with some concern that the *Lady* seemed cumbersome. Her hold was too full. If pirates did attack him, he wouldn't stand a chance, he reflected. They could fight, but one well-placed shot broadside and the *Lady* would be done for. He frowned.

Perhaps his desire to make an extra profit from the sandalwood had gotten in the way of good common sense.

It was almost dusk, the most hateful time of day for sea captains bent on reaching port unharmed. It was almost impossible to see clearly what lay ahead—which made it the most advantageous time for pirates to attack. Luis turned the *Lady* in the sultry breeze as he ordered his men to climb into the shrouds and watch the seas.

As the days wore on, Luis's apprehension increased. He was sailing in dangerous waters, waters familiar to pirates and unfamiliar to him. What chance would he have in the event of an attack? If he could just make Cape Town and unload most of his cargo, he would feel safe. Two more days, he told himself over and over. Just two more days.

The *Silver Lady* was no more than twelve hours from Cape Town when Luis spotted the ship off his starboard bow. "Sail ho!" came the cry from above. "She's black and she carries no colors!"

Luis pressed his eye to the round circle of glass, but in the failing light he couldn't distinguish colors. "All hands, prepare for attack!" he shouted.

"All hands ready," Julian shouted back.

"She's traveling at five knots, Cap'n," called the mizzen watch. "She sees us but isn't changing course! She's going to pass us by!"

Luis stood on the bow, the glass to his eye. It was a frigate, black as ink with sails to match. The hairs on the back of his neck prickled as he waited and watched. He didn't realize he'd been holding his breath until the frigate sailed ahead, paying his ship no mind.

The crew was on deck, clustered around him, jabbering. They'd all heard the tales of the magical black ship and her long-legged female captain.

"Men in the rigging—"

"A man at the wheel—"

"No sight of a woman—"

"She carries no flag or name. Is it the . . . ?"

"I don't know," Luis growled. "Carlos, fetch Julian. Tell him to report to me here on deck!"

Moments later the first mate faced the captain in the eerie, yellow lantern light. "It gave me a bad turn there, Cap'n. I never thought I'd see that ship again."

"*Is* it the same ship, Julian?" Luis demanded. "How can you be sure?"

"In twenty years, Cap'n, this is the first time I've seen a black ship. I can't swear it's the *same* ship, but it put the fear of God in me, I can tell you that!"

"Did anyone see a female aboard?" Luis called out. To a man, the crew shook their heads.

"What does it mean, Cap'n?" asked Julian.

"I don't know," Luis replied. "But I'm damn sure going to find out the minute we reach Cape Town." He thrust the glass at Julian. "Keep your eye dead ahead. I'll be in my quarters."

The door closed securely behind him, Luis drew a deep breath. So, it wasn't a fairy tale after all. His eyes narrowed as he stared sightlessly at the navigational charts spread out before him. How many black ships with black sails could there be? As far as he knew, there had been no reports of any in the previous twenty years. He tried to swallow past the dryness in his throat.

There really was a black ship.

The black frigate sailed on under close-reefed sails toward Saianha, her new home. In the moonlight, skimming over the breakers, she gleamed a deadly silver—as deadly as the owner who waited impatiently for her delivery.

Chapter Five

Cape Town

Amalie's attitude was one of proper subservience as she waited for the ladies of Cape Town to give their approval. Although she appeared calm, her insides were churning. Just the evening before, she'd practiced her poses for hours, taking long, deep breaths, casting her eyes downward, placing a gentle hand on one of the younger children's shoulders to show protectiveness, allowing a small, winsome smile to touch her lips. She was tired now with the strain she'd been under for the past several days. In a few minutes the women, with their pursed lips and disdaining glances, would either approve of her as guardian to the children or shake their heads, indicating other arrangements would have to be made.

Amalie raised her eyes, meeting those of the woman closest to her, the spokesperson of the small, tight group. Her expression gave away none of the hatred she felt for these women with their flowered dresses and ugly hats and sensible shoes, their smug, self-righteous faces. She drew an imperceptible breath when the biddy nearest her spoke.

"Everything seems to be fine, the sleeping area is adequate, your food storage area free of vermin, and the hymn and lesson books properly marked. I see no reason why you cannot continue as you have been. I think all of us agree that you're doing a fine job with the children.''

Amalie watched as each woman nodded agreement. This time she allowed her timid smile to flourish, not out of gratitude, but rather at the long hairs jiggling at the corners of the woman's mouth. "Whiskers," she blurted out aloud, unable to stop the word from escaping her lips.

"I beg your pardon?" the woman said stiffly.

Amalie smiled, showing perfect pearl-white teeth. "Forgive me. My Dutch is not so . . . bad . . . good?" The little girls at her side giggled knowingly. Amalie's command of the "master tongue," they knew, was perfect.

Heads held high, the dowagers hiked up their skirts and marched back to their waiting carriage. Amalie waved cheerfully as they drove off without a backward glance, and the moment they were out of sight she broke into gales of laughter. To the children's delight, she mimicked the town women, down to tweaking a set of imaginary whiskers. When she had had enough of her little frolic, she clapped her hands.

"Enough! Back to work, and there shall be a treat when I ring the bell." The children scattered, each to an assigned job.

It was over and done with, the visit she'd dreaded for weeks. Now she could breathe easier and get on with the business at hand. She looked around, pleased with what she saw. The stone cutters were making wonderful progress on the house. Another two months and her father's house would be restored. In just one month Lucy, the oldest of the girls, had transformed the surrounding jungle into a profusion of brilliant, fragrant flower beds. When the house was finished she would have flowers in every room, on the veranda, too. A pity, though, that it took so many hours to weed and cut back the jungle.

Amalie's tawny cat's eyes looked to the sun; it was time for her daily walk to the cove, to search the waters for some sign of her ship. It should arrive today, tomorrow at the latest, if they were on schedule.

She hurried back inside, into the kitchen, where she searched for and found the footgear she'd bought in town two weeks before. One pair of ladies' opera pumps, in sumptuous black silk, and a set of high walking boots in soft black leather . . . She loved them, but she hated the way they felt on her feet. The children had giggled and teased her when she paraded in front of them, turning her ankle with each step. Each day she forced herself to wear them for a little while, first the silky black shoes with the narrow heels and then the buccaneer boots, which encased her legs up to the thighs in leather, rubbing and chafing against her tender flesh. Already she had several blisters on her feet, but it was worth it. Soon she would be able to wear the dainty black shoes with ease—just as the town ladies did.

Amalie slipped on the leather boots and reached for her father's spyglass, which she kept on the kitchen shelf. Each time she used the glass she knew she was one day closer to seeing her ship arrive. The knowledge sustained her though all the long hours of waiting and watching. It had become a ritual—walking down to the cove and watching for her ship—and, like most rituals, it was now an end unto itself.

The footpath was neat and well tended, flowers on each side, to guide her through the jungle. Each day, as they worked, the children managed to cut away a little more, clearing away the vines and plants that seemed to grow overnight. In another week the entire path to the rise where she stood sentinel each afternoon would be free of growth.

Today there was one less worry riding her slim shoulders, one added cause for jubilation. The thin-lipped,

narrow-minded Cape Town ladies were back to minding
their own business and would stay out of her affairs—for
the time being. When next they came to call—*if* they did—
she would be able to meet them at her guarded gates
dressed in her finest and tell them what they could do with
their good intentions. She laughed, a devilish sound that
sent the birds squawking and fluttering to the tops of the
emerald-leafed trees.

By the time Amalie set foot on the rise that afforded her
a clear view of the cove, she was drenched in perspiration
and had to drop to her haunches to rest. All about her the
jungle steamed in the midday sun, sending out spiraling,
heady, intoxicating scents.

Amalie loved this little sanctuary, as she referred to it.
No one, not even the children, could find her here once
she'd left the portion of the path that had been cleared.
She'd discovered this copse with its wild ferns and brilliant
jungle flowers long before she'd embarked upon her present course, but even then it was a place to daydream and
make plans. This was where she had come to read her
father's journals; here she'd always felt like a queen. Once
she'd come at twilight when the first stars dotted the velvet
blanket of night. Childishly she'd called on the heavens to
avenge her for her mother's sake . . . to grant her the power
to destroy those who would stand in the way of her rightful
inheritance. For hours she'd cried out her anguish—begged
and pleaded, bargained and wheedled—and in the end
she'd returned to the mission convinced that it wasn't
enough simply to wish for what you wanted. You had to
scheme and plot and then act on your plans the way she
was doing. And, she mused, you had to be prepared to
eliminate anything and anyone who stood in the way. The
determination to succeed was what had brought her to
where she was.

On her feet now, oblivious to the steaming jungle and

her own sweat-drenched body, Amalie brought the spy-glass to her eye in search of her ship. Blue sky merged with sun-spangled ocean as she scanned the horizon. Nothing.

Angrily, she shook the spyglass and looked again. Dam-nation, where were they? Was it possible she'd made a mistake in trusting Wilhelm to get her ship to her in time? Of course, weather conditions hadn't been the best of late, and repairs had probably taken longer than anticipated. She'd wait a few more days before she sent out an inquiry. What else could she do?

Amalie tossed the spyglass to the ground and followed it there. Glum-faced, she watched as a brilliant feathered parrot flew down from its perch in the jungle shrubbery to peck at the glass with his beak. Then, with a sigh, she turned away to contemplate the horizon. Her wonderful new future seemed to be growing more elusive with each passing day. Was it doomed to failure? The thought had never before entered her mind, but what if—

Suddenly she bolted upright, squinting into the dis-tance. Startled, the parrot squawked loudly, ruffled its em-erald plumage, and flew off to a nearby branch. Amalie snatched up the spyglass and focused it carefully. Yes, there it was—a small dark dot on the distant horizon. It had to be her ship; it just *had* to be! She waited, hardly daring to breathe. The moment her eyes could see the ship without the aid of the spyglass, she let out a whoop of pure joy.

The black ship was finally here.

Her black ship.

Amalie rushed to the edge of the rise, forgetting about the parrot now sitting serenely in a low-lying cluster of colorful frondlike branches. He squawked once and then again as Amalie's wildly swinging arms knocked him from his perch. Instantly he retaliated by diving at Amalie's left arm. His beak ripped into her, digging tenaciously at the soft flesh on her inner arm, and he was dragged with her as she tumbled over the side of the rise and rolled to the bottom. Screaming in pain and outrage, Amalie tried to shake him loose, but he only clung harder, his beak buried in her flesh. The moment she rolled to a stop, the parrot gave a vicious tug, tearing her arm all the way to the inside of her elbow before freeing himself and flying high to safety in the trees.

Her eyes filling with horror, Amalie stared at her injured arm and at the blood spurting in every direction. Hurriedly she tore at her skirt to bandage the wound, leaving dirt and bits of leaves clinging to the edges of the jagged opening.

It was a good ten minutes before she had calmed down enough to think rationally. She knew she could bleed to death if she didn't close the wound and wrap it tightly. But first it would have to be cleaned. With water. . . .

On that thought she leapt into the cove and thrust her arm into the cool, clear water, shivering in the sunshine as all around her turned pink with her blood. Then she waded out, trying to keep the wound closed while she searched the underbrush for a plant with healing properties. In a frenzy she slapped three pale green leaves onto the bleeding wound, unsure if they would help or not, then bound her arm, using her teeth to pull the cloth into a tight knot.

Eyes full of alarm, she watched as blood continued to soak through the makeshift bandage. The next moment— just as the black ship weighed anchor—she was back in the cove, floundering in the water with her arm submerged. Again the sea around her turned pink. Amalie moaned. She could feel herself growing weak from fear and loss of blood; if she fainted, she might slip under the water and drown. The realization made her scream, the sound carrying over the water like an eerie wail. She thought she saw one of the men from her ship dive overboard just before she surrendered to darkness.

When Amalie regained consciousness, she was on the ground and surrounded by several of the scurvy-looking men she'd hired to crew her ship. All wore looks of confusion. She fought off a wave of dizziness as one of the men helped her to her feet. Her arm, she noticed, was neatly bandaged with a filthy rag. "Has the wound stopped bleeding?" she asked hoarsely.

"Aye, but it needs tending," the man holding her said gruffly.

She tried to see his face in the fading light. He was the youngest of the crew and the least verbal, if she remembered correctly. Later, when she wasn't so weak, she'd think about the fact that he and the others around her had probably saved her life.

"I have to return to the house," she said, "but I don't think I can walk."

"Aye, we thought of that. I'm to carry you," the young man said in broken Dutch. Portuguese, Amalie decided as she allowed herself to be cradled in the man's arms. She turned her head in the direction of the crew.

"Stay with the ship until I tell you otherwise," she ordered them, then sank back with a moan and allowed herself to be carried away.

There was disgust on the faces of the men as they marched to the jolly boat waiting at the shallow end of the cove. Delays for whatever reason meant money lost—and all because of a woman's weak stomach and faint heart.

"She damn well better be prepared to make us rich," grumbled the oldest of the crew, a man named Miguel.

"Women are good for one thing and one thing only,"

sneered another. He massaged his groin openly to make his point.

The others smirked as they remembered the way Amalie's thin, wet shift clung to the curves of her body. Miguel fished his one and only coin from the knot in his blouse. "Her nipples are this big!" He pursed his mustached lips into a round O. "When the time is right, lads, we'll all have a piece of her, and that's a promise!"

"What's your name?" Amalie asked the young man who was carrying her so effortlessly.

"Cato, miss. Are you feeling stronger?" He liked the way she felt, all warm and wet with her long hair swirling about his bare arms. He'd never had a woman the way the others had, although he'd boasted about it along with the rest of them. "I see lights up ahead. Would you rather walk now?" he asked tentatively.

Amalie smiled. "I think I can walk if you'll allow me to hold on to your arm. It was kind of you to carry me home. Are you the one who bandaged my arm?"

"Aye, miss. You lost a lot of blood. The dressing should be changed right away. The saltwater helped to clean the wound, but then you put those dirty leaves on. . . ."

"I didn't know what else to do. I was so afraid I would bleed to death that I did the first thing I could think of. I'll have one of the girls clean and dress the wound. I'm sorry you had to ruin your shirt," Amalie said softly as she looked at the man's bare arm.

Cato shuffled his feet as he stared into the clearing. The large house looked grand to him in the yellowish light, grander than anything he'd ever seen.

As Amalie neared the house, the four girls from Christabel's ran up to her, smiling shyly at Cato. "It's all right, Clara," Amalie said quietly. "This is Cato. He's a friend. Lucy, fetch some food for him before he leaves." She turned to Cato. "I'll send word to the ship when I'm ready to sail. Thank you for helping me."

Cato shrugged and shuffled his feet, refusing to meet Amalie's gaze. As he was led away, he glanced back at her, his gut churning as he remembered the way the crew had leered at her limp body when he'd pulled her from the cove.

"Handsome and dashing, even if he's a common seaman," Clara crowed as she removed the bandage on Amalie's arm. A moment later she exclaimed in horror at the sight of the open wound. "Mother of God!"

She ran off to the kitchen for medical supplies and was startled to find Amalie laughing wildly when she returned. "What is it? What's the matter?" she asked, alarmed.

"Fetch me my father's journal, Clara, I want to show you something," Amalie said. When Clara returned a moment later with the tattered book, Amalie leafed through it until she found the page she wanted. "See this!" she cried delightedly.

Clara gazed down at the drawing of a woman in scanty attire, her left arm poised in midair as she brandished a cutlass. Down the inside of her arm ran a jagged-looking scar, which the artist had magnified with red ink. Her eyes widened as they returned to the site of Amalie's injury.

"If I'd planned it, I couldn't have done it better," Amalie told her, grinning. "Some things, I've come to learn, are better left to chance."

"Is there much pain?" Clara demanded as she sprinkled on the healing powder brought along from the mission.

Amalie shook her head. "It's a pain I can live with. Go to bed, Clara. If I need you, I'll call. Tomorrow we have much to do now that the ship is here."

"I'll stay until you're asleep," Clara insisted. "You

thrash about in your sleep, and you might injure your arm.''

The moment Amalie had drifted into a sound sleep, Clara left the room with the journal in her hand. In the kitchen, she turned up the wick in the lamp and stared down at the drawing. This wasn't God's hand, of that she was sure. It was the work of the devil. God's wrath was going to come down on all of them, she was sure of it. She blessed herself.

She owed her life to Amalie, as did the others. Without her intervention the four of them would still be working in Christabel's brothel. She'd prayed to God on a nightly basis to be freed from Christabel's bondage, and nothing had happened until the day Amalie appeared. Was she one of God's emissaries, or had she been sent by the devil?

The others, younger than Clara, saw Amalie only as a savior and didn't think beyond the fact that they were finally free of Christabel and had a roof over their heads and all the food they could eat. Should she talk to them? She wondered, frowning. But what could she say? Was it wrong of Amalie to want what was rightfully hers? No, she decided, but it was a sin to plunder ships at sea. Of course *she* was a sinner too. They were all sinners. But they'd been forced into sin. This plan of Amalie's was deliberate.

Clara squeezed her eyes shut and prayed. *Please, God, forgive us for what we're going to do. And as soon as Amalie has enough to restore this fine house, make her stop so we can all live simply and honestly.*

Her hands trembling, Clara walked down a long hallway to Amalie's room. Satisfied that her benefactress was sleeping peacefully, she left the journal and returned to her own pallet, where she said a rosary before falling into a restless slumber.

* * *

It was a full week before Amalie was able to move about with ease. Tired and weak from a three-day fever, she allowed the girls to coddle, admitting only to herself that she rather liked the attention. Clara insisted that she spend part of every day sitting in the shade of a banyan tree, her wounded arm free of its bandage, to receive a dose of the sun's beating rays. "It will help heal and dry that monstrous scab," she said knowledgeably.

After several hours, when her arm started to itch badly, Clara would move her to the veranda and pour whiskey over the wound, wincing when Amalie screamed in agony. But it had to be done. And as the days passed, Amalie found that the process grew less painful, a sure sign that the wound was almost healed.

One afternoon, after she'd awakened from a brief nap in the sun, Amalie became aware of a commotion at the far end of the veranda. The children were squealing with delight. They had a visitor.

She stared at the stranger through narrowed eyes. He was taller, more muscular, than any man she'd ever seen. More handsome in his fine lawn shirt and ink-black trousers. What was he doing here? she wondered. What did he want? Her heart took an extra beat when the man turned to stare in her direction. He was devilishly handsome.

When he continued to wave his arms and point in her direction, Amalie swallowed fearfully. Surely Clara and the others wouldn't allow him near her. She didn't want to see anyone. Nervously she waited as Clara approached her, certain the jeweler's death was about to be laid at her feet.

"What is it, Clara?" she called out. "Who is he, and what does he want?"

"His name is Luis Domingo, and he's from Spain," Clara replied, eyes sparkling. "He said the Spanish Crown paid him to bring a trunk here to you. And you have to sign this paper because he has to return it to Spain. He's a sea captain on his way to Java. He wants to talk to you, Amalie.''

"No," Amalie said, shaking her head. "I don't want to talk to him. And I can't use my hand yet—you'll have to sign the paper for me. Here, stand in front of me so he can't see what you're doing. Did he say what's in the trunk?''

Her tongue caught between her teeth, Clara signed Amalie's name in a shaky hand. "No, it has a seal on it. He's handsome, isn't he? Are you sure you don't want to talk to him?''

"I'm sure. You told him I was ill, didn't you?" Clara nodded. "Good, now return this paper to him, thank him, and offer him a cool drink. And while he's drinking it, find out what he's carrying on his ship. Be vague, as though you're making polite conversation.'' She watched with narrowed eyes as Clara hurried away.

Luis Domingo gazed admiringly at the manicured gardens as he waited for the cool drink the young lady was bringing him. Relieved at last to be rid of the huge trunk, he glanced down at the spidery signature on the heavy vellum. Amalie Suub Alvarez must be very old—old and waiting to die. He allowed his eyes to sweep the grounds and the shrouded figure reclining on the cane chair under the spreading banyan tree. He thought he smelled death.

The drink was cool and tart, and Luis gulped it down in two long swallows. He wiped at his brow, aware that his neck and armpits were soaked with sweat.

"I'll walk with you to your wagon, Señor Domingo," Clara offered.

Luis looked over his shoulder. "Is she going to die?''

Flustered, Clara stammered, "Wh-who?''

"The old lady. Is she going to die?"

"Ah, no, no, she . . . No, I don't think so. Tell me, Señor Domingo, what do you carry in your ship? Jewels, spices, silks? My mistress likes me to . . . to tell her little stories. I'll make one up about you and tell it to her this evening before she goes to sleep."

Luis laughed, a sound that carried on the breeze across the garden to Amalie, whose eyes popped open. She liked the deep, masculine sound.

"Well," she demanded peevishly after Luis had left, "what did he say?"

Clara clapped her hands in excitement. "Everything, all manner of riches! He's so handsome, isn't he, Amalie? He's sailing to Java and then back to Spain to sell everything he's picked up in his travels. Isn't that romantic? And bringing you that trunk all the way from Spain—and then delivering it *personally*! What do you think is in it?"

Amalie's brow furrowed. "It's probably papers and ledgers of my father's. I don't even want to look at it. Have the boys carry it down to the cellar. Now, tell me, when is Señor . . . Domingo leaving for Java?"

"Two days. He said he would sail with the tide." Clara hesitated. "Amalie, you aren't . . . you wouldn't . . . But you aren't well enough yet!"

Amalie smiled. "In another two days I'll be fine. Now, Clara, I want you to go to the cove and ask Cato to come here. But first have the boys take the trunk to the cellar. I want it out of my sight." A trunk full of the trash of her father's life. Why would the authorities think she would want such a thing? To be rid of it, of course. Chaezar Alvarez had been a blight on the Spanish Crown. Well, she didn't want his wretched refuse, either. She had more important things to worry about.

Two days . . . just two more days . . .

* * *

Amalie set foot on her ship shortly before she gave the order to set sail. She had come aboard with little gear beyond the scanty costume she'd recreated and the high buccaneer boots, which she'd secured in her cabin. She would have plenty of time to don them once Domingo's ship was sighted, and she had no desire to let her crew see her naked legs before she absolutely had to. Now, looking around at the surly faces of her crew, she knew she was about to make her first concession.

"No seaman worth his salt sails on a ship that carries no name. It's bad luck," Miguel snarled. "We don't care about colors, but we do care about a name." The others lined up behind Miguel and chorused their agreement, even Cato.

Amalie was on uncertain ground. She knew nothing about naming a ship, but it was obviously a matter that had to be settled immediately or she would have a mutiny on her hands. That she did understand. She struggled to come up with a meaningful name, one that would strike fear in her crew and those of the ships they accosted.

"From this moment on," she called out, "the ship will be called the *Sea Siren*! If there's one among you who objects to this decision, he may leave now." When no one moved, she nodded. "So be it."

This was the moment the crew had waited for—the moment she herself had waited for. Could she do it?

"To your posts," she cried, her hands tight on the wheel, heart beating wildly. Book learning was quite different from real-life experience, she was discovering. She forced herself to relax, the warm salt air a balm to her body. Gradually she began to feel confident and exhilarated.

The frigate skimmed out of the deep-water cove, over the white-capped breakers, and into open water. Amalie caught the smirk on Cato's face as he faced several of the

crew. Obviously a wager had been placed on her capabilities, and she'd come through a winner—as had Cato. She
liked the idea that he had not bet against her, and her eyes
thanked him before she turned the wheel over to Rego,
her first mate.

Now it was time to walk about *her* ship. She'd lied,
cheated, stolen, and killed to arrive at this moment. She
smiled as she strolled the deck, aware that the crew's eyes
were on every step she took.

The newly named *Sea Siren* was a sleek, three-masted
frigate that was skillfully demonstrating her prowess in
what Amalie thought of as her maiden voyage. She sported
fresh decks scrupulously scoured and a sterncastle whose
varnish was just beginning to dry. And it was all hers. No
one was ever going to take it away from her.

Amalie turned and swayed on the rolling deck. She took
a deep breath and then another; she couldn't afford to get
seasick, not when things were going so well. Any sign of
weakness on her part would be seized by the crew as jus-
tification to take matters into their own hands.

Cato appeared out of nowhere, startling her. "It takes
awhile to get your sea legs. It'll help if you eat something.
If you like, I can bring a bit of food to your cabin. Miguel
says we should sight the Spaniard by nightfall."

Amalie looked into Cato's anxious blue eyes. "So
soon?" The young man nodded. "Very well, fetch me
some fruit and a little bread. I'll be in my quarters."

Amalie had never before set foot aboard a ship. It was
all a new experience for her, but one she liked . . . very
much. Her cabin was small with a bunk, a chair, and
several shelves. It was clean and smelled of soap and the
sea. The bundle on her bed drew her eye. Soon it would
be time to don the costume.

She tested the hard bunk, then sat back with an uneasy
sigh. Everything she'd planned was about to happen. What

if the men aboard Domingo's ship put up a fight and she lost her crew? What if the Spaniard captured her and turned her over to the authorities? Her resolve hardened as she recalled the anticipation on the faces of her men. None of them had any intention of backing down or putting up a weak fight. If need be, it would be a bloody battle with no quarter given, of that much she was certain.

Amalie drew in her breath as she buttoned the stark white blouse. She was nervous, unsure of herself, and she didn't like it at all. Even the sight of the rapier didn't comfort her, and the cutlass only made her wince. With her injured arm there was no way she could hold it, much less wield it. She could, however, attach the cutlass to the belt at her waist and carry the rapier. Two weapons might even enhance her resemblance to the notorious Sea Siren and force Domingo's crew to think twice about fighting back.

She pulled on the boots, grimacing as the leather abraded her blistered feet, then hobbled out the door and up the ladder. Once secure on deck, she struck the classic "Sea Siren" pose—legs astride, rapier in hand—and silently dared her crew to comment.

Watching her, Cato drew in his breath with a sharp hiss. She was magnificent. Her long hair streaming behind her in the gentle breeze, the black kid boots cuffed at the knees, the soft white shirt tied in a knot at her waist, those long, slender legs . . . Jesus, he wanted her, as did every man aboard ship, and he would fight to the death for her. He had heard tales of the infamous Sea Siren, and he'd bet a year's wages that there wasn't a man at sea who could tell the difference.

Amalie did her best to hold the spyglass steady as she scanned the horizon. She forgot about everything—her uneasiness with the crew, even the stinging pain of her blisters and chafed thighs—the moment she sighted the minuscule speck in the distance. "Sail, ho!" she cried.

"Where away?" Miguel shouted.

"Straight ahead," came a reply from high in the rigging.

Amalie swallowed past the lump in her throat. "Loosen sail, full speed. I want every minute to count. Remember what I told you—our attack is to be quick and deadly if necessary." She leapt down from the bow and raced to the stern, where she climbed onto a pile of rigging atop a water barrel. With her legs spread to steady her, she was a Valkyrie, the frigate her Valhalla. She threw back her head and laughed, the sound ripping across the water like the wind.

The *Sea Siren* drew ever closer to her prey, and Amalie knew the moment Luis Domingo had focused on her with his glass. She read the fear and loathing in his face and laughed again, this time in triumph.

"Make no false moves, Captain," she called out as the two ships came within hailing distance, "or my men will make short work of you and yours!"

In reply Luis Domingo brought up his cutlass and lashed out at Amalie's men as they leapt aboard the *Silver Lady*. It took all of thirty minutes for Amalie's cutthroats to subdue Domingo's nine-man crew. Outnumbered and pinned to the mast by Cato, Domingo could only curse his revenge as he watched his cargo being carried off. His eyes spewed hatred at the beautiful creature on the stern of the ghostly black ship.

An eternity later Amalie gave him a low, sweeping bow, her rapier slicing through the twilight. Luis tried to blink the sweat from his eyes, staring in disbelief as the long-legged creature blew him a gentle kiss with her fingertips.

"I'll kill you for this!" he shouted. "I'll hunt you down and rip you limb from limb!"

"You aren't man enough," Amalie called out, chuckling. "This little assault was nothing compared with what I could have done if you had angered me. As it is, I'm feeling charitable, so I'm allowing you to keep your sandalwood, your ship . . . and your life. You have much to thank me for, Captain."

"I'll die before I thank you, you thieving bitch!" Luis spat out.

"That can be arranged, too." Once again she offered him a mocking bow. "Perhaps next time. Until we meet again, Señor Domingo, thank *you* for your generous contribution to my well-being."

It was fully dark by the time the black ship had melted into the night.

For hours Luis swore he could hear the Sea Siren's evil laughter as he cursed and stormed about his ship. "All of this," he snarled, "and not a shot was fired! Pinned to my own goddamn mast! She'll pay. I swear before God that she will pay!"

"We were outnumbered, Cap'n," Julian said nervously. "It was like this when she attacked the *Spanish Princess*. We had no time to react, and we were loaded down with cargo. Only that time the Siren sank the ship. Today she was generous." He peered out into the night and shuddered. "You don't suppose she'll come back and ram us, do you, Cap'n?"

Luis snorted. "She won't be back. She's sailing off to dispose of my cargo, God only knows where. Pirating is a handsome business, all profit." He turned to glare at his first mate. "You're sure that woman was the same one who struck down the *Princess*?"

"I swear on my mother, Cap'n. Did you see those long legs and that midnight-dark hair? Her laugh is the same, too. My blood ran cold when I heard it."

"It's easy to laugh when you're victorious, Julian. But she won't always be victorious; I'll see to that," Luis said, his voice so deadly quiet, so ominous, that Julian crossed himself involuntarily.

"Aye, Cap'n." It was on the tip of his tongue to tell Luis that his father, the elder Domingo, had said the same thing before he died.

"Swab these decks and get me a Bible so we can give the dead a Christian sea burial. . . . Three good, honest, hardworking seamen cut down—I swear I'll make her pay for this!"

"Ay, Cap'n," Julian said, sighing as he watched his captain stride away. How did a person exact revenge on a ghost? For twenty years had passed since her attack on the *Spanish Princess*, and the Siren was still as young and beautiful as ever. No, she was an evil ghost, and mere mortals would never stop her. The only thing to do was pray.

All night long Luis Domingo prowled the decks of the *Silver Lady*. It was all true, every word the old man had said.

The Sea Siren lived.

Chapter Six

Java

Dawn, Fury thought, was always a happy time for her parents because it signified a new day, a day to be cherished and lived to its fullest. She, too, had come to think like her parents, rising early to watch the sun ascend the heavens. Today, however, she would have preferred the impenetrable mask of night—a Stygian ally to hide her shame and bewilderment. Shame, because somewhere deep inside her she was relieved that the bishop had denied her entrance to the convent. Bewilderment, because now she had nothing to do until her parents arrived. *If* they arrived. Her parents, she knew, were not creatures of schedules. They could very well decide to stay in the Americas for years.

The early-morning dew soaked Fury's delicate slippers as she strolled through the garden, but she barely noticed. She gazed about in the soft grayness, knowing that in just minutes the garden would be ripe with color and scent. All around her would awaken to greet the new day, as had she, but to what end? Without a purpose in life, and the means to fulfill that purpose, one day was much like another—empty and joyless. She was sick to death of needlework and books. Prayer, too, had become a chore that rarely soothed the agitation of her mind. It wasn't that God wasn't responding to her devotions; it was that she had no patience to wait for that response. Everything was in God's time. Time . . . How she hated the word. Time could be an eternity. It was entirely possible that she could wither away and die of . . . loneliness, she thought morosely.

Fury wiped at her eyes, certain the tears shimmering on her lashes would spill over. She knew she was indulging in self-pity, and determined at once to make every effort to change her empty days and evenings. Today, for example, she would go into town to visit with Father Sebastian and offer her services to the parish. It was the least she could do.

By now it was full light, the slight breeze warm and flower-scented. Fury drank deeply of the early morning; in a short while, the air would be heavy and hot. But she was getting used to that. In the month since her arrival, she'd found herself adapting to her old home with ease. Boredom was her only problem. There were simply too many hours in the day.

Her arms full of fragrant blooms, she made her way back to the house to change and by midmorning was ready to leave for town. The sun beat down upon her as she climbed into the flat wagon and nodded to the djongo who would take her to Father Sebastian's rectory. She was dressed simply in a yellow-sprigged muslin dress with long sleeves, her ebony hair pulled back and swirled on top of her head. She knew she should be taking a hat or at least a parasol to ward off the fiery rays, but she loved the way they tinted her fair skin to a rich honeyed hue.

By the time they'd reached the village, Fury was limp with the heat and soaked with perspiration. But at least here the air was slightly cooler, and a gentle breeze blew in off the village quay. She drew in a deep breath, savoring the tang of salt air.

The village was small and laid out along the tiny waterfront. Many of the gabled rooftops were tiled, giving them a sense of permanence. This village, crowded as it was between jungle and water, seemed to have a timelessness about it, unobtrusive in its surroundings. As the wagon rounded a bend in the dusty road, the hamlet disappeared. The small parish church was nestled at the end of the long, narrow street, and to its right sat Father Sebastian's house. In another minute she would be there.

They were just passing the Dutch East India offices when Fury gasped in horror. The djongo turned his head, startled.

"What is wrong, missy?" he queried.

Luis Domingo . . . here, in Java? It wasn't possible! Yet there he was, going into the Dutch East India offices. "Faster, Ling, make the horse go faster," Fury ordered. He can't see me like this, she thought wildly. Dear God, what must I look like?

"Horse hot, missy, no go faster."

"Yes, yes, I know. I'm sorry. . . ."

There was no place to run, no place to hide. He was turning now at the sound of the wagon wheels, and she was close enough to see his frown of puzzlement. Obviously he was trying to remember where he'd seen her before. Then, mercifully, they were past him. "Turn around, Ling, and see if that man is staring at us," Fury said breathlessly.

"Much look, strange look, on man's face," Ling reported. "Man still looking," he added a moment later when he turned for a second look. "Padre's house, missy. You wait, I help you down. Horse need water and shade tree. I wait over there," he said, pointing to a small lot on the opposite side of the road.

Fury almost swooned as the old priest led her into his cool study. Concerned, he immediately ordered a cool drink and then had his housekeeper lead her upstairs to "freshen up." The child needed to talk to him, that much was obvious; but why now, he wondered, wringing his hands in agitation, why at this particular time of day? Luis Domingo would be arriving within minutes. And Domingo, unlike the delicate young lady upstairs, was in a murderous frame of mind and hell-bent on revenge. And he knew why. Father Sebastian peered out the window nervously. The moment he'd heard about Domingo's experience with the infamous Sea Siren, he'd personally canvassed the town until he'd found Jacobus—who was now, this minute, secure in the rectory sleeping off his last jug of wine. God alone knew what would happen if Domingo accosted the old sea barnacle now, in his current state. Better to keep them apart, at least for the time being.

"Merciful Father," the old priest murmured, fingering the beads of his rosary, "grant me the wisdom to help Señor Domingo, and show me the way to protect Jacobus . . . and," he added, eyes twinkling, "if You have the time, allow me a little insight into Miss Furana."

The priest started when the garden bell tinkled and Fury reentered the room at the same time. In a matter of minutes Luis Domingo would walk through his door.

"There's no time for explanations, Furana," he said hurriedly. "Go upstairs immediately and stay there until I call you. Señor Domingo will walk into this room in a few seconds, and I—I doubt he will take kindly to your presence at this time. He's rather . . . overwrought."

Fury's eyes were full of questions, but she knew better than to argue with the gentle priest. Without a word she headed for the rectory staircase and took the steps two at a time, the way she had when she was little and her brothers had chased her about the house. She reached the top just as Luis Domingo announced himself.

What was he doing at Father Sebastian's? Fury wondered. Flattening herself against the stairwell wall, she listened as the Spaniard repeated the story of his ruin at the hands of the nefarious Sea Siren. . . .

An hour later, after Luis had finally calmed down enough to listen to reason, Father Sebastian blessed him and showed him out. Instantly Fury descended the stairs, her face full of shock, eyes disbelieving.

"It's not true, you *know* it isn't, Father," she cried. "The Sea Siren . . . Father, it's impossible! Why would he tell such a lie? You should have said something, told him that my mother is in the Americas. Why didn't you?"

"Child, listen to me. It's understandable that you're upset, but think for a moment. How would it look if I suddenly appeared to know so much about the Sea Siren? I admit I was fearful of giving away some of my knowledge. It is imperative that I protect those who have seen fit to take me into their confidence. All Señor Domingo knows is that he lost his cargo to a woman dressed as the infamous Sea Siren who captained a black ship that was identical to the *Rana*." The priest rubbed his eyes wearily. "When I first heard the story in the village, I immediately brought Jacobus here. It was Jacobus who told Luis Domingo his version of the Sea Siren months ago, in exchange for a jug of rum. I think we should put our heads together and—"

"And what, Father?"

"I don't know, child, I don't know," Father Sebastian said, gnarled fingers clutching at his rosary as if to a lifeline.

Fury shook her head. "I don't understand why he came to you. You're a priest, what would you know of pirates and cargoes?"

Unconsciously, the priest began to knead the hard beads. "Comfort, words of wisdom. Why did you come here, Furana? You yourself seek comfort and a solution to your . . . problems. Why should Señor Domingo be any different?''

Of course he was right, thought Fury. She was reacting emotionally, something her mother had always cautioned her about. ''I assume the whole town knows now,'' she muttered. She threw up her hands and started to pace the tiny study.

''I'm sorry now that your parents confided in me,'' Father Sebastian said softly. ''But when your father became ill, Sirena thought it was because of her . . . activities on the high seas. Even though Regan isn't of our faith, I prayed with your mother for days on end.'' He sighed. ''Lord, I wanted to tell that young man he was mistaken, but I am bound by the promise I made to your mother.''

Fury nodded. ''Yes, of course. But we must do something, Father. We can't allow these tales to flourish, and yet we can't openly defend the Sea Siren. That would cause suspicion. I—I need time to think.''

''What do you want me to do, Furana?'' the priest asked quietly.

Fury paused, frowning. ''If you could go to the Dutch East India offices and see what Mynheer Dykstra knows, that would be most helpful, Father. . . . And then I'd like you to bring Señor Domingo to the casa tomorrow evening for dinner. Together we might be able to clear up this whole sorry dilemma.'' She cocked her head to one side, considering. ''Tell him only that's he's been invited to the van der Rhys casa for dinner. He'll assume that my parents issued the invitation, and I would prefer it that way. I rather think this meeting between us should come as something of a surprise. It's entirely possible that the man is lying. Other sea captains have plundered their own ships for personal profit. He could be doing the same thing.''

''I'll pray for a solution to this problem,'' the priest said, suddenly feeling out of his depth.

Fury spun about, eyes glinting dangerously. "You do that, Father. Perhaps praying will work for you. It certainly hasn't for me, of late. As far as I can determine, God has forsaken me. And now He's seen fit to burden me with this very *earthly* problem—quite fitting, don't you think, Father?"

"That's blasphemy, child," Father Sebastian said, aghast. "You're distraught. You must not denounce God because of this unfortunate incident—or for *any* reason. Hell is—"

"Right here, Father. I'm walking in hell now and have been for the past month. You might pray about *that*, if you've a mind to!" Her face flooded with indignation, Fury fled the parish house. It wasn't until she was safely back in her room at the casa that she regretted the way she'd spoken to the priest.

It had to be a lie, a trick of some sort. The question was: Why would Luis Domingo pick Java of all places to fabricate such a tale . . . unless he was up to something? Nothing else made sense. The man had to be acting on the tales Jacobus had told him, salvaging his cargo for his own personal gain—*in the name of the Sea Siren*. Damn his eyes!

By God, she'd find a way to stop him. All she had to do was sit down with a clear head and figure out a way to end the tales of her mother once and for all. First, though, she'd begin a journal, while things were still fresh in her mind. Tomorrow, after dinner with Domingo, she'd have a detailed report for her mother to read so she'd know her daughter had acted in good faith on behalf of the Sea Siren.

It was late afternoon when Fury retired to the garden to gather more flowers for the house. She felt better having committed her thoughts and anxieties to paper. She'd also planned a simple but tasteful dinner for the following evening. Her dinner gown would be simple, too, since all her good clothing had been left behind in Spain. Perhaps she could find something appropriate among the things her mother had left behind.

When her basket was full, Fury retraced her steps to the house down a long, winding stone walkway. A circling breeze forced her eyes upward, and she watched as Pilar and Gaspar sailed down to perch on the banister of the garden terrace. Setting the basket on a glass-topped table, Fury walked over to the hawks, stroking their silky heads and crooning soft, warm words of affection. Both birds ruffled their feathers. Gaspar inched his way across the banister until he was even with the basket of flowers. One talon reached out for a soft purple bloom. Daintily, so as not to crush the delicate flower, he inched his way on one talon back to Fury and Pilar.

Fury held her breath. Who was the flower for—herself or Pilar? Please let it be for Pilar, she prayed. It was a game she'd played with the birds back in Spain. Before, the flower had always been for her. Now she nodded slightly to Gaspar. He offered the bloom to Pilar, who seemed to take an eternity before deciding to accept it. A minute later it was Pilar who inched her way toward Fury to offer the mangled bloom.

Fury laughed in delight and clapped her hands. "Wonderful! Now you understand about giving and receiving." She placed the flower in her hair over her ear and bent low so the birds could observe what she'd done. "Well done, Gaspar. Thank you, Pilar."

The hawks preened, their feathers whispering to each other before they soared upward. Fury danced her way into the huge kitchen to hand over the flower basket to the cook.

Later, on her way upstairs to her room, she decided she

would wear a flower in her hair when she dined with Luis Domingo and Father Sebastian.

Fury was exhausted when she woke the following morning. She'd dreamed all night, terrible dreams. First her mother and father had spent hours screaming at her, berating her for not redeeming Sirena's good name. Then Luis Domingo had taken over, accosting her with a wicked-looking cutlass and threatening to kill her mother. In her nightmare she'd run from the Spaniard until she was breathless, searching desperately for the cave where he'd stashed his cargo. And then, just as she'd been about to uncover his lair, she'd awakened.

Thieves always tried to blame someone else, Fury decided as she threw open the windows and savored the flower-scented air. Overhead in the thick umbrella of green leaves, she heard a soft rustling. Her beauties . . .

She called to the hawks and was rewarded by the sight of a sleepy Pilar parting the branches overhead with her wing tips, her glossy head peeking through the emerald leaves. Fury waved listlessly, and within moments both birds were perched on the balcony railing, eyes glittering and intent. They remained motionless as she stroked their heads, murmuring soft early-morning words of greeting.

"I wonder," Fury mused, "if there is a way for you to . . . spy on Luis Domingo." She must be out of her mind, she thought. The hawks were intelligent but certainly not capable of spying. Still . . . "It would be nice if you could follow him and report back. You know, scratch me a message or bring me something to prove he really was attacked by a pirate." She giggled, her usual good humor returning. Gaspar's wing wavered and then wrapped itself around her shoulder. A moment later Pilar, the less affectionate of the two birds, followed suit. "I know, I know," Fury gurgled, delighted, "you are going to take care of everything. Well, I'm going to take care of you right now and give you your breakfast, and then we're going to take a look at the *Rana.*''

Fury wondered what could possibly be accomplished by running down to the cove where her mother's old ship was berthed. The *Rana* must be rotted through and through by now, probably unsafe to board. Still, it would be wonderful to see her again and know once and for all that no pirate had restored her and taken her out to sea to pillage and plunder. At the very least, seeing the ship would reassure her.

Buoyed by the prospect of taking action—any kind of action—Fury dressed, breakfasted, and fed the hawks, then strode out to the stables.

She had always loved the pungent smell of this place. As a child she had played and romped and hidden in the straw, daring her parents to find her, squealing in her high, child's voice when her father pretended not to know which particular pile of straw she was hiding in. So many pleasant, wonderful memories.

"I'll take Starlight," she told a young stable boy. "Fetch her out and I'll saddle her myself." Starlight was a spirited roan mare with a perfect white blaze and three white stockings. Fury loved her and tried to ride out with her for at least a little while every day.

The stable boy, no more than twelve years of age, stood back as she threw on the saddle and secured the cinch. His eyes almost popped from his head when the two hawks swooped down, their talons spread to secure a perch on the back of the leather saddle. Fury laughed, her long hair billowing backward between the two birds as she spurred Starlight to a fast canter. The boy stared after her, blessing himself as the huge birds flapped their wings and screeched.

After a minute or two Fury tightened the reins, forcing

Starlight to a trot. The humidity was at its heaviest, and it would be at least an hour before they came to water. She kept her eyes to the ground as the roan picked her way daintily through the vine-covered trails. This particular track held years and years of growth, so much so that at last she was forced to slip from the roan's back and tether her.

She wasn't absolutely sure of her way, but she seemed to recognize certain outcroppings and fern glades. The thatched hut where her mother had hidden things she wished to keep secret. It was just a lean-to now. Fury had been to the cove only three times—once with her mother, once with her father, and once with all four of her brothers. That time, the five of them had sneaked off without telling anyone, and as they'd stood on the rise looking down at their mother's ship, they'd played a game, each of them getting the chance to be captain. At the end of the day they'd all been in agreement—none of them would ever fill their mother's shoes when it came to pirating games on the sea. They'd all been punished upon their return, and Fury had cried, heartbroken—not because she'd been sent to bed without dinner, but because she would never be the Sea Siren.

The hawks were overhead now, working what little breeze there was to stay as close to her as possible, both of them screeching their displeasure at these strange new surroundings. Fury felt like screaming herself as she beat at the vines and vegetation choking off the path. She was sweating profusely, and her long hair was hanging in lank strings about her face. She ripped at the neck and sleeves of her dress to bare her arms and shoulders to the stagnant air. It occurred to her that she was making a mistake: all this time and trouble merely to look at a decaying, rotting ship. But she plowed on determinedly, wiping her face with the tattered sleeves of her dress. Above, the birds circled lazily in the blazing sun.

A minute later she felt a cooling breeze wash over her and knew she was almost to the rise above the cove. She stopped, her heart hammering in her chest. Please, she prayed, let the ship be there.

The hawks were ahead of her now; even at this distance she could see they were ready to swoop down and meet her at the rise. She ran then, not even feeling the branches that scratched her bare arms and legs. Another few feet and she would be in the clearing.

Like a child, Fury covered her eyes, delaying the moment of discovery. Finally, unable to stand the suspense a moment longer, she took her hands away—and stared in disbelief at the frigate. Even from this distance she could see that the ship was in perfect condition, her decks and railings gleaming. And black as tar.

Fury swayed dizzily. It was impossible; the *Rana* was supposed to be safely anchored and rotting away to nothingness. God in heaven, how was this possible?

Should she scramble down the bank and swim out to the ship? One look at the sun told her she had to head back to the casa or she would be late for dinner. Tomorrow she would return—properly dressed. She needed time to think, time to consider. . . .

All the way back to the house Fury's mind raced. Someone had kept the ship in repair; more than that, she was completely outfitted and ready to take to the sea. But who? Was it the same person who had plundered Luis Domingo's ship? Was it perhaps Luis Domingo himself? Soon she would have her answers.

Fury galloped into the courtyard at full speed, reining Starlight so abruptly that the mare reared back, her front hooves pawing the air, the hawks screeching as they dived downward and then up. As the stable boy ran to help her, she slid from the horse and dashed to the kitchen doorway.

Inside the house, she tore up the stairs like a whirlwind, calling over her shoulder, "Juli! Draw me a bath and get my clothes ready," and shedding her torn gown at the top of the stairs. She left her petticoats and both shoes in a pile outside her door.

Juli came hurrying over, eyes dancing with amusement. "Everything is in readiness and has been for some time," she said tartly. "I am well aware that the van der Rhys women tend to do things at the last moment. Rest easy, Miss Fury, your mother always said it was fashionable to keep a man waiting."

"Not this lady," Fury muttered as she slipped into the tub of steaming water. "Ooooh, this is hot!"

"How else will we get all the . . . What *are* you covered with?" Juli demanded. "And what are we to do with your hair? It will never dry!"

"It's dust, Juli—dust and sweat and Lord only knows what else. Oh, *how* will I ever be ready in time?" Fury wailed. "What—"

"I'll think of something, Miss Fury. Now hold still while I . . ." Juli frowned in concentration as she dunked, rubbed, and scrubbed Fury within an inch of her life. When she stepped from the tub she was again rubbed and patted until her skin glowed. Powder permeated the air, as did a fragrant scent that made Fury's head reel. At last Juli smiled. "Intoxicating! You'll have to dress yourself while I see about . . . Ah, I have just the thing for your hair. Your mother left it behind. Many times she, too, would return late from one of her excursions, and her hair, like yours, took forever to dry. Your father never suspected. I'm so glad I saved it."

Thirty minutes later Fury was fully dressed in a rich tangerine silk dress with long, loosely cuffed sleeves and gores of silk swirling about her ankles. She felt elegant and quite grown-up, especially since the dress had belonged to her mother and fitted her perfectly. No jewelry was needed to adorn the timeless elegance of the gown, but she definitely wanted a flower in her hair—only it was soaking wet.

"I found it, I found it!" Juli cried exultantly from the doorway. "It's just as dazzling as it was the day your mother wore it for the first time. It's called a skullcap," she said, fingering the delicate circle of fabric. "I remember when she had it made. It took hours to sew these tiny pearls and brilliants over the silk. See the way it curves here at the edges. You can either cover your ears or . . . Try it on, Miss Fury."

A moment later Juli clapped her hands in delight. "You look like a royal queen! Remember to hold your head up because the crown of the cap is the heaviest. As your hair starts to dry it could slide off."

Fury frowned. "It is heavy. Perhaps a coronet of braids . . ."

"There's no time," Juli said, shaking her head. "Father Sebastian and a very handsome gentleman are waiting for you on the veranda. And now that you aren't going into the convent," she added meaningfully, "it wouldn't hurt you to . . . flirt a little. You are your mother's daughter, after all."

Fury flushed. "How did my mother tolerate your brazenness?" she demanded.

"Your mother taught me to speak my mind. If she were here, she'd tell you the same thing."

"Is he really that dashing?" Fury asked, giving herself one last look in the full-length mirror. "I met him only once at my birthday ball months ago. He didn't . . . what I mean is . . ."

Juli giggled. "He didn't make your blood sing, eh? Well, he will tonight, young lady. He will tonight."

Luis Domingo's manners were impeccable, his eyes glowing with admiration as he bowed low over Fury's extended hand. "You cannot be the same young lady I escorted to dinner a few months ago," he murmured.

"Oh. And why is that, Señor Domingo?" Fury asked coolly.

"You were merely pretty then. Tonight you are ravishing." He pressed her hand once, lingeringly, then let it go. "Then you were but a sweet child; now you are a formidable young woman."

Flustered, Fury remained silent as she led the way into the house, where Juli served wine in elegant crystal goblets. The moment they were seated, Fury fixed her gaze on Luis and spoke directly. "Father Sebastian tells me that your ship was attacked by . . . some woman."

Father Sebastian's jaw dropped, his eyes flying first to Fury and then to Luis Domingo. With a sinking heart, he saw Domingo's jaw tense.

"Not *some* woman," Luis replied, "The infamous Sea Siren herself. She plundered my ship and made off with all my cargo, with the exception of some sandalwood."

"Come now, señor," Fury said casually, sipping her wine, "even I remember the stories about the Sea Siren, and I was only a child. If there is such a person, she must be quite old by now. You described a beautiful young woman to Father Sebastian. How do you explain that? I, too, have seen the picture that hangs in the Dutch East India offices, and Mynheer Dykstra, a good friend of the family's, told us that picture is over twenty years old."

Luis shrugged. "I cannot explain it. I can only tell you what happened. My men were present. She was there and she was real and the frigate she sailed was black as Hades," he said coldly.

Fury decided to try another tack. "Señor Domingo, there must be hundreds of black ships that sail the seas. You did say this attack occurred at dusk, the deadliest time of day for sea captains. Perhaps it was the lighting that made the frigate look black."

Luis's eyes darkened. "Would that same lighting also make white sails turn black? And how do you explain the woman herself? She talked to me—I didn't imagine *that*. I tell you, she was real and she was beautiful, much the same as she was described to me."

The priest sipped his wine and regarded Luis thoughtfully. "How close were you to this female pirate, señor," he asked, "and how old would you say she was?"

"Stern to stern," Luis replied, "and young. Beautiful, deadly . . ."

"And an impostor!" Fury said, waving her hand in the air. "Surely a man of your vast experience has reasoned that out by now. Fairy tales, señor, are for children, and this particular tale has been told over and over until it's become real. The Sea Siren is either dead or, more likely, retired from the sea."

Luis was on his feet, his mouth a tense, grim line. "Am I to understand you're calling me a liar, señorita?" he said quietly.

Fury remained seated and offered Luis a serene smile. "No, señor, I am merely saying I *think* you're mistaken. An able impostor is the only logical explanation."

"How is it you know so much about this scourge of the seas?" Luis demanded.

Fury flushed. "Señor, the Sea Siren was no scourge! It is true she wreaked havoc on my father and almost ruined the Dutch East India Company. If anyone is an authority on her, it is my father. She never plundered for cargo; she had a mission, and when that mission was fulfilled, she retired. It's that simple. Your female pirate is an impostor, and I simply cannot believe otherwise!''

''I'll be goddamned to hell!'' Luis exploded. He turned to Father Sebastian. ''Is that what you think, too, *Padre*?''

The elderly priest hesitated; clearly this discussion was not to his liking. ''Twenty years, señor, is a very long time for a woman not to age,'' he said reluctantly. ''On the other hand, you and your men were *there*—and you seem so sure . . . Tonight I will pray for a reasonable explanation.''

''In the meantime,'' Fury said sweetly, ''let us put such talk aside. I believe our dinner is ready. Señor . . . ?'' She beckoned, motioning to his chair.

Luis struggled with himself, but in the end common courtesy and gallantry prevailed, and he took his seat without further comment.

Midway through the meal, Fury realized that Father Sebastian was the only one at the table actually paying attention to the food. She and Luis were merely going through the motions for the sake of propriety. Conversation consisted of the weather, the beautiful gardens, and the mysterious trunk he'd delivered to Saianha. At the mention of Chaezar Alvarez's wife, Fury's eyes widened. Even Father Sebastian stopped eating.

''Señor Alvarez had a wife?'' he asked incredulously.

Luis nodded. ''Does that surprise you?''

Father Sebastian shrugged and resumed eating.

''Señor Alvarez was a competitor of my father's years ago. It was said that he was enamored of the Sea Siren, as was every man in Batavia, even my father.'' Fury stared into Luis's dark eyes. ''My father never once mentioned his having a wife.''

''Perhaps it is my mistake.'' Luis proceeded to relate the terms of the Spanish commission and the delivery he'd made to Saianha. "I merely assumed it was his wife. The name on the manifest was Amalie Suub Alvarez. The woman appeared to be quite advanced in age and in ill health when I delivered the trunk. I did not actually meet her, however. I don't suppose it matters one way or the other."

"No, I don't suppose it does," Fury said thoughtfully.

Luis regarded Fury just as thoughtfully in the ensuing silence. She was every bit as beautiful as her exquisite mother, he reflected. And as sharp-tongued. Nothing would get by this one. Earlier, he'd been quite open in expressing his thoughts and losing his temper—which he wished now he'd controlled—and she'd shown a depth of spirit in matching him that he'd had to admire.

"Tell me, Miss van der Rhys," he said abruptly, "if I'm not being too presumptuous, why did you have a change of heart in regard to the convent?"

Fury crossed her fingers under the table. "I decided I couldn't give up the outside world. I thought I had a noble religious vocation, but I was proved wrong once I returned here to Batavia. Isn't that so, Father Sebastian?" she asked quietly.

"Hrumph, yes, quite so," the priest replied, forking a large piece of fowl onto his plate.

Luis's eyes narrowed. Something was going on between the priest and the girl—a secret of some sort. "What will you do now?" he asked nonchalantly.

"I plan to help Father Sebastian in the parish until my parents return from the Americas," Fury told him.

"So you can stay close to God, I assume," Luis muttered.

"Yes." Fury glanced at the open doors leading to the wide veranda. Luis's eyes followed her gaze, and he heard a slight rustling noise from among the trees outside.

"It's very warm this evening, don't you think?" Fury asked sweetly.

Luis nodded. He wondered suddenly if he was falling in love with this beautiful young woman. He'd been attracted to her the first time he'd met her, although then she'd seemed no more than a delightful child—and one promised to God, at that. Now, however . . .

Fury looked up at that moment and caught him staring at her. The flush on her cheeks made him smile inwardly; he was responsible, he knew, for the color creeping up her long, slender throat. What would it feel like to caress that delicate column of ivory? he wondered. To follow it with his lips, down . . . down . . .

Breathless, Fury tore her eyes away and placed her napkin across her plate, the signal that dinner was at an end. She wondered if she dared to take the Spaniard for a stroll through the garden with the hawks on the veranda, then decided it would be most unwise under the circumstances. Instead, she led the way into her father's library, where Juli served coffee and offered cigars. Both men declined the tobacco but accepted brandy with their coffee.

"I hope you won't think ill of me, child, if we make an early departure," Father Sebastian said, placing his coffee cup on the silver tray. He stood and took her hand in his.

"Of course not, Father," Fury said warmly, "but you're welcome to stay the night if you like." She turned to Luis. "Señor Domingo, must you return to town also? But you'll want to see about your cargo, of course. What will you do? Can you possibly recapture what was taken from you?"

"I plan to put a price on the Siren's head," Luis declared bluntly. "I have all the time in the world now to search her out and bring her to justice. Believe me when I tell you there will be no mercy shown her."

Fury smiled. "I believe you, Señor Domingo, but first

you have to find her. I wish you would believe me when I tell you it is an impostor who ravaged your ship. In any case, I wish you success in your endeavor. If I hear any news from Mynheer Dykstra, I will be sure that you are informed.''

At the wide front doors, Luis brought Fury's hands to his lips, his eyes boring into hers. ''I thought you were beautiful when I first met you, but here in this lush tropical paradise, I realize you are exquisite. You remind me of someone I've seen somewhere,'' he said thoughtfully.

Fury blushed furiously. Her hands were trembling so badly, he had to be aware of it. ''My mother, perhaps. People say we look very much alike.'' Her voice was as shaky as her hands. No man had ever had this effect on her before.

He nodded and released her hands, stepping back to don his cape. ''Perhaps. *Buenas noches, señorita.*''

Fury nodded and smiled. ''Perhaps you will return when your emotions are . . . calmer,'' she said, one eyebrow lifted suggestively.

He bowed low before her. ''I'd like that very much.''

The moment the darkness swallowed the two men, Fury ran to the kitchen, her cheeks on fire. ''Juli!'' she called.

Juli came hurrying in, her eyes dancing with mirth. ''Is your blood singing, miss?'' she asked playfully.

''Of course not,'' Fury blustered. ''But he *is* handsome, isn't he? He said *I* was exquisite. And he kept staring at this . . . this cap on my head. For all I know, he thinks I'm bald.'' Both women doubled over in peals of laughter. Fury handed the sparkling headpiece to Juli.

''I watched from the kitchen,'' Juli told her. ''He hardly ate, and his eyes never left you. Definitely enamored. You could probably twist him around your finger—if you wanted to, that is,'' she added brazenly.

Fury laughed. "I have to admit I was flattered. Tell me, did you listen to what he had to say about the Sea Siren?"

"Every word," Juli said, nodding. "I'd say the señor is quite intelligent and able to make sense of the puzzle you've set for him. You must be very careful. . . . Now," she said, clapping her hands, "I want to hear about your trip to the cove. How did you find the *Rana*?"

Fury was somewhat puzzled by the teasing manner in which Juli asked the question, but she was too excited to pursue it. "Oh, Juli, you won't believe this, but the ship is moored out there! She's *seaworthy*. I expected her to be a hulk and rotting from top to bottom. It's been so many years! Who could have . . . Someone found her and . . . Why are you smiling, Juli?" she demanded, unable to stand it a moment longer. "What do you know?"

"As you know, Miss Fury, I have many brothers—seven, to be exact," Juli began, eyes twinkling. "When your mother started sending me all those gifts and purses of money, I wanted to do something for her in return. So, I talked the matter over with Father Sebastian, and he suggested we condition the ship and careen her. My brothers did it. And they did a wonderful job! She's as seaworthy as she was in your mother's day. But this I swear, Miss Fury—whoever it was who attacked Señor Domingo's ship did not to do so with the *Rana*. No one but your mother would dare to take her down the River of Death."

"Then who attacked Señor Domingo?" Fury asked.

Juli shook her head. "I have no idea. But if you should decide to take matters into your own hands—to hunt down the impostor who is posing as your mother . . . well, you now have the means to do it."

Fury swallowed past the lump in her throat. "Juli, I've never sailed a ship on my own. I've taken the wheel, but my father and mother were with me. When I was younger

I sailed with my brothers. A ship the size of the *Rana* needs a goodly crew. I can't . . . I couldn't . . ."

"Who else?" Juli said forcefully. "You are your mother's daughter. When Sirena was tested, she found she had the strength, the will, the determination, to overcome everything in her path to reach her objective. You are no different. We could wait to see if this impostor plunders other ships. I can have my brothers frequent the harbor and saloons. They're bound to pick up some information, if there's any to be gathered. If the piracy of Señor Domingo's ship is an isolated incident, the whole matter would best be forgotten. But if not . . ." She felt no need to complete the sentence.

Fury's heart fluttered in her chest. Juli was right: she could study her mother's navigational charts, brush up on her seafaring skills—and wait to see if this impostor struck again. If she did, the *Rana* would be ready to exact revenge . . . with an able captain at the wheel.

"Would you like me to make you some hot chocolate before you retire?" Juli asked, watching her. "If you plan on riding out to the cove tomorrow, you'll want a good night's rest."

"I am tired," Fury agreed. "Chocolate would be wonderful, Juli." Warm chocolate to soothe her, she reflected, with her mother's navigation charts and thoughts of Luis Domingo to keep her company. . . .

Fury sighed. She'd be lucky if she got any sleep at all.

While Fury sipped at her chocolate and pored over the *Rana*'s charts, Luis Domingo was sipping wine with Father Sebastian in his study, wine that Juli had added to the basket of food she'd sent along with the priest.

Father Sebastian was tired, and he was worried. Life, he decided on the way back to town, had been far too quiet. This man was going to turn everything upside down.

He just knew Fury was going to do something foolish, something that might later come back to haunt Sirena van der Rhys, and ultimately he would he held responsible. Dear God, how will I ever explain this to Regan? he wondered, shuddering at the thought.

"Are you all right, Father?" Luis asked with concern.

Father Sebastian swallowed the last of his wine and immediately poured a second glass. If nothing else, the Madeira would help him sleep. "A little tired, my son, but the trip out to the van der Rhyses' estate always makes me feel good. Tell me, what did you think of Furana?"

Luis paused to consider the question. "She's beautiful. Spirited, I'd say. I didn't see that in her the first time I met her. Then she was . . . perhaps 'peaceful' would be the right word. Now she seems to be fretting over something. I'd like to see her again when my affairs are straightened out. But I've no intention of . . . distracting myself until I've tracked down the Sea Siren and brought her to justice."

Father Sebastian blanched. "How do you intend to find her? I don't see what you can possibly do now. The woman is gone, along with your cargo. If—and I say if—she's as proficient as the Sea Siren, you will never find her."

"Then I'll set a trap for her."

"What sort of trap, Señor Domingo?" the priest asked, frowning.

"I think it wiser not to voice my plans, even to you, Father," Luis said apologetically. "I would like to ask you a question, however."

"Yes, my son?"

"In all the tales you've heard of the Sea Siren, do they always refer to a scar on the inside of her arm, a scar so wicked it defies description?"

The priest nodded. "I believe so. From here to here," he said, rubbing the inside of his arm from wrist to elbow.

"Then she shouldn't be too hard to find," the Spaniard said, his eyes narrowing.

Father Sebastian felt a prickle of alarm race up his spine. Fury's arm was scarred as badly as her mother's. "The Sea Siren is dead!" he said harshly.

"And I tell you she's alive," Luis insisted. "I saw her with my own eyes!"

"No, my son. You saw a woman *pretending* to be the Sea Siren." He was on his feet now, weaving his way to the staircase. "I'm very tired, Señor Domingo, so if you would take pity on an aging man and see your way out, I would appreciate it."

The Spaniard regarded the priest with eyes as cold as death. So, he thought, the holy man did know something! "Wait, *Padre*," he called out. "Please, just a moment more."

Father Sebastian paused and then turned to face Luis, his hands feverishly working the beads around his waist. "Yes, Señor Domingo?"

"Father, what I said to you moments ago, my confession as to my plans, I'd like you to consider it just that— a confession. A sacred trust. Never to leave this room."

The priest nodded, his eyes infinitely weary. "You need not worry. I have never broken any of my vows in all my years. Your . . . plans are safe with me. Now, if you'll excuse me . . ."

Luis's eyes smoldered as he watched the gnarled figure make its way to the staircase. "We'll talk again. *Buenas noches,* Father."

Luis Domingo closed the door quietly behind him. The night was warm and dark. He stood on the stone step, savoring the flower-scented air before he reached into his pocket for a cigar. When the tip glowed brightly, he began his long walk back to the *Silver Lady*.

Turning at one point to take a last look behind him, he

saw two yellowish lights wink on the second floor of the parish house. The good Father and . . . who else? The drunken old man from the tavern, no doubt. Earlier in the day the tavern owner had told him the sea salt had trudged off with the priest.

Luis drew deeply on the cigar. Now, what possible connection could a priest and an old sailor have in common? He stopped in his tracks and blew a cloud of blue-black smoke in the still air. An old man, a nervous old priest, and a young girl who'd just changed her mind about entering the convent . . . A conspiracy?

As he strolled down the hard-packed road, Luis allowed his thoughts to drift. Nothing else made sense. It had to be a conspiracy. Clearly he would have to interrogate the officers of the Dutch East India Company and anyone else who could remember back to the Sea Siren's reign of terror.

By the time he boarded his ship, his thoughts had turned inward. Grimacing, he tossed the remains of the cigar overboard and headed to his cabin. What kind of man was he that he would suspect a priest, a memory-fogged old man, and a sweet, innocent young woman? He cursed himself for his shabby, uncharitable thoughts, and wondered what would happen in heaven if the good Father, Fury van der Rhys, and he bombarded God with prayers that were in direct conflict with one another. Whom would that unfathomable Spirit help? The holy man, of course, and the young religious woman.

"Son of a bitch!" he said as he climbed into his bunk. Then he threw back his head and laughed bitterly. "Son of a *bitch!*"

Chapter Seven

Luis Domingo struggled with the rage that threatened to engulf him. Exactly thirty days earlier the *Silver Lady* had been attacked and plundered, and he was no closer to finding the pirates now than he was on that fateful day. No other sightings had been chronicled. He knew the captains and crews of the ships he'd questioned, as well as the government officials and town merchants he'd interrogated were wondering by now if he'd lost his wits. He was the nightly topic of dinner conversation, but he was too angry to care. For weeks he'd done nothing but seek information, and at last he was forced to acknowledge that there was none to be had, a realization that only increased his anger. No man liked to be made a fool of.

He was standing at the harbor now with the rest of the tradesmen, watching a brigantine limp into port. He wondered what account her captain would give when he set foot on land. His ship carried a monstrous-size hole in her stern; apparently the attacker had gotten off a good shot broadside. The Spaniard hated himself for hoping the marauding pirate had been the sea slut, as he now referred to her in his mind. But if it was the same woman who'd attacked the *Silver Lady*, Batavia would finally have to take him seriously. And if the brig's cargo had been meant for the Dutch East India Company, they would go after the pirate themselves.

Luis let out his breath in an exploding sigh when, the instant he set foot on land, the captain started to babble almost incoherently about the famous Sea Siren. All heads turned in Luis's direction.

Luis moved closer to the Dutch East India's manager. "What was she carrying, Dykstra?"

He shrugged bitterly. "A goddamn fortune in cloves, nutmegs, and silks. . . . Look, now is as good a time as any for me to apologize for doubting you. Twenty years is a long time . . . you can't blame people for being skeptical about the sudden reappearance of a legend."

"What are you going to do?" Luis asked.

"What I would do myself if I weren't too old—hunt her down and bring her back in irons." He turned to Luis and smiled. "Which is just what I'm going to hire you to do."

Luis laughed mirthlessly. "I cannot conceive of any commission I'd rather undertake. You may consider me hired."

There was no answering laughter from the Dutch East India's manager. "Excellent. Señor Domingo, if you'll follow me back to the office, I'll be glad to discuss terms with you. I have full powers here, and I'm a fair man, as fair as Regan van der Rhys, who held this job before me. The last time the Siren was in these waters, the company was almost ruined because we waited too long to act on the information we had. I won't allow that to happen this time."

Luis bit down on his lower lip. "I, too, consider myself a fair man. I think we'll be able to come to an agreement."

"This time I want the woman captured," Dykstra emphasized. "You're going to have to forget about being noble because of her sex. There's no such thing as courtesy on the high seas. I don't care what condition she's in, as long as you bring her in. Do we understand each other?"

Luis nodded. "How much time do I have?" he asked.

"As much time as it takes," Dykstra said, mopping at his flushed face. "Within reason, of course." If there was one thing he wanted to avoid, it was to retire from the Dutch East India Company under a cloud. He wasn't sure Luis Domingo was the right man to send after the Siren, but he was the only man available. He was almost certain Regan van der Rhys would approve his choice.

Luis mopped at his own brow as he and Dykstra left the docks. "I'll need to talk with you at length. I want to know everything you know about the Sea Siren and the parts you and Regan van der Rhys played during her reign of terror. He brought you into his confidence, did he not?"

"Of course," Dykstra wheezed, struggling to keep up with the Spaniard's brisk pace. "We were . . . are the best of friends. Regan van der Rhys is the man who . . . I wouldn't have this position if it weren't for the mynheer. Come, have supper tonight at my house. I have an excellent cook, and later if you . . . feel . . . have the desire, we can . . . ah, visit another very old friend of both Mynheer van der Rhys's and mine."

Luis smiled. "Are you referring to Clarice's . . . establishment?"

Dykstra laughed. "So you know Clarice. Of course everyone knows *of* Clarice, but there are few people who *know* her, if you take my meaning."

"Perfectly." Luis inclined his head in acknowledgment. "I'd be honored to join you for supper. I'll look forward to a pleasant evening, then."

Alone in his offices, Dykstra stared moodily at the patch on the wall where the picture of the Sea Siren had hung for so many years. He would miss looking at it every day now that Domingo had just left with it, claiming it as his own. The portrait had somehow become quite dear to him; he'd almost come to regard his possession of it as a sacred trust of sorts, bequeathed to him by Regan van der Rhys as his successor, so to speak. But there was no way in hell he was going to believe the Sea Siren of his early days was back in business. It simply wasn't possible. Regan had personally given him his word that the infamous wench had retired from the sea.

Dykstra leaned back in his chair and hooked his booted feet over the edge of his desk. He should be in a flap of rage over the sacking of the company's ship, but he wasn't. This was what had been missing in his life—the excitement he and Regan used to experience when the Siren was at sea. He liked the feeling of anticipation, of single-minded purpose. Domingo was going to be another Regan, he could sense it. He threw back his head and laughed when he thought about how Clarice would probably give him pretend virgins for the rest of his life as thanks for introducing Luis to her "girls." Clarice was always properly grateful, he reflected fondly. Goddamn, life was suddenly interesting again.

All the way home, Dykstra fantasized about the evening ahead—he and Luis Domingo . . . and Clarice's women. By the time he walked through the front door of his tastefully furnished house, he'd bedded all of Clarice's nubile virgins, leaving his leftovers for the rest of the town's patrons. In his mind he was a happy man. What a story he'd have for Regan when next they met!

At the thought of his old friend, Dykstra turned unexpectedly moody. He remembered how badly Regan had wanted to capture the Sea Siren—so badly, he hadn't been able to think about anything else. Dykstra had never understood Regan's decision to let her go. When pressed, Regan had merely said that one could not hold a spirit captive. There had been something in the man's eyes that had puzzled him at the time, something he'd mulled over for many years. It wasn't like Regan to let anything get away from him if he wanted it, and he'd wanted the Siren so badly, he would have killed anyone who stood in his way.

The bottle of rum on Dykstra's desk beckoned. He was on his third glass when he slapped at his unruly gray hair. "Oh, God, no," he muttered as he sorted feverishly through the papers in his desk. Somewhere he had a miniature of Regan and Sirena. Hell, he didn't need the rendering to remember what Sirena looked like; all he had to do was look at their daughter. He threw his hands in the air and yowled his outrage.

They were close, he and Regan, the way men are who boast about their conquests. Regan would never have let the Siren out of his clutches, which could mean only one thing: *Regan had had the Siren in his clutches all along.* Goddamn, why hadn't he ever figured it out before?

Sirena van der Rhys was the Sea Siren! She retired from the sea when Regan married her. What a stupid clod he was! How Regan and Sirena must have laughed at him—no wonder Regan had never endorsed him for the governorship.

But if Regan's wife was the infamous Sea Siren, what did it mean? he asked himself, trying to think everything through clearly. For one thing, he allowed, the story about Fury going into the convent could all be a ruse. Regan and Sirena were too protective of Fury; they would never have allowed their only daughter to come all the way to Batavia to enter a convent alone.

"Son of a bitch!" Dykstra bellowed suddenly. *Fury* was the mysterious legend come to life—a true reincarnation of the infamous Sea Siren. How could he have been so blind?

Dykstra fingered the rum bottle clumsily, then set it aside. He'd had more than enough to drink. Domingo would be arriving soon for dinner, and he'd need his wits about him when entertaining the Spaniard. His eyes narrowed as he contemplated the evening ahead. Should he apprise Domingo of what he suspected or keep his thoughts to himself until they could be proved? Everything came down to proof, and there *was* some sort of proof, something he couldn't remember, something Regan had told him . . . what was it? Damn the rum, he wasn't thinking clearly! Coffee. He still had time for plenty of thick, black coffee.

Dykstra struggled to his feet. The proof . . . what was the proof? he persisted, his pulses pounding with the effort. Perhaps if he stopped thinking about it, it would come to him. He made his way to the kitchen and ordered coffee from his startled housekeeper. "Fetch it to my bedroom. I'll take it while I change for dinner," he growled over his shoulder.

Goddamn it, what was the proof?

Relaxing in his bath, Dykstra forced his mind to blankness so he could restructure his thoughts. It wasn't the Siren's legs or her breasts, although Regan had gone on and on about how beautiful they were. So what in the goddamn hell was the proof?

Dykstra's hand slapped at the soapy water. The scar! *That's* what it was. Of course, how stupid of him to forget. Regan had said he'd observed the vicious, wicked scar when he fought with the Siren. It ran the entire length of her arm, and that's why she always wore long sleeves. Indeed, he could not remember a single instance when he'd seen Sirena's bare arms. All her gowns bore long sleeves. Dykstra's bushy brows furrowed. Fury's arms, too, had been covered the day she'd appeared in the Dutch East India offices. Was it part of their plan? he wondered.

"*What* plan?" he asked himself, disgusted. He could sit in his bath all night and still be wondering come dawn. Maybe Regan had nothing to do with any of this. Maybe it was all Sirena. The possibilities seemed endless.

Goddamn it, he realized sourly, now he had a pounding headache. If he didn't get rid of it, he'd have a miserable time at Clarice's.

* * *

Luis sensed a change in the Dutchman when he arrived. He was pensive and morose, then almost surly whenever he spoke. Never one to let things simmer if he could bring matters to a boil, he spoke harshly. "Are you having second thoughts about hiring me, Dykstra?"

Dykstra looked up, startled. "Not at all. I simply have a damnable headache. I've been realizing that my—my superiors will no doubt pressure me for a swift resolution to this . . . this wretched business, and with my retirement imminent, and the governorship opening up . . ." He smiled sheepishly. "Well, you may just imagine how this is going to look on my record. It has nothing to do with you, Domingo. My offer still stands."

Luis nodded. "As does my acceptance."

"Excellent. In that case," Dykstra continued, "there's something else I wanted to tell you—a piece of information I'd forgotten until today. The Sea Siren has this scar . . . Regan told me he'd actually seen it once. Apparently it runs the entire length of her right arm. That will be all the proof you'll need in verifying . . . when you capture the witch."

It was almost midnight when the two men left Dykstra's home and headed for Clarice's establishment.

"You flatter me, Mynheer Dykstra, by bringing this dashing young man to my house," whispered Clarice, a ravishing, voluptuous woman of indeterminate age. She turned to Luis with a wide smile. "Obviously, señor, you are a man of culture who knows his own mind. I like that. How may I be of service?"

Luis threw back his head and laughed, a deep, resonant sound. "I'd like a very long-legged young lady whose breasts are no more than a handful," he drawled. "Eyes as blue as sapphires and hair as black as sin. A pretty smile. A woman versed in *all* the ways of pleasuring a man. And when she grows tired, have five or six others form a line outside my door. Any questions, madam?''

Clarice shook her head. "I believe we can accommodate you, señor. I knew a man like you once with appetites much the same as yours. He never left this house unsatisfied.''

"We'll see," Luis called over his shoulder as he made his way to the second floor.

"My God, where did you find this one?'' Clarice hissed to Dykstra the instant the Spaniard was out of hearing. "He cannot be serious in his request—I need all my girls; tonight is one of the busiest nights of the week. I'm going to charge him by the hour," she hissed again. "Who will pay for this night of debauchery, Mynheer?''

Dykstra shrugged. "Señor Domingo is my guest, so I will pay. It is of no importance. Now, to *my* wants . . .''

"I know, I know, three virgins," Clarice purred. "Do you think they grow on trees, Mynheer? But for you, anything.''

"How old are they?'' Dykstra asked, one eyebrow lifted skeptically.

"Old enough," Clarice replied with a casual wave of her hand. "They just arrived yesterday. I've been saving them for you.''

It wasn't until he was removing his trousers that Luis realized he'd described Fury in telling Clarice what he wanted in a woman. The one she'd sent him was called Naula, and it didn't take him long to learn that she was hellfire and damnation when she wasn't being angelical and ethereal.

Within minutes Luis found himself moaning as he throbbed and pulsated, nearly out of his mind with desire. Naula transported him to such dizzying heights, he soon gave himself up totally to her expert ministrations. Up, up, up she led him, until finally he exploded into slick wetness. He was aware of Naula's smiling face as he relaxed into the soft bedcovers.

"Devil," he managed to gasp.

"Yes," Naula whispered. "Will you tell Clarice I pleasured you?" she teased, her fingers trailing intricate patterns down his chest.

"Jesus Christ, hell, yes . . ." He moved to lie on his side, his dark head nuzzled between Naula's creamy, round breasts.

"What shall I tell the other . . . young ladies waiting outside your door?" Naula asked coyly.

"Tell them to . . . to disappear."

Naula's laughter tinkled about the room. "That's what Clarice said you would say. Mynheer Dykstra said *he's* the only man here who can . . . service *all* of Clarice's young ladies." She laughed impishly as she worked her tongue inside Luis's ear.

Luis's long legs were suddenly over the side of the bed. "They said *that*? Then maybe we should play a little trick on Clarice and the mynheer."

Naula leaned over and trailed her fingers down his back. "The kind of trick Mynheer van der Rhys used to play with Mynheer Dykstra?"

"Which was?" Luis asked, curious.

"They always boasted of their prowess, but the truth was quite the opposite . . . you understand, señor? The girls kept their little secrets because they were generous men. And since Mynheer Dykstra is paying for your night's entertainment, I see no reason why you can't turn his own trick back on him. If you like," Naula said, nibbling at his shoulder, "I can help you."

Luis's heart skipped a beat. He *knew* this young woman could very well kill him with her bedroom skill. He wondered how it was that Dykstra was still alive.

He was on his back again with Naula leaning over him,

one round, pink-tipped breast sliding back and forth across his lips. Desire swelled in him a second time.

"What shall I tell the others?" Naula whispered, pressing the length of her silky body against his own.

"To come in, of course," Luis groaned. "I'll think of something."

Naula pouted as she walked naked to the door and motioned for the others to enter. The girls, one more beautiful than the other, giggled when Luis drew the sheet up to his neck.

One of them, more brazen than the rest and sinfully beautiful, walked over to the bed and pulled back the sheet. Luis's erection died immediately. A second clucked her tongue in disapproval, while a third wagged a playful finger under his nose. A fourth crept to the edge of the bed, her breasts spilling from their gossamer covering. "If you like, señor, we can make this a night you'll never forget," she murmured.

Luis swallowed and tried to speak, but his tongue had grown thick and somehow incapable of forming words. He settled for a nod. Goddamn, Dykstra certainly knew how to make a man happy.

Naked bodies whirled about him as the covers were thrown from the bed. Every inch of his body was oiled and massaged. He felt himself being poked and prodded in some places while others were reduced to lacy, shivering trails of ecstasy. Just when he thought he couldn't stand it another second, he felt five pink-tipped tongues lapping the sweet-smelling coconut oil from his entire body. At some point his ankles and wrists were pinned to the soft mattress as one deft pink tongue trailed the length of his entire body. His growl of pleasure was so intense, the women smiled knowingly as he struggled to free himself. The moment Naula's sheath imprisoned him, the others freed his wrists and ankles and tiptoed from the room.

Luis was aware of the droplets of perspiration on Naula's face as she rocked over him, bringing them both to a dizzying crescendo of fulfillment.

From somewhere far away he heard a faint whisper. "You'll sleep like a newborn babe, señor." A whispery kiss feathered his parted lips. "Very few men have given me as much pleasure as you have."

The moment the door closed behind her, Luis was wide awake, wondering if making love to Furana van der Rhys would be half as satisfying as this. His last conscious thought before drifting off was to wonder what it would be like to make love to the Sea Siren.

Luis woke at midmorning to a light tapping at his door. He mumbled something, then immediately rolled over and went back to a half sleep. A moment later he became aware of muted noise and activity in his room and jerked to wakefulness, thinking Clarice operated a day shift of sorts.

They were lined up, all five of them, dressed in proper day attire and looking every bit the same as the town ladies. Only their eyes were merry and devilish when they pointed to the tub full of steaming water.

Of course, he needed a bath! He reeked of himself and Naula, not to mention the coconut oil. He was aware for the first time of the bits and pieces of feathers from the pillows sticking to his oiled skin. Willingly he allowed himself to be led, by five giggling females, to the inevitable.

An hour later he was so clean, he literally squeaked. Every inch of his skin had been prodded, poked, rubbed, and scrubbed. He squinted at his glowing skin. In his entire life he'd never been this clean.

Breakfast, they said, would be served in the dining room. Luis dressed quickly. Clarice, he decided, managed a full-scale operation that ran smoothly. He'd been in many a brothel, but none like this.

It was past the noon hour when Domingo and Dykstra

tripped down the whitewashed steps of Clarice's establishment. "How was your evening?" Dykstra asked him.

"Superb," Luis said, shielding his eyes from the glare of the sun. "And yours?"

"Equally superb. Clarice certainly knows how to treat a man. We must come back again."

"By all means." Luis grinned.

"Meanwhile, back to business," Dykstra said coolly. "Before leaving the office yesterday I gave orders to have one of the company's frigates readied for the evening tide. If you are ready to begin, that is. If not, tomorrow will be soon enough. I think we covered everything last evening. If there's anything else . . ."

Luis rubbed his chin thoughtfully. "No. From here on in I'll manage. I'll be aboard the *Silver Lady* until it's time to sail, should you need to get in touch with me. Otherwise, I'll plan to sail with the tide. The sooner I get matters under way, the sooner this will be resolved."

"Remember, Domingo, I want her—one way or the other!" Dykstra said as they parted at the Dutch East India offices.

Luis nodded and strode off. One way or the other . . . If necessary, could he kill a woman, even one who'd robbed him of his dream? He prided himself on being a gentleman. A poor gentleman, thanks to the sea witch.

As he leapt on board the *Lady*, he decided he could kill a woman if his life was in danger. But the woman hadn't yet been born who would ever get that advantage over him again. No woman was as strong and powerful as a man. This he believed implicitly.

While Luis Domingo was transferring his belongings to the Dutch East India's ship, Fury van der Rhys was slipping and sliding down the rise that bordered the *Rana*'s berth. She looked back to the top and waved to Juli, who was busy untying a bundle from her stiffly starched apron.

"Hold out your arms!" she shouted. Without thinking, Fury stretched out her arms and caught the packet.

"What is it?" she called up. Juli brought her hand to her forehead in the age-old maritime salute. Fury laughed excitedly as she slipped into the water. Minutes later she was climbing the rope ladder that would lead her onto the *Rana*'s decks.

Dripping water, the bundle tied around her neck, Fury hauled herself up on deck and looked about her, her face full of awe. This was *her* ship now. Strange feelings rushed through her as she touched first one thing, then another. Her mother's ship . . . Her mother had fought and killed aboard this ship to avenge her sister's death. She'd made love down below with Fury's father. How many times, Fury wondered, had she cheated death on these same decks? Suddenly the urge to swim back to shore was so strong, she had to grip the rail to keep from bolting. She dropped her hands to her sides when she saw Gaspar and Pilar work their way down in the warm breeze. "You're a welcome sight," she called. She stroked the birds' sleek heads, laughing as Pilar pecked at the bundle around her neck. "I don't know, maybe it's a mid-afternoon snack. I suppose we could eat it now."

How curious they were, these beauties of hers, she thought as she undid the twine around the bundle. The hawks rustled beside her quietly, their black eyes glittering with alarm at her gasp of surprise as she withdrew her mother's costume from the bundle. She could imagine Juli smiling at the thought of her reaction. She brought the fine lawn shirt to her cheek and swore she could smell her mother's scent. The birds inched down the brass railing, their eyes never leaving her face. "Stay here," she ordered, "I'll be right back."

In her mother's old quarters, Fury shed her wet clothing. Above deck she could hear the birds and knew they wondered what she was doing. She herself was wondering the same thing. Whatever it was, she knew it was something she *had* to do. What she was feeling, right now, this very minute, was quite different from what she'd experienced when she'd first dressed in the costume—the day she'd arrived at the estate. That had been amusing; this was real. So real, in fact, that she raced up to the wheelhouse and gripped the wheel the way her mother had hundreds of times, the way she herself had when she'd brought her father's ship into port with the aid of Gaspar and Pilar.

Where were they? Frantically she looked around and saw Gaspar take wing and soar straight up out of sight. Pilar remained on the railing. She frowned; the two hawks never separated from each other unless they had to—or in case of danger. She raced to the bow of the ship, her eyes searching for Gaspar.

In the distance she saw Juli, who was waving frantically, as though trying to tell her something. Fury shielded her eyes and saw the housekeeper sweeping her arms about in wicked, slicing motions. Of course, the rapier. She remembered seeing both the rapier and cutlass below. Juli must have had one of her brothers bring the weapons on board earlier. She ran to the cabin and brought the weapon back on deck. Razor-sharp and wicked as sin, it was; she flexed it, her stance secure as she danced back and forth across the deck. "En garde!" she cried as the blade nicked and sliced at the warm air.

She was the Sea Siren.

On the rise Juli smiled her approval. "Now, little one, you'll know what it's like to feel alive." She watched the pantomime below with bated breath, her eyes taking measure of the young woman who feinted, dipped, and slashed at an imaginary opponent. "You are your mother's daughter," she whispered at last.

Down below, Fury was filled with a sudden fierce pride. She was instantly all things—courageous, beautiful, daring, accomplished—all the things her mother was before her. She *was* the Sea Siren.

"Quarter!" she shouted triumphantly. "Quarter and your life is spared, señor!" Of course she would spare the Spaniard's life, the way her mother had spared Regan's. How could she do less? she thought, elated. She laid aside the rapier and ran below again to return with the heavy cutlass that was her father's.

Fury's thoughts were swept away when she noticed Gaspar circling overhead, working the wind to descend. She shielded her eyes from the sun and saw something gleaming and sparkling in his talons. In the blink of an eye Pilar was off the rail to catch the shimmering bangle. A second later she was holding it out to Fury.

"My garter! Gaspar, wherever did you get this!" she cried as she fingered the glittering diamonds. "The last time I saw this was the night of my birthday celebration. Gaspar, you took it! How wonderful! You brought it all this way." Tearfully, Fury nuzzled the bird's sleek head. "You could have given this to me any time since I've been here, but you waited till now. Why?"

Both birds cocked their heads and regarded her with keen eyes.

Fury sighed. "I won't pretend to understand, but it's obvious that you mean me to wear this." Quick as a flash she secured the glittering circlet around her thigh. "Ooohhh, I feel so deliciously wicked," she purred. "And now I understand. Before I was . . . pretending. This garter makes me real." She clapped her hands to show her approval and watched as the birds soared high overhead. They would play now, delighted with their little trick.

Vivid blue eyes stared down at the winking diamond garter. Long, tawny legs flashed in the sun as Fury brandished the heavy cutlass, nicking and slicing the air about her.

A long time later, exhausted at last, she returned to her cabin to shed her costume. When she walked back on deck she was Fury van der Rhys.

"I watched you. You *were* the Siren," Juli said excitedly. "I want to hear what it was like walking about the ship. And what did those damnable birds give you?"

"Juli, it was the most wonderful experience!" Fury exclaimed. "I felt as if I were bewitched for a time, and then when Gaspar brought the garter, I was me again. Oh, I can't explain it! I was slicing at Señor Domingo and making him beg me—I was going to spare his life the way my mother spared my father's. I never felt like that before. It was make-believe, a pretend game. And now it's over," she concluded sadly.

"Hardly," Juli muttered. "I think it's just beginning. If we're lucky, your clothes will dry before we reach the house. Tomorrow is another day, Miss Fury."

Fury nodded. "Yes, another day."

She was on her way up the stairs to retire when Juli came running up to say that Father Sebastian had just arrived and was waiting to speak with her on the veranda. Fury hurried out to him.

"Father, what is it?" she cried anxiously. "What's happened?"

"I'm not sure, but I thought you would want to know. The talk in town is that Mynheer Dykstra hired Señor Domingo to find the Sea Siren. The señor sailed with the tide on one of the Dutch East India's ships. Yesterday, a brigantine belonging to the Dutch East India Company limped into port. Her captain said she was attacked by the Sea

Siren. She was shot broadside and all the Dutch East India's cargo plundered. It's just like before. The town is . . . they're saying all manner of things. The merchants are putting a price on her head and the Dutch East India Company is adding its own. Every able-bodied ship is going to sea to hunt her down—dead or alive, they say.''

"Did anyone actually see the . . . the impostor?''

"The entire crew of the plundered ship, and that makes Señor Domingo's story true. We never should have doubted him,'' the old priest said sourly.

Fury considered his words, brows furrowed in a pensive frown. "Father, don't you find it just a little bit strange that Señor Domingo is the one hired by the Dutch East India Company to find the Sea Siren?''

"Not in the least. He's young and strong, and he actually had words with the woman. He was the logical choice. Mynheer Dykstra is too old to be hunting down the likes of this woman. It makes sense.''

"Not to me, it doesn't,'' Fury snapped. "Perhaps they're in this together. *That's* logical.''

"Furana!'' cried the priest, shocked. "Mynheer Dykstra is your father's old friend. He would never do anything so base. You should apologize for such a wicked thought. Although—'' he hesitated.

"What?'' Fury demanded.

"Both men were seen coming out of—''

"Where?'' Fury prodded when he seemed disinclined to continue.

"Clarice's . . . establishment. At midmorning. Today.''

"Oh . . .'' The information was a blow to Fury's pride. She knew her face was scarlet as she led the way into the library, where she rang Juli for refreshments.

"You'll stay the night, Father. I insist.''

"Yes, thank you, child. I don't think I'm up to the trip back this evening.''

Over coffee, Fury and Father Sebastian discussed other, inconsequential matters, but Fury's mind was whirling with thoughts of Luis Domingo in Clarice's establishment. True, her own father had gone to Clarice many, many times—or so her mother had said. But the idea of Luis Domingo in the arms of an experienced whore made her body hot all over.

"Have you ever seen the women who work for Clarice?" she asked at last, unable to stand it a moment longer.

"My, yes—and it would be hard to tell they weren't town ladies," the priest said piously. "Quite elegant they are when they shop. Only the finest. Very young and pretty."

"How pretty?" Fury asked, wanting to bite off her tongue for voicing the question.

Father Sebastian leaned back in his chair, his eyes far away. "Very beautiful, I believe. The prettiest one is Naula. Clarice considers her a prize among all the girls." He turned away then, embarrassed at the turn their conversation had taken. "Why are we talking about this, child?"

Fury tossed her head defensively. "You brought up the subject, Father. I have no interest in brothels or the people who frequent them. Señor Domingo's personal affairs are of no interest to me whatever," she added, eyes flashing.

"I thought we were discussing Mynheer Dykstra and the Spaniard," the priest said fretfully. "Am I . . . did I forget something?"

"No, of course not. You're just tired. I'll ring for Juli and have her show you to your room. Good night, Father."

"Sleep well, child."

A few minutes before midnight Fury rapped softly on Juli's bedroom door. "These brothers of yours," she asked when Juli beckoned her inside, "all seven of them, where are they?"

"In town. Why, Miss Fury? Has something happened to Father Sebastian?"

"No, no, nothing like that. If your brothers can crew my ship, I can sail on the morning tide. We need to send someone into town and arrange with them to meet me at the ship."

"Who? Are you sure you want the servants to know . . . Oh, I see, you want me to go into town. You are like your mother," Juli grumbled as she began to dress. The housekeeper's eyes widened when she took a good look at Fury and realized she was dressed and planning to make her way through the jungle in the darkness. "Miss Fury! You can't possibly—"

"The moon is bright, and I'll take Gaspar and Pilar with me. The stable boys think me daft as it is. A moonlight ride won't surprise them at all, and I'll try to be quiet. You'll have to send someone to care for the horse, though.

"Promise your brothers they'll be well paid," she whispered as Juli slipped out the door.

Later, on her way to the stable, Fury wondered where she was going to get the money to pay Juli's brothers. Perhaps Mynheer Dykstra would advance her some money without asking too many questions.

Fury saddled the mare and led her into the courtyard. Then she clapped her hands lightly and was rewarded with a *swoosh* of dark air. Somewhere in the darkness the hawks were waiting for her.

Fury didn't like the darkness. She never had. On the ride to the cove she tried to pray but soon gave it up in favor of an easier task—imagining the face of the whore Naula described by Father Sebastian. Beautiful, he'd said. Well, there was no one more beautiful than her mother. If the faceless Naula were half as pretty, she was indeed worth looking at. Had the famous Clarice assigned Naula to Luis Domingo? Probably, Fury decided. He was the type of man who would command only the best, the most experienced women. Lord, she hated her thoughts. Luis Domingo meant nothing to her, and if she sailed the *Rana* out to sea in search of him, she'd be endangering her life.

Fury's throat constricted as she thought of all the others who would be looking for the Sea Siren—Luis Domingo would not be alone. What chance would she have against a gaggle of cutthroats eager to claim the price on her head? And it was *her* head. Nowhere in this world was there a woman who could even come close to impersonating her mother . . . except for herself.

Fury followed the jungle slope down, finally reaching the tiny beach that cupped the cliff-framed cove, and approached the ship. It took only minutes to pasture the horse and swim out to the *Rana*.

Soaking wet, she made her way to the wheelhouse and the maps and charts she would need to steer down the river and out to sea. She prayed that twenty long years had shifted the rocks that gave the River of Death its name. If not, she would need every ounce of skill to somehow skirt the killing rocks at the ocean's edge.

Fury's touch was reverent as she unrolled first one map and then another until she found what she wanted. If she was unlucky enough to be seen, she would sail around the west tip of Java. "Anyone in pursuit will think the sea swallowed me whole," she muttered. This map of the eastern isles was going to be a blessing.

Her slender fingers trailed across the old maps her mother had sailed by. There was no reason to believe she couldn't manage the trip. Still, she didn't feel at all as confident as she had the previous day when she'd come aboard. Of course, then she'd had the costume and the weapons. They made the difference. Dressed as she was now, she was a lady, a visitor on board ship. It was a feeling she didn't like at all.

Below in her cabin she stripped off her wet clothing and slipped into the costume she'd worn the day before. As if by magic, the same feeling returned. Before she allowed herself to think about her transformation, she was on deck, cutlass in one hand, rapier in the other.

Confident now, she strutted up and down the teakwood deck, getting the feel of the black boots, the diamond garter winking in the lantern light. Suddenly she stopped, eyes wide with the realization that she was different here aboard the *Rana*. Her hand measured the weight of the rapier, and she knew in that second she could wound, maim, or kill if she had to. Furana van der Rhys might flush, blush, and simper in the presence of Luis Domingo, but not this seafaring hellcat.

She was striding again, the heels of her boots thumping on the deck as she tried to make sense of what she was thinking and feeling. Long ago, when her mother rode the seas, she lived under a dual identity, an identity that served her well. She was able to transform not only her outward appearance, but her personality as well. On land she was as capable as at sea, and she didn't need the scanty costume or the *Rana* to be the Sea Siren. Fury, however, needed both to assume her mother's old identity. "And that doesn't say much for me," Fury muttered, one hand still clutching the hilt of the rapier.

The peaceful cove was a haven . . . for now. Fury leaned on the railing and stared across the moonlit water. She could still change her mind if she wanted to. She could forget about the impostor riding the seas and Luis Domingo as well. She could even go back to Spain. So many choices. . . .

Suddenly the hawks grew restless from their position on

the mizzenmast, and Fury picked up the sound on the water at the same moment. A boat was headed their way.

The boat was small and crowded, the occupants' whispers carrying across the water. Immediately Fury dropped the rope ladder over the side of the ship. All but Juli climbed aboard.

"I'll secure this vessel at the deepest end of the cove," Juli called up. "Good luck."

Fury's heart pounded as she greeted Juli's brothers. All were young, agile, and in the darkness she was unable to read their expressions. She called out to Juli, her voice betraying the anxiousness she was feeling. "Juli, how much did you tell them . . . what are their feelings . . . what did their wives . . . Juli, you can't leave me like this and not . . ."

Juli closed the distance between the *Rana*'s bow and the jolly boat she was in. "They are not afraid, if that's what you want to know, Miss Fury. They are big, hulking men, as you can see, and even if they were afraid, they'd never voice their fears in front of a woman. We have their wives to thank for allowing them to sail with you. *They* understand what it is you are doing. I gave away no secrets, if that is what you are fretting over, although one would have to be very stupid not to know what is going on. The less voiced the better. I will tell you this: they fear those damnable birds."

"Gaspar and Pilar!" Fury said in a shocked voice. "But they won't harm your brothers. Speaking of harm, Juli, each day that goes by, there are more and more people who know . . . for years this was the best-kept secret in the world, and now all seven of your brothers know, Father Sebastian knows, and it wouldn't surprise me at all if Luis Domingo knows, not to mention the imposter who roams the seas."

Juli's voice turned thick with displeasure. "My brothers, to a man, will swear allegiance to you. There is no one else who can be trusted. If you are having second thoughts, now is the time to voice them," she growled.

"No, no, I guess I'm just nervous. It will be light very soon and time to sail."

"Godspeed," Juli called over her shoulder. "I'll pray for your safe return."

Fury turned to face her crew. They were clean and freshly shaved, and had curious, honest eyes. Immediately, Fury regretted her words to Juli. They were there to help her. All were young but none as young as herself. All were married with children, Juli had told her several days earlier. The wages she would pay them would not make them rich but would make their lives more comfortable. None of them seem surprised at her scanty costume, and none were leering at her. She felt safe and realized one source of her anxiety was gone. Now it was time for business.

If her crew of seven felt uneasy, it wasn't noticeable to Fury as the *Rana* skimmed out of the cove beneath her sure, if unpracticed, hands—down the winding river, over the white-capped breakers, and . . . into open water. She hadn't expected such a rough sea, and it took all her strength to hold the frigate steady. Above her she could see Gaspar and Pilar, sentinels on the mizzenmast, their jet eyes on the rolling breakers. Over and over she told herself that she was the *Rana*'s master.

Two hours later a wild wind started to blow in from the west, signaling an impending storm. Excitement coursed through Fury as she gripped the wheel. She felt Gaspar and Pilar swoop down to perch on the high-backed chair that was bolted to the floor, their talons digging into the heavy mahogany. Their presence gave Fury renewed strength. If she could bring the *Java Queen* safely into port, she could certainly ride the *Rana* through any rough weather.

The course she plotted was one of pure instinct, one she felt a man such as Luis Domingo would follow. If she was wrong, she'd have to live with her mistake. She hoped that Father Sebastian's information was accurate. She had to assume that the Spaniard would set sail in one of the Dutch East India's brigantines, which would give her a definite advantage. If she was mistaken—if he was sailing a frigate much like her own—he would be making top speed. She had to outmaneuver as well as outguess him.

Where would he head? If there was a storm, the brigantine wouldn't heave to under a reefed main topsail. Instinct told her the Spaniard would take the northern shore to reach Sumbawa while she was following a course along the southern shore of Java. Most likely he'd head for the shore off the island where the last Dutch East India ship was attacked. Weather and speed permitting, she could rendezvous there with the angry sea captain. Bali, she decided, the most beautiful island off Java's eastern tip, was his destination. Now it was hers as well.

The storm was savage in its intensity, but of short duration. Fury rode it out under her own prowess, the crew cheering her on. When she turned the wheel over to Mandu, Juli's oldest brother, there was open admiration in his eyes. "Well done, Capitana." Fury beamed her pleasure at his words. Her mother's old crew had called her capitana, too. "I'd be obliged, Capitana, if you'd take . . . your feathered friends with you," Mandu added uneasily.

Fury laughed and snapped her fingers. The birds spread their wings with a loud swish before they sailed upward among the rigging. Mandu turned his head to look over his shoulder.

"Think of them as being on *our* side, *our* protectors,

not just my own,'' Fury suggested, smiling. ''As long as you do nothing to alarm them in regard to me, they are quite docile.''

Mandu gave a brief nod. ''Aye, Capitana.''

Out on deck, Fury called for all hands. ''*We* did well, men,'' she told them. ''Another day, and if my predictions are right, we should meet up with our quarry. Bali would be my first thought, but he may make Sumbawa, depending on his headwinds. For now we've earned a brief rest.'' She turned away, dismissing her small crew. ''I'll be in my cabin.''

Down below she grinned gleefully. Shorthanded as they were—a frigate generally required a crew of at least twelve—they'd done better than she had a right to expect. Good men, a good captain, and a good ship were all that was needed. Now she could relax for a moment.

On deck, the crew whispered among themselves. For a woman, this young lady had handled the frigate as well as any man. For once their sharp-tongued sister had been correct in her assertions. All they had to do now was secure the ship and allow the warm trade winds to spur them onward.

Ten hours later a cry of ''Sail ho!'' came from the rigging. The spyglass was in Fury's hands in a moment.

''Does she sport a Dutch flag?'' she shouted.

''Aye, Capitana, and she's tightened sail. She's spotted us. Her captain is on the stern.''

''All hands on deck! Mandu, steer this ship directly broadside.'' To the others she shouted, ''I want no shots fired until I give the order. We aren't here to fight. Do you understand?''

Never in her life had she experienced such excitement. Her heat thundered in her chest and her pulses thrummed. Something niggled at her, some little-known thing she should have done and now couldn't remember. . . . Lord, of course, the lip and cheek color!

In the blink of an eye she raced to her cabin and dabbed from the little pot Juli had added to her satchel at the last moment. It was Juli who remembered her mother scrubbing the vermilion paint from her cheeks on her return.

Back on deck, Fury raced to the bow of the ship. Feet firmly planted and slightly apart, her hair billowing behind her, she waited, a smile on her face.

"Remember now, veer off at the last moment," she called to her crew. "I want the captain to think we're going to attack, until the very last second. She's loosening sail. The men are in the shrouds. I can see them unfurling the sail! We have only a few moments of daylight left. We're almost broadside!"

As the last vestige of daylight relinquished its hold on the dark gray of early night, Fury felt her hand caressing the hilt of the cutlass at her side.

Luis Domingo, captain of the *China Jewel*, stood on the stern, his face full of shock at the figure of the woman outlined in the murky yellow light. Cutlass in hand, she made a low, mocking bow in his direction.

"We mean you no harm, señor, unless it is your intention to fire upon us," she called to him.

He should give the order to fire; he couldn't understand why he wasn't. He knew his men were ready and waiting for this female witch to make some move that would warrant an attack. He also knew the *Jewel* could not outrace the sleek black frigate. So he waited, his dark eyes narrowed to slits. "We carry no cargo; this is a scouting voyage only," he called.

"I'm not interested in your cargo, señor. I've been tracking you since you left port. Take a good look at me, señor!" Fury ordered. "I am not the pirate who plundered the *Silver Lady*! You were mistaken, and I demand an apology.''

''You'll get no apology from me, you sea slut,'' Luis snarled. ''You robbed my cargo. I saw you, I talked to you. No woman makes a fool of me!''

''You'll regret those words, you miserable Spaniard!'' Fury cried. She didn't stop to think. She was a whirlwind of motion as long legs flexed and then leapt. In a split second she was aboard the *China Jewel*, the tip of the cutlass pointed six inches below the Spaniard's belt.

Stunned, Luis stepped backward, followed by the scantily clad woman wielding her cutlass. ''I could kill you this very second,'' Fury said, her voice ominously quiet. ''All it would take is one downward stroke. But I told you I meant you no harm. You should have believed me.''

She inched closer, the cutlass secure in her hand. ''Listen to me carefully, señor. I never killed for the sake of killing. I never plundered for my own benefit. My reign on the sea was a cause, and when that cause was laid to rest, I retired. Until today I have not been aboard that frigate out there for twenty years, nor have I attacked any ships.''

''Then how do you explain the Dutch East India's brigantine?'' Luis snapped.

''She was beset by an impostor, as were you. I don't know who, or why this . . . this person chooses to masquerade as the Sea Siren, but I shall find out.''

Fury took a step backward and lowered the cutlass a fraction. ''And now,'' she said mockingly, ''I believe I came aboard for a reason . . . an apology. Proceed, Captain.'' When Luis remained silent, she whipped up the cutlass to slice the buttons from his shirt, then returned it to point directly at his groin. ''I'm losing patience, señor.''

Grim-faced, Luis shook his head. ''No apology, Sea

Siren, not from my lips. I know what I saw, I know what I experienced. What you say may or may not be true; I am, however, willing to concede your point—if you will but *show me your arm.*"

Fury drew away, startled and at a sudden loss for words. At that moment there was a loud, *swoosh*ing noise from above. Both Fury and Luis looked up in time to see Gaspar and Pilar swoop down, then soar upward again, their wings rustling as they circled the Spaniard in a menacing orbit.

"What the goddamn living hell is *that*?" Luis shouted as he doubled over.

Fury laughed. "*That*, señor, is called retribution. Those birds can kill you as quickly as I can. Right now they're quite angry, as you can see. If I *ever* hear you or your crew refer to me as a sea slut again, I'll unleash them on you so fast, your head will spin."

Luis observed the circling hawks for a moment or two, then returned his gaze to Fury, eyes glinting with rage. "Another time, another place, Siren, and we'll face off again."

"On your knees, señor!" To the birds, Fury called, "Watch him till I'm back aboard."

Luis stared, mesmerized, as incredibly long legs leapt high above him. He sucked in his breath when she landed gracefully aboard the black frigate. The sound of her laughter raised the hackles on the back of his neck.

"Admit it, señor, I outmaneuvered you!" she called, offering a salute with the tip of the cutlass.

"Never!" he cried passionately. "I could have drilled you broadside. But I was in a charitable mood."

Again Fury's laughter tinkled across the water. Her crew as well as Domingo's knew she was the victor, no matter what he said.

The hawks swooped down with deadly intent, only to

sail upward in their own wake as Fury called, "Enough!" He watched in amazement as both birds flew into the black ship's rigging.

Until this moment he'd been unaware of the fog rolling in. Even now it shrouded his decks, creeping upward. All he could see of the woman aboard the black frigate was the diamond garter twinkling in the misty light. Then . . . nothing. *She always disappears into the mist,* the old sea salt had said.

A long time later, a tankard of ale in his hand, he asked his first mate, Julian, for his opinion. "Was it the same woman?"

Julian frowned. "I don't recall seeing that diamond garter on the woman who attacked the *Queen,* and I know there were no birds. . . ."

"What about the first time, when she attacked the *Spanish Princess.* Did you see a garter or those damnable birds then?"

"It was so long ago, Captain, and my memory isn't what it used to be. The birds I would remember, but the garter, I'd have to say no. Women . . . acquire baubles and wear them at a whim. It's possible she confiscated it from somewhere. She is more beautiful than I remember. The red lips and cheeks I remember, and those long legs . . . aye, Captain, a beautiful woman."

"How old do you think she is?" Luis asked.

"You would be a better judge of that than I, Captain. Young, I'd say."

Luis's brows knitted in thought. "No more than twenty, I'd say. The real Siren would be in her fortieth year or thereabouts." He threw up his hands in disgust. "Women!"

"You saw the scar?" Julian asked.

"No, but it's my gut feeling it's there. She must be real, she has to be real."

"Flesh and blood?" Julian demanded fearfully.

"As real as you and I. I could feel her breath on my face. I want her," Luis growled.

"As does every man jack aboard this ship," Julian said. "She's a devil angel if ever there was one. She strikes the fear of God in me, I can tell you that."

Luis sat alone for the rest of the night, secure in the knowledge that his ship was in Julian's capable hands. He searched his mind for ways he could have reacted differently, things he could have said and done. She hadn't exactly made a fool of him, but she'd definitely had the advantage. Only a fool would have attacked the odds once she boarded the *Jewel*.

Beautiful honey-colored legs, eyes that were more blue than the sky. So very beautiful, more beautiful than any woman he'd ever met. Strong, capable, sense of humor. Her remembered laughter sent chills up his arms. His last thought before retiring to his cabin was that this was one woman not to be taken lightly. As he drifted off to sleep, he wondered once again what it would be like to make love to the exquisite sea creature.

In her bunk Fury lay still, trying to stem the trembling that threatened to overtake her. It was over; she had successfully carried off her plan. She truly believed she was the victor, although no battle had been waged and no blows struck for either side.

Not until dawn was she able to give definition to what she was feeling: her blood was singing, and all because of Luis Domingo.

Chapter Eight

Saianha

Amalie leaned against the cave opening, her pose one of nonchalance. It was backbreaking work carrying the cargoes of the many ships they'd plundered to this safe, secure cave, not that she was doing any of the work. As each crate or barrel was stored inside, she logged it in one of her father's old ledgers. Later, when she felt it was safe, she would dispose of the goods to the highest bidder, preferably in Spain. She wondered idly when and how much; she had no idea what the contents of the cave would yield in the way of money. She also had to allow for the crew's share. No matter, it was close to a fortune.

It was a beautiful evening, warm and star-blessed. She was glad to be on land. While she liked the sea and the rolling ship, she knew she could not create a life for herself on the water. This was where she belonged; the ship and the sea were merely the means to insure that the rest of her life would be charted to her satisfaction.

The note she'd made in the margin of the ledger irritated her. In order to transport the contents of the cave to a ready market, she would need a brigantine, perhaps a galleon, possibly two. There was no way she could purchase the ships, since she had no ready money and nothing to trade for them. She would have to commandeer them at

187

some point and drive the crew overboard. But where would she secure the ships until it was time to sail for Spain?

Another problem, and one she thought about constantly, plagued her as no other. How long would her crew be content with things the way they were? Already they were grumbling about money and the risk to their lives every time they accosted a ship. For six months now she'd been able to calm them, promising them anything she could think of to ward off a mutiny. The only alternative was to kill off those who became too verbal in their complaints or demands.

Amalie logged a cask of coffee beans and another of nutmeg, the men cursing as they rolled and dragged the heavy barrels into the recesses of the cave. Tomorrow they would sail on the morning tide in hopes of overtaking a galleon with an escort of two, all heavily loaded with ivory, a prize that was unequaled among their current plunder. A prize the Dutch East India Company could ill afford to lose. Amalie smiled in the darkness. Their loss—her gain. If she could just find a safe hiding place for the galleon and brigantines, she could keep the cargoes on board and not have to go through this time-consuming ritual of loading, unloading, and logging in.

She smiled again, grimly this time, when she thought of the price on her head. She knew in her gut there wasn't one among her crew—save, perhaps, Cato—who hadn't speculated on turning her in. That amount of money, plus all the cargoes, would make them rich for life. The whole fine mess was taking its toll on her, and she knew it. She slept little, and when she did, it was lightly. The least little sound woke her. Most of the time she was irritable and angry with the crew's sly looks and open greed. She knew she was going to have to do something soon to set an example, one they wouldn't forget.

Minutes later Amalie snapped the ledger closed and sig-

naled her men that it was time to leave. She was last in
line to slip and slide down the steep incline that led to the
small harbor where her ship was anchored. Cato was directly in front of her. The tension between her shoulder
blades told her that something was up. Miguel and some
of the others must be plotting to waylay her, she reflected,
or, worse yet, kill her so that all the cave's contents and
her ship would be theirs.

"Cato, look at me," Amalie said. "This damned crew
is planning something, aren't they?"

Cato kept his eyes fastened to the scrubby terrain and
treacherous vines. "I'm not sure," he answered, his voice
low.

Panic swept through Amalie. She needed these men,
needed them desperately. She swallowed past the lump in
her throat and tried to speak normally. "I'll cut out their
gizzards, yours, too, if you align yourself with them."

Still, Cato did not respond. Desperate now, Amalie tried
a different tack. "Cato, do you recall the conversation we
had on deck one night while the others were sleeping and
you were on watch? I meant every word I said. When my
father's house is finally restored, I will live like a queen—
and a queen needs a king. You and I could be very happy
. . . as long as you don't cross me and do something foolish that we'll both regret."

Cato turned at last to speak to her—and in doing so lost
his footing. Amalie reached out, her grip on his arm like
a vise, and pulled him upright. "There now," she said
softly, releasing his arm, "you're steady on your feet. Remember, I want to know your decision before we sail."

Cato nodded, his young gaze full of admiration. Amalie's
strength and stamina never ceased to amaze him. But he'd
be a fool to side with the woman against Miguel and his
cutthroats. She would be sadly outnumbered, of that he
was sure. He would tell the others, his friends, that they

would be princes, and because he would be king he would grant them whatever they desired. She hadn't said anything about crowns, though, he worried. A queen and king always wore crowns and elegant robes. His spirits soared almost immediately when he remembered seeing the trunk with its heavy lock and emblem of the Spanish Crown. Crowns and costly robes would be kept in such a place. His spirits plummeted. His young, curious voice carried back to Amalie. "Where will you get a throne?"

Amalie chuckled deep in her throat. "I already have . . . two of them. They belonged to my father. Solid gold," she lied. "In need of polishing. It will be your first . . . kingly duty."

It never occurred to Cato that kings didn't do manual labor. He smiled in the darkness. Already, he could feel the costly robes about his shoulders. He would have to give some thought to the crown and how it would stay fastened to his head. Gold was heavy, and if the crown were studded with priceless gems, it would weigh even more. Wearing a crown was probably something one had to get used to, he thought smugly. He racked his imagination to come up with something he could tell the others princes wore. Possibly neck cuffs studded with rubies, emeralds, and diamonds. He almost choked on his own saliva when he thought of the others as his loyal subjects. He knew at that moment he would do whatever Amalie wanted him to do, even kill.

In her cabin Amalie changed from her coarse dress to the abbreviated costume responsible for Miguel's slobbering mouth. Cato was so young and probably no match for Miguel and his cohorts. She had doubts about her own abilities but refused to dwell on them. The impending confrontation was inevitable, had been from the start. Miguel's greed exceeded only her own. It would happen in open water, of that much she was sure, which didn't give her much time to prepare for the onslaught. An hour, perhaps two at the most, before the crew made a move. Her heart pumped madly in her chest with the realization the crew would openly attack her and try to kill her. How she defended herself and how victorious she was would set the precedent for her reign at sea. The previous altercations were what she considered necessary exercises to prepare her for the really important attacks like the one she was anticipating today.

Amalie flexed her injured arm. Daily she'd exercised with the heavy cutlass until she thought she would drop with fatigue. She was confident that she could outfight any man bent on attacking her.

The attack, when it came, was stealthy and deadly.

Amalie swiveled, cutlass in her hand, at the precise moment Miguel raised his arm to strike her down. The seaman's body had reflected off the shimmering water when the glass was to her eye, which gave her the split second she needed to square off against the hateful cutthroat. All about her were shouts of outrage and curses of rebellion as she brought up her arm to fend off Miguel's wicked blade. Up and down, to the left and to the right, she feinted, her agile body dancing away to thrust and jab.

"Kill me, will you?" she cried. "Not likely, you pig!"

The surprise and a quick moment of fear showed in Miguel's eyes as Amalie's lightning-fast movement sent him reeling backward. She pressed her advantage, parrying with an expertise he'd not known she possessed. His eyes widened when her blade sliced down, then upward, ripping not only his trousers, but his filthy shirt as well. The sight of his own blood brought obscenities spewing from his mouth. His own cutlass sliced through thin air as Amalie danced backward and then to the left, her cutlass whacking his arm at the elbow. She laughed when his ugly face contorted in pain.

"Whore!" Miguel roared, his blade lashing out at Amalie's scarred arm.

"Son of a whore!" Amalie countered as her blade sliced upward, ripping Miguel's ear from the side of his head. "You swore your allegiance to me and turned mutineer, and for that you and the scum that follow you deserve to die!"

Miguel's eyes were murderous with rage as he swung his cutlass, missing Amalie's own ear by a hair. Amalie thrust blindly, off balance as the seaman tried to pin her against the railing. Curses and dark mutterings rocked in her ears as she thrust the cutlass straight out, piercing Miguel in the middle of his stomach. She heaved mightily, ripping the blade upward toward his chest. Blood gushed from the gaping wound.

Amalie whirled then, her eyes glittering as she faced the circle of men that had formed around her and the unfortunate Miguel. She crouched, her hand beckoning the next volunteer who wanted to do battle. "Now, do it now, or from this day on you'll never know a moment's peace," she cried, "for I no longer trust you. I'll kill you when you sleep, when you're high in the rigging, when you're sotted with ale, or when you're playing a game of cards. I'll come up behind you and slice your head from your neck."

When no one moved, she straightened to her full height. "I see that wisdom has struck all of you suddenly. From this moment on you will never again question my authority. You belong to me now, body and soul. You will do what I say when I say it. And the first man who looks at me crossways will find himself shark fodder like Miguel," she warned them. "Now get rid of this vermin and scour these decks till they sparkle!"

The silence roared in Amalie's ears as she strode to her quarters. The moment the cabin door was closed and locked, she rushed to her bunk and buried her face in the pillow to muffle her cries of triumph.

She'd won. *She'd won!* She was now in total control of her ship and the men aboard. There wasn't one who'd have the guts to start a fight with her. Over and over again she played back the scene with Miguel. The exhilaration was overpowering, running like fire through her veins, until she realized what it was she was experiencing: the need to prove herself even more. And the only way she could do that was with a man.

Cato. Cato, with the young, strong body and dark, burning eyes. She would devour him, satiate herself, and make him a willing slave to her bidding. It would be a simple matter to drug the young man with her charms until he was addicted to her body as well as to her mystique. All she had to do now was wait until he brought her a mug of coffee and his hourly report on conditions topside.

Within minutes of the hourly bell, Cato arrived at her cabin carrying a steaming cup of coffee, and meat and bread on a tray. Amalie—or his queen, as he now thought of her—was sitting on the edge of her bunk, smiling at him. He returned her smile and gingerly set the tray on the small table next to the bunk. There was something very different about the way she was looking at him, almost as if she wanted him . . . to touch her. A core of heat curled in his stomach and then fanned outward to suffuse his cheeks with color.

"I want to thank you for—" Amalie jerked her head to indicate the upper deck. Cato nodded and turned to leave. "Wait, don't go," she called. "Come, sit here by me and tell me what the crew is saying. Have I anything to worry about?"

He wanted to tell her she would never have to worry

about anything; he wanted to tell her he would protect her from the likes of Miguel and any others who might have the same intentions. He wanted to tell her how beautiful she was; how he admired her strength and the way she'd attacked the man who was now feeding the sharks . . . But he didn't. His tongue was too thick in his mouth for words, and his body was raging with desire. Dare he tell her what he was thinking?

Hands trembling, he sat down next to his captain. "I . . . the men, they have all sworn allegiance to you, and this time they mean what they say," he began. "Miguel was . . . has always been . . . They're glad he's dead. You have nothing to worry about. I promise to keep my eyes and ears open."

"Thank you," Amalie said, and touched his arm in a gentle caress. Cato flinched as though he'd been struck.

"Would you like to touch me the way I'm touching you?" she asked softly.

Cato nodded, his callused hands reaching out almost of their own accord.

Amalie laughed deep in her throat, the sound primitive and sensual, demanding. "No, not my arm. Here . . ." She pointed to the cleavage between her breasts.

Cato closed his eyes as he buried his face in the twin mounds of creamy flesh, only half aware of Amalie's fingers fumbling with the buttons on her shirt. When at last her breasts were totally free of their confinement, she stretched and leaned back, relishing the artful working of his tongue, moaning her pleasure as she drew his head upward. Their lips met in a searing kiss that left both of them gasping. In a second their clothing fell to the floor as their bodies met and locked with each other. Amalie felt herself crying out as Cato's hands stroked her body, slowly at first and then urgently. She could feel a roaring in her head as the urgent caresses unleashed the wild, clamorous passion she'd so long held in abeyance.

Blood raced through Cato's veins as Amalie clawed at his back, her mouth burning beneath his. Frantically, low moans of pleasure and desire shaking her, she writhed beneath his hardness.

"Hurry, hurry," she murmured, tearing her mouth from his. With one hard thrust from Cato she arched her back, involuntarily crying out, her head rearing into the pillow.

Stunned with what she'd just experienced, Amalie clasped Cato's head to her breast as she crooned words of satisfaction. Minutes later she whispered, "Again, please, again." This time she moved to lie on top of him, her breasts crushing against his chest. Ever so slightly she brought her bruised lips to his, her tongue darting in and out of the warm recesses of his mouth.

Cato, his body slick with perspiration, his heart drumming, silently offered himself up to his queen.

Moaning with pleasure at her ability to arouse him with a mere touch, she crouched up onto her knees, straddling his firm body, her breathing hard and ragged, her motion rhythmical, drawing him deeper into her web.

Cato reached for her breasts with trembling hands. A low, fierce growl of ecstasy ripped from his mouth as Amalie once again brought him to the brink of exploding passion—only to stop all movement, leaving him burning for release.

"Beg me, plead with me," she whispered. "Tell me you want me, all of me, tell me there is no other like me."

Cato's eyes glazed as he repeated the desired words from the depths of his soul. "Don't leave me," he whispered as he drew her to him, their bodies entwined. "I need you," he gasped, surrendering to wave upon wave of passion. He could feel his heart hammering in his chest, every nerve in his body clamoring for satisfaction. "Please," he moaned.

"Yes . . . *Now* . . ." she whispered. They rolled as one, her powerful hands pulling his full weight down onto her.

He rode her like a wild stallion, hard and fast, plunging, withdrawing, until neither of them could stand the exquisite pain a moment longer. Amalie rocked her slick body against his, meeting each explosion of his passion with a tortured cry.

Cato had no idea how much time had passed until Amalie stirred next to him. He didn't care if he never went on deck again. This was what he wanted; this was what he would never forget. He reached out to stroke Amalie's face, and she smiled against his hand. "Did I please you?" he whispered huskily, his heart bursting with love. "Will I make a fitting king for you?"

Amalie smiled again, curling her naked body like a cat. "Of course," she whispered, and realized she meant the words. Cato was so innocent. She'd pleasured many men, more than she cared to remember, but not one had been interested in pleasing her. Only Cato. She tweaked his cheek playfully, wanting to bring a smile to his face.

"Will . . . will we do this again?" he asked in a hushed, pleading voice.

"As often as you like," Amalie replied. She gurgled with laughter when, minutes later, Cato swaggered from her cabin. In no way would she ever think of him as a boy again. In her heart she knew he'd never breathe a word of what had transpired between them. It would make little difference to her authority over the other men if he did, but it was nice to know he respected her enough not to boast about their lovemaking.

Stretching luxuriously, Amalie savored the feeling of satisfaction that welled within. She could still smell the musky scent of Cato, and it pleased her. With a little work, a little refinement, he just might be the perfect king for her domain. She detested the word *slave*, but Cato would make a willing one. She pressed her face deep into her pillow and imagined she was holding him in her arms, kissing him, making love to him. She remembered the way her body felt when he was deep inside her. Right now, this very moment, she wanted that feeling again and knew she would never have enough now that her passions had been aroused. Hours and hours . . . days, possibly weeks of doing nothing but making love and eating. Could one exist only on love? She wanted to find out, needed to find out, and she would.

Amalie slept then, her dreams filled with a tall, dark-eyed Spaniard who in no way resembled Cato. When she woke, it was fully dark, a bright orange moon shining through the mullioned window in her cabin. As she dressed she tried not to think about her dream and what it meant.

The moment her booted feet touched the deck, she heard the cry of "Sail ho!" from high in the rigging. Her heart leapt in her chest at the thought of another battle, especially now, when she didn't feel like fighting. Uneasily she took notice of the low, swirling fog. The smoky lamp pots added eerie shadows everywhere she looked. Perhaps it was an omen of some kind, a warning. . . .

Almost immediately she discounted the thought. A fog was a fog, and the smoky lantern pots were lights, nothing more. But she would have them extinguished in any case—lights could be seen even in fog.

"Where away?" she shouted, cursing when the spyglass offered nothing but swirling fog. She ran to the bow and brought the glass to her eye a second time, then craned her neck backward to peer into the rigging. "You're sure?"

"Dead ahead, Captain. She's traveling at five knots,

perhaps a little less, and she doesn't know we're on her stern,'' the seaman called softly, knowing full well that voices carried over the water. "She's heavily armed."

Darkness, Amalie decided, could either be one's enemy or one's friend. "Douse all lanterns," she ordered. The only thing in her favor right now was the fog and darkness, since she was sailing in unfamiliar waters. One good shot could scuttle her frigate, and they'd all be joining Miguel.

At last she sighted them—the galleon and her two brigantines . . . loaded with ivory and perfect for her needs. She couldn't afford to make a mistake. Swiftly she motioned to Cato.

"We'll attack from the jolly boats," she told him. "I want a dozen men in the water swimming alongside. The galleon won't expect such a feeble attempt—surprise will be in our favor. As soon as we have cloud cover, over we go. Have everyone gather round while I explain our plan. . . .''

Amalie's heart pounded as the jolly boats set out under cover of the thick gray fog, one to the left, one to the right, and the third directly in the wake of the galleon. The plan, she'd explained, required strict silence. Having her crew attack by stealth while she rendered the captain helpless would be their one main advantage. They were sadly outnumbered, and what she was planning was foolhardy. But she gave each man his orders and the promise of an extra dividend when splitting the prize. Bloodthirsty by nature, they could hardly wait to get their hands on the small convoy.

"Directly ahead," whispered one of the men from the water.

Amalie looked about but could see nothing save the eerie yellow glow of the galleon's smoke pots. Another few moments and it would be time to board. This attack, she thought excitedly, would double or perhaps triple the price on her head. Three ships at once! She almost laughed aloud as she slid over the side of the jolly boat.

Everything was going according to plan; even the thick, dark clouds cooperated, sailing across the sky to give her all the cover she needed. The moment her feet touched the galleon's deck, she crouched down, straining to make out the deck in the thick fog. One of the men jabbed his forefinger in the direction of the wheelhouse, and Amalie sprinted off in a half crouch, all senses alert to anything that might hinder her progress.

Seconds later one of the smoke pots hissed loudly in the water, her signal for them to attack as one—and all hell broke loose.

"All hands on deck!" the captain shouted into his horn. "To your stations! Attack! *Attack!*"

Amalie smiled in the darkness as she crept behind the captain. A minute later she had his hands pinned behind his back and her arm locked around his throat. "If you want to stay alive, Captain, order your crew to cease and desist. I want these ships. If you force us to kill your men, it will be your doing."

The captain tried to speak, but Amalie's arm was slowly cutting off his air supply. When he struggled, she merely increased the pressure. "Quietly, Captain, or I'll snap your neck. Now—order them into the jolly boats."

"Jolly boats?" the captain rasped.

"Of course. Do you think for one moment the Sea Siren would leave you in open water to die? I told you, I want these ships, not your lives. Make your decision *now*." Amalie released her hold on the captain and thrust him forward. She watched through narrowed eyes as he picked up the horn to obey her command.

It was all too easy, she thought suspiciously. Something was wrong. "I want to see your log," she told him, "and then I want a roll call—on deck. And if you do anything out of the ordinary, Captain, I'll run you through and pin you to the yardarm.''

The captain was a fat man, his steps jerky and faltering with fear. Amalie jabbed his buttocks with the tip of her cutlass as she marched him to the quarter deck. Soon the crews from all three ships were howling their outrage at the near-naked long-legged apparition issuing orders in a voice stronger than any they'd ever heard from their own captain.

It was a bloodless battle for the most part, with only three men of the galleon's crew carrying slight wounds. To a man, her own crew emerged unscathed. In her excitement, Amalie searched for Cato and gave him a jaunty salute with the tip of her cutlass. "Well done!" she called. "Well done indeed."

"I never believed the story until now," the captain muttered.

Amalie turned to him with a smile. "What story is that, Captain?"

"That you were real. There were some who said you were a legend. Once before you all but ruined the Dutch East India Company. Are you here now to finish the job?"

Amalie merely shrugged. Let him think what he wanted. By the time he reached port—*if* he did—his story would be so outrageously magnified, she'd be hard-pressed to recognize it anyway.

The captain struggled to stand at his full height. He couldn't go over the side without one last attempt at bravado. He needed to show his crew he was not a coward. "They'll kill you, you know. There's a price on your head now that will increase when we reach port. The Dutch East India Company has hired a man, a crew, to ride these seas and capture you."

Amalie laughed. "You're all fools! There's no man out there," she said, motioning to the open water with her cutlass, "who can kill me. I'm a legend. Am I real, Captain, or am I a ghost? How is it that none of my men were hurt? How is it that I captured *you* so easily? If I were flesh and blood, could I do all these things? Think about *that* when you make your report to your company's officers."

The captain's eyes bulged with fear. A spirit, a ghost? He looked around at his crew, who were eager now to go over the side. By the time he turned back to Amalie, a low bank of fog had rolled across the deck, obscuring her form within its thick, swirling tentacles. The captain reached out to her with a trembling hand, but she stepped backward, to be enveloped completely by the heavy mist. It was as if she'd never existed.

Giving a low groan, the captain spun around and threw himself overboard. There followed splash after splash of water as his crew did the same. Amalie had to clamp her hand over her mouth to keep from laughing aloud.

"Secure these ships and make ready to sail!" she hissed to her crew.

"Aye, Captain."

Amalie watched the beginning of a new day from the bow of her ship, a steaming mug of coffee in her hands. There was a smile on her face as she admired her three latest acquisitions . . . a marvelous night's work. The ivory alone would make her richer than she ever dreamed. A few more ships to her credit, and she would soon have a flotilla. An *armed* flotilla.

Cato came up behind her. "Are we sailing home?" he asked quietly.

Amalie turned, her eyes softening in the early light. "No," she said. "Soon, though."

"What will you do next?" he asked. He was remembering the hours he'd spent lying next to her. He wanted to be there again, in her bunk, shutting out the world.

Amalie pretended to consider his question as she sipped her coffee. "I think we'll wait for the . . . person the Dutch East India Company hired to find me. He can't be far away. And I suspect he won't be as foolish as our fat captain. Silent and deadly, I'll wager. If he's who I think he is, then he feels he has a score to settle with us for sacking his cargo."

"The Spaniard?" Cato asked.

She nodded. "It makes sense, doesn't it? Who else would be angry and poor enough to take on the fruitless task of finding the Sea Siren? Remember, too, that we attacked his ship off the coast. For all we know, he could be sailing blind. He doesn't know we're in his waters, so to speak. He's either captaining his own ship or one belonging to the Dutch East India Company," she mused. "Until then, though, our immediate problem is where to hide these ships."

"The outer islands are riddled with hideaways and caves," Cato said, frowning. "If we found one, we can find others. Surely your father's maps will yield a suitable place. Perhaps a deep harbor, the one he used to store the unlimed nutmegs you told me about when we were in Saianha."

"I told you about that!" Amalie said in puzzled surprise.

"It was when I carried you to your house after you injured your arm. You spoke of many things then. I remember all of them," he said softly, proudly.

He was so boyish, Amalie thought, and yet manly at the same time. Her eyes warmed as she handed him her mug. "Have one of the men bring some food to my cabin. I want to go over those charts again."

Cato shuffled his feet on the deck. "Have someone bring

food to my cabin'' meant he wasn't to do the bringing.
Steaming with jealousy, he stalked away, aware that
Amalie's eyes were boring into his back. When she wanted
him, she would let him know. If he wanted her, he would
just have to wait until she was ready. Lovemaking on command. He spit over the side of the rail to show his displeasure. Maybe living as a king wasn't going to be so
wonderful after all.

In her quarters, Amalie spread out the old maps and
charts on her bunk, knowing full well it was going to take
every bit of concentration to decipher her father's faded
markings. Hours later her eyes burned with strain and her
shoulders ached with tension. What good were the ships
if she couldn't find a safe harbor for them? And the ivory—
was it a good idea to leave it aboard the ships, or should
she secure it in the caves with the rest of the booty they'd
plundered? Her head reeled with all the possibilities. Becoming rich had been the easy part. The hard part, she
now realized, was keeping the riches secure.

Returning to Saianha would be the simplest solution. In
her own waters she might fare better, but then, what should
she do with the plunder they'd already stored? She couldn't
have two bases of operation, and yet . . .

Her head started to pound. If her crew became aware
of her indecision, they might decide to take matters into
their own hands. What captain would sail blindly with no
destination in mind? She had to come up with something
before she went on deck. She bent over the maps again.

Amalie could barely keep her eyes focused when, an
eternity later, she sat back with a satisfied sigh. After hours
of painstaking scrutiny, the oldest of the maps had yielded
the perfect sanctuary: a deep cove at the end of the River
of Death. There was something in her father's journal about
the deadly river, something to do with the real Sea Siren.

Volcanoes and rocks . . . "the only explanation," he'd written in his cramped hand. But explanation of what? According to the chart in front of her, the mouth of the river had been closed off when twin volcanoes had erupted years before.

Amalie massaged her throbbing temples before she returned to the maps. Bits and pieces of her father's journal flashed before her, committed to memory. Of course! "The only explanation" meant the Sea Siren had sailed her ship up the River of Death, and that was how she'd outwitted all who'd been determined to capture her. Amalie felt giddy with the realization. How else could the female renegade disappear at will? If the mouth of the river was blocked at some point, surely over the years the elements had created another opening.

Her best calculations, allowing for a stint of heavy weather, placed her approximately seven days away from the river. She'd give the order to change course and head directly for it; with luck, the tides and currents over the years had rendered it passable. She could only pray that she wasn't making a mistake.

Amalie felt almost invincible as she strode up and out to the deck. How wonderful the balmy air felt, how clean and fresh! The throbbing in her temples eased with each long-legged stride. She had accomplished a feat the equal of any the Sea Siren had performed. And she'd become a woman in the true sense of the word. This strange, intoxicating elation had to be . . . happiness. It was unlike anything she'd ever felt before.

Hours later she was still on deck, her perch on a pile of rigging secure. Overhead, millions of tiny stars winked down at her while dark clouds, as soft as gossamer, sailed across the sky like graceful dancers. She'd lost all track of time and knew only that it was the dead of the night. She should have been sleepy, but she wasn't.

"I thought I'd find you here," Cato said softly. "You should be asleep." He reached out to caress her hair, and Amalie shivered beneath his touch.

"I don't want to sleep for fear I'll miss something," she said. "If I had my way, I'd never sleep. It's such a waste of time. We live only once, and every hour, every minute, should be savored. Sleep robs us of those precious hours and minutes."

Cato pondered her words. "In these hours, nothing of importance happens. Darkness is a time for . . . many things."

Amalie laughed throatily, the sound tinkling seductively across the rippling water. "One night we'll make love here on the deck under the stars. Would you like that?" He nodded. Amalie knew that even now he was consumed with passion for her. All she had to do was crook her finger and . . .

"There's a time and a place for everything, Cato," she said, smiling, touching his cheek. "Soon. . . ."

A bank of dark clouds scudded across the moon, blotting out the winking stars. "You see, if we were below decks, we would miss this blessed darkness," she murmured, gazing up at the heavens. "It's as though someone tossed a coverlet across the sky, bathing us in this dark velvet. Now we have only scent and feeling. The smoke pots are low. Once they're extinguished the blackness will be complete." She looked at him. "Does that frighten you?"

"No. Does it frighten you?" Cato asked curiously.

"Somewhat. If a ship were to come upon us, how would we see and retaliate? We would have to rely on our senses of smell and touch. A little difficult if one is to do battle, do you agree?"

Cato shrugged. "Unlikely."

"The moment we make a safe harbor, I want the galleon's weapons transferred to this frigate. It was foolish of me even to think of sailing this ship without cannon, but I did it, and it's not a mistake I want to repeat. Two expert gunners are all we need, providing they have excellent eyesight.'' Amalie could feel Cato's shudder.

"If I'm to die, I'd rather die at a man's hands,'' he said stoutly. "A man whose face I can see.'' His tone softened then. "If you wanted this frigate outfitted with cannon, it should have been done in port. It's going to be an awesome task, and there's going to be a war among the crew. Give some thought to unloading the ivory from the brigantine and sailing her. It will be a simple matter to paint the ship black if that's your intention.''

"No,'' Amalie said harshly. "This is my ship. The *Sea Siren* belongs to me. It wouldn't be the same; I must sail *this* ship. At one time it carried its own cannon, but those bastards in town made off with them, thinking this ship would never be seaworthy again. It can be done, but until then I think we should sail only under cover of darkness. We have three ships to worry about now as well as our own, and we're short handed. We're ripe for the picking if another pirate ship accosts us. I have no intention of giving up what I have, Cato. I want you to apprise the crew of this. If there's any dissension, let me know.''

The last of the oil in the smoke pot sputtered out, bathing the deck in total darkness. For a moment all was silent, and then suddenly Cato whirled about, his words hissing in the quiet moonlit night. It took a moment for Amalie to realize that he was talking to one of her men. A strange sail had been sighted three leagues westward, said the crewman, flying two colors, Dutch and Spanish.

The words whipped from Amalie's mouth. "Do we assume she's armed? How high does she ride? Cargo?''

"I recognize her,'' the seaman reported. "She's the backbone of the Dutch East India Company and is deployed to convoy cargo vessels and to fight off pirates. She's three-masted and carries square rigging. It's doubtful she's carrying cargo, she rides too high."

Amalie peered about her in the darkness, seeing nothing. The night could work for her or against her, since the same darkness cloaked the unknown ship to the west. Her mind raced, and for the first time she felt unsure of her course. "Has she spotted us?"

"Aye, but she probably thinks we're from her own company since her true colors still fly. The night is too dark for her to see us clearly."

"Can we overtake her?"

"Aye, if we change course and leave the other ships behind," the seaman said. "But then we have no cannon."

Attack or not attack? Perspiration dotted Amalie's brow. "Conditions are not . . . appropriate for an attack," she said, swallowing past the lump in her throat. "We'll stay on course."

"There are weapons aboard the brigantines," the seaman said boldly. "We can be aboard in minutes."

"To what end?" Amalie snarled. "A ship with an empty hold will do us no good. We have to find a safe harbor for the three ships we have now. A fourth, if we're lucky enough to snare her, will only compound our problem. She's no good to us. Pass the word, we stay true on our course."

"What if she attacks us?" Cato asked quietly.

"That's a different matter. If it happens, we'll deal—"

A volley of thunder ripped through the black night, drowning out Amalie's words and putting an abrupt end to her hopes of sailing on unseen. "All hands on deck!" she shouted as pungent black smoke whirled upward from the galleon. "She's been hit broadside. All hands to the brigantine. Over the side. *Quickly!*" A second volley of shots rocketed through the night and then a third, none of them finding their target.

The frigate was alongside the brigantine in minutes. Amalie leapt aboard, shouting orders to fire on the three-masted ship. "Shred her sails! Rupture her bow! Splinter her stern! I want that ship gutted and sunk! Move fast, men! The fool fires on his own ships!" She pointed to several scurrying seamen. "You, you, and you, shore up this ship—and be quick, or that beautiful ivory will sink to the bottom of the sea, where it will do us no good."

"You fire like women with babies on their hips!" Luis Domingo shouted above the cannon shots. "Do I have to come down there and show you how to do it? Open your eyes and fire on the target. Shot that goes to the bottom of the sea does us no good." Roaring with rage, his face white as sheeting, he glanced over his shoulder just in time to see a pair of beautiful long legs leap gracefully from the bow of the brigantine and land just inches from where he was standing. The Sea Siren!

"Enough!" she cried. "Give quarter or we sink this ship with all your men aboard! Think fast, señor, you have only seconds!"

"Never!"

"Never is a very long time. Never could very well be your eternity. I'll ask you again—give quarter."

"I said never!" Luis snarled. "I'll kill you before I yield. First you robbed my cargo with your cutthroats, then you had the gall to accost me a second time and tell me that it wasn't you at all but an impostor pillaging and plundering in your name." He took a step forward and spat in front of her, eyes murderous. "Liar! Sea slut!"

What was he talking about? For the briefest of seconds Amalie's blood ran cold and she wavered. "I—I had no intention of attacking your ship, señor. You fired first. As for your cargo, if you aren't man enough to defend what is yours, you deserve to be bested. Now fight like a man or go over the side! I gave you your chance and you ignored it.''

Amalie's cutlass lashed upward and then down quicker than the volley of shots ripping through the night. She feinted to the right, the tip of her blade slicing through the air. Suddenly a jolt of pain ripped up her arm into her shoulder as the Spaniard's cutlass met her own. She sidestepped neatly, drawing the blade down the length of his leg. Taken by surprise with the force of her strength, Luis staggered backward. Amalie seized the advantage and brought up the cutlass, using both hands to hack at the weapon in her opponent's hand. Recovering quickly, he jabbed at her midsection, but she stepped aside nimbly, her weapon arching upward. She feinted to the right and then the left, lashing out in every direction, hoping to make contact in the darkness. Again steel met steel, but this time she felt herself being driven backward, farther, farther, until she was forced against the ship's railing.

''Now it is *you* who will give quarter,'' Luis growled, drawing his cutlass against hers and pressing the weight of both to her heaving breasts.

''You speckled-shirted dog, I'll never give you quarter!'' Amalie gasped, and brought up her knee with all the force she could muster to trounce the Spaniard in the groin. He reeled backward, doubling over with pain. Amalie held the cutlass high overhead, about to bring it down on Luis's neck, when Cato appeared next to her.

''There's no need,'' he cried, staying her arm. ''You've won. His crew and yours know you are the victor. They've all been disarmed; you'll have no further trouble with them. We can be on our way unmolested—why not let them keep their captain?''

Luis snorted at Cato's report. ''Why don't you have

those goddamn black birds finish me off if you don't have the guts to do it yourself,'' he hissed.

Amalie paused, caught between Cato's declaration of victory and the Spaniard's puzzling words. *What black birds?* Suddenly she felt his hand on her arm, the fingers running up and down the heavy welt of the scar on her arm.

"Lying slut!" he roared. "If my life depended on what you call the truth, I wouldn't believe you. A fine tale it was! Send in your killing birds and be damned!"

Amalie lowered her cutlass, exasperated. "I don't know what you're talking about, señor. I don't want you and I don't want this ship. You fired on me. Ask yourself why I would attack a ship with an empty hold."

"I'd rather ask why you travel with a Dutch and Spanish escort," Luis countered. "Those ships belong to the Dutch East India Company. What are you doing with them?"

"I might ask you a question, señor," she said, ignoring his demand. "Why would you fire on your own ships? You ride these waters looking for me, and yet it's your own company's ships you shot at, not mine. Are you that poor a shot, or is it that you're afraid to fire on me directly since I scuttled the *Silver Lady*?" She laughed with the triumph of a conviction, then backed away from him until she'd reached the bow of the ship. "I have no more time to converse with you further, señor. Be sure it's a pretty tale you spin when you return to Batavia, and be sure to spell my name correctly on the wanted posters."

Luis watched as she leapt from his ship to the bow of her own. His eyes strained to pierce the darkness, trying to make out her diamond garter. He saw nothing save a flash of steel as she sheathed her cutlass. "Let's hope that diamond garter is still aboard these decks," he called loudly. "It might make all this worthwhile."

Amalie could hold her tongue no longer. "You've done

nothing but talk in riddles this past hour, señor. If you have a passion for killing birds and lust after diamond garters, look elsewhere. *Buenas noches, señor.* The next time we meet I'll kill you for no other reason than to please myself.''

''Twice! Twice she bested me. Or was it three times? Goddamn bitch!'' He'd see her dead before . . . Christ, what was the matter with him? He'd had her in his clutches and let her go. He'd believed her when she said she meant him no harm . . . the birds, where were the goddamn black birds? And where was her garter? ''All hands on deck!'' he shouted. ''Scour this ship! Find that diamond garter! Now!'' he thundered.

''You saw the garter, Julian! Where the hell is it?'' Luis roared his anger as he dabbed at the blood dribbling down his chest.

''Captain, I was too busy fending for myself. It's dark and I saw no garter on the sea witch's leg. I did see it when she came broadside at your last meeting. Perhaps she took it off herself. The sea witch is no different from other women. One day they put gemstones in their ears and around their necks, the next day they tie on velvet ribbons. The sea witch is a woman with flights of fancy. If you wish, I'll help the crew search for the garter. When you spoke of it to her, she didn't show any concern that I could see, which makes me think she simply wasn't wearing her bauble this night.''

''You can't trust women,'' Luis spat out. ''I went against my better instincts. I never should have believed her. She's right, I am a fool.''

''Why do you think she didn't—''

''Kill me? I don't know, unless she was enamored of my charms,'' Luis said bitterly.

''I saw it all, Cap'n. You could have taken her at any

time," Julian said loyally. "You held back because she was a woman, isn't that right?"

"She's incredibly strong," Luis hedged. "And skilled. I had no idea she'd be that good. Not even our first encounter . . ." He spun around to his first mate. "But she lied, Julian! I was halfway to believing her. . . ."

"We fired first, Cap'n," Julian muttered. "She did say she was staying true to her course."

"Then what in the goddamn hell was she doing with three ships belonging to the Dutch East India Company? Who the hell could see that dastardly black ship in this darkness? It could have been any ship. Tell me, Julian, did you see . . . sense anything different about this woman?"

The first mate shook his head. "Not a thing, Cap'n. Beautiful as sin. I suppose it's possible that she's going to escort the Dutch East India's ships back to port . . . safely." He shrugged.

"The day that happens they'll get whiskey in hell," Luis snarled. Frowning, he leaned over the rail to stare into the murky waters below. Was Julian right? Had he held back because the Siren was a woman—or had she bested him? To others he could lie, but not to himself. He searched his mind for ways he'd held back, given in to the strength of the woman, but only because . . . because . . . he wasn't sure in his own mind if she was the real Sea Siren or the impostor. Yes, he'd held back; he was certain. His breath exploded in a loud sigh of relief.

"Julian, I don't believe she was the Sea Siren," he said. "No birds, no garter . . . But whether I'm right or not, the next time *any* woman confronts me on the open seas, I'll forget what a gentleman I am. The next time I'll . . ."

The first rays of dawn saw Luis Domingo in his quarters with every map owned by the Dutch East India Company spread before him. He'd find the sea witch if it was the last thing he did. It was dusk when he flexed his shoulders and called for his first mate.

"I do believe I found the slut's lair," he drawled nonchalantly, pointing to a chart so old the edges were frayed and yellowed.

Julian peered down at the ancient chart, his face draining of all color. "The River of Death!" he said in a trembling voice.

Luis nodded. "Don't you see, it bears out everything that old sea salt told me months ago. Think back to the Siren's beginning reign of terror and destruction of the Dutch East India Company. Somehow she was privy to sailing dates and cargo manifests, which means she sequestered that damnable black ship somewhere in a deep harbor or hiding place that only she had the nerve to sail into. And what better place than the River of Death? Those simmering sister volcanoes would hold any sea captain at bay." He turned to his first mate, eyes glinting in the dim lantern light. "I'm convinced now that there are two Sirens. The question is: Which one is the impostor? Believe it or not, we've met both of them. Which is your choice?"

Julian paused, clearly taken aback. "I can't be sure, Cap'n, but the one tonight was damnably strong, and there was something about her voice, as though she knew something . . . knew her own power. They called her arrogant back then, so arrogant she believed she was—"

"Invincible. Exactly!" Luis jabbed a finger under Julian's nose. "She could be invincible and arrogant only because she knew she was safe and could disappear almost at will. The volcanoes created a vaporous black mist—the one the old sea salt referred to. Examine all this information, and the answer is right in front of you. If you recall, the Siren retired from the seas when the sister volcanoes erupted. See—on this map and this one, the entrance to the river was blocked, probably sealing her ship inside her sequestered cove. Now, this map"—he pointed to a recent rendering—"shows that the river is open. Quite natural with the various tides and currents. It's still narrow and would take much skill to skirt the rocky formations on either side. A frigate could make it, but it's doubtful a brigantine could sail past the opening. I plan to travel that river in one of the jolly boats."

Luis tossed his marking chalk on the rough table and clapped Julian on the back. "Better yet, the River of Death is so close to Batavia, I think we'll change course—sail for port and trade in this ship for another, one of those sloops with the rapierlike bowsprit. Dykstra was to take delivery of several on behalf of the Dutch East India Company; he probably has them by now. They say the bowsprit on those sloops is almost as long as the hull. The parade of canvas she sports makes her more nimble than a brigantine or frigate. And the square topsail, in favorable winds, gives an extra measure of speed, which is what I'm going to need. Eleven knots is nothing to sneer at. Dykstra said they were to be outfitted with twelve or fourteen cannon. Six would do us fine, less weight in favor of maneuverability.

"Yes," he went on, tapping his chin, "that's exactly what we're going to do. Give the order to change course now. We'll lose two days at the most and, hopefully, pick them up once we have the sloop. What do you think, Julian?" Luis asked as he rolled the charts and maps into goatskin pouches.

Julian nodded. "I can think of no better explanation, Cap'n. But what if there is no black frigate once you're past the River of Death? How will we know if it's her haven?"

"We'll know," Luis replied. "When people think they are safe, they become careless. There will be some sign,

I'm sure of it. If there isn't, we're no worse off. The most we lose is seven days either way. But I feel it here''—he pounded his chest—"those waters are her home.''

Julian left the captain's quarters to give the order to change course. Up on deck, he strode from bow to stern, savoring the warmth of the evening air. He could imagine no life other than this one. The sea was his mistress, the clear, star-filled night his wife, the elements his children, the captain his superior. . . . Still, now and then he wondered if he would ever see his mother country again. If the captain was smitten with the Sea Siren, it could be the death of all of them.

He wondered then, and not for the first time, why the Siren hadn't run the captain through. She had to be the real Siren because of her boast that she did not kill for the sake of killing. Nothing else made sense . . . unless she was the impostor and smitten with the captain herself. Damnation, he was developing a pounding headache. Women always gave him a headache; they were such demanding and unpredictable creatures. Diamond garters, black birds that killed, near-naked women who could fight better than most men . . . The world was changing too fast for him. Truly, he belonged at sea.

Chapter Nine

Batavia

Peter Dykstra nervously fingered the ends of his lace collar before knocking at the door of the casa. His heart thumped in his chest at what he was about to do: spy on and try to trick his good friend's daughter. Once and for all he was going to bring this puzzling matter to a conclusion. Whatever happened afterward would be in other hands, not his own, he decided miserably.

Over the dinner table, Dykstra was glad that poor eyesight was not among his various ailments. Fury looked ravishing in the candlelight; if he didn't know better, he would have thought he was sitting across from her mother. He warned himself to be careful with his questions. If what he suspected was true, he didn't want to alert the young lady. He remembered well her mother's hot temper, and there was no reason to believe the daughter wasn't similarly gifted.

"I'm so glad you could come to dinner, Mynheer," Fury said graciously, sipping from her wineglass. "I've become very lonely here. Gathering flowers to grace the rooms is not my idea of a productive life. How fortunate that you are a man and can do as you please. When I was a child I wanted to be a boy like my brothers and do all the things they did."

The perfect opening. "Good Lord, child, do you mean you'd like to go to sea or be a merchant?" Dykstra asked. "Did your parents ever tell you tales of the Sea Siren?"

Fury felt a hard nudge to her back as Juli removed the first course plates. "Of course, Mynheer Dykstra. My father openly admits to once being obsessed with the famous pirate. I thought it such a romantic story." She smiled dreamily. "I can't even begin to imagine what her life must have been like. So strong and powerful, men lusting after her, none strong enough to kill her. Conquistador, they called her. A better sailor than any man. What did you think of her, Mynheer?"

Dykstra hesitated. Obviously she knew what he was after. As wily and ingenious as her mother. "I always envied your father's meetings with her. There were many, you know. Of course, we have only his word for what happened during those meetings," he added.

"Your words seem to carry a double meaning, Mynheer," Fury said quietly.

"Oh, no, it's just that Regan and I were such fast friends, and both of us liked to boast . . . the way men will do with one another. I tend to think your father gilded his stories a little. I would have done the same in his circumstances." He shook his head. "It wasn't like Regan to let her go. I've never understood why he allowed it."

Fury's eyes narrowed. "He didn't *allow* her to flee, Mynheer. She escaped. He searched for years, every chance he could, until . . . my mother called a halt to his wanderings. And, eventually, she retired on her own—as I've been given to understand. My parents felt much admiration for so accomplished a woman. There aren't many women walking this earth or sailing the seas who can bring hundreds of men to their knees."

Dykstra felt himself bristling with suppressed rage. "She was no lady! Good women don't do the things she did. She deserved to be punished for her cruel deeds," he said coldly.

Fury flushed. "On the contrary, Mynheer, my father said the Siren was more of a lady than all of the women together in Batavia. With the exception of my mother," she added hastily.

Dykstra paused and took a steadying breath. "It sounds like you condone the Sea Siren's actions," he said, striving for a light tone.

"Mynheer Dykstra, the Sea Siren reigned over twenty years ago, before I was born. I admire what she did . . . and all for a cause that otherwise would have gone unpunished—" Fury broke off to stare directly into Dykstra's eyes. "Why are we talking about the Sea Siren now, at this particular time? Is it because of the bogus pirate who is sailing the seas? You'll never convince me she's the Sea Siren."

"How can you be so sure if, as you say, you weren't even born during her reign of terror?"

Fury could feel her skin prickling. Dykstra had something, some news, or else he was baiting a trap for her. "Mynheer Dykstra, this impostor is a direct contradiction to all the Sea Siren stood for. I wouldn't cross this one if I were you—she might come on land and run you through just for the pleasure of it. You see, that is the difference between the two; the real Sea Siren would never do such a thing. She's an honorable woman!" Smiling coldly, she placed her napkin on her plate and rose. "We can have coffee and brandy in my father's study, if you like."

Without a word Dykstra followed her into the study, his hand in his waistcoat pocket. She was suspicious—so suspicious, she was letting her tongue run away with her. It was time to close in for the kill.

In her father's library Fury did her best to relax and

play hostess as Juli placed the silver tray on a low table. "Sugar, Mynheer?"

"Please. . . . Fury, I have something I want you to look at."

"You sound very mysterious," Fury said lightly. She could feel Juli stiffen in the study doorway.

"When Señor Domingo first told me of the attack on his father's ship, the *Spanish Princess*, I was, of course, skeptical, as were the other men in town. But when he described the woman so carefully, I had to pay strict attention. For he *was* describing the Sea Siren—or at least the Sea Siren whose picture hung in the Dutch East India offices." Fury nodded to show she was following the manager's story.

"Well," Dykstra continued, "several days ago I was rummaging in my desk for something and came across this miniature painting of your parents, one your father gave me when he moved his family to Spain. I don't know what possessed me to alter this, but I did. Would you like to see it?"

Fury nodded, struggling to control her emotions. She knew full well Dykstra was watching her with sharp eyes.

"But this is outrageous, Mynheer!" she exploded a moment later. "My father will never forgive you for your . . . suspicions. You're making my mother out to be the Sea Siren! Where did you come by such an idea? No, no, it isn't possible."

"It's not only possible, it's probable," Dykstra declared. "And I'll take that probability one step further. I think you've taken her place."

Fury had the presence of mind to look astonished. "But why? After all these years, why would you think . . . for what purpose? Oh, it's too preposterous to even give credence . . . I'm appalled, Mynheer, that you would even *think* me—"

"Mynheer, where would Miss Fury get the Sea Siren's ship?" Juli interrupted, forgetting her place. "It's been said it was scuttled, rotting at the bottom of the sea. And Miss Fury has never left this house except to go into town. You can speak with any of the other servants if you don't believe me."

Dykstra ignored the housekeeper's outburst, his eyes on Fury and the color creeping into her cheeks.

"Mynheer Dykstra, it's a coincidence that I'm here in Batavia at this time," Fury continued, wary now. "I was to enter the convent, but matters were taken out of my hands when the sisters were sent away. There was nothing I could do. I'm waiting for my parents to return from the Americas later this year."

"When one practices to deceive, one must spin a web of lies and enlist cohorts to aid and abet the deception," Dykstra said gently.

Fury's eyes were furious as she stood to show the evening was at an end. "May I ask to whom you have told this ridiculous tale?"

Dykstra rose as well. "I'm afraid that's my business, Furana. From now on this house will be watched. Once and for all we will discover the Sea Siren's identity."

"How dare you!" Fury gasped. "Please leave this house—now! I will never forgive you, nor will my mother. My father's wrath I leave to you!"

The moment the door closed behind the Dutchman, Juli ran to Fury. "My God, how did he find out? What are we to do? If he has the house watched . . ."

"I suppose it's down the trellis for me under dark of night," Fury said shakily.

Juli giggled. "This is so exciting! Just like when your mother was roaming the seas. I never knew what each new day would bring. I knew it was going to be like before; I just *knew* it!"

"It's not as simple as Mynheer Dykstra makes it sound," Fury said thoughtfully. "I think there's more to all of this than he's let on. He and my father have been friends for over thirty years. Why is he turning on us like this? It doesn't make sense . . . unless he feels he's going to be passed over for the governorship, and is trying somehow to build up his reputation at my expense. He never would have dared to say such things, much less even think them, if my father were here. Do you think my defense of the Sea Siren was too strong?"

"Justly so." Juli shrugged. "He can't prove anything. Even if he suspects, he has no proof. For now you will simply do what your mother did when things became . . . difficult."

"What did she do?" Fury demanded.

"Took to her bed and said she was on a religious retreat. Locked her door and went down the trellis and out to the cove." Juli smiled, remembering. "The more dangerous it was, the better she seemed to like it. She positively bloomed when she was 'on a mission,' as she called it."

Fury placed a hand on Juli's arm, bringing her back to the present. "You said you had something to tell me?" she said gently.

Juli frowned. "I had something to . . . Oh, yes! And very important it is, too. My second brother's wife, Drucilla, cooks for a gem merchant's family in town. It seems this merchant has a brother in town who is also a gem merchant. Drucilla told me she overheard the merchant talking to Mynheer Dykstra about a shipment of *thirty* pounds of diamonds that is due to arrive here any day now."

Juli paused for breath. "Now, let me see if I remember this," she continued slowly. "It seems the diamonds belong to the Viceroy of Karwar, Dom Ignacio Carlos Xavier de Reness, third count of Surat. The merchant said the count obtained the diamonds in private trading and signed aboard as a paying passenger. It's the *Nightstar* and due to make port, as I said. She carries a very valuable cargo of Chinese silks, porcelain, textiles, and all manner of exotic products. Drucilla said the plan was to sew the diamonds into the count's clothing so that, in case of a pirate attack, only the cargo will be plundered. The count will be disguised as a seaman. It's his intention to return to Spain, where he hopes to restore his family's fortunes. But that's not all, Miss Fury!'' she cried as Fury opened her mouth to speak. ''Drucilla says Mynheer Dykstra has asked Señor Domingo to *pose* as the count and carry the diamonds himself. What do you think of that!''

Fury sank down onto one of the chairs, stunned. ''Thirty pounds of diamonds! If they're perfect gemstones, they'll be worth a king's ransom. That must mean the Dutch East India Company is accepting responsibility for safe transport. Obviously the count, whoever he is, is not capable of fending off deadly pirates if Señor Domingo is to assume his identity.''

''Has this information helped at all, Miss Fury?'' Juli asked anxiously.

Fury massaged her temples to ward off the headache she felt coming on. ''Matters like this have a way of becoming public knowledge. I don't think I would wager my diamond garter that the bogus Sea Siren is ignorant of this news.'' She rose and began to pace the study floor.

''All those diamonds,'' she muttered. ''Perhaps I should think along the lines of an escort for the *Nightstar*. I'll stay a respectable distance, and none need know I'm sailing a protective course. At the same time, I'll be returning home to Spain, for I seriously doubt my parents will come here to Java. . . . Yes, yes, I think I've arrived at the perfect solution.'' She turned to Juli. ''What to you think?''

Tears gathered in the housekeeper's eyes. ''You are your

mother's daughter through and through," she said softly. "I truly believe she would have made the same decision. I understand your desire to return home. And I am proud and happy to be a part of all this."

There was no doubt in Fury's mind that she could provide safe conduct for the faceless count and his diamond fortune, and Luis Domingo. No doubt at all.

At midmorning the following day a white-uniformed djongo arrived at the casa. He shuffled his bare feet, his eyes cast downward while he waited for Juli to take the invitation he held out to her.

Fury raised her eyebrows as she read, a smile tugging at the corners of her mouth. "Fetch me a pen," she ordered one of the maids.

"A soiree," Juli said, peering over Fury's shoulder. "The entire board of governors of the Dutch East India Company. What does it mean?"

"I think they are ready to choose my father's replacement, and since the logical choice is Mynheer Dykstra, they'll want my views—or rather, my father's views," Fury replied, scribbling a note of acceptance and thanks to her hostess, Matilda von Klausner. "Which might or might not explain his actions last evening. I'll have to think about that later. For now I'll have to think about a gown." She waved the djongo away and closed the door. "Juli, whatever shall I wear? I brought nothing suitable with me."

Hands on her ample hips, the housekeeper peered at Fury with speculative interest. "Are you handy with a needle, Miss Fury?"

Fury shook her head. "Are you?"

"I'm afraid not. And a week isn't very much time."

"Is there any material in my mother's trunks?"

"Oh, yes. There are two bolts of China silk that are

exquisite. Both are in perfect condition, but what good will it do us?''

"What about your brothers' wives?'' Fury asked hopefully.

Juli snorted. "They mend. Where would they learn how to sew for fine ladies? No, there is no one—not even in town. Every seamstress will be overworked.''

"Then we must improvise,'' Fury said briskly. "Show me the material. Perhaps something will come to us.''

"Something?''

"A solution,'' Fury said tightly.

"Hrumph.'' Juli snorted.

Minutes later Fury's bedroom was draped with the costly bolts of material, one an emerald silk shot through with silver, the second a lovely plum embroidered with gold thread. "The emerald one, I think,'' Fury said, frowning. "The plum is lovely, but I prefer the green. You were right, Juli, it's magnificent! Now, if we just put our minds to it, I think we can come up with a solution. . . .''

An hour later the two women were still staring at each other and the fabric. Suddenly Fury gathered the handsome bolt of emerald silk and draped it around her entire body. She swayed seductively for Juli's benefit. "What do you think?''

"That's perfect, Miss Fury! A sari, the kind women of India wear. We won't have to sew at all,'' Juli said in relief, "providing we can cut a straight line with the scissors.'' The brilliant silk was unwrapped and rewrapped around Fury's slender form. "See, we'll drape this here as a sleeve of sorts to cover your scarred arm. Your other arm and shoulder will be bare. You can wear the diamond garter on your bare arm, like this,'' she said, circling Fury's upper arm with her hand. "And diamonds in your ears will add just the right touch. What do you think?''

Fury grinned. "I think I wouldn't be able to get along

without you. If we make a fringe at the edge, we won't even have to sew a hem. It's absolutely perfect.'' Fury pirouetted slowly, glancing behind her to catch the effect of the billowing fabric. ''I wonder if I will know anyone at the soiree beside Mynheer Dykstra and a few of the governors,'' she mused.

''I'm sure Señor Domingo will be there,'' Juli said slyly.

''That would be nice, I'm sure. He's never seen me in anything as breathtaking as this. The dress I wore to my birthday ball was fashionable, but of schoolgirl quality. And at our dinner I wore one of Mother's gowns. This will be something that will—''

''Make *his* blood sing,'' Juli giggled. ''We'll have to give you an elaborate hairdo and color your lips and cheeks as well.''

''For a public appearance?'' Fury gasped.

''Of course. Your mother loved to shock the local inhabitants. And she succeeded time and again. Your father would turn white with jealousy when men dropped at her feet. Yet he knew in his heart she was his. It was a game they played. Your father would huff and puff, and your mother would flirt so outrageously, it was sinful. It was all so wonderful back then.'' Juli sighed happily with her memories.

Fury sank down on the bed. ''I want to be like my mother, but I want to be myself, too,'' she said slowly. ''All the things I know about her and all the things you've been telling me confuse me sometimes. I don't want to impersonate her, Juli. On shipboard it's different, but not here. I have to be me, Fury.''

''But you are!'' Juli exclaimed. ''You picked the fabric you most admired. Your coiffure will be of your own choice. The garter is yours; your mother never wore one. It will be Fury van der Rhys who attends the soiree, not your mother.''

Fury hugged the older woman. "Thank you, Juli, you're a wonderful friend. I truly appreciate your help."

"It's my pleasure, Miss Fury."

Somehow Fury managed to while away the rest of the day walking in the garden and reading from an old book of poetry. She fed the hawks and had an early dinner, then retired to the privacy of her bedchamber.

As she undressed, she realized that she'd lied to Juli earlier when she'd said she was tired. She wasn't the least bit tired. In fact, she felt more alive—now, this minute—than she'd felt at any time since arriving in Batavia. She'd learned something, something she needed to think about seriously.

The silky sheet pulled up to her chin, Fury braced herself in her nest of pillows, the heady flower-scented evening air wafting through the open balcony doors to tease her nostrils. Now, at last, she thought she knew the answers to the questions that had plagued her all her life.

She loved her mother and as a child had tried to emulate her, taking pleasure in the compliments that compared her prettiness with her mother's. "So like your mother in every way." In every way . . . except one. In the beginning she'd savored the comparisons, especially when her father uttered them, but she always knew in her heart that there was only one Sirena. And at some point after the death of her brothers, she'd consciously tried to change her physical appearance—her hair, her nails, her mode of dress. But she couldn't change her features. With each passing day, she grew more and more to resemble her mother. Her expertise with the rapier, her sailing skill, all as good as her mother's. Her social graces she knew now had been sabotaged deliberately . . . by herself.

Her decision to enter the convent had been a last attempt to reclaim her own identity—to herself, not Sirena van der Rhys's daughter, not an exact replica of her mother, but

Furana van der Rhys, postulant, novitiate, and finally nun. Fully, totally committed to God.

All those prayers, all the rosaries, all the sore knees, weren't for God, they were for her—selfish prayers that would allow her to be separate from her glamorous, glorious mother. And the more her parents had argued with her, the more determined she'd been.

Fury sat up in bed as the hawks called gently to her from the balcony railing.

"Yes," she murmured as she crept from the bed. "You knew, didn't you. I don't know how, but you did; otherwise you wouldn't have followed me. You've been wonderful—true and loyal friends to me." She reached out to stroke them. "I don't know if I am meant for the convent. Perhaps it was an excuse for me to find a life for myself, a life of my own. I love my mother, but I don't want to be her. I want her to be proud of me for my own accomplishments. Clearing her name is something only I can do. And with your help I know I can succeed."

She laughed ruefully. "You see, I'm still uncertain how far my abilities will carry me. I've never had a price on my head, and I've never fought a life-or-death duel. I know I don't want to die, at least not yet. I want to love and be loved. I want my blood to sing when I wake in the morning, and I want it to be singing when I fall asleep at night next to the man I love, but my commitment to God . . . I don't suppose you understand a thing I've been saying, and that's all right as long as you're here. It's taken me ages to learn about myself, and tonight was my time to begin."

Gaspar's wing tip fluttered softly as it inched up to caress Fury's cheek. Not to be outdone, Pilar stretched and spread her wing around Fury's shoulder, her glittering eyes warning Gaspar that this was a woman's moment. Fury laughed with delight when Gaspar inched his way down the balcony. "Thank you," she crooned, then gently made *swoosh*ing motions with her hands for the birds to retire for the night.

Sleep proved to be elusive, however. So many words, so many thoughts . . . The explanation was too simple, Fury thought in dismay. How could she wipe away her commitment to God and the church in just a few hours, and with mere words?

Instantly contrite, she leaned over the side of the bed and fumbled for her rosary on the night table. "Holy Father, I haven't forsaken You," she prayed. "For so long I believed . . . still believe I am meant to serve You in whatever capacity I can. I will never again believe that You have forsaken me, this I swear. You are all about me. Show me what it is You want me to do. I can give up this life, I know I can. Forgive me, Merciful Father, for my sins. . . ."

The week passed slowly for Fury. She was aware of the men watching the casa and herself but refused to be intimidated by them. Each day she saddled Starlight and rode out to the rise to gaze down upon the *Rana*. She did nothing out of the ordinary, however, and Juli always reported to her when she returned that the men had not left their posts. She felt she was setting up a valuable pattern from which to draw on in the coming days.

On the morning of the soiree she sat gazing longingly at the bolt of China silk in her bedroom. She couldn't wait to be wrapped in its silky softness; she wanted to feel a man's arms—Luis Domingo's arms—about her, crooning sweet words under a bright moon and winking stars. She wanted so to attend this soiree, wanted to see Luis Domingo again. She wanted . . . craved . . . needed . . .

It was possible she was tormenting herself needlessly, for she didn't know if the handsome Spaniard would even be there. But that possibility was too painful to contemplate. He simply *had* to be.

Fury could feel tears of shame stinging her eyes at her lustful thoughts. But she couldn't stop them. Over and over she wondered what it would be like to make love with Luis Domingo.

"You aren't considered a real woman until you bed a man, and it doesn't matter if you're married or not," a school friend had whispered once. She had been the most knowledgeable about the man-woman union, as she called it, although neither Fury nor the other girls at the convent school had ever challenged her as to the source of her knowledge. "Men's tongues are like weapons on a woman's body," the young lady had declared authoritatively, adding that women had to be as aggressive as men in bed and make known their wants. "You must tell them what feels good, here and here," she said, pointing to various parts of her anatomy. "Can you imagine letting a man undress you and looking at *all* of your naked body!" Fury *could* imagine, and *that* had been the problem.

She was startled from her burning thoughts when Juli poked her head in the doorway. "Everything is ready, Miss Fury. My brother brought your garter from the ship early this morning. We should be leaving soon. You did say you wanted to stop by the parish house to see Father Sebastian. The sooner we start, the sooner you'll be conversing with the *padre*," she said cheerfully. "We can ask him if Señor Domingo will attend. Surely he'll know."

"It's of no importance," Fury said, as if it made no difference to her whatsoever. She could feel Juli's eyes on her but refused to meet her gaze.

"Of course it's important," the housekeeper chided. "You will be the most beautiful, sought-after young lady at this soiree. All of Batavia will be talking about the stunning, exquisite Señorita van der Rhys. I want that

Spaniard's eyes to pop from his head when he sees you. You wouldn't be a woman if you didn't want the same thing.''

Woman . . . Fury's heart thumped in her chest. ''You make it sound like a contest,'' she grumbled.

Juli nodded. ''In a manner of speaking it is. All the women try to outshine one another. And there is always a winner. Men flock around you in droves, they shoot daggers with their eyes at their friends when they're luckier than themselves, and you favor them with a dance. Even the married men have roving eyes. My advice is to flirt outrageously with one and all. With the ladies who will want to scratch your eyes out, be demure and polite, respectful of their ages and their corsets.'' This last bit of advice sent Fury into peals of laughter. Juli grinned. ''But if you plan on taking a breath of air, make sure it's with Señor Domingo and no one else, or tongues will wag for weeks. You want only the most handsome, the most eligible man, and he is the catch of the season.''

''There is one problem I think we've both overlooked,'' Fury said, standing. ''How am I to dance in this tight dress we've created? I can just see it unraveling while I'm on the dance floor. My petticoat will be such a shock.''

''Petticoat . . . petticoat . . . you don't wear a petticoat with . . . absolutely not. You'll look . . . fat and dumpy, like the ladies with corsets. No, no, no, the material must swirl and drape, there is no room for underpinnings.''

''None?'' Fury gulped. ''What if it comes loose by some . . . fluke . . . men are so clumsy . . . my God, I didn't think . . . no, I must wear . . . stop laughing, Juli. I could be exposed . . . good Lord, now what am I to do?'' Fury wailed.

''It's too late to do anything, so you might as well stop fretting about what *could* happen and concentrate on making it not happen. If you really don't want to dance, say you hurt your ankle. You'll think of something," Juli said loftily.

Fury's stomach turned sour when she thought of herself dancing unaware of the emerald silk unwinding until she was stark naked in Luis Domingo's arms, the guests hooting with delight. Dear God. She must have been crazy to accept this invitation and go along with Juli's idea for the dress—or was it her idea—damnation, she couldn't remember anything today. She turned to Juli and said sweetly, "I will personally throttle you with my bare hands if this dress so much as moves on my body." Juli blanched and shrugged.

"If it does, there will be hundreds of men wanting to make an honest woman of you." She almost hoped it would happen; nothing would stir up the party like a naked woman. Then she thought about Fury's promise. "I forgot to tell you that my brother said the prettiest girls from . . . you know, Clarice's place, are to be among the governors' escorts. Can you imagine! Of course the town *ladies* don't know they've been invited, because this time, it seems, the men are organizing the soiree." Juli laughed and clapped her hands with glee. "I can't wait to see the expressions on the faces of those dowagers!"

The town whores at the soiree! Fury felt light-headed. Father Sebastian had said Naula was the prettiest of Clarice's girls. Certainly she would be at the soiree on the arm of one of the governors. The idea of Clarice's girls at the party was so outrageous, Fury found herself laughing.

"I can't imagine what protocol is in a matter such as this," she sputtered, wiping her eyes. "Does one acknowledge them? No doubt the governors will expect a certain amount of . . . camaraderie among the women! My God, Juli, I never would have believed this. Perhaps there's no need for us to stop by the parish house now— undoubtedly Father Sebastian will be attending the soiree himself, if for no other reason than to keep the guests from tearing one another apart!''

While the two women laughed about Father Sebastian's role at the soiree, the good *padre* himself was finding nothing amusing in the situation, although he knew he could perform his duties as long as he kept his gaze lowered. However, it wasn't the evening's festivities that bothered him, but the letter he held in his hand.

The words on the stiff, crackly parchment were already committed to memory, but still he opened the letter and read it again, fingering the heavy gold seal that identified to the reader, as surely as the cramped, narrow script and ponderous signature, the source of the correspondence. The elderly priest was sorry that he'd petitioned the archbishop himself to grant Fury entrance to the convent. That permission had now been granted, thanks to his pleas—temporary entrance two weeks from Sunday.

Sighing, he slid the letter between the pages of his Bible and plodded wearily into the kitchen. Why couldn't he have left well enough alone? Now he would have to tell Furana . . . and he didn't want to.

"Say the rosary, say the rosary," came a squawk from the kitchen windowsill. "Pray for the living, pray for the dead. Sins are the devil's work, oh, yes, oh, yes, praypraypray!"

"Shut up," the priest grumbled, glaring up at the brightly plumed caged parrot. A moment later he hurried off as a knock sounded at his front door.

It was Furana and her housekeeper. Father Sebastian's eyes flew to his Bible. Not today; he couldn't tell her today. Tomorrow, perhaps, or the day after. "Lies are sinful, lies are sinful!" the parrot screeched as the priest opened the door.

"What a wonderful surprise," Father Sebastian said

hoarsely. "Thank you," he said, taking a basket of food from Juli. "I'll just take this inside." He made his way down the hallway to the kitchen, where he immediately threw a rag over the parrot's cage.

"Death to all sinners!" shrieked the bird before darkness descended.

"Tea, ladies?" the priest asked, returning to the parlor.

"No, Father, we stopped only to deliver this basket. We're on our way to Mevrouw von Klausner's house for the soiree this evening. I trust you will be there to give the opening blessing," Fury said, biting her lips to keep from laughing.

"Yes. I was rather surprised, but then, I am the only religious in town at this time. Tonight is . . . uh, rather unusual, but they—the governors, that is—have asked me specifically . . . and they have been most kind to many of my poor, unfortunate parishioners. . . ."

"Will Señor Domingo be in attendance?" Juli asked, rescuing the poor man from his obvious discomfort.

"Why, yes, I believe so. He was in port yesterday. I'm sure he will be there. Nau—uh, he needs some respite, as do most men."

Fury took pity on the priest. "Perhaps you shouldn't attend. I know it's going to be difficult for you. I could explain to Mevrouw von Klausner that you aren't feeling well."

Father Sebastian smiled warmly. "It's kind of you, Furana, but I'll be fine. You ladies had best run along now. I know how much time it takes for you to prepare yourselves for these occasions."

"Thank you, Father. Rest now, we can see ourselves out. And Father," Fury called over her shoulder, "I know your blessing will be appreciated by . . . everyone."

"Poor dear," she murmured as they made their way to the von Klausner house at the end of the street. "He's so torn between what is right and wrong. He will suffer torments over this.'' She giggled.

''We're going to be the first to arrive,'' Juli grumbled. ''Your mother always said it was fashionable to be late, and people pay more attention when you're the last to arrive. Our timing is . . . inadequate.''

Fury shrugged. ''Even if we're the first to arrive, I can make sure I am the last to be announced. It makes no difference.'' *He's going to be here,* she thought, heart pounding. *I'll see him again.*

Excitement coursed through Fury as a clutch of djongos carried their small satchels and escorted them to their assigned rooms.

''Missy wish bath?'' the djongo queried.

''Yes.'' Juli nodded briskly as she set about laying Fury's clothing on the bed. ''Quickly, quickly.'' She frowned as the djongo minced his way out the door.

Fury's transformation was about to begin.

Every nerve in Luis Domingo's body quivered with exasperation at his circumstances. Here he was sitting aboard the *Silver Lady* smoking a cigar like one of Batavia's fat merchants instead of sailing the sea searching for the Sea Siren. He had Dykstra and the brood of governors from Amsterdam to thank for his idleness. Thanks to Dykstra, he would also be attending the soiree at the von Klausner house, an affair he wasn't looking forward to. He wasn't in the mood to salivate over coy woman and dominating mothers who thought him a good catch for their aging daughters. Of course he could have refused the invitation and sailed on the early tide, but he hadn't. The Dutch East India Company had hired him, and in their employ he would do as instructed.

Luis's stance, as he leaned against the mainmast, was one of unconscious grace. He blew a perfect smoke ring as he stared out at the deep blue of the ocean. He itched to take the wheel and sail until he came to the mouth of the River of Death. Nothing would stop him tomorrow; he would sail with the tide—under his own colors or those of the Dutch East India Company.

He hated to admit it, but he had the feeling that something was about to go awry, something he had no control over. He gazed out to sea, shielding his eyes against the sun's brilliant glare, searching for something—anything—that might give him a clue. He felt as though he were carrying a hundred-pound yoke on his shoulders, and he didn't like the feeling.

The sun dimmed momentarily, and Luis glanced upward. The sky had been blue without a trace of a cloud. He sucked in his breath as two dark shapes, wings spread, flew directly overhead, blocking the sun. *The goddamn black birds!* He swiveled to follow them with his eyes and was stunned a moment later to see them nest in the breadfruit tree at the von Klausner house. "Son of a bitch!" he muttered.

The hundred-pound yoke disappeared. The Sea Siren—the real one or the impostor—was nearby, either on land or hiding in a deepwater cove. He cursed himself for allowing Dykstra to talk him out of sailing to the River of Death. Instantly he was off the *Silver Lady* and boarding the ship he'd just brought into port yesterday. In moments he had his maps and charts out of their goatskin protection, his narrowed gaze tracing the route he would take tomorrow.

Nothing had changed since he'd looked at them last. Again his finger traced the route, up the river, farther, farther, until he came to the deepwater cove he was certain sequestered the deadly, sleek black ship captained by the Sea Siren. She was close; *this* was what he'd been feeling.

Once again his finger traced the cove, this time until he

came to the wide half-circle and solid wall of rock and jungle on each side. There was no reason to *sail* up the River of Death, he realized. He could ride at least part of the way and use his feet the rest of the time. He could leave now and find that goddamn black ship before nightfall. He had to. Time was his enemy, with the Spanish ship due in any day.

It was the diamonds, of course. She was after the diamonds, so there was no point in wasting his time searching her out; *she* would find *them*. And she was here: he could feel her. Close, by God, she was so close!

Fifteen minutes later Luis was riding hard. An hour later he realized he was hopelessly lost. All about him was steaming verdant jungle. To his eye, there was no sign of a trail or footpath. The horse, lathered and panting, was about ready to drop. Luis looked upward at the startling blue sky, expecting to see the black birds circling overhead. But the expanse remained serene and beautiful.

Ten minutes later he dismounted and tethered the weary animal. The blazing sun beat down on him as he struck out on foot, his hands ripping and beating back the choking jungle growth. Time soon lost all meaning, but he tramped on regardless. At one point he was aware the sun was well over his shoulder and that he should start back. Another thirty minutes, he pleaded with himself, just thirty more minutes.

Suddenly he found himself sniffing like a dog at a smell he would have recognized anywhere. Water . . . wonderful, glorious water. And something else: the faint sound of voices. He dropped to a near crouch and inched his way to the small sandy beach directly ahead of him. A cove, probably one of many, but would the Siren's ship be anchored in this quiet spot? He slithered to the edge of the beach under full cover of the thick, lush foliage.

Luis's heart thundered in his chest until he was certain

the men laughing aboard the black frigate would hear it. Black frigate. The Sea Siren's ship! His eyes searched out the battering ram on the bow. That he would never forget! By God, he'd found it, he'd succeeded where hundreds of others had failed.

He strained to hear what the voices were saying, then blinked in disbelief. They were having a discussion about children and furniture! Chatting and drinking coffee from a huge iron pot on deck. These were not common seamen. Christ, was it possible he'd made a mistake? He continued to listen, one eye on the setting sun.

A deep, pleasant laugh carried across the water as one of the men discussed his sister. The others seemed to know her, for only complimentary words were being used. Was the sister the Sea Siren? Luis wondered. A moment later he knew he'd found the right ship when another of the men mentioned "the *capitana*" and the sister in the same breath. "Even if she feeds those devil birds for the *capitana*, she's as fearful of them as we are." There was a chorus of agreement among the men. Luis found himself pounding the ground triumphantly. "I wonder if the birds will chaperone the party this evening," the man continued. "Can you picture that scene?"

Luis had heard enough. He crawled backward until he felt it was safe to stand erect. Then he spun around and tore down the path he'd created earlier. The inky night settled about him just as he sighted his horse. Breathing raggedly, he leaned against the animal's broad flanks.

By God, he'd found her . . . almost. He'd found her ship, and that was every bit as good as finding the she-devil herself. All he had to do, he thought as he climbed into the saddle, was alert the Dutch East India Company and block the entrance to the River of Death. Position men all along the perimeter of the cove to cut off any means of escape. Then he'd have her!

A sudden thought made him rein in the horse. Which one *was* she? Who was the real Siren—the one with the damn black birds or the other one? Both women had a scar; he felt somehow confident of that, although he hadn't seen them and had felt only one for sure. But on which arm? That was the secret . . . which arm? Left? Right?

Angrily Luis wiped his sweating forehead with his shirt-sleeve as he spurred the horse onward. By night's end he'd have his answer. And he would remain quiet and not tell Mynheer Dykstra what he'd just discovered. For now.

The moment he reached the smithy he slid from the horse's back and handed the animal to a stable boy. He raced down the street to the town's one boardinghouse. Inside, he shouted for a hot bath as he flew up the stair-case, ripping at his shirt along the way.

The startled bath boy rolled his eyes heavenward when Luis started to whistle. The señor was a happy man, he decided as pail after pail of water doused the Spaniard.

Luis was still whistling when, one hour later, he strolled down the plank streets dressed in a natty white linen suit, a fragrant cigar between his fingers. He was the only man to have found the Siren's lair, the only man. The knowl-edge was more powerful than any aphrodisiac.

Yes, Luis Domingo was a happy man.

Chapter Ten

Juli clapped her hands to shoo the von Klausner servants from the room with their empty water pails. She turned to Fury, who was sitting on a stool wrapped in a length of soft sheeting. "And now, Señorita van der Rhys, it is time to turn you into the most ravishing creature in all of Batavia. First, your hair. . . . Hmm, you smell divine, better than the entire garden at the casa."

Fury watched in the mirror as her hair was pulled and tugged, swirled and twirled, until she was barely able to recognize herself in the pier glass. Suddenly she was totally different from the proper young lady who had graced her previous life. She held her breath as Juli touched coloring to her cheeks and blended it on her high cheekbones.

"Now, do this," the housekeeper said, stretching her mouth into a wide grimace. She ran her index finger deftly over Fury's lips and blotted the excess. "See how white your teeth look against the color of your lips? Perfect! Just perfect," she pronounced. "And now the earrings. . . ."

A moment later Fury took a look at herself and gasped. "I don't look like me *or* my mother!"

"That's why it's perfect. Men will be groveling at your feet, all those crusty old Dutch governors with their . . . women. Señor Domingo will probably drag you off to his ship in front of everyone and make wild, passionate love to you all night long,'' Juli predicted, grinning.

Fury giggled. The prospect was not without appeal, although she didn't say so to Juli.

Musical chords from the spinet in the ballroom wafted upward to drift through the open French doors. ''I do believe the party is beginning,'' Juli said. ''Even up here I can hear the guests being announced. Oh, Miss Fury, you will create a stir when you walk in alone, more regal than any queen. Quickly now, we must drape this silk to perfection. I have it timed perfectly. Don't squirm, don't even move,'' she ordered. Fury's face burned as Juli deftly wrapped the luxurious silk all about her naked body. The housekeeper had insisted she wear no undergarments at all, and she'd been right: no matter how thin, they would have thrown off the look of the fashioned gown.

''Short steps only, Miss Fury.'' Juli walked slowly around Fury, inspecting every curve with a critical eye. ''You can do it. Just remember that every woman in the room will be green with jealousy, and every man desperate for your favors. And now I have a surprise for you,'' she said, her eyes fairly dancing with excitement. ''When I went downstairs for extra bath sheeting, I peeked at those little cards for the dinner guests, and guess who your partner is! Señor Domingo!''

Fury's heart began to pound. That meant she would have the handsome Spaniard all to herself for well over an hour. She laughed delightedly and pirouetted for Juli's benefit.

Juli tapped her chin with a stubby finger. ''By next week I do believe we could sell this creation by the hundreds. We're the only ones who know it hasn't been sewn. We should give it serious thought. Now, remember, short steps or you'll fall flat on your face,'' she said tartly.

Fury twirled one last time in front of the pier glass, her

eyes drinking in the sight of her long, slender form. Suddenly the room was awash with sound and motion as the hawks swooped in to perch on the bedposts. Fury affected a low, sweeping bow, and Pilar fanned her wings in approval. Gaspar tilted his head to the side, then sailed across the room to land on the dressing table. He extended one claw, and Fury saw something sparkle in the clutch of his talon.

"The garter!" Juli cried. "You get it, Miss Fury. I'm not going near those birds."

Fury held out her hand, and Gaspar dropped the diamond garter into her palm. "They love anything that glitters," she said with fond indulgence as she fastened the garter on her upper arm. "Now what?" she asked Juli as the diamond circlet slipped to her wrist. "It's too big. . . . "

"Allow me." Juli unfastened the garter, one eye on the hawks as they watched her every movement. "See, we'll fasten it higher and move it to catch on this link. The little tail will be on the inside of your arm. No one will notice. . . . There! It's perfectly exquisite!"

Pilar's wings rustled and fanned out as she lifted herself up to hover above Juli and Fury. Gently, one wing tip lowered to tickle Fury's cheek. Gaspar flapped his wings until he, too, had a suitable draft to rise, and then both birds *swoosh*ed through the open doors leading to the balcony. Juli sighed with obvious relief as she ushered Fury to the bedroom door.

"Have a wonderful time, Miss Fury," she said, giving her a hug. "I'll try to peek from the landing."

Fury blessed herself as she walked out to the staircase that led to the wide central foyer. She told herself she was a make-believe fairy princess on her way to a ball where she would meet a handsome prince—and that was exactly what she was doing, she thought triumphantly.

Fury drew a deep breath when the von Klausners'

houseman announced, "Señorita Furana van der Rhys. . . ." She heard the collective gasp as she made her way down the receiving line—and she reveled in it. Head held high, she moved off to the right side of the room so designated for ladies, where she was immediately claimed by a gallant Spanish don who insisted on fetching her a glass of wine. While she waited for him to return, she allowed her eyes to search the room for a glimpse of Luis Domingo.

At the moment of Fury's announced entrance to the ball, Luis Domingo was being introduced to the board of governors from the Dutch East India Company and their charming escorts. He made a show of bowing elaborately over Naula's hand and received a brazen wink in return. Chuckling, he straightened—just in time to witness Fury's entrance.

"Regan's daughter," murmured one of the governors.

A second nodded appreciatively. "Exquisite creature. More beautiful than her mother. . . ."

"Magnificent gown, and I know nothing about women's clothes," pronounced a third governor.

The ladies, too, had much to say with their eyes and low-voiced mutterings.

"The gown must have cost a fortune. . . ."

"Absolutely nothing underneath . . ."

"Flawless gems . . . worth a king's ransom . . ."

"Scandalous use of face color . . ."

And then Naula's statement put it all in perspective for Luis:

"If that gorgeous silk were mine, I'd have made it Chinese style with an opening up to here." She pointed to the middle of her slender thigh. "Just high enough for a garter to show through the opening when I took a step."

Instantly Luis excused himself and made his way across

the room to Fury. His heart pumped furiously as he bowed low over her hand, his dark eyes glittering with admiration. Christ, she was beautiful. More beautiful than any woman he'd ever met. And possibly more dangerous as well. It was time to find out.

"Señor Domingo, how nice to see you again," Fury murmured. Her blood wasn't just singing, it was boiling in her veins.

"And I you," Luis said gallantly. "But don't you think it's time you called me Luis?"

The laughter around his eyes puzzled Fury, but she smiled and nodded. "Will you be in port long?" she asked. The handsome don, approaching with a long-stemmed goblet, glowered at Luis, then abruptly changed course and drank the wine himself.

Luis smiled. "I think I just intimidated the man who was fetching your wine. My apologies. Would you like me to—"

"No, thank you. He was merely being polite. It must be obvious to you, Señ—Luis, that the ladies here this evening are . . ."

"Jealous? But of course. They pale beside you, and isn't that something no woman wants to have happen?"

"I wouldn't know," Fury said airily.

Luis laughed. "Come now, I thought every woman"—he emphasized the word—"recognized envy as the highest form of flattery, particularly when exhibited by members of her own sex. Would you like to hear a bit of gossip concerning your gown?" he teased.

"Oh, dear, am I perhaps too . . . ?" She glanced down at herself in sudden apprehension.

"On the contrary. All of the . . . ah, governors' *escorts* were breathless with their comments. The one with black hair said if she had a length of silk, she would have fashioned it Chinese style, with a slit up to here, and worn a *garter.* The others seemed to agree with her taste." Luis watched Fury's eyes for any sign of agitation.

"How interesting," Fury said coolly. "And what is your opinion?" *My God, he knows, and he's baiting me. Damn you, Gaspar, if it weren't for you, I would have forgotten to wear this bauble.*

Luis pretended embarrassment. "I like a length of thigh as much as the next man. I think I'd vote for the garter. They must be all the rage in feminine wear. The Sea Siren wears one. But then," he added lightly, "women are creatures of whimsy, and fashions change so quickly these days. Don't you agree?"

"Absolutely." By now Fury wanted desperately to flee but knew she had to brazen this out and pretend to take Luis's words at face value. "I think I would like that wine after all, Luis. If you don't mind . . ."

"It will be my pleasure," Luis said, and moved off to the far corner of the room.

By God, she *was* the one! He had her now *and* the place where she kept her ship. As he waited for a white-liveried waiter to pour wine into two long-stemmed crystal goblets, he began to laugh, remembering the look on Fury's face when he mentioned the garter. She thinks I suspect, but she isn't sure, he reflected. By God, it was the coup of the century!

Suddenly he sobered, recalling that whatever her game was, Fury van der Rhys—the Sea Siren of the diamond garter and black birds—hadn't harmed him when they'd met at sea. She'd merely said *she* had come out of retirement to seek the woman posing as herself, and he hadn't believed her. It was the other one, the impostor, who'd plundered his ships and then accosted him a second time. Christ, he was going mad with all this subterfuge!

"Thank you," Fury said demurely when he returned

with her wine. "I don't believe you responded when I asked how long you'll be in port."

"Another day at least. I have something I must do tomorrow, and if I finish, I'll sail with the tide."

Fury smiled. "You make it all sound so . . . mysterious."

"I suppose it is in a way. I think I've discovered, and this is just between us"—Luis lowered his voice—"the Sea Siren's lair."

Fury's fingers clutched the stem of the wineglass in a white-knuckled grip. "How . . . how interesting. Perhaps you might confide in me? Of course I won't breathe a word. I did live here for some of my younger years. I might know where this lair is."

"Would you believe it's possible to navigate the River of Death? I think that's how the Siren gets away. The volcanoes create a mist, and the steam from them mixes with the river to form a black mist they say she disappears into. Of course, my maps say the mouth of the river has been blocked for years. The volcanoes erupted during the Siren's reign of the seas. That's why she retired; she couldn't travel the river any longer."

"You almost make me believe you, Luis," Fury said sharply. "But everyone knows the river is still blocked. No one is brave enough to take a ship up that river. I think your theory is interesting, but not feasible."

"Tomorrow I plan to test it. The Dutch East India Company has a new sloop that will sail through with ease. I think the river's been open for years now. The currents and tides . . . you see, it's the only explanation."

"Tomorrow, you say?" Fury purred.

Luis nodded. "Tomorrow."

Fury sipped her wine. "Tell me, have you spoken of your theory to anyone else?"

"Good Lord, no. Do you think I want to give away the

biggest coup of my life? Then there's the reward, of course, and handsome it is. But I know I can trust you.''

Fury smiled grimly. ''Have no fear, Luis, my lips are sealed.''

''Not forever, I hope,'' Luis said lightly. ''Someday I should like to kiss those lips.''

Fury's throat closed, and her eyes smarted with tears. Frantically, she glanced toward the stairway for some sign of Juli.

''Oh, there's one other thing,'' Luis said, watching her intently. Again he lowered his voice. ''Apparently the Siren sails with two huge black birds, deadly creatures. This afternoon I saw them fly overhead and nest not far from this very house. That can mean only that the Sea Siren is in one of the coves or inlets off the river. Don't you agree?''

Fury shrugged. ''What would I know about such things? Deadly black birds, diamond garters, the River of Death . . . I only hope you aren't wasting your time. They say the Siren can outthink and outmaneuver any man.''

''I've heard that, too,'' Luis said mockingly. ''I'll keep it all in mind. Now, would you care for a stroll in the garden? It's much too warm in here. You *can* walk in that dress, can't you?''

''Not very well, but yes, I would like to take a stroll. First, however, I'd like to go to my room for a handkerchief. If you'll wait for me, I'll join you on the veranda.''

It seemed to take Fury forever to make her way across the room and out to the candlelit foyer, where she spotted Juli talking in rapturous tones to the von Klausners' houseman.

''I have to talk to you. Now!'' she spat out, taking Juli by the arm.

''What is it?'' Juli asked, alarmed.

''Luis Domingo knows. He's been baiting me all evening. Somehow he's figured it all out. You have to go to the cove and tell your brothers to take the ship out and down the river. He knows it's no longer blocked, and he said he's going upriver tomorrow. We can't wait until then—it has to be done now! I hate to ask you to do this, but I can't leave, he's too suspicious as it is. I wouldn't put it past him to leave now just to satisfy his own curiosity. For all I know, he may already have been to the cove.''

''Where should I tell my brothers to take the ship? I see you haven't given that any thought. Well, give this some thought, Miss Fury, the man on the steps is starting to make my blood sing.''

''Tomorrow is another day,'' Fury said airily. ''I expect you to bring back information. Your brothers have always lived here. Surely they know places. . . . I'll leave it to you, Juli. I have to get back before Luis suspects something. Oh, and Juli, take Gaspar and Pilar with you. Simply tell them to follow you and they will. Go along now,'' she said in her mother's firm voice.

''Dear Aldo, there's something my mistress wants me to do. I'm afraid we'll have to postpone our dinner in the kitchen. Perhaps we could breakfast together if you have a mind to. My mistress is soooo demanding,'' Juli simpered as she backed herself up the stairs. It wasn't till she was all the way to the top of the stairs that she realized she would either have to go down over the balcony or descend the stairs and go past Aldo, who would surely wonder where she was going at that time of night. And where was she to find the damn black birds?

He was so close, she could smell the faint scent of cigar smoke on his clothing, a scent reminiscent of her father. He had her elbow in the palm of his hand as she took dainty little steps in the tight gown. She could feel herself shivering in the warm air, shivers that had nothing to do with the balmy air.

The garden was exquisite, with colorful lanterns illuminating the intricate footpaths. A slight breeze carried the heady scent of jasmine to Fury's nostrils. She began to relax, savoring the feel of the air and the touch of the handsome man walking by her side.

They would miss the board of governors' announcement if they stayed in the garden, she thought, then realized she didn't care if she missed it or not. This was what she wanted. And she didn't want it to end.

Be bold and brash, Fury decided. She bent down to pick up her skirts only to realize there was no excess silk to hike above her ankles. She gave a light tug at the clinging wrapped silk—and immediately toppled over to land flat on her face in the grass. A furious flapping overhead in the darkness made her bury her head in the lush greenery to stifle her laughter. She knew the hawks would circle harmlessly and then return to their perches.

Luis was grinning from ear to ear as he reached down to help her up. "I guess I have to thank you for wearing that scandalous dress, for if it weren't for the dress, I wouldn't be about to . . ."

His lips were so close that Fury could feel his warm breath on her cheek. She closed her eyes in anticipation of the kiss she knew was coming. She wanted him to kiss her, expected it; after all, that's what this evening was all about. Another moment and his lips would be on hers. She would swoon, be all light-headed and warm all over. What was taking him so long? Perhaps he was staring at her, memorizing her face or simply drinking in her beauty. She opened one eye and then the other. He wasn't drinking in her beauty or memorizing her features at all. He was staring at something behind her. Something that was high in the air. The birds! She turned and almost lost her footing a second time. She should have fainted, she thought sourly.

"Isn't that your housekeeper hanging from the balustrade?" Luis drawled.

"My housekeeper!" Fury shrilled. "Absolutely not! Why would my housekeeper hang from . . . that woman doesn't look anything like . . . my . . . my housekeeper. How can you think such a thing? It's a trick of lighting, the lanterns . . ."

"Something seems to be attacking her . . . do you hear that noise?" Luis chuckled deep in his throat, a sound Fury took to be fear. "It must be those damn killer birds! You stay here while I get help!"

"That's not my room!" Fury lied brazenly.

"I don't think that matters right now. What matters is getting the poor woman down before she kills herself. Do you want her death on your conscience?"

"Well, no, but . . . look, she's got a foothold and is . . . she's over the side and back on the balcony. See, your anxiety was for naught. Poor woman was probably trying to get away from . . . from someone," Fury said weakly.

"Did you see those damnable birds?" Luis asked gruffly.

"No, I didn't see any birds, and I could barely see the woman," Fury said huffily. "I think we should go indoors. I feel a chill and I think I have a headache coming on."

"I wonder why that doesn't surprise me," Luis drawled.

"I beg your pardon, what did you say?" Fury asked fretfully as she started to mince her way on the garden path.

"What I said was we should get back to what we were doing before that ridiculous woman decided to escape from her lover."

Fury could feel herself stiffen as Luis gathered her into

his arms. She closed her eyes, knowing this time he *was* memorizing her features. His lips were so close, almost on hers. She could feel her heart begin to pound—or was it his? His lips were soft, gentle, and full of promise. She could feel his hand on her bare arm, the fingers trailing down, down . . . And then those same gentle fingers were on her back and working their way down her draped arm. Another second and they would find their way to the inside portion of her arm.

Suddenly, deep inside her a warning sounded. She didn't want to heed it, she wanted to remain in Luis's warm embrace, their bodies pressed tightly together. But some instinct prompted her to tear herself away. She took a few steps backward, a flustered look on her face, and then ran—ripping at the confining fabric of her gown, loosening it slightly. At the French doors she stopped to regain her composure, then smoothed back her hair and walked into the ballroom.

No one was paying attention to her; all eyes were on the dais, where the governors were about to make their announcement. She heard the words, and later they would sink in, but not now. Dykstra had been passed over for the governorship, and some faceless man she'd never heard of was being mentioned for the position.

He knows, he knows, he knows!

In her room, Fury unwrapped the shimmering emerald silk from her shoulder, tied it to the bedpost, and then twirled until she was standing naked in the darkness. She'd never felt this hot, this burning fire that was consuming her. Fear? Luis Domingo? In minutes she was dressed and on the balcony, peering into the darkness for a vine or trellis. There were none. Heart thudding in her chest, she climbed over the balustrade. Poor Juli. Poor Fury, she thought grimly as she closed her eyes.

* * *

Luis Domingo stood in the shadows, his dark eyes narrowed in amusement. Did she dare to jump? She could kill herself. When he saw her kick off her slippers, he moved out of the shadows and ran, knowing he didn't want the young woman to hurt herself no matter who she was, no matter what she'd done.

Fury squeezed her eyes tight and leapt, her arms flailing the air. At the same moment Luis stretched out his arms and caught her, his body jerking backward with the force of her weight.

"My God . . . what . . ."

"I have to assume this is a new cure for a headache," Luis drawled from beneath her.

"My God . . . what . . ."

"You already said that. . . . I think an explanation is in order, but if you prefer to . . . ah, ignore this situation, I can and will keep my lips sealed."

He knows and he's laughing at me. Sparks spewed from Fury's eyes. Damn, what would her mother have done in a situation like this?

She realized then that her body was literally covering his. She was so close to him, her lips almost on his. "Actually," she murmured in a shaky voice, "I was . . . was looking for you. Obviously you were closer than I realized." She cradled his dark head in her hands and brought her lips to his in a searing kiss that sent shock waves through her entire body. Luis's arms tightened around her, straining to bring her even closer.

She didn't care then if his fingers caressed her arm; she didn't care about anything but his lips on hers. Her body was demanding, ordering her to explore, to search . . . to seek and find.

"No," Luis said hoarsely as he thrust her from him. Fury blinked and looked at him, confused. "You don't know what you're . . . No. I can't. . . ."

Fury blinked again, then shame rushed through her. He'd been playing with her, he didn't want her at all! The kiss was . . . the same kind he'd given the whore Naula. Damn him to hell—he thought she was no more than a common wanton!

She was on her feet in an instant, her face fiery red. "Good night, Señor Domingo," she said coldly.

Luis could only stare after her, too stunned to move. The moment the darkness swallowed her, he cried her name, again and again.

Tears streaming down her cheeks, Fury ran through the dark, quiet streets until she came to the parish house. She didn't bother to knock but thrust open the door, calling the priest's name in a voice so tormented, the good father—who'd long since left the soiree for the comfort of his own bed—was downstairs in an instant, tripping on his nightshirt as he went along.

"What is it, child? What's happened? What time is it?"

"He knows, Father, he knows! I'm sure of it!"

"Who knows what?" the old priest demanded fretfully.

"Señor Domingo. He suspects who I am. My scar . . . the hawks, the diamond garter . . . I sent Juli to get the ship out of the cove before sunup. There is no other hiding place for her." Fury began to pace up and down the foyer, wringing her hands. "It's all over, Father. Everyone will know shortly. I suppose you know that Mynheer Dykstra was passed over for the governorship for someone I never heard of. He will never forgive my father and mother, or me, for that matter. Do you know why they wouldn't accept him, Father?"

Father Sebastian sighed. "Because he is getting on in years. They want a younger man, or at least that's what I think. I can't prove it. I saw the mynheer's face; he took the announcement badly, I thought. I tried to speak with him, but he stormed out of the house. He said if he isn't good enough to be governor, then he is resigning as the manager of the Dutch East India Company. The mynheer is a very bitter man and I can't say I blame him. I devoted an hour of prayer for his soul.''

''Yes, yes, that's all well and good, Father, but about my problem. If Luis Domingo tells Mynheer Dykstra, the . . . they could send me to prison, Father. My mother, too.'' The thought of her beautiful mother in prison turned Fury's face white. She herself knew about prisons; she'd been planning on entering one.

The elderly priest shook his head. ''They have to have proof, Furana. A scar on your arm isn't going to convince the authorities you're anything but who you are, a young lady sent here to enter the convent.''

''A young lady who was *rejected*. Father, the authorities will see it as a simple ruse. My mother's ship . . . I can't let it be confiscated, she'll never forgive me. Once I secure it, I'll return here and decide what I am to do.''

He should tell her now, the old priest thought. He should walk over to his Bible and show her the letter from the archbishop. But he knew he wouldn't do any such thing. ''What can I do, child?''

''If Luis Domingo is half as astute as I think he is, he knows this is the only place I'd come to at this late hour. Would you—would you tell him I came here to make a confession because of my . . . my wanton desires?''

''Do you think he'll believe you came here in the middle of the night to confess your sins?'' Father Sebastian asked gently.

''It's up to you to make him believe it, Father. The casa is being watched by Mynheer Dykstra's men. I was going to sail the *Rana* to provide Luis with an escort back to Spain—at a safe distance, of course.'' She told him then about the diamond consignment. ''I have to go back to the von Klausner house now,'' she concluded, ''and believe me when I tell you it's going to be much harder to get in than it was getting out. I have no idea how I'm going to explain my absence. The story will be all over Batavia. God only knows what Mynheer Dykstra will do.''

"You are your mother's daughter, Furana. Whatever happens, I'm sure you'll do the right thing," the priest said loyally.

Fury whirled. "I'm sick and tired of hearing I'm my mother's daughter! That sort of thinking is what got me into this predicament. Listen to me, Father. I will do whatever I have to to keep this secret. No one—not Mynheer Dykstra, not Luis Domingo—will reveal it. *No one. Now*, Father, you can pray for me!''

Fury had her hand on the doorlatch when Father Sebastian called to her. "Do you love Luis Domingo?''

Fury's bitter laughter sent chills down the old priest's back. Why, he wondered miserably, had he expected an answer?

Half in the shadows, Luis settled himself on an iron bench to await Fury's return. He could have followed her, but he'd wanted to remain in the garden and think about those few tantalizing moments in the grass. Whoever would have thought that the demure religious could be so passionate? Christ Almighty, he could have taken her right there! He still didn't know where he'd found the strength to stop himself.

A strange feeling settled over him. He tried to put a name to it, and when the elusive words finally surfaced, he almost choked on the thick gray smoke from his cigar. Protectiveness and love. For Fury van der Rhys. The thought was so mind-boggling, he rose and began to pace in irritation. It wasn't possible he could be falling in love with the young woman . . . it couldn't be! Yet his eyes kindled with desire as he recalled her entrance to the party. Every man in the room had wanted her, and he was no exception. He still wanted her, for all the good it was going to do him. He conjured a vision of himself, old and gray, unmarried and childless, living on his memories while Fury, in a nun's habit, prayed for his everlasting soul.

Luis stomped off through the garden in search of total darkness and solitude. As he turned to toss away his half-smoked cigar, he saw Fury out of the corner of his eye, contemplating the second-floor balcony. His heart began to pound. He wanted to go to her, tell her he would keep her secret and help her get back to her room, but he couldn't move. Forty minutes later he heaved a mighty sigh of relief when he saw her slide over the balustrade. He continued to watch, and twenty minutes after that the housekeeper appeared, pondering the same problem of reaching the second floor unseen. It was all Luis could do to keep from showing her the various footholds Fury had found. "First of all you have to hike up your skirts," he whispered, "there to the right, that's it, grab hold, now inch your way, little by little, ah, that's it, now to the left, slowly, there you have it . . . straight now . . . ."

The attack, when it came, was so silent, so deadly, Luis barely had time to dive for cover. His heart pumped madly. From somewhere deep inside him words came, words he later could barely remember uttering. "I mean her no harm, for Christ's sake, I think I love her!" Did he say the words or did he—the sudden silence roared in his ears. He knew his hair was standing on end in the breeze the birds created. "Jesus Christ!" he fumed as he got to his feet. They were overhead, each working the gentle breeze, waiting, waiting for him to . . . what? for Christ's sake. Explain? "I'd never hurt her," he whispered. "I won't give away her secret. I won't," he said fiercely. "If you're going to do something, for God's sake, do it now!'' he commanded. He watched in horror as Pilar seemed to soar straight up in the air, her wings flapping in a frenzy in the light from the colorful lantern. She circled, her wings fanning the air, and then before he could blink his eyes she descended to within an inch of him, hanging suspended in the air, her wing tip feathering out to touch his cheek. So gently. ''Take care of her,'' he said softly.

''Hawhawhawhaw,'' came Gaspar's cry overhead.

''And on that note, I think I'll say good night to my hostess,'' Luis muttered in relief.

Luis wasn't at all surprised, a short while later, to find himself at the parish house. He looked longingly at the second-story windows. It was almost sacrilegious to wake the old priest at this hour, but he needed to talk to someone who wouldn't lie to him, someone who knew Fury van der Rhys, Peter Dykstra, and Fury's parents. His feet seemed to have a mind of their own as they walked up the path and onto the small porch of the parish house. He knew the door wasn't locked. The parish house as well as the church were never locked to those in need of prayer and a kind word.

Inside, Luis settled himself on the one comfortable chair, leaned back, and closed his eyes. Perhaps he'd missed his calling and should have entered the priesthood. It was so peaceful here. He imagined he could see tiny angels flitting overhead, plump little cherubs praying and singing. Because he believed in the *padre*'s God he knew there were such things. He found himself grinning when he patted his shoulder where he knew an imaginary angel hovered.

He could sit here all night; the *padre* wouldn't care. He had no desire to return to his boardinghouse or to the ship.

In fact, he'd even lost the need to talk with the good Father: best let him sleep.

Poor Father Sebastian, Luis thought, stretching comfortably. He was at the end of his life span; just yesterday he'd noticed the man's bowed back, his bent, gnarled hands. Was he in pain? Probably, Luis decided. Yet he'd never seen anything but compassion and goodness in the old man's face. No doubt at the end of the day he would sit in this chair and read his Bible, deriving comfort and the strength to endure one more day. Luis smiled, a sweet, gentle smile, and asked the Lord to allow the priest to live to be a hundred.

Would he be trespassing if he picked up the priest's Bible and read a verse or two? Perhaps he would find answers in this holy book. Or were the answers within himself? What exactly was it that he was seeking? Vengeance . . . yes, he was bent on vengeance for the death and ruination of his father. He'd almost forgotten about *that*. He'd been so intent on the future, he'd shelved the past.

Sudden anger ripped through Luis, driving all his peaceful thoughts into oblivion. He slammed the Bible onto the table. Honeyed words weren't going to change past injustices or make him forget about his father and what Fury's mother did to him. For in his mind now he was convinced that Sirena van der Rhys was the Sea Siren.

He should return to the ship and try to get some sleep. At least in sleep he wouldn't be tormented. He gazed around at the moonlight spilling into the room, and then, sighing, he righted the Bible on the little table, aware for the first time of the crackly paper underneath. Idly he opened the stiff paper and read the flowing script. He sat for a very long time, the words burning into his heart. When he at last folded the religious decree, he felt as though he'd been kicked in the stomach by a mule.

On stiff legs he made his way back to his ship, his thoughts as unyielding as his bones. There would be no sleep for him this night—and probably not for several nights to come.

Fury was lost to him . . . not that she'd ever truly been his, but this evening, for a few brief moments, she'd been ready to offer herself to him. And what had he done? He'd goddamn well turned away from her. If he lived to be a hundred, he'd never forget the look of shame and humiliation on her face—not at what she'd been prepared to do, but at his reaction to it. "You're a bastard," he muttered. "A low-down, scheming bastard!"

When the gray-laced dawn crept over the horizon, Luis was on the deck of the *Silver Lady* cradling a mug of three-day-old coffee in his hands that was so strong he could have eaten it in chunks.

The trade winds were cool and balmy as they rippled across the deck, but even they couldn't ease his tortured thoughts. Perhaps he should cut his losses and sail the *Silver Lady* back to Spain, begin all over. He had the rest of his life to make a fortune. He would probably never marry now, so he didn't have to worry about building a fine house and supporting a family. He could live at sea and call the *Silver Lady* his home.

As for the real Sea Siren, let her rest in peace. Her daughter would soon be peaceful enough in the convent, praying for all their wicked souls. The bogus impostor could have his cargoes, and may she never know a moment's peace from them. The hell with Dykstra and the Dutch East India Company. The hell with the diamond merchant he was to escort back to Spain. He would sail with the evening tide.

But before then, he decided, he'd take one last ride back to the cove, prove to himself once and for all that Fury really was impersonating her mother. If nothing else, he wanted to carry that proof back to Spain with him. It was important to him, and he wasn't sure why.

The sun was creeping into the sky when Luis began his trek through the jungle. Somehow he felt sure that he would find the cove serene, with no trace of the hateful black ship. Certainly he'd given Fury plenty of time to sail her out to open water. He wondered if she would ever realize what he'd done for her. On the other hand, she might realize full well that it was within his power to sign her death warrant. Even if he chose not to expose her and her ship, but sailed away without telling a soul, mightn't she convince herself otherwise? She would assume her ship was no longer safe here in the cove—and with no place to hide, she'd be open prey to any marauder on the seas.

Minutes later he reached his destination. Sure enough, there was no sign of the ship that had rocked so gently in the calm cove waters the night before. Any doubts about Fury's identity were now washed away, he thought grimly.

Over and over on his ride back to the harbor he asked himself if he could turn his back on Fury. It was his fault she'd rushed to move her ship, and it would be his fault if she didn't survive to enter the convent two weeks from today. Could he live with that?

The small town was alive with bustle and noise as Luis reined in his horse at the parish house. All the von Klausner guests were departing for their homes after a huge breakfast, as was the local custom. He wondered where Dykstra was. The entire board of governors would be leaving Clarice's about now, their morning baths and huge breakfasts a pleasant memory. Past memories were best forgotten, he thought sourly.

"Señor, will you join me for lunch?' the priest asked, opening the door in greeting.

"Yes, thank you," Luis replied. "But, Father, I must talk with you, it's very important."

"Can we talk over lunch, or would you prefer my study?"

"It doesn't matter. Father, you must speak with Fury. . . ." All his hopes and ambitions spilled out, along with the past evening's activities and his recent trip to the cove. "I was here last night, Father, I needed to talk with you. I was going to read a verse or two from your Bible, and the . . . the letter underneath fell to the floor. I don't know why I read it, there's no excuse I can offer for invading your privacy. I do apologize," Luis said gruffly.

"She doesn't know . . . about the letter, that is," the priest said fretfully. "She and her housekeeper left the von Klausners' just as the sun came up. I intend to ride out to their casa myself when the sun sets and tell her then. I'll give her a message if you wish."

"Tell her the cove and her secret is safe with me. She has nothing to fear from me. I'm sailing this evening."

"You have time to ride out and tell her yourself," the priest said.

"If you don't mind, Father, I'd rather not. In fact, I think I'll forgo lunch as well." Luis extended his hand. "Perhaps we'll meet again one day."

"If not in this life, then in the next one," the elderly priest said, walking with him to the front door. "I wish you a safe journey, Señor Domingo, and have no fear, I will deliver your message to Fury just as you instructed. Godspeed."

Father Sebastian watched the handsome Spaniard until he was out of sight. He didn't have much firsthand knowledge about love between men and women, but what knowledge he did have told him Luis Domingo was in love. Fury had been acting the same way, her face flushing any time the Spaniard's name was mentioned. The thought of her in a convent for the rest of her life was so upsetting, he walked into his kitchen and ripped the cloth from the parrot's cage. "Go on, say it!" he croaked petulantly.

"Say your prayers, say your prayers," the parrot babbled.

"Shut up!" he ordered, throwing the cloth back over the parrot's cage. "I don't need you to tell me to pray, it's all I do; it's what I do best." To his housekeeper he said, "I'm leaving now. I won't be here for dinner, I may not even return this evening. If you see me, I'm here; if not, I'm not here."

"Are you all right, Father?" the old woman asked, bewildered.

"No, I'm not all right, but don't concern yourself," he grumbled. "Just give me a jug of water to take with me and that umbrella you never use. I'm too old for this hot sun. And before you can say it, I don't care if the town thinks me daft or not."

Chapter Eleven

The River of Death

The sky overhead looked evil somehow, Amalie thought fearfully. Low gray clouds scudding together formed a thick blanket that dipped lower and lower until it was impossible to distinguish the fog from the cloud bank. But if she showed fear in any way, her crew would forget about Miguel and the allegiance they'd sworn to her. Open water at least gave a captain and his ship a fighting chance. Navigating this narrow river known for so many deaths would take every ounce of skill and determination. Amalie wanted nothing more than to squeeze her eyes shut and not open them until she had secured her ship in the first deepwater cove she came to. But she was hell-bent on a course from which there was no turning back.

Amalie was steering what she hoped was a straight blind run with one of her crew on the bow to warn her if she came too close to the dangerous rocks on either side of the narrow river.

Her hands gripped the wheel so fiercely, her knuckles showed white. She wanted to think about the real Sea Siren and the whispered diamond consignment her crew had picked up on that was due to arrive in Batavia. Until now it had all been so easy, a game of sorts; but no longer. The Spaniard's riddles finally made sense to her. The woman her father had written about in his journal was back on the high seas—and seeking revenge. Revenge against *her*, Amalie, for plundering the seas in her name.

Dare she set sail after the Dutch ship and the diamond consignment? Of course she dared; the diamonds were the reason she was steering this very ship up the River of Death. If she was successful, she, too, would retire from the sea. She'd return to Saianha a wealthy woman, able to live in luxury until she died.

The plan when they weighed anchor was for Cato to pilot the jolly boat into the harbor and sign on to the Dutch manifest. Seamen talked when they were full of grog. Rego would be in town waiting for Cato to inform him of the sailing time. But she'd have to be careful. The real Sea Siren, if she knew of the diamond consignment, would be on watch. She might even be noble enough to provide an escort for the Dutch ship. The thought was farfetched but not impossible.

Amalie's shoulders ached with the strain of constant vigilance. They were close now, almost there. . . . She watched, grim-faced, as Cato reached out and touched a jutting rock. They were all a hairbreadth away from disaster, and everyone aboard the ship knew it.

"Never again," she muttered to herself. "I never want to be this close to death again."

When at last Cato shouted, "We're clear, the cove is dead ahead!" Amalie did her best to straighten up, to look confident and assured. Fortunately only Cato knew how weak she was, how terrified.

"All that matters is you did it," he murmured. "Don't think back, think only of the present. We'll weigh anchor, and at first light I'll make my way back down the river and into town. I'll take the jolly boat as far as it's safe and travel the rest of the way on foot. Rego will return with the boat when I have the information you need."

Below decks in her cabin, Amalie gave in to her emotions. She huddled in her bunk, shivering uncontrollably. Tears of frustration, of fear and relief, coursed down her cheeks. She wasn't the Sea Siren. She was an impostor who couldn't even come close. That woman had been nerveless, her ability lawless. The Siren had relied only on herself, while she, Amalie, was dependent on her crew and others for information. Hers was a mission of pure greed; the Siren had sailed to avenge a wrong. There was no comparison no matter how much she wanted to believe she was every bit as capable and talented as the famous Sea Siren. "Even in death you robbed me, you bastard," she hissed to the four walls. "I wish you could hear me, Father," she spat out.

Amalie wanted to pray then, to the God she'd learned about in the mission. If she said the words she learned and remembered, it would be sacrilegious and only compound her spiritual being. That God would not forgive what she'd done.

When Cato looked in on Amalie, just before setting out in the jolly boat, she was sleeping, her tears drying on her cheeks. She looked so beautiful, he thought, her hand cupped under her cheek. Peaceful and saintly . . . He felt his loins stir, and he ached with his need. Softly he turned and closed the door behind him. He had his own mission now, one dictated by his love.

Juli clucked her tongue at her mistress. "You need sleep, Miss Fury. There's nothing you can do until one of my brothers brings word. Use that time to rest. Warm milk, warm chocolate," she coaxed.

Fury shook her head and continued her restless pacing. A sudden clatter in the courtyard sent her flying to the balcony doors. "It's Father Sebastian," Fury muttered as she turned from the window. "What do you suppose . . . ?"

"Nothing good, I'm sure," Juli said sourly as she moved out of Fury's way.

Fury threw open the heavy front door to stare anxiously at the priest. "What is it, Father, has something happened? Why have you come all this way so early in the morning? Juli, fetch a cool drink. And set the table for breakfast."

"No, child," the priest said, mopping his forehead. "No breakfast, but I would like a cool drink. Please, let us sit down. My bones grow older each day."

Fury waited in an agony of impatience as Father Sebastian drained his drink. At last he sighed heavily and leaned forward, his face so earnest she almost swooned with fear. Something had happened to her parents, she thought wildly. The elderly priest looked so sad, so forlorn.

"It's my parents, isn't it?" she blurted out. "Something has happened to them. That's why you're here."

"No, child!" cried Father Sebastian, obviously upset that his behavior had so misled her. "That's not why I'm here. . . . Last night, quite late, Luis Domingo came to the parish house. He entered, but he did not wake me, although he needed to talk. Instead, he . . . sought solace by picking up my Bible, and he . . . he read this." The priest drew out the parchment letter from the archbishop. "I meant to tell you about it earlier, child, but I couldn't. I so wanted you to enjoy the soiree and not concern yourself with this until it . . . This doesn't mean you have to . . . Forgive me, Furana," he concluded lamely.

Fury reached for the crackly paper, but the priest hesitated. "Before I give you this," he said, "I want you to know something. Señor Domingo asked me to give you a message. He said he'd been to the cove and seen your ship. He said your secret is safe with him. He's sailing with the evening tide. He read this letter while I slept and later apologized to me for having done so. You'll never see him

again, Furana.'' The good father sighed heavily. ''I fear
we've both misjudged the man. Mynheer Dykstra, however, will not be as generous as Señor Domingo. With him
the matter is much more personal, I believe.''

''The letter, Father. Give it to me,'' Fury demanded.
Her face betrayed no emotion as she read the contents.
''This says I have . . . two weeks . . . two weeks to
do . . .''

''Whatever you want. Two weeks is fourteen days. A
person could sail quite far in fourteen days. This time of
year the trade winds are a sailor's dream. When one leaves
the outside world for a religious vocation, one must leave
his old world in peace, with no emotional ties. I . . . I
told Señor Domingo he should come out here and tell you
himself, but he declined. I wanted to say something to
him that would ease his mind, but I couldn't say what he
needed to hear. He knows who you are, Furana. And he's
carried his vengeance against your mother for so long.
He's turning his back on everything—his chance to seek
out the impostor, his chance for a handsome commission
to escort the diamond merchant back to Spain, everything.''

''We all make decisions we have to live with, Father,''
Fury said softly.

''He must love you very much to make such a decision.'' Father Sebastian felt his old heart quicken at the
look of pure joy that settled on Fury's face. Her eyes were
like stars, her smile as radiant as the sun. He wanted to
cry when the stars and sun left her features. ''Child, I have
no idea what you feel for the Spaniard. What does a man
of God know about love between a man and a woman?
But I know what I saw in Señor Domingo's face, what I
heard in his voice. And I must assume that God, in His
infinite wisdom, has given me the insight to interpret his
emotions. I believe he is in love with you. What you do

with this information is up to you, of course. Now, if you wouldn't mind, I'd like to impose on you for a short nap before I return to the village."

"Of course, Father," Juli said, holding the door open, her eyes on Fury. She wondered smugly if her own eyes were as star bright as her mistress's. Aldo would arrive, if all went well, after dinner. Her feet literally danced up the long staircase. What was Fury going to do?

"The good Father is tucked in with a cool drink on his night table," she reported on her return to the study. "He'll sleep well; I closed the draperies. Now!"—she regarded Fury narrowly, hands on her ample hips—"what was *that* all about? It's just a letter, it didn't come from your pope. You don't have to obey it if you don't want to. If you have doubts, you shouldn't even *consider* obeying. I heard what Father Sebastian said, and I saw your face, Miss Fury. Does the wind have to blow you over before you wake up to what's in front of your eyes? Do what your heart tells you to do!"

"Juli, in case you haven't noticed, I no longer have a ship in the cove," Fury snapped. "I couldn't do anything even if I wanted to—at this time. Until one of your brothers arrives with information, we have to be patient."

"You could be making plans," Juli persisted. "Don't you want to see him one more time? That place you're planning on entering, it will be dark and dreary . . . his handsome face could be the sunshine in your thoughts."

Fury flinched. "I'll be too busy to think about Señor Domingo. Besides, it's unholy to think of a man when I've given myself to God."

Juli gave her a withering look. "You haven't given yourself yet. You still have two weeks to do whatever you want. Two weeks, Miss Fury!"

"I'll just have to live with that, won't I? The woman posing as my mother probably has knowledge of the diamond consignment and has heard that Señor Domingo is to sail with the diamond merchant. Now that he sails on his own frigate, she won't go after the Dutch ship. She'll probably think it's a trick of some sort and go after Luis . . . I mean Señor Domingo. She'll never get the diamonds, and he—well, he can take care of himself,'' she concluded defiantly.

The silence between the two women grew unbearable. Fury refused to meet Juli's eyes, although she knew the housekeeper was staring at her, waiting. . . .

"You have no guts!" she burst out at last.

Fury was on her feet in a second. "I resent your remark, Juli!"

"And well you should," Juli responded. "You were play-acting before, enjoying yourself and the drama you created. Now, when it's time to do what your mother would do, you have no stomach for saving the man you love. You love him, admit it, Miss Fury!"

"I'll admit no such thing. You forget your place. Perhaps my mother allowed you to speak to her in such a manner, but you will not talk to me like this!"

Juli stomped her way out of the study, calling over her shoulder, "Your mother was a woman in every sense of the word. You hide behind a holy facade and mumble prayers that do not come from your heart. You're afraid to become a woman!" She slammed into the kitchen and began to hack away at a chicken on her table, muttering angrily all the while.

Moments later Fury thrust open the door. "Juli, I'm sorry. I never should have spoken to you as I did. Please, forgive me. You've been a wonderful friend to my mother and myself. I don't know what I would have done without you. Listen to me, I have to make you understand. I'm committed to God. I'm meant to enter the convent. Of course it isn't going to be easy, I know that. There's every possibility I may fail in my vocation, but I have to try. Can't you understand? All my life . . . God is my life."

Juli sniffed and bent over her chicken without looking up. "The way I see it, Miss Fury, is you're cheating your God. You'll never convince me you don't have worldly feelings for the Spaniard. If you wish to dupe yourself, that's fine with me. Even those damnable birds haven't touched him. That should tell you something. You say they're attuned to you, so therefore they must know he's . . . good for you."

"You think I should go after him . . . and do what?" Fury asked, spreading her hands wide. "Somehow I don't think Señor Domingo will think kindly of me when I tell him I'm sailing along as an escort to protect him," she sniffed.

Juli brought the blade down across the chicken's wing joint with a vicious slam. "You don't have to tell him *that*. When you catch up to him, tell him you want only to warn him. A man will think kindly of a woman if she tries to apprise him of trouble. All men know we women have a sixth sense."

"How much of what you've just said is your own insight and how much is my mother's?" Fury demanded. She laughed bitterly as Juli refused to meet her gaze. The chicken lost its leg with a loud *whack!*

"Cook that," Fury said, pointing to the unfortunate fowl, "and give it to Father Sebastian. I don't want any lunch. Don't ever give me chicken again. I'll be in the garden."

"Thinking, I hope," Juli muttered as the knife severed the remaining leg from the carcass.

Out among the lush greenery, Fury headed for the nearest shade tree to reflect on the events of the past twenty-four hours. What was she to do? How foolish of Juli to assume there were choices for her to draw from. Could she go after Luis Domingo, warn him, and then head back to port and enter the convent? Two weeks wasn't much time. If there was a storm or if another ship accosted her, she could be delayed. If she didn't appear at the convent gates at the appointed time, she might be denied entrance. If she did go to sea and got herself killed or maimed, she could never enter the convent—or anyplace else, for that matter.

Overhead, the branches of the lush breadfruit tree rustled. Fury peered upward into Gaspar's glittering gaze. "I don't know what to do," she whispered. Her eye sought the sun as she tried to calculate how long it would take her to ride horseback into town. If she went by way of the cove, she might make the harbor at high tide.

Juli watched her mistress from the kitchen window. "It's better than nothing," she mumbled as she dropped the pieces of chicken into the boiling water. If Fury's God was on her side, she'd arrive in town with minutes to spare.

Fury gave no mind to her appearance as she spurred Starlight through the trampled jungle path. Within minutes her hair was free of its pins, streaming behind her in damp tendrils. Overhead, the hawks kept pace with her, working the air as they flew directly in her path. The horse's galloping hooves beat to the rhythm of her heart's refrain: Why am I doing this, why? Why? *Why?*

Because I damn well want to! She answered at last. I don't care if he thinks me wanton. He stirred something in me, something I've never felt before.

Juli was right, she could do whatever she pleased until the moment she walked through the gates of the convent. And this damn well pleased her. Telling Luis her thoughts concerning the impostor—even apologizing to him for her mother—was just an excuse. She wanted to see him again. She needed to say good-bye.

An hour later she was within walking distance of the

cove. From there she led Starlight on foot to save her strength for the hard ride along the sandy beach and then back through the jungle to the harbor.

The sound of voices coming from the beach carried to her ears. She noticed then that the hawks had worked their way down and were perched on Starlight's saddle, their dark eyes sparkling in the sun. Fury brought the horse up short and strained to hear what was being said down below. Juli's brothers must have brought her ship back to the cove, she decided. Thank God, the *Rana* was safe—safe, providing Luis Domingo kept his word. She was about to call out when she heard loud cursing in what sounded like Portuguese. Instantly she tethered the horse, then set out, crouching low as she scrambled down the familiar terrain.

The blazing sun was beginning to make her light-headed. The jungle sounds were quiet now, evidence that someone was walking about. Would they recognize the signs of an alien presence? When there was no break in the conversation, Fury sighed in relief, then cautioned herself to move stealthily.

Panting with her efforts to remain unnoticed, she peered below for her first glimpse of the *Rana*—and sucked in her breath at the sight before her eyes. The black ship loomed ahead like a specter, but it wasn't *her* black ship. How . . . ?

Was this the ship Luis Domingo had seen? Or had he sighted the *Rana* herself? It had been scant hours since her frigate had sailed down the river. Suddenly she grew angry. Why should she be so surprised to see the impostor's ship here? she asked herself caustically. If Luis Domingo had figured out her hiding place, certainly the Sea Siren's impersonator could have done the same. After all, it was the perfect—if not the only—sanctuary in the vicinity. So much for thinking herself clever at covering her tracks.

Fury squinted to observe the ship more closely. Armed. A good-size crew if the number of men on deck was any indication. Where was the captain? Below decks, obviously. Should she stay in hiding to observe movement, or . . . She cast a critical eye at the sun. If she wanted to see Luis, she would have to leave now. But if she wanted to discover the identity of the impostor, she would have to remain.

Moments later Fury had reached a decision. She wasn't meant to see Luis again—circumstances dictated but one course of action. She wasn't leaving here until she saw the infamous poseur with her own eyes.

Settling herself behind the dense jungle growth, Fury waited, the sun beating down on her with a vengeance. Her mouth was parched, her wet clothes drying on her back. She brushed at hundreds of insects determined to suck her blood. She was itching from head to toe. If only she could slip into the cool cove water. But no, she had to think, to plan. . . . If the impostor had sailed up the River of Death, she was as apt as the real Sea Siren. And would be equally adept at sailing with the tide, unless . . . unless . . . *The mouth of the river had to be blocked.*

One clenched fist pounded the soft, loamy ground, releasing black specks and bits of greenery. A loud squawk of outrage from a jungle bird permeated the air. Immediately the men below quieted. Fury held her breath.

The voice she was waiting to hear was husky, alluring. Sultry. Fury parted the thick emerald leaves. "A jungle parrot," the woman sneered. "The same kind of jungle bird that gave me this!" She brandished her left arm for all to see.

Fury clamped a hand over her mouth, her eyes widening in surprise. No wonder Luis and the others had mistaken her for the Sea Siren. She wore an identical outfit, had the same long, streaming, dark hair, and had a scar on her arm that obviously passed for her mother's. With one crucial exception: the impostor's scar was on her *left* arm, whereas her mother's and her own were on the right.

But she was beautiful, Fury admitted. Achingly, gloriously beautiful. With the sun glittering down on the deck of the black ship, she looked like a golden goddess. Fury could see the men leering at her, but with one murderous glance she sent them back to their game of cards. Fury inched her way backward, grasping at vines and leaves to prevent herself from sliding forward.

Juli was waiting for her at the stable when she returned. In a choked voice she told the housekeeper what she'd just seen. "Did Father Sebastian leave?" she asked.

"Hours ago. Why?"

"I wanted to tell him to alert the Dutch East India Company. The mouth of the river has to be blocked. There's no other way for the impostor to get her ship out. None of them would last a day in the jungle on foot. I have to bathe and go into town. This will finally clear my mother's name. I can hardly believe it."

"You realize you missed Señor Domingo's departure, don't you?" Juli demanded as they walked back into the house.

"What would you have me do, Juli? I did my best. I thought it more advantageous to find out what I could about that miserable woman. She's in the *Rana*'s cove, don't you understand? I must warn the governors about her."

"I suppose so," Juli said reluctantly. "At least we no longer have to worry about the two men Mynheer Dykstra's had watching the house. They left at midafternoon. I suppose now that he has no chance of being made governor, Dykstra's lost interest in playing detective and building up his reputation at your expense."

Fury looked at Juli and grinned. "It's almost too bad, in a way. I was looking forward to using that balcony. . . ."

* * *

The town was dark when Fury reined in her horse at the parish house. She was on the ground in an instant, straightening her dress and smoothing back stray tendrils of hair that escaped the knot on top of her head. She strode off briskly toward the harbor, hoping against hope that the *Silver Lady* would still be at the wharf. Her heart sank at the sight of the empty slip.

"Looking for someone, little lady?" asked the harbormaster, coming up behind her. Fury whirled to find a kind looking old man with pure white hair staring at her with concern.

"The *Silver Lady*? Did she sail with the tide?"

"Aye, that she did. It was a busy hour this night. The governors left, as did Mynheer Dykstra. Man up and resigned his post—just like that."

Fury bit down on her lower lip. "I suspected he might. Are the offices empty?" she asked.

"Aye, and they'll remain closed until the new manager arrives. That's what the sign in the window says," the harbormaster said jovially.

"A poor way of doing business, if you ask me," Fury said tartly. "When my father was manager of the company, the doors were never closed."

The harbormaster shrugged. "It's getting late, little lady. You best be getting indoors before some of these scurvy seamen mistake you for one of . . . well, before they think Clarice let you out for a stroll. I'll walk with you if you have a destination in mind," he offered.

"The parish house," Fury said, looking about her curiously. Sure enough, she noticed a few seamen here and there, watching her with open interest. The same kind of seamen she'd seen in the cove.

When Fury knocked at the parish house door, Father Sebastian received her with stunned surprise. What young lady traveled about in the darkness doing God only knew what? Furana seemed to make a habit of it.

"What is it, child?" he asked, alarmed. "What's happened?"

Fury babbled then, the way the parrot in the kitchen did the moment his cage cover was removed. "So you see, Father," she concluded, "I can't alert the burghers. They will block the entrance to the river, and while it will seal the impostor's ship in the cove, it means I will never be able to return the *Rana* to her resting place. I don't think my mother would ever forgive me if I allowed that to happen. Oh, I truly don't know what to do. On the way into town I was convinced blocking the mouth of the river was the only sensible thing to do. Now the thought seems ridiculous. What am I to do?"

"Child, I wish I knew," the priest said wearily. "It all seems like a bad dream."

"Father," Fury said softly, her voice tinged with regret, "Luis—Señor Domingo was gone when I finally arrived at the harbor. Do you . . . were you there when he left?"

The old priest nodded. "I gave his ship and two others my blessing before they set out to sea. I don't believe sufficient stores were loaded on any of them. Mynheer Dykstra sailed his own ship. There was a diamond merchant with him, and a fine dandy he was. The governors, too, set sail, with much fanfare. At the last moment there was a delay when a young seaman left Mynheer Dykstra's ship and asked to sign on the *Silver Lady*. Mynheer Dykstra was most upset when the man refused to sail with him. But Señor Domingo was the first to leave." Father Sebastian spread his hands wide. "I'm sorry, Furana, I have nothing else to tell you."

"I'm going around in circles," Fury muttered. "Why is it so hard for me to make a decision? I feel that the impostor is going to attack Señor Domingo's ship . . .

needlessly, Father, because the diamond merchant is now carrying the gems himself, aboard Mynheer Dykstra's ship.'' She shook her head in confusion. ''Oh, it's all happened too quickly.''

''If Luis Domingo doesn't have the diamonds, he can't very well produce them for the impostor. All he has to do is tell her they're on Mynheer Dykstra's ship.'' The priest rubbed his gnarled fingers to ease the pain. ''What do you want me to do?'' he asked.

''Delay my . . . plead my case with the Mother Superior by way of the archbishop. If I sail after Señor Domingo, there is no guarantee I'll be able to return in time to enter the convent. I don't even know where Juli's brothers have hidden the *Rana*. It could take days for them to return and that much time again to set sail. Señor Domingo will have too much of a head start. A spell of bad weather could delay me even more. Will you intervene, Father?'' she pleaded.

''I'll do my best, child,'' Father Sebastian promised.

''That's all I ask,'' Fury said, relieved. ''If things don't work out, if I'm denied entrance to the convent for some reason, then I'll have to take it as a sign from God that I'm not to pursue my vocation.''

''Yes, that sounds reasonable to me.'' He wanted to beg her to stay the night, knowing full well no lady ever traveled alone in darkness—on horseback, no less. But this lady, so like her mother, did not follow the rules of propriety. And she was obviously determined to return to the casa.

''Thank you so much for listening to me, Father,'' Fury said, walking with him to the front door. ''I feel much better now. I'll have Juli or one of the other servants apprise you of whatever I decide to do.''

The night was inky black with a sprinkling of stars overhead. The sultry breeze blowing off the ocean tickled Fu-

ry's cheeks and neck. The streets were quiet, the houses
dark. For the first time she became aware of the late hour
and the long ride looming ahead of her. She'd come to
town on a fool's errand, but how was she to know the
Dutch East India Companys' manager had sailed on the
tide along with Luis Domingo and the governors? Why
had they left so soon? she wondered. Her father had told
her they sometimes stayed for months at a time. And Dykstra—how strange that he should leave on such short notice. Did he simply plan to abandon his house and his
holdings in Batavia? Did he plan to return? Who was to
succeed him in the Dutch East India Company's offices?
Why had the governors closed the offices?

Fury sat down on the parish steps, her elbows propped
on her knees, and tried to fathom the day's events. Dykstra, if he truly did suspect her mother's identity, wouldn't
let the matter fade away to nothing. He was an astute business manager, and as such he might have tried to strike a
bargain with the governors. Maybe he hadn't really been
passed over as governor; maybe it was just meant to look
that way.

The moment Fury was secure in the saddle, the horse
galloped off, nostrils flaring, mane whipping across her
tight hold on the reins.

There was a plan, she was certain of it. All she had to
do was puzzle it out. And she would start with Luis Domingo.

What man, she wondered, would give up a handsome
commission to return home to Spain with only sandalwood
in his hold? Dykstra had first hired him to set a trap for
the Sea Siren, and then he'd hired him to guard the diamond merchant on his trip back to Spain. As far as she
knew, Luis Domingo was not a rich man, and the commission would have been handsome. But he'd given it up,
or so he'd said. He'd also said he was not going to reveal

her identity or her mother's. Why? Because of Dykstra? But Dykstra wanted the Sea Siren, badly. How good was Domingo's word?

Then there was Peter Dykstra, who'd been passed over as governor in favor of a younger man, Father Sebastian said. That didn't make sense. The Dutch East India Company favored older, experienced men like her father and Dykstra. In ordering Luis Domingo to capture the Sea Siren, Dykstra could have been acting from personal interest alone. If so, mightn't it have had to do with revenge against her father, her mother, and herself? Yet, her father and Dykstra were the best of friends, and had been for years.

Third, the arrival of the governors was not, by itself, unusual. But the timing of their visit and their abrupt departure were. All details worthy of her attention.

And where did the diamond merchant fit into all of this? Fury wondered. Whose ship was he really sailing on? Or were the diamonds on one ship and the man on another?

So many questions, so few answers. What she had to do now was examine all the details and come up with answers. They, in turn, would lead her to a conclusion.

By the time she reached the casa Fury had a pounding headache. But she also had her answers. Upstairs, she looked longingly at her bed but knew she had to commit to paper her conclusions before she surrendered to sleep.

The diamonds, she wrote, were obviously worth more than she imagined. Possibly a million pesetas if the gems were flawless. Luis Domingo was carrying the diamonds, possibly in his seaman's bag, to throw off suspicion. The board of governors had indeed appointed Dykstra governor, but because of the Sea Siren's "reappearance" they'd come up with the ruse that had been enacted at the von Klausner soiree. Because, she scribbled, the resulting furor would draw attention away from the diamond consignment. Furthermore, the woman posing as the Sea Siren had already accosted Luis Domingo twice and knew he was sailing with only sandalwood in his hold, sandalwood she didn't want. The diamond merchant was sailing on Peter Dykstra's ship, the governors on a third ship. A small convoy, of sorts, but who would be escorting whom?

Fury leaned back in her chair, her temples throbbing. Something niggled at her, something the priest said. A detail, an important one. Fury massaged her temples, knowing the answer would come to her if she could just relax and think about something else for a little while.

She thought of her parents and the games she'd played with her younger bro— The young man who had signed on Luis's ship at the last moment! Father Sebastian had said Mynheer Dykstra had been upset. That little detail had to mean something.

Fury was off her chair in a second, twirling around in a dizzying circle. Of course, he was a member of the impostor's crew! He'd changed ships at the last moment to allow someone at the harbor to inform the impersonator that the diamonds were aboard Luis's ship.

She had it all now. The question was, what should she do? What *could* she do? There was no way to overtake the small convoy at this time. She could sail in a jolly boat down the river and into the cove and attack the impostor. But it was such a foolhardy idea, she felt disgusted with herself for even thinking of it. Her other alternative was to wait for Juli's brothers to return and take her own ship. Somewhere en route she'd lie in wait for the impostor and attack her ship, thereby granting safe conduct for Luis and the convoy.

Fury threw herself on the bed, burying her face in the pillow. "I'll never see him again. He'll never know for certain I am my mother's daughter. Someday," she cried into the pillow, "he might hear a story of this coming battle and remember me."

A stiff breeze ruffled the bedcovers as Gaspar sailed into the room, his talons searching for the bedrail. His wings rustled and fluttered as he inched his way to the pillow Fury lay upon. "I tried to see him again," she whispered brokenly. "I wanted to see him, but it wasn't meant to be. All I can do now is try to make his journey as safe as possible. He . . . I could love him," she sobbed. "Now I . . . I couldn't even say good-bye." She rolled over and sat up, tears streaming down her cheeks. "And what will become of you and Pilar when I go to the convent?" A fresh wave of sobs broke out.

Gaspar moved one talon until he had a corner of the sheet gripped securely. He brought it up gently, offering it to Fury as though it were a prize of great value. She sobbed all the harder.

An angry *swoosh* of air stirred in the room as Pilar took her place next to Gaspar. The hawks stared at the sobbing girl, then Gaspar moved, his wing tips gently wiping the tears from Fury's cheeks. She broke down completely then, throwing herself deeper into the pillow. The startled birds looked at each other, their wings fanning the bed furiously. Pilar lifted her wings until she was satisfied with the draft she created and sailed straight up and out through the open doors, Gaspar in her wake.

Up they flew, into the dark night, high above the jungle trees, and out over open water, their wings flapping together as their jet eyes searched the vast expanse of dark water.

Two days later, as the sun prepared to dip beyond the horizon, Juli's youngest brother arrived at the casa. He was overwrought, wild-eyed. "I saw . . . I couldn't believe my eyes . . . I knew I'd just left your ship and my brothers, but there it was—the black ship sailing from the River of Death. I couldn't see clearly, but the woman at the wheel . . . I swore she was you. I almost killed myself getting here. It was the woman posing as you, Capitana!'' the young man said breathlessly.

Fury nodded. "How long ago?''

"A little past first light. It will take us three days to rendezvous with your ship if we leave now.''

"Juli, I . . .''

The housekeeper had a sudden vision of her brother returning to the casa with Fury's dead, broken body. She threw her arms around Fury in a fierce hug. "You could encounter the impostor. I have every confidence in your ability, but . . .''

"But what?'' Fury asked quietly.

"If she wants the diamonds as badly as we think she does, she'll do anything. Her men are seasoned cutthroats. My brothers are husbands, family men. They can defend themselves, but a fight to the death, if it comes to that . . . They're no match for such men.''

Fury nodded. "I've thought of that. I plan to discuss it with them once I board my ship, give them a chance to remain onshore without any loss of face. I'll have Gaspar and Pilar with me.''

"In case you haven't noticed, Miss Fury, those evil-looking creatures have been absent for two days.''

"They often disappear for days at a time,'' Fury said lightly.

"Since when?'' Juli demanded. "They hover about here like bees at a honey pot. Even at night I hear them.''

"I'm not worried, Juli, and I don't want you to worry. I'll be back here before you know it, in plenty of time to . . . to do what I have to do. Now, fetch my things so we can be on our way.''

How young this boy was, she thought, and his wife about to give birth to their first child. She smiled at him, seeing the relief in his face at the knowledge he would be returning to his small cottage and his family.

Where were the hawks? Her stomach lurched at the thought of sailing completely alone, something she knew she couldn't do. Everything was wrong; she could feel it in her bones. Every instinct in her warned against this voyage. Give it up, this is a foolhardy thing you're doing. You can't possibly overtake the impostor, do battle, and win . . . not singlehandedly. *Oh, Gaspar, where are you?*

"I hate it when you cry, Juli," Fury said as she prepared to take her leave. "Only weak women cry; women who can't take charge of their destinies. You of all people should know that. Now, when I return I expect to see that handsome houseboy of the von Klausners—what's his name? Aldo?—on your arm proposing marriage. I promise to spend all my time thinking about a suitable wedding present," she teased.

"You take care of her!" Juli growled to her brother as they rode away. "Don't shame me. Tell the others what I've said, too!"

The moment Fury stepped aboard the *Rana*, her confidence returned. "All hands to the quarter deck," she shouted, her eyes on the sky for some sign of the hawks. When her crew was assembled, she made her announcement. The brothers all looked at one another, shuffling their feet.

At last the oldest spoke. "Does the capitana think we aren't capable men?" he asked brusquely.

"Not at all," Fury replied. "I think you're more than capable, and I'm proud to sail with you. It's your families. . . . I don't think I could live with myself if anything happened to you. Juli would never forgive me. There's no telling how much of a fight this impostor will put up, and I've no idea whether I can best her. We might be evenly matched in a fight, but . . . what I mean is, I know you are capable men, but . . ."

The oldest of the brothers grimaced. "We're with you, Capitana, and I don't think you need concern yourself with our well-being. All of us have been to sea and can defend ourselves as well as one another."

Fury looked from one to the other, warmed and gratified by the stout confidence, the allegiance, she saw shining in their eyes. At last she smiled and nodded. "All right, then. We sail a westerly course through the Sunda Strait to open water and then a northwest course. We have a stiff breeze now and can possibly make up some time."

She brought the glass to her eye to scan the sky overhead. "Gaspar, where are you?" she murmured. She'd been watching for hours, the bright sun blinding her, but still she searched. She should never have allowed herself to become so attached to them. "Please God," she prayed, "let them be safe; they belong to You, as do all creatures great and small. Keep them safe and return them to me this one last time. When I leave this worldly place to join You, I will give them up to You. Until that time . . ." She sobbed deep in her throat and ran below to her cabin, where she wept in private—great heart-wrenching sobs at her loss. "Be merciful," she pleaded. "They aren't wild birds any longer, they can't fend for themselves. They need me," she wept into her pillow. "And I need someone to need me, to want me, beside You."

The *Silver Lady* sliced through the crystal blue water at a speed approaching eleven knots, the Dutch ships trailing in her wake at less than nine. It irritated Luis that Peter Dykstra and the governors of Amsterdam considered the *Silver Lady* an escort, while in truth the Dutch ships were *his* escort.

"Carry the diamonds aboard the *Silver Lady*, and my

lips are sealed regarding the Sea Siren's identity,'' Dykstra
had promised. It was his final offer. Luis had argued with
Dykstra, called himself every name he could think of, be-
rated himself, cursed himself . . . but in the end he'd
agreed to bring the diamonds aboard. At this moment they
rested in a velvet-lined cask marked VINEGAR in crude
black letters.

All he wanted was to return to Spain in a healthy condition so he could lick his wounds and start over. He didn't
want the Dutchman's commission or his damnable diamonds, but he was stuck with both, thanks to his feelings
for Fury van der Rhys. He hadn't meant to fall in love,
but he had. And now that love would be his undoing.

"Women," he snorted, "should be put together on an
island so they could make one another miserable instead
of wreaking havoc with men's hearts.''

He should have gone to the casa; he'd had the time to
say good-bye. Why hadn't he gone when the priest suggested it? Because, he told himself, he didn't dare gaze
upon Fury's beautiful face. He knew he would have
begged, like a fool, to . . . to . . .

Luis whipped the glass to his eye, more to drive the
thoughts from his head than to scan the waters surrounding
him. He felt bruised, battered, and sad of heart at his loss.
Would there ever be another woman who could stir him
as Fury had done?

"Captain, Captain . . . look! Overhead! What is it? Jesus Christ! It's those devil birds! Captain! Look!''

"I see them. Quiet!'' he roared. He watched, mesmerized at the sight of the black birds in the distance. A chill
raced down his arms. Wherever the birds were, Fury was
close by. . . . They were closer now, their wings fanning
the air, their screeches carrying on the stiff breeze.

Soon the hawks were directly overhead, circling the mainmast at a dizzying speed. Luis's heart began to pound. Why were they here? Where was Fury?

Up, up, up they soared in a straight line until they were almost out of sight. Luis brought the glass to his eye and could see only the brilliant blue sky. Then, suddenly, he saw both birds descend at a speed equal to a cannon shot. He swallowed, his heart in his mouth, when Gaspar checked his descent in midair, his wings flapping to create his own breeze, before he settled on the ship's quarter rail, just inches from where Luis was standing. The moment Pilar took her position nearby, he let his breath out in a long, explosive sigh.

"What . . . what do they want?" Julian asked fearfully.

"How the hell do I know!" Luis muttered. "Bring some meat, they could be hungry." He waited until Julian had returned with a slab of salt pork, then advanced toward them.

"Hawhawhawhaw," the birds chorused.

"And I'm supposed to know what that sound means," Luis grated out.

Their glittering eyes boring into him, Luis advanced with the pail of meat Julian handed him. The birds ignored the food. Gaspar's wing tip feathered out to touch Luis on the shoulder, and Pilar worked hers until she could trace a pattern in the distance. Luis's eyes widened. He turned to face the east, his eyes full of questions. When Gaspar's talon reached out to grasp his arm, he felt no pain and realized the bird's intention was not to hurt him, but to make him turn until he was facing the two Dutch ships sailing in his wake.

In an instant the birds were off the railing and swooping upward, their wings flapping angrily, their screeches keen and shrill. He watched as the birds circled overhead before flying off in an easterly direction.

"We're changing course," Luis ordered. "Turn this

goddamn ship around. Now!'' Overhead, the hawks called their approval before descending to the mizzenmast, where they clung wearily.

"No man touches those birds!'' Luis thundered. "Full speed. All hands on deck!'' To the Dutch ships he was about to pass, he roared again, "Continue or follow me, it's your choice!''

"What in the goddamn hell do you think you're doing, Domingo?'' Dykstra shouted.

"What does it look like I'm doing? I changed course. I have some unfinished business to take care of. If you want your cargo, come alongside. Be quick about it!''

"I'll do better than that. I'm coming aboard,'' Dykstra roared.

"Suit yourself, but if you miss your footing, I've no time to fish you from the water.''

"Where the hell are you going?'' Dykstra called a second time.

Luis ignored the question. "What's it to be, Dykstra? Do you want your cargo or not? You can follow me if you want.''

Listening to this exchange, Cato almost fell from his position in the rigging. What was he to do? If the Dutchman came aboard, he himself would stay. If the cargo was shifted to the other ship, he would give himself away if he tried to board her. Filled with anxiety, he waited for the Dutchman to make his decision and almost fainted in relief when Dykstra gave the order to change course. The diamonds would remain aboard.

Suddenly he whirled, the hackles on the back of his neck rising. Until this moment he'd thought the devilish birds were high in the mast. If he moved, even slightly, they would be on him in a minute. Christ, he hated them, hated their beady black eyes. It was some kind of omen, he was sure of it.

An hour later Cato was in the same position in the rigging, the hawks only inches away. Luis's eyes narrowed as he watched the birds watching the young man. If they wanted to, they could have toppled him in a second; instead, they chose to keep an eye on him. Why?

Pilar's feathers rustled ominously. Gaspar's head dipped slightly as he prepared to fan out his wings. He was in the air in a second, Pilar working the light breeze he created to follow. "I'll be goddamned!" Luis muttered. They understood what he was saying. Half his brain negated what he'd just observed, but the other half believed implicitly. Cato's white face told him he too was a believer.

Luis watched Cato as he moved off, his head jerking backward with every few steps he took. He looked around sheepishly before he spoke. "If you're as tired as I think you are, then you should rest. I'll keep my eyes on the boy. Your food is on the quarter deck."

"Hawhawhawhaw," Gaspar responded.

"I'll be goddamned," Luis muttered over and over as he strode about the ship. "If I didn't see it with my own eyes, I wouldn't believe it." Craning his neck for one last look at the birds clinging to the mainmast, he wasn't surprised to see their glittering eyes follow his every step.

Now, alone in his cabin, he could think about what the hawks' arrival meant. Fury must be in danger. Either she'd sent the birds after him, or they'd come on their own, which left her without their protection. Luis could feel his stomach start to churn. The hawks seemed content to nest in the mainmast and sail at eleven knots, which had to mean she was in no immediate danger.

The relief Luis felt was so sudden, so overwhelming, he tripped over his own feet, sprawling crossways atop an extra water barrel stored on deck. His curse was ripe and flowery until he saw Gaspar take wing and sail down in his direction. "Son of a bitch!" he muttered, certain the hawk was going to attack him. Instead, Gaspar worked the breeze and seemed to float in the air over his head. When he felt the slight feathering on the back of his neck as he struggled to his feet, he realized the bird was hovering *protectively*.

"I'm all right," he said helplessly. In disbelief he watched the huge bird fan his wings and sail upward in the breeze he created for himself.

A long time later Luis smiled to himself. What was the beautiful, elegant Furana van der Rhys going to say when she found out her goddamn birds were enamored of him? More important, what was his crew thinking about him? He'd seen their sly looks and their fear whenever the birds appeared. They think I'm insane, he thought, and they could be right. What sea captain carrying a fortune in precious diamonds would change course because of two black birds?

One of these days, when the time was right, he'd give his crew a lecture on trust—birds and . . . women. But for now he would content himself with seeking out the newest member of his crew for a . . . chat.

Chapter Twelve

The moment Rego arrived, Amalie set sail for the Sunda Strait, her destination Sumatra, where she would lay in fresh stores and then head for open water. The galleon and brigantine ivory remained behind in the thick gray mist at the mouth of the river, unmanned and ghostly.

Amalie felt paralyzed with fear, an emotion she hated but seemed unable to conquer. She was shaking now, her stomach churning as she contemplated what might happen to her. For some reason she'd always thought she would grow old regally and die in her bed, bedecked with jewels and all her servants in attendance.

The moment Cato left the ship she'd been assailed with doubts of every description. Her instincts told her to give up the diamonds, take what booty she'd salvaged, and return to Saianha. The ivory alone would make her a wealthy woman for the rest of her days. But just when she'd been about to follow through, a vision of the diamonds had appeared before her—a small mountain of them, all shimmery and sparkly. Worthy of a queen and belonging to a kingdom. She couldn't give them up.

Amalie's throat closed at the thought of meeting up with the real Sea Siren, the one her father was so obsessed with, the one who had killed him in the end. *She has no equal*, her father had written. On another page he'd said no man was capable of besting her. He'd died for his efforts, and here she was, foolish enough to think she could succeed where so many others had failed.

For days now she'd been debating with herself about telling the crew what she was after. If they knew of the diamonds, they would fight with her and for her, but when it was all over they would kill her. If the diamonds were divided among her men, they could live in splendor for the rest of their lives.

It was too late for anything now save forging ahead. If she did anything else, she would lose Cato, which would be even worse than losing the diamonds. That particular thought had made her blood run cold. Never, until now, had she believed love would rule her mind and her heart.

Then a second thought struck her, one she'd done her best to ignore for days. If she was caught, she would be turned over to the authorities and either hung or imprisoned for life. Her stomach fluttered warningly at the prospect. Perhaps she should give it all up and return home. Cato knew where she lived. Somehow he would find her.

"Bitch!" she spat out, disgusted with herself. "I want those diamonds, and I mean to have them!"

Seething, Amalie stomped her way from the wheelhouse to the deck. Her crew scattered on sight, busying themselves with the endless task of keeping the frigate seaworthy. She leaned against the quarter deck rail and watched her men go about their duties, lulled by the sounds of water slapping against the hull of the ship. She was calmer now, her breathing deep and regular. Her eyes strayed to the top of the mizzenmast, and she wondered what it would feel like to climb to the top and survey the ocean. Exhilarating, no doubt, but she would not do it. Nothing, she thought morbidly, would drive away this accursed fear. *Too late* . . . it was too late to do anything but stay on course. Whatever was going to happen would happen.

It was dark, she realized suddenly. She'd missed the sun

sinking red-gold behind the horizon. How had she failed to notice the end of a day? She lifted her face to the open sky, relishing the crisp tang of the salt sea as a million stars winked down upon her.

"Mount a square topsail," she shouted. "I want speed, this wind is too favorable to lose. We can make eleven knots easily." Damn their eyes, she hated every one of them. Dirty, filthy drunkards, red-faced from rum and grog.

Amalie's anger drove away her fear as she watched her men mount the topsail. "I could do it faster myself," she shouted.

"Then come up here and do it," came the surly reply.

In a frenzy Amalie scrambled her way up the mast to the insolent seaman. Unsheathing her cutlass, she lashed out at him, slicing the man's arm from shoulder to wrist. He bellowed in pain and fear as he toppled down, down . . . to land on the deck in a crumpled heap.

"Throw him in irons!" Amalie screamed. "I'll have nothing less than respect on his ship. Hear me well, you scurvy lot. The next man goes over the side!" She could hear their muttered curses as they dragged the bleeding man below.

For six days Amalie prowled the decks of her ship like a tiger in search of food. She had not been able to sustain her anger, and her fear was as ripe and rotting as week-old fruit. The need to cry was overwhelming at times. She wished constantly for Cato.

On the seventh day there came a shout from the rigging. "Sail ho!"

"Where away?" Amalie called.

"Dead ahead, thirty knots. She appears to be at anchor. Possibly repairs."

"In the middle of the ocean?" Amalie cried, incredulous.

"She's weighed anchor," came the stubborn reply.

Amalie ran to the bow of the ship and brought the glass to her eye. Damn his eyes, he was right. Only one ship. Where was the Dutchman's escort? Unless the ship didn't belong to the Dutchman, but to someone else, the only person brave enough to weigh anchor in the middle of the sea to . . . lie in wait. She knew in her gut that the ship was black, and the moment the clouds passed across the sun, she would have all the proof she needed.

Now that there was virtually no breeze, her ship's progress slowed. By the time they were within a five-knot range it would be dark. Amalie could feel herself start to tremble.

"Rego, come here," she called softly. "Pass the word, the moment we're within range I want that ship fired on. The shots had damn well better make their mark, or the gunners will be swimming home. Pass the word and do it quietly, voices carry over the water. If we've spotted her, she's spotted us."

"I see her on our stern," Fury called jubilantly. "The wind's dying. One hour, two at the most, and she'll be close enough to fire upon. All we need is two good shots, one on her bow and one broadside. Hoist the anchor. I don't want to make it too easy for her. Quickly now, men. We can't give her the advantage."

"Aye, Capitana. Do you have a mind to play a little game with the black ship?" her first mate inquired in an amused voice.

Fury's soft laughter tinkled across the water. "In a manner of speaking. The cat is always faster than the rat."

Her first mate laughed with her. He had every confidence in this strange young woman with her scanty costume. He listened with interest as she described what she was going to do.

"We'll sail like a bolt of lightning, this way and then that way, a jagged pattern, so to speak. Let her think we're limping and making repairs. She'll think she frightens us. Dawn will provide us with all the light we need to bring about a confrontation. This matter is going to be laid to rest once and for all. She'll never plunder those diamonds in my mother's name,'' Fury vowed. ''If I have to, I'll kill her.''

Amalie watched Fury's zigzag pattern through the glass, the smoke pots creating eerie yellow circles on the water. ''She's playing a game. She's been lying in wait for us. It's to be cat and rat at first light. We'll hold our own, never fear,'' she called to Rego, who passed the word down the line of nervous crewmen.

Amalie cringed when she heard a sound she couldn't identify at first.

''She's laughing at you,'' Rego said. ''I've heard tales of the Sea Siren's laughter, musical as a bell, they say.'' He hunkered into himself.

''You're a gambling man,'' Amalie declared in return. ''Who do you wager will win this . . . confrontation?'' Rego took so long in answering, she lashed out at him with her booted foot. ''I suppose the others are of the same opinion,'' she sneered.

''She's been sailing the seas for over twenty years,'' Rego said hesitantly.

''That makes her an old woman, Rego. Can an old woman best me? Miguel didn't fare too well against me, and I'm a mere woman. What do you have to say to that?''

''I say . . . you will need all the good-luck charms and prayers you have at your disposal. There will be no mutiny on this ship, if that is what you fear. We fear the wrath of the woman on our bow. You would do well to fear the Sea Siren,'' Rego said brazenly, not caring if he upset his captain or not. He wanted to live, and at this moment he didn't give a whit about the cargo she was bent on capturing. Cato, his best friend, had whispered to him that the cargo she was after was a fortune in diamonds and had sworn him to secrecy, promising to appoint him a prince in Amalie's kingdom. He'd just wiped away that promise with his bold, honest opinions. Besides, he didn't believe for one minute that Cato was going to be a king. He didn't believe his captain was going to be a queen either. Kings and queens wore crowns and royal robes. His young face puckered in disgust at his friend's fairy-tale beliefs.

Men were all alike, Amalie thought bitterly. The little skirmishes she'd participated in to prove herself to her crew were nothing in comparison with what would happen shortly. If only she knew for certain that it was the real Siren lying in wait for her, she would . . . do nothing differently than she was doing, she decided.

The thought occurred to her that she could weigh her own anchor or change course, but if she did that, the Siren could come at her from behind or broadside. For the moment she had the advantage—an advantage she intended to keep.

Luis's neck ached with the strain of holding his head steady to peer through the glass. He felt as if he'd been dragged over rough terrain by a runaway horse. For more hours than he could remember he'd done nothing but keep his eye pressed to the glass, and the strain was starting to affect his position with the crew. And now it was almost a new day, he thought tiredly as he accepted a mug of steaming coffee from his first mate.

"If you like, Captain, I'll take the watch," Julian offered. "A wash and a shave will go a long way to easing your tiredness."

Luis nodded and handed the spyglass to his first mate. The moment he closed the wheelhouse door behind him, his shoulders drooped. A wash and shave would feel good. A clean shirt wouldn't hurt, either, he decided.

The faint breeze circling about him felt good. He looked up and noticed the first gray streaks of dawn. A second later he realized the breeze wasn't coming from the ocean, but from the rigging. He arched his neck to see better in the grayish light, and his blood ran cold at the sight of the black birds sailing straight up into the air at a dizzying speed. They continued to circle the topsail, their wings fanning the air furiously. A moment later they were higher than he could see. His eyes burning, he ran from the wheelhouse for his spyglass, all signs of weariness gone.

"Where the hell are they?" he roared minutes later when the gray sky remained clear. He heard them before they came into sight, diving toward the ship faster than a thunderbolt. Gaspar, his wings feathered inward, plunged straight to the bow where Luis was standing. The Spaniard sucked in his breath as the bird fanned his wings and swept outward, away from the railing, just as Pilar rocketed behind him. They worked the breeze to stay aloft at eye level until Luis raised his hand to show he understood. He watched as both birds arrowed a westerly course.

"I'm changing course," Julian shouted before Luis could issue an order.

Luis brought the glass to his eye, straining to see in the early light. There was no sign of the hawks, nor had he expected any. They were on their way to Fury. Their temporary visit was at an end.

He could feel his heart pounding in his chest. Fury was close now. The hawks had come to him for help. If she were in mortal danger, they wouldn't have stayed with him so long. Whatever was about to happen was going to happen soon.

"Tighten sail, full speed!" he roared. He wished then that he, too, could soar and fly to Fury as the hawks had done.

"Now, what the hell are you doing?" Peter Dykstra raged across the water. "You're following those goddamn birds, aren't you?'' He shook his fist in the air. ''I want you to turn your ship around and sail a steady course. Stop this foolishness immediately!''

''This is my ship, Dykstra, and if you don't like what I'm doing, fire me,'' Luis called back. ''I never wanted your job in the first place. If you want your cargo, I'll lower it in one of the jolly boats. I have no intention of getting myself killed so you can live to be a rich man. The Sea Siren is out there, or maybe I should say both Sea Sirens are out there. One way or another, she's going to come after your cargo. It's my decision to meet her head on. She won't be expecting this kind of maneuver.''

''You're insane,'' Dykstra said hoarsely. Yet in his heart he knew the Spaniard spoke the truth. He lowered his eyes until he was facing the scurvy crew he'd hired at the last minute. To a man, they would cut him down the moment they discovered the true contents of his cargo.

''Follow him,'' the diamond merchant called in a feeble voice. ''I'm paying you to take my orders, and I'm *ordering* you to follow Captain Domingo!''

''I'm filing charges against you the moment we reach Spain, Domingo,'' Dykstra blustered. ''You won't like languishing in a Spanish prison.''

''Then you'll be right alongside me,'' Luis snarled. ''And my countrymen will not be kind to a Dutchman. Think about that, Mynheer.'' He turned to Julian. ''Tie the vinegar cask to the jolly boat and lower it.''

''No, no, no!'' the diamond merchant screamed. ''I'm paying *you*, not Mynheer Dykstra. I've made no demands on you. I want you to continue!''

Luis was gracious in his acquiescence. ''But I want your assurance that our bargain is sealed,'' he called to Dykstra.

Dykstra bristled. ''I'm a man of my word!''

"Dykstra, you're a man of *many* words. Just one will do this time. Is it a bargain?"

"*Yes*, damn you!" Dykstra bellowed.

"Sail ho!" came the cry from the rigging.

"I see two sets of sails," came a second cry.

"Where away?" Luis shouted.

"Dead ahead on our bow, Captain. She's sailing at seven knots."

"Man your stations," Luis ordered. "Fire only when I give the command!"

"She's gaining on us, Capitana. We're ready to fire when you give the order," Fury's first mate shouted excitedly. "Capitana, look, to the west!"

Fury whirled, the glass to her eye. "Gaspar!" she cried. "Pilar! You came back!"

Faster than a cannonball, the hawks were on the ship's railing, their talons curled securely on the shiny brass, their glittering eyes fixed on Fury's excited face.

"Where have you been? Oh, I don't care where you've been, only that you're here safe and sound. I knew you'd come, I knew it! It's not time for me to leave you . . . yet." She bent low, her head between the two birds as she stroked their silky backs. "Go up, Gaspar, high in the rigging in case shots are fired," she urged. "Pilar, stay with him."

"Sail ho! On our bow, three ships. I can see the Spaniard on the bow. The frigate on our stern is gaining. What should we do, Capitana?" shouted the youngest of Juli's brothers.

"Those on our bow are . . . friendly. I think," Fury muttered. So *that's* where the hawks had been; they'd gone after Luis! She laughed, a sound of pure joy. Leaping to the stern, she nicked the air in a salute to the birds perched on the mizzenmast.

"Hawhawhawhaw," came the response.

The sudden roar of a cannon shot split the early-morning dawn. "Fire!" Fury shouted. "She's in your sights. Rip her bow to splinters. Broadside now! On the count of three!"

Black smoke spiraled upward on the gentle trade winds, obliterating all view of the pirate ship. Her own ship rocked crazily beneath her feet. "We've been hit, Capitana, our stern!"

"Shore up this ship!" Fury ordered as a second wave of cannon fire thundered through the air. This time the volley of shots came from the Spaniard's ship.

"Try hitting the ship instead of the water, señor!" Fury called to Luis. "You do me no good if you can't knock her guns out."

"Ungrateful bitch!" Luis muttered as he gave a second order to fire. His own ship took a volley of shots then, splintering his bow just beneath his feet. "Fire, goddamn you!" he raged. "Not this black ship, the one on her stern. Drive her into the sea!"

"All hands on deck!" Fury shouted. "Mount the shrouds and yardarms. I'm going to steer this ship directly astern at full speed, and our bow will puncture hers. She won't have time to turn her sail. She's taking on water; one of us got off a good shot. *Fire!*" The impostor was dead ahead, and Fury could see the men scrambling on deck as she shouted orders.

A deafening crash sounded as the cannonball made contact with the enemy ship. As the ram punctured her bow, large splinters of wood flew in the air. Men toppled overboard as other seamen rushed to secure the cannon that was no longer stationary. The crackling and rendering of the ship was ear-splitting.

Fury raced to the bow, her hand on the hilt of the cutlass as several of Amalie's men leapt aboard her frigate. Out of the corner of her eye she saw Juli's brothers defend themselves with an expertise she hadn't known they possessed. Once she risked a glance in the direction of the Spaniard's ship. The entire crew was gathered at the rail, watching *her*, waiting to see if she needed their help.

"I want to see you before I kill you!" she shouted to Amalie, who was standing on what was left of her stern. She was truly magnificent, Fury thought, every bit as beautiful as her mother must have been years ago as she, too, had stood in just such a position, ready to do battle. It never occurred to her that she was equally as magnificent to those watching.

Amalie leapt aboard the *Rana*, landing less than a foot away. "You aren't old at all," she exclaimed, brandishing her cutlass.

Fury laughed. "Why should I be old?" she said. "I'm not real; I'm a legend you refused to let die, and for that *you* will die." She smiled at the rage in the impostor's eyes.

"You're as real as I am!" Amalie snarled. "Blood will spout from your veins just as it will from mine. You're no spirit!" Fury smiled grimly as she unsheathed her cutlass.

"Do something!" Dykstra shrieked to Luis.

"I believe the situation is well in hand, Mynheer Dykstra," the Spaniard called back. "We have only to wait for the outcome. Your cargo is safe."

Dykstra was so upset, he fairly jittered in response. "Look *again*, Captain!"

Luis shaded his eyes to see through the thick black smoke circling upward from the impostor's ship. He'd been so intent on watching Fury and her adversary, he'd ignored the pirate's men, who were now attacking from all directions. Bedlam broke out as Dykstra's crew joined in the battle, followed by the governor's men. Luis and his own crew were the last to leap into the fray.

"Look to your back, Siren!" he shouted over to Fury, who turned with the speed of a cat and slicked her cutlass with a high, wide arch. She watched in horror as her attacker's arm as well as his cutlass rolled across the deck. She whirled back just in time to see Amalie bearing down on her.

All about her the air was filled with shouts and screams as metal clanged against metal. Shots seemed to come from nowhere, and most neither knew nor cared whom they were killing and wounding.

Great black clouds of pungent smoke rolled about the cluster of ships, making visibility almost impossible. Fury rubbed her eyes and backed away to search for firmer footing, all the while intent on the advancing figure of the impostor.

"I want those diamonds," Amalie said hoarsely.

"No," Fury shouted. "Your days of plundering in the Siren's name are over. Give quarter now and I'll spare your life. Prison is better than dying here, with this scurvy lot you call a crew. What's it to be?"

"Never!" Amalie brought up her cutlass.

Slowly Fury raised her own weapon. "So be it," she said, her voice deadly calm. Flexing her knees and lashing out with a sudden thrust, she drove Amalie backward. Amalie recovered quickly, slashing upward at Fury's cutlass. Stunned with the force of the blow, Fury stumbled but recovered quickly and jabbed straight for Amalie's midsection. Daintily she sidestepped, then lashed out again, this time glancing down the side of Amalie's scarred arm to draw blood.

Hatred spewed from Amalie's eyes as she jabbed upward, knocking Fury against the railing. She crouched and with both hands on the cutlass whipped the blade up and down and down again until Fury was bent over the railing, her weapon held crossways in front of her. "I'll kill you for this, you miserable bitch!" Amalie screamed.

Suddenly she sensed a presence behind her and dropped

to her haunches, swiveling as she lashed upward to drive the weapon from Luis Domingo's hands. Her shrill laughter echoed off the water as the Spaniard stumbled backward, losing his footing. Immediately two of Amalie's cutthroats were on him as Fury lashed out, slicing close to her opponent's skull. She feinted to the right and thrust downward, missing Amalie's back by a hairbreadth. But the momentum carried her forward, and she slipped and lost her footing, the cutlass flying from her hands. Frantically she scrambled for her weapon as Amalie bore down on her.

In a sudden burst of speed, Gaspar swooped downward from his perch in the rigging, Pilar in his wake. Wild, shrill screeches ripped from their mouths as Gaspar dove straight for Amalie's slender back.

Amalie threw up her arms to ward off the deadly attack, her eyes filled with terror. She shrieked with pain as Gaspar raked her shoulder with his talons. Blood spurted everywhere. Pilar circled around her, her screams more shrill than Gaspar's. In the blink of an eye she had Fury's cutlass in her talons, offering it to the young woman as if it were a precious prize.

With a frenzied shake of his feathers, Gaspar outstripped the wind as he plunged upward in preparation of a killing dive that would render Amalie helpless.

Breathing raggedly, Fury crouched low as she prepared to leap over the pool of blood. Out of the corner of her eye she saw Luis fighting for his life. "Pilar!" she screamed. "Over there!" She jerked her head in the Spaniard's direction.

"This places me in your debt," Luis called as the hawk distracted his opponent long enough to enable him to heave his cutlass upward in a mighty thrust.

"They're leaving!" Fury spat angrily as the governors' ship hoisted anchor. "They value their precious lives more than they value honor! Dykstra is leaving, too. He wants to live to enjoy his new role as governor. Tell me, señor, whose ship carries the cargo?'' Fury demanded raggedly. "In case you haven't noticed, we're outnumbered. Give it up before more of your men are killed. These scurve will fight to the death!''

In a makeshift cell in the hold of Luis's ship, Cato worked at his bonds. Amalie's scream of terror was still ringing in his ears. Already his wrists and hands were slippery with his own blood, fingers numb with his efforts to free himself. When the rope slid over his hands at last, he leapt up and raced to the galley for the vinegar cask. Up on deck, no one paid him any mind as he leapt over wounded bodies in search of Amalie. Suddenly he stopped, watching in horror. Gaspar, sleek as an arrow, was hovering over Amalie menacingly as Fury approached, cutlass in hand.

Amalie, one eye on the black bird and the other on Fury, cast away all fear the moment she heard Cato call out to her. Drawing on every ounce of strength left in her body, she lashed out at Fury with her cutlass, knocking the blade from Fury's hand with unbelievable force. She crouched, feinted, and leapt in the air just as Gaspar's talons crunched down on her neck. The force of his descent pulled her backward, and as she groped to remain upright, her blade sliced into Gaspar's chest. The sleek bird dropped to the deck with a cry of pain that pierced Fury to her soul.

The sound carried on the wind to Pilar, who turned in midair, circling the frenzied melee. Up she swirled, higher and higher, screeching her own cry of pain, then she swooped down, ripping and clawing as she raced back and forth across the bloodied decks.

"No, Pilar, she's mine!'' screamed Fury, her eyes

blinded with tears. The hawk halted and dropped to the deck, her wings feathering out to protect her fallen mate.

Every curse, every epithet she'd ever heard, ripped from Fury's snarling mouth. "Kill my bird, will you! I'll run you through till your blood covers these decks. Murdering bitch! I'll slice every inch of flesh from your body, I'll gouge your eyes till you're blind, and while you're dying, I'll laugh! No quarter!" she snarled, her teeth bared in hatred. Luis gawked and moved backward, noticing that the odds of battle had dwindled to his and Fury's benefit, thanks to the avenging black birds.

Luis watched, his heart in his mouth, his eyes filled with admiration as Fury battled with Amalie. To his first mate, Julian, he roared, "Drive these cutthroats over the side. There's to be no interference. No quarter!"

Glazed, hate-filled eyes glittered at Fury as she slashed out again and again. Up and down the cutlass slicked until Amalie's blouse was in shreds, her bare breasts exposed to the men on deck. "Whore!" Amalie shrilled, stumbling backward.

Fury's blade lashed out again, faster than lightning, curling a streak of rushing blood on the impostor's breast. "The *S* is so you'll remember this moment as you die!" Fury cried, laughing maniacally. Amalie's blade sliced upward, but she danced nimbly away. "Now, Pilar! Pin her to the rail!" she screamed as she drove her opponent backward.

Pilar rose on her talons, her wings fluttering dangerously as she sailed upward to obey her mistress's command.

Her breast heaving, Fury brought up her cutlass one last time. Amalie's weapon dropped to the deck, her hand slick with her own blood. Blood streamed down her face as her mouth spewed obscenities, her bare breasts heaving with the effort it cost her to speak. Suddenly her head was jerked backward as Pilar pulled and tugged. She groped for the rail, trying to unleash the deadly talons holding her prisoner.

"No! Leave her be! *No!*" Cato cried as he skidded across the deck, still holding the vinegar cask. He slipped on the blood-slick surface and dropped the cask. Diamonds glittered ruby red as they rolled across the deck.

"Fool!" Amalie snarled—and in that moment Pilar's talons drove her over the side.

Cato's mad, glittering eyes brought Luis to his side in an instant. "Don't even think about picking up her weapon," he snarled.

With a mighty heave, Cato sailed over the railing to land in the water, searching frantically for a sign of his love. Water bubbled all about him from the cannon shot as he reached out and made contact with a pair of flailing arms.

It was over.

Fury was on her knees, her hands cradling Gaspar's head. "Please, Gaspar, don't die," she pleaded. "Not here, like this. I can't let you give up your life for me. . . . Luis, please help me," she cried, looking up. "Please! I don't care about my mother's secret; you can tell the world, if you'll only help me. He can't die. Tell me what to do, please!"

Luis dropped to his knees, his fingers gentle as he probed the bird's bony chest. When he raised his eyes he was smiling. "It's a clean wound, Fury, straight between his ribs. He won't be able to fly for a while, but he'll mend. I can fashion a dressing with some ointment to ward off infection. If we can keep him at rest, he'll live to soar through the heavens again."

Fury dropped her head in her hands and wept, great heartbreaking sobs of relief. "I didn't kill her, the impostor—she was alive when she went over the side!" she cried. Luis smiled at her outburst, knowing she was reacting with her emotions, as a typical female, now that the crisis was past.

Her eyes shimmering with tears, Fury looked up in time to see Pilar's wing tip feather out against Luis's cheek. The sight made her wail, a high keening sound.

"What is it, what's the matter?" Luis asked, touching a lock of her hair.

"They like you. Pilar does that only to me. You've stolen their affection," she moaned.

Luis chuckled. "I guess they know what a sterling person I am. I never meant you harm, I told them that; little did I know that they understood me. I will never forget the day they arrived on my ship. My crew thought me daft for changing course. I knew something was wrong and that they'd come to fetch me. Now, who is to carry this gallant bird to a clean, calm resting place?"

"I want to," Fury said softly. "He'll rest on my bunk until he's better." She bent down to pick up the injured hawk.

How gentle she was, Luis thought, watching her. It was almost impossible for him to reconcile the bloodthirsty, hard-driving combatant with this delicate young woman who would weep over an injured bird. It must be why God chose her to serve Him. His heart shattered with the thought.

"Clear these decks and scrub them till they shine!" he ordered. "Lower all jolly boats!"

"Aye, Cap'n. What's to be done with the diamonds?" Julian asked as he bent down to pick up a sparkling gem.

It was a good question, Luis thought. "What happened to the diamond merchant? Did he sail with the governors or with Dykstra?"

Julian laughed. "Neither, Cap'n. When the fight broke out he went over the side in one of the jolly boats. I saw him paddle off with my own eyes. I've been thinking about those diamonds, Cap'n. I believe they were stolen. He could have taken them with him; he knew they were in the vinegar cask. But he valued his life more than he valued his stones."

Luis nodded. "Sounds right to me, Julian. I myself had serious doubts about our cargo. Mynheer Dykstra pushed my back to the wall, and we struck a bargain. I had no other choice but to carry them on board. I guess they can be considered salvage."

"That's what we thought you'd say, Cap'n," Julian said, reaching into his pocket for a handful of the sparkling gems. "This is your share, and it'll more than make up for your lost cargoes, and your father's cargoes years ago. You could probably live the rest of your life in luxury with the remainder." He drew closer and lowered his voice. "And, Cap'n, I finally remembered what it was about the Sea Siren I wanted to tell you. She didn't kill your father, and she didn't destroy his ship. Aye, she boarded and demanded to see all our hands. But she was satisfied the man she sought was not one of our crew. The shot that was fired and sunk our ship came from a marauder that she went after. Your father toppled over the side. She tried to pull him back on board, but he was a large man, and his weight was too much for her. In my mind and fear, all I could remember was her at the rail with your father. When I saw the lass at the rail, I remembered. It's true, Cap'n, the Siren never killed for the sake of killing. And this lass has that same trait. Her secret is safe with me and this crew. No word of this will ever pass our lips."

"She was magnificent, wasn't she?" Luis said softly.

"Aye, Cap'n, magnificent she is. A man would be a fool to let such a creature escape his clutches. I saw the way she begged you to save that damn bird. There was love in her eyes, Cap'n."

"For the bird, not for me," Luis said gruffly.

"You're a fool if you believe that, beggin' your pardon, Cap'n." Julian grinned. "I know what my eyes saw. The tears were for the bird, the love was for you."

Luis shook his head. "She's going into a convent. I can't . . . she's meant for a life of—"

"The older a man gets, the more foolish he becomes," Julian said tartly. "I think I'll have the crew tidy this ship, shore her up good, and then we'll retire to the *Lady*. Tall tales and rum will be the order of the day, if you've no objection. With us out of your way, you'll have a chance to get to know the young lady before she . . . You understand, Cap'n?"

Luis grinned and winked at his first mate. "Perfectly! Her crew, are they hale and hearty? She'll want to know."

"A few minor wounds that'll be forgotten the moment they receive their pocketful of stones." He saluted smartly and turned on his heel. Luis nicked the air with the tip of his cutlass. "You're a man among men, Julian," he said lightly.

Julian turned. "All I need is a good woman who will know how to spend all my money." His delighted laugh rolled off the decks.

The *Rana* was scrubbed down with holy stones, from bow to stern, and by sundown no trace of the bloody battle remained. A pot of simmering salmagundi stood ready in the galley, compliments of Julian and the crew of the *Silver Lady*. Gaspar was resting comfortably, with Pilar standing guard.

Fury stood on the stern of the *Rana* dressed in a white muslin dress. Luis thought she looked like an angel. It was hard for him to believe she'd fought as valiantly and gallantly as any man he'd ever served with. Now he had questions to ask, questions that required answers. His stomach heaved at the thought of causing this beautiful creature even one moment of discomfort.

When the first star appeared, he fetched two cane chairs and set them side by side. Fury looked up and smiled wanly.

"A diamond for your thoughts," he teased. The rhythm of his voice remained light as he continued. "I—I need to know why you came after me. When the birds came, you weren't in danger. They were content to sail with me in the rigging. I didn't understand then, and I don't understand now."

Fury shrugged. "I can't answer for the birds. I thought they'd deserted me; they were gone so long. They'd never done anything like that before. There are times when they seem to be so attuned to me, it's almost frightening. I came after you because . . . because I wanted to warn you, to see you one last time. I suppose I wanted to say good-bye. You left so abruptly the last time I saw you. . . . I—I should apologize for my behavior when we—"

"You should do no such thing," Luis said harshly. "It's I who should apologize. I acted like an idiot. . . ." His voice softened. "And I'm most heartily sorry, Furana."

The night was coal black, sultry, and sea-scented. Overhead, a silvery moon vied with the diamond-bright stars for illumination. Fury found herself wishing for cloud cover. When the low, swirling fog drifted in from the sea, she knew her prayers had been answered. Soon the only light would come from the smoky yellow lanterns hung about the ship. She smiled in the darkness. "I accept your apology."

"You do!"

"Of course. But I also apologize for lying to you about my mother. I think you . . . deserve to know about her and why I went to the lengths I did to protect—"

"No, I don't want to hear. That's one secret that should remain a secret. I'll carry what I know to my grave," he whispered, laying a gentle finger against her lips.

"In my heart I knew you would say that," Fury murmured. "I have so little time . . . I must sail for Batavia tomorrow. Weather permitting, I shall arrive in time to . . .

But tonight—tonight is mine. There will be no prayers to ask forgiveness . . . no regrets. I want to . . . I must be certain in my own mind that I'm doing the right thing. It isn't fair to you . . . it's all I can think of to do.''

"Shhh,'' Luis said, drawing her close. "This is no time to talk.''

Fury was aware of him as never before. He was so lean and hard against her, so warm and strong. She felt his hand under her chin, gently turning her face to his as the soft gray fog obliterated the moon. His mouth was on hers, sweet and gentle. She pressed herself against him, her arms circling his broad back, her mouth trembling beneath his. She felt him growl low in his throat and knew she was responsible for the sound of pleasure. It seemed to her a tidal current rivered between them as his warm breath caressed her cheek, her neck. She regretted the fog now, wishing only to see Luis's desire for her in his eyes and for him to see her own. She felt him smile against her cheek as his hands fumbled with the buttons on her dress. Her own hands felt clumsy as she searched for the buttons on his shirt.

"I've never done this before,'' she murmured.

"I know.'' Luis chuckled deep in his throat. His voice was thick and husky, her own sounding the same. Suddenly he lost patience and ripped at her camisole. She reveled in his touch, welcomed it, demanded more, and he obeyed, his head dropping to the softness of her breasts. This was no dream, she told herself, this was what she'd dreamed of for so long; what she'd craved. She arched her back, drawing him closer.

She felt beautiful and desirable as Luis murmured her name over and over, his lips trailing down, down, until they reached the flat plane of her stomach.

Their clothes lay next to them, discarded and forgotten. He was against her, the length of him. She writhed with pleasure as she pressed her body against his. He kissed her cheek, her throat, her breasts, his fiery tongue scorching her body. She felt his name escape her lips again and again as his hands reached out, circling her bare back, luxuriating in the satiny warmth of her skin. His mouth was drawn to the place where her neck joined her shoulders, and she was aware of her own shudder of delight and the anticipation that coursed through him. A tear fell from her eye and slipped down her cheek. Seeing it, Luis kissed it away, tasting the salt of it, as though it had come from the sea.

He moved just slightly from her—only far enough for his eyes to focus on her through the soft mist, needing to commit her face to memory so that she would live in him for the rest of his days. How bittersweet this love, he thought as he drew her close again.

Magic spun a web and cloaked them from the world; they were in love this night. His hands caressed down the length of her body, loving her, worshiping her. Their passion, he knew deep in his heart, was a gift from God. A gift for this night only and to be treasured unto eternity.

Fury rolled over, pulling him against her, into every curve, as she fought to keep from losing herself in the fierce, hot joy spreading throughout her body. She felt light, soft nibbles against her lips. The pressure of his lips on hers was increasingly demanding, persuasive. Her breathing became his as he explored her mouth with his probing tongue. His hands on her body were fluid, hypnotic, touching her intimately, spreading fire throughout her entire body. Her arms moved naturally to encircle his broad back. She felt his hands cradle her head as her wealth of ebony hair fell over their faces. She began to moan softly as his hands tantalized her with their gentle, sensuous caresses. The warmth of his body and the rippling muscles beneath her hands so delighted her, she crushed her lips against his, demanding he return her ardor. Her heart pounded as she heard him emit low animal groans of passion.

"I need you," he panted as his mouth came down against hers, crushing her, driving the breath from her body.

His lips were hungry, demanding that he be satisfied by her. She strained toward him, willing him to demand more of her so that she could feed his insatiable appetite. Her lips parted, and she tasted his sweetness as she felt his hands continue to explore her body. She moaned with pleasure when his fingers found the way to the soft, silky place between her thighs.

The searing heat of her desire washed everything else away. Everything was forgotten, all her promises, all her religious longings. All she wanted now was to be near him, to have him be a part of her. He whispered soft endearments that were barely audible as his lips blazed a burning trail from her mouth to her neck to her breasts, his hands tender yet searching. Nothing matters, Fury told herself as she sought his devouring lips and the delicious feel of his body next to hers. Passion rose in her in waves as she felt him stiffen against her.

"Now," he whispered huskily.

Fury gazed at him with passion-filled eyes. He wanted her, needed her as much as she wanted and needed him. God help her, she meant to have him, no matter what the cost. Her eyes flooded with tears as she nuzzled her head into the hollow of his neck.

The prick of pain as he entered her was minuscule as her overriding passions rose and fell to match the rhythm of his thrusts. Suddenly, unexpectedly, the core of her being shattered, flooding her entire body with hot, scorching release.

Spent, they lay in each other's arms. Fury sighed deeply. So this was what it was like to be a total woman, the kind of woman she'd heard whispered about at the convent school. She closed her eyes, reliving each exquisite moment of their lovemaking. How, how was she to give this up? How was she never to think of this again? Her sinful flesh had betrayed her. Could she atone? Tomorrow she would think about atonement. For now she wanted to lie in this man's arms and whisper all the words lovers whispered to one another.

They slept then, their cheeks pressed close together. Fury smiled in her sleep, her dreams sweet and gentle, and when the last tendril of fog lifted to expose the silvery moon and twinkling stars, she woke, her silky lashes fluttering against Luis's cheek.

"It's not morning yet, is it?" he whispered anxiously.

"No. The fog has lifted," Fury murmured. "Perhaps we should wish on a star. Do you think wishes come true?"

"Not this one," Luis said through clenched teeth. How many more hours, he wondered, before he would have to give her up? He didn't want this to end, not ever. How could he give her up? He wasn't made of stone; he loved this beautiful young woman. He'd proved his love, and she'd matched his ardor with her own. What was she thinking, feeling? he wondered.

"My wishes always came true before," Fury said wistfully. "Of course, I never realized as a child that my parents were responsible for making them come true. . . . I'll never forget you, Luis."

"Nor I you," Luis said, stroking her hair. "I want only your happiness, and if I'm not the person to grant you that happiness, I can at least wish you . . . You know what I'm trying to say," he said gruffly.

There was no way she could explain her feelings. She didn't understand them herself. She only knew that she would never be able to drive him from her heart. In her

dark cell at night she would think of him and in the morning she would offer prayers, asking forgiveness.

The silence between them seemed more eloquent than
words. When Luis reached down to take her hand in his,
she sighed with happiness as she felt her body being drawn
to his. She was ever aware of his leanness, his maleness.
Her flesh tingled with the contact of his. She felt her body
move into the circle of his arms as his mouth became a
part of hers, and her heart beat in a savage, untamed
rhythm. In their yearnings they strained together, mount-
ing obstacles of the flesh to marry spirit and soul, united
for eternity.

In the quiet moonlight they devoured each other with
searching, hungry lips. At last Luis tore his mouth from
hers, his breathing ragged and harsh. But it was Fury
whose sensibilities returned first, and she moved away
from him, her eyes sleepy, almost content. She moistened
her lips, and her bruised mouth tasted sweet to her tongue.

When Luis pulled her to him again, Fury responded by
crushing her mouth to his, demanding more. The banked
fires burst into flame as she felt his searching hands explore her body. His touch was scorching, searing, as her
own hands caressed his high cheekbones and luxuriated in
his lustrous raven hair. Moan after moan escaped her as
she strained against him, her mouth mingling with his, her
tongue darting to conquer his.

Luis drew in his breath at the sight of Fury's body bathed
in silvery radiance. His face was inscrutable in the ghostly
rays, but his gaze was almost tangible; she felt it reach
her, touch her, and she became aware of the all-consuming
fire that raged through her. Her body took on a will of its
own as Luis caressed and explored every inch of her. She
moved to the rhythm he initiated and felt him respond to
her in a way she had never dreamed possible. Flames
licked her body as she sought to quench the blazing in-

ferno that engulfed her. He kissed her ears, her eyes, her moistened mouth, murmuring tender words of love, his hands traveling down her lithe form, arousing, teasing her, until her breath came in short gasps and her body writhed beneath his touch.

His lips clung to hers as he pressed her down into the coarse blanket on the deck. He buried his hands in her silken hair, twining the thickness, holding her head still as he kissed her savagely. Fury strained against his muscular chest as she responded to his passion with an urgency that demanded release. He caressed her again and again, cherishing her, desiring her, imprisoning her body with his.

He felt her flesh grow warm and taut beneath him; his avid mouth worshiped her, tracing moist patterns on her creamy skin. His dark head moved lower, grazing the firmness of her belly, down to the silky smoothness between her thighs. He parted her legs with his knee and felt her respond to him, arching her back to receive him. Her parted lips were a flame that met his raging, tumultuous mouth. She welcomed him, accepted him, his hardness, his leanness, his very maleness, as he drove into her.

He lay upon her, commanding her response, and she offered it, writhing beneath him, exulting in her own femininity as she caressed his broad back and crushed her lips to his. The unquenchable heat that was soaring through her beat in her veins, threatening to crescendo into a raging inferno. The pounding of her heart thundered in her ears—or was it Luis's that beat and roared about them? Her breathing ragged, she prepared herself for him. And when at last the searing ache erupted within her, she was consumed in the explosion—a soul-shattering cataclysm that carried Luis with her over the brink.

They clung tightly to each other like children fearful of

being separated. "I'll always love you, Luis," Fury whispered.

"And I you," Luis murmured, his lips in her hair.

"It will be light soon, we have to get dressed." For the first time Fury realized that they were lying out in the open on a coarse blanket.

"Who will see us?" Luis teased.

"Those on your ship."

"She's drifted off, a good distance. But you're right, it's time to get dressed. Fury, I . . ."

"Shhh, no words, Luis, please. What we had . . . have . . . will stay with us always. It's time for you to continue with your journey home, and I must . . . continue mine. Please, flag your ship while I see to Gaspar and Pilar. Please, Luis, don't make this more difficult for me than it already is," Fury said through her tears. "Adios, my love. . . ." A moment later she was gone, down below with her protective birds.

Luis never felt so alone in his life.

"How can I live without him?" Fury demanded of Pilar, who was standing guard over her mate. "You must understand what I feel. You battled those in your way to get to Gaspar. You can't bear to be without him, I know you can't. I feel that way about Luis.

"Oh, I'm so selfish," she wept. "I want to have everything, but I can't. I'm promised to God. It's my destiny. There are no choices. Already I've betrayed my God and my faith and will spend the rest of my life atoning for my . . . last night."

Fury washed and brushed her hair, donned clean undergarments and a fresh dress. Tears filled her eyes and streamed down her cheeks. The ship was moving now, no longer drifting, which meant in a matter of minutes Luis would board the *Silver Lady*; Juli's brothers would return, and they'd change course for Batavia. She felt as though her heart had been ripped from her chest.

The moment she heard Juli's brothers on board, she wiped away her tears and ran up onto the deck, racing to the stern. Hair billowing behind her, she waved once, twice . . . and then once again as the man on the stern of the *Silver Lady* saluted her in return.

When the *Rana* was safe in her berth at the cove, Fury, drawn and haggard, issued her last orders. "Clean this ship from top to bottom, see that her repairs are first rate, scour the decks one last time with holy stones, and repaint the ship. Fix her right name on the bow. Last but not least, fashion a litter for Gaspar and I'll carry him to the casa. Adios, my friends. I'll tell Juli you're well."

The brothers banded together and stared at their captain. The eldest spoke, his voice gruff yet gentle. "We know it's not our place, but the Spaniard loves you very much. If you let him go now, he'll never be the man he's destined to be, just as you will never be the woman you are destined to be. Your life will be a world of holy words without meaning." He glanced at the others, then down at his feet. "That's all we have to say, Capitana. . . . Oh, yes, one last thing. Give these to our sister, one from each of us."

Fury accepted the handful of brilliant gems and did her best to smile. "I want the mouth of the river blocked once the ship is secure," she said. "Can you do that for me?"

"Aye, Capitana. We'll send word when it's sealed. Adios."

"Adios," Fury whispered.

It was done.

"You look like death!" Juli grumbled as she ushered Fury up the stairs to her room. "Fetch up the hot water!" she ordered one of the maids.

Fury grimaced. "I know what I look like, Juli. I don't need you to remind me."

"Tomorrow—"

"I know what tomorrow is," Fury snapped. "I'll be ready. Has Father Sebastian been here? Is he going to accompany me?"

Juli nodded. "He doesn't want to, but he will. It's a mistake. Everyone but you knows it's a mistake, and still you persist in this foolishness. You aren't meant to enter that damn convent!" She grumbled as pail after pail of water was poured into the tub.

"I'm committed to God—you can't change that with words!" Fury cried. "Now I don't want to talk about this ever again. Do you hear me?"

"Everyone in the casa can hear you," Juli retorted. "Tell me something, Miss Fury, have you given any thought to the fact that you could be . . . *enceinte*?"

Fury turned slowly to stare at the matronly housekeeper. "What did you say?"

"You heard me. Those things happen when a man and a woman . . . You should think about *that* before you enter the convent, or you will shame everyone—your parents, those good, holy women, and yourself."

Fury sat down in the tub with a loud splash. She cursed then, long and loud.

Juli covered her ears and turned so Fury wouldn't see her smile. "Where did you learn such words? Not from *my* brothers! Although," she added thoughtfully, "I seem to recall your mother using those very same words whenever your father angered her." She chuckled. "Your God will never forgive you."

"As of this minute, Juli, you are no longer in my employ. Take your damn diamonds and go away. Go to Aldo—or go to hell! I don't care. With those jewels you can live in splendor for the rest of your life! . . . What are you waiting for?''

"Your apology and then I'll go. You see, you're upset, and the only reason you're upset is because of Señor Domingo. You know what you're planning is wrong, yet you're still going to go through with it. You lack the courage to admit you made a mistake. You should never have let him go; now you'll never see him again. He could be killed at sea by other marauders, have you given that any thought?''

Fury's eyes filled with tears. "I want to be alone, Juli, please, leave me to my misery. And yes, I'm sorry for what I said. You can stay on here if you like.''

After Juli left, Fury sat in the tub until her skin puckered. Then she crawled into her bed, pulling the light coverlet up to her chin. Through the window she could see Gaspar in his litter in the sun, Pilar perched nearby. A happy ending for everyone but her and Luis.

She beat her fists into the pillows, tears of self-pity drenching the lacy covering. Eventually she slept, but it was a sleep invaded by dark dreams of a squawling baby in her cell at the convent, begging for wholesome food and sunlight. She woke exhausted, with dark shadows under her eyes that no amount of powder could cover.

As she dressed she found herself wondering if she really could be pregnant. It simply wasn't possible, she thought. She was obeying her calling, her destiny was preordained. Her sins of the flesh would be obliterated. God was all-forgiving. She would serve Him for the rest of her life.

Father Sebastian was downstairs; she could hear his voice, subdued yet anxious. Juli would be telling him all the details of her sea voyage, possibly even the intimate details she thought she knew. Fury's face burned as she remembered the things she'd done, the emotions she'd felt. Perhaps she should make a confession before she left for the convent. Her heart thudded at saying the words aloud to the priest. No, she would wait and make her confession at the convent.

"Damn!" she muttered. She should enter the convent free of sin, pure and holy. She was none of those things. "Please, give me some sign that You want me," she whispered. "I will honor my commitment to You, Holy Father, if this is what I'm supposed to do."

She walked out to the balcony to say a last good-bye to the hawks. They were quiet, too quiet, she thought as she stroked them. They know where I'm going. They know they'll never see me again.

"When Gaspar is well, I want you to find Luis and stay with him," she told Pilar. "He'll take care of you, I know he will." She sobbed then, hard sounds of pure grief that neither bird appeared to acknowledge. Pilar's glittering eyes remained on Gaspar, whose own shiny dark eyes remained closed. "Good-bye, my friends," she whispered, and ran from the room, her satchel bobbing against her legs.

Pilar's diamond-bright eyes followed Fury until she was out of sight. Gaspar's eyes snapped open, and he struggled to raise himself but felt Pilar's wings pressing him back down on his bed. She flapped her wings, admonishing her mate to remain where he was, before she spiraled upward and out through the open French doors that led to the balcony. Instead of following the priest's wagon, the hawk flew toward port and then out to sea.

It was hours before Pilar spied the ship she was searching for. She circled in a pattern that only she and Gaspar knew before plunging downward to land next to Luis on the stern. He showed no surprise at her arrival. Pilar watched him intently, waiting for him to speak.

"I can't let her go," he said hoarsely. "I have to try to make her see it's me she needs. I'm not going to ask her to forsake God. I'll beg if I have to. I told her I loved her, but I didn't tell her how much. I had to come back to tell her I can't live without her. Once she walks through the gates, there is no turning back. But I can't make this ship go any faster, and the wind is dying. I need more time, hours at least. There's no way I can make it in time, I know that, but I have no choice. I must try." He looked at Pilar and slowly shook his head. "Why am I telling you all this? You can't possibly understand what I'm thinking and feeling."

Pilar gave a piercing cry as she spiraled straight up over his head. Luis watched until the hawk was out of sight. He cursed at the sea, his ship, and the dying wind. He knew he was torturing himself by continuing, but he couldn't live if he didn't at least try to convince Fury that he could make her happy.

"We're picking up a stiff breeze, Cap'n," Julian called to him. "A storm is following us. If we can outrace it, we'll make ten knots and be in port by sundown."

Luis raised his eyes, convinced he would see Pilar hovering overhead. Instead, a bolt of lightning raced across the sky, followed by thunder that deafened him.

"Thank You," he whispered.

The sun was merciless, Fury reflected as she shifted her parasol to offer shade to the priest at her side. They'd said little to each other, but she knew he was aware that she'd been crying. Now, though, her eyes were dry, all her tears shed. She was resigned to her fate, her destiny. She wouldn't dwell on the fact that this should be the happiest day of her life.

"Oh, no," she exclaimed suddenly as she was jolted from her seat in the priest's wagon. "Father, the wheel's come off!"

"So it has," Father Sebastian muttered. He reined in the horse and offered the reins to Fury while he climbed from the wagon. He lowered his head, his wide pancake hat shielding the smile that tugged at the corners of his mouth.

A moment later he threw up his hands in a helpless gesture. "The wheel's cracked. I suppose it was bound to happen sooner or later."

"Can't you fix it?" Fury asked.

"Child, it's split in two. See for yourself." It hadn't been easy to replace his original wheel; the blacksmith had looked at him suspiciously when he'd insisted on the cracked one.

"We'll have to walk," Fury said firmly.

"In this blistering heat!" the holy man cried incredulously.

"We were riding in this heat; walking will make no difference except to our legs," Fury pointed out. "If you prefer, I can make my way alone. There's no need for you to accompany me."

As stubborn and strong-willed as her mother, Father Sebastian thought. "You won't arrive in time, Furana. The Mother Superior will not open the gates after dark. Even if you ran all the way, I doubt you could arrive in time."

"I'll take the horse, then," Fury said desperately. "If you wait for the sun to set and walk slowly, Father, you can make it back to the casa. But this is my last chance, I must take it. Please, say you understand."

"Oh, I understand," the priest said, nodding. "I hope *you* understand that this is an old horse. There's no speed or adventure left in him."

"I have to try," Fury said through clenched teeth. "I'll leave you the food and water and my parasol."

A moment later she was on the horse's broad back, urging him forward. The animal moved off so slowly, she wanted to scream. An hour later she was convinced she would make better time if she walked. She dismounted and smacked the horse's flanks, watching him clop off in the direction from which he'd come.

Fury trudged on, her rosary in one hand, her satchel in the other. For hours she limped along, every bone in her body protesting the abuse she was inflicting upon it.

Shortly before sundown she saw the imposing convent in the distance. Her heart thudded as she glanced up at the setting sun. She had several miles yet to go, and most, if not all, of her energy was depleted. She dropped her satchel and kept on walking. She'd come into the world with nothing, and she would leave it the same way. She prayed for the energy to continue. The moment she finished her prayer, she felt a sudden burst of energy and ran as fast as her legs would carry her. She would arrive in time. Darkness had not yet cloaked the outside world.

She could see the habits of the nuns as they walked from the convent courtyard toward the gates. In minutes she would be able to see their faces clearly. She ran faster, the heels of her shoes leaving clumps of earth in their wake. On and on she ran, her breathing ragged, her lungs burning. She could see their faces now, so serene and peaceful-looking, their dark habits so protective. One of the nuns carried a lantern, the other a huge brass key. Another minute and she would be there, she thought exultantly. Despite everything, she'd actually arrived in time. It was meant to be.

In the near darkness she heard a sudden rush overhead. She ran faster, her heart thundering in her chest. The nun's lantern light was so close, she could see Pilar clearly as she sailed downward in her own draft to fall at Fury's feet with a soft thump.

Fury heard the key clank into the iron gate's monstrous lock as she dropped to her knees. She stared at the nuns for a moment before her eyes lowered to Pilar. From somewhere far off she thought she heard the sound of hoofbeats. Father Sebastian, she thought; he must have found a way to make the old horse pick up his feet and actually move. They were looking at her. She could feel their eyes on her, but hers were on her faithful friend. "She's hurt, may I bring her inside?" she pleaded.

"No, child, the bird belongs to the outside world," the oldest of the nuns said gently. "Come, it's time."

"I can't leave her, she's hurt. She'll die if I leave her here. Father Sebastian won't know what to do for her. She doesn't know him," Fury pleaded. "Please, just until she's—"

"No, child."

Fury sobbed. "But Pilar is one of God's creatures. How can you turn your back on—" They were closing the gates. She could hear the rusty sound of the old hinges in the darkening night. "Wait!" she screamed.

Luis watched from a distance, his heart in his mouth, waiting for the girl's decision.

"If you can't leave your worldly possessions and . . . friends behind, child, there is no place beyond these gates for you," said the old nun.

"I won't leave her behind. The God I pray to would never forgive me if I . . ." The sound of the key in the lock was so loud in Fury's ears, she thought she would faint. "You're right, Sisters, I don't belong behind these gates," she called to the retreating nuns.

Pilar was on her feet in an instant, strutting about Fury, her wings fluttering softly in the darkness. Fury sank down beside her, stunned. "You tricked me," she said slowly. "You weren't hurt at all. Why, why did you . . . come here, you wonderful friend." She sat cross-legged in front of the convent gates, cradling Pilar, something the hawk had never allowed before. She lost all sense of time as she sat in the moonlight contemplating her future. Luis would be part of it—if she cared to return to Spain. Her heart fluttered at the thought of living without the handsome Spaniard. It might be years before she saw him again. What a fool she'd been. She should have listened to her heart. God in His infinite wisdom had shown her the destiny that was to be hers.

"It's time to go home, Pilar," she murmured. "Gaspar is waiting for you. I'll find my way, have no fear. Somewhere out there in the darkness Father Sebastian is waiting." She clapped her hands, a signal for Pilar to take wing. "Tell Gaspar I'll be along shortly," she called happily as she strode off into the darkness.

"I have this fine steed, Miss van der Rhys. He has a broad back and can carry the both of us with ease, if you have a mind to join me, that is," Luis said huskily.

"Luis!" Fury cried, running to him. "How did you . . . Why . . . Oh, I don't care how it happened. I'm so . . . You must have ridden like the wind . . . did you?"

"Don't you ever finish a sentence?" Luis laughed as he slid from the horse to take her in his arms.

"Only short ones. I love you," she murmured against his broad chest.

"And I love you," he said, stroking her hair. "I told myself I wouldn't interfere, that I would abide by your decision. I thought I would die when I heard those gates creak open. And when they closed I wanted to . . . do what I'm going to do now," he said, and brought his lips down on hers.

Hovering in a circle overhead, outlined by the moon, Pilar voiced her approval before streaking off to her mate. "Hawhawhawhaw!"

Epilogue

Saianha: Two years later

The bone-thin woman swathed in snowy blankets on the veranda stared straight ahead. Her face was heavily scarred, and small patches on her head were shiny where new hair refused to grow. She was ugly now, shriveled and skeletal in appearance. She didn't speak and had to be spoon-fed. She never turned her head to see the splendor of her house, so lovingly restored by Cato with the handful of diamonds he'd taken from the vinegar cask.

Cato was in her line of vision, but Amalie gave no sign that she was aware of him. Soon there would be a fresh vase of flowers next to her chair—flowers she neither saw nor smelled.

Amalie Suub Alvarez existed; she no longer lived.

"You said you were going to open the trunk today, Cato," Clara said anxiously. "You said when the plantation was restored to its original splendor you would open it for Amalie. I had the servants bring it to the veranda. Perhaps the contents will evoke some response in her. Shall we do it now?" she asked as she linked her arm with Cato's.

Clara was heavy with child, his child. His prince or princess, he thought happily. "Yes, let's open it now," he said, helping his wife up the wide veranda steps.

The trunk was old, the makeshift lock older and made to last an eternity, Cato thought as he pounded at it with an iron bar. He looked at Amalie to see if there was any sign of recognition. She continued to stare ahead, her gaze unblinking. It took both Cato and Clara to lift the heavy lid.

"My God!" Cato whispered as he stared down at a king's ransom in jewels and gold coins. He filled his hands and offered them to Amalie. "It was all for nothing, Amalie," he cried. "You were richer than any queen and you didn't know it. You could be wearing these now, dressed in the finest gowns. You would truly be a queen. It was all for nothing." His shoulders slumped when he remembered the back breaking months and years of work it took to bring all the pillaged booty from the caves back to Amalie's kingdom.

Amalie's black eyes glittered malevolently as she stared at Cato's hands. His head was bowed, his eyes downcast, when she brought both of her clenched fists down on his neck. He died instantly.

Stunned, Clara could only stare at her husband's body with fear-filled eyes. She never saw Amalie's foot about to strike her in the throat until it was too late.

Cato's child was born within the hour, a handsome blond-haired male child.

"You will be king," Amalie proclaimed, her mad eyes devouring the child. "All these riches will be yours. I will be your queen!" Her shrill, evil laughter wafted through the trees, carrying to the four corners of her plantation.

There was none who voiced an objection to her proclamation.

"Long live the queen!" she cackled.

Casey held her breath as she walked through the double doors of the elegant Tu Do Street Princess Hotel in downtown Saigon. The cool air blasted her. The small suitcase she carried with the blue dress inside was a child's case. It was bright red with a colorful picture of Mickey Mouse on the front and brought smiles to the faces in the lobby. She felt silly, but exhilarated, a megawatt smile on her face.

She saw him then. He was getting to his feet, but he was moving slowly as though he were afraid. His eyelashes were still incredibly long. He was as tanned as she was. And then she saw his smile, saw the warmth in his eyes. "You made it," he said hoarsely.

"I would have walked," Casey said simply.

"Me, too." Mac grinned.

"Have you been waiting long?"

"All of my life," he said.

"Me, too."

"I only have eight hours left," Mac said.

"I have seven."

He was dressed in clean jungle fatigues. She couldn't wear the blue dress after all, it was too fancy. Her heart thumped. "I can be ready in fifteen minutes," she said breathlessly.

"I can carry your bag to the room," Mac said in a strange voice he barely recognized as his own. "I'll come back down here to wait for you," he added hastily. "You look just the way I remember."

"You do, too. I told everyone about your long eyelashes. I didn't think we'd ever . . . what I mean is I hoped, but . . . the pilots, they're just super. If it wasn't for them, I wouldn't be here."

"Thank God for the Bamboo Pipeline," Mac said, handing her the Mickey Mouse bag he'd been carrying. He shuffled his feet. "The shower is great. Don't take too long, Casey."

"I won't. Wait for me." She smiled.

"You bet. Fifteen minutes."

He walked on air. He felt the same way. She was the same. Everything was the same as it had been in San Francisco. The only difference was they were half a world away from California. He shivered, a delicious feeling of triumph coursing through him. *They* were the same. Casey thought so, too, he could see it in her face.

God, she was beautiful, just the way he remembered. Her hair, bleached almost white from the sun, was like a nimbus around her head. He liked it piled up with all the wispy curls about her face. He literally danced his way to the elevator so he could touch her the moment she stepped through the door.

What would they do, where would they go? He'd have to ask her what she wanted to do. If it was left up to him, he'd take her to the fanciest restaurant in town and stare at her for seven straight hours. He'd hold her hand, smile, and they'd talk the way they had the last time. "You lucky bastard," he said to himself.

The moment Casey stepped into the lobby Mac swept her up in the air. "I had to do that." He grinned. Casey laughed, a delightful trilling sound. "What shall we do?" he asked.

"I have this list. . . ."

"I do, too," Mac said, waving a crumpled piece of paper under her nose. "Let's get the shopping out of the way. Then, I want to be alone with you, just the two of us, so I'd suggest the Zoo and Botanical Gardens. It's a weekday and there won't be many people there. And, it's safe. Of course, first we have to eat. . . . The time will go by so fast we . . ."

"I know, so let's not waste time. I also have to drop a letter off at my roommate's parents' house. It's only two streets away from the hotel, so we can walk. Hurry, Mac, let's get all the chores out of the way." She couldn't believe she was being so bold. She linked her arm with his.

"You look lovely," Mac said. "That's a pretty dress."

She told him about the dress her friend in Paris had sent and how she'd planned to wear it until she saw his fatigues.

"You should have worn it. Blue's my favorite color. Sorry I screwed up."

"Next time, when we have more time."

On the walk to Lily's house, Mac said, "The chopper pilots told me about you nurses and how hard it is on you. They say all you nurses should get medals. How do you do it? I see death, but not the way you do. I don't understand how you can . . ."

"We make a difference. In the beginning it was . . . a nightmare. After a while you sort of get numb. You do what you're trained to do. You do the best you can. For a while we were working with outdated penicillin. There are days when

I think it's all a bad dream and I'll wake up in my own bed. But it's *real*, so real I constantly find myself questioning my own ability, my training. How do you handle what you're doing?''

"For a while I didn't think I would be able to cut it. Sitting behind a desk in the Pentagon did nothing to prepare me. Like you, I've been doing my best. I've lost some men. I've learned to hate. I don't know if that's good or bad. The hate has kept me alive.''

"It's a pretty house,'' Casey said, pulling on the bell outside the walled garden. "We have houses like this in the south of France. We call them villas. I think it looks a little like the mission houses in California.''

"Are you sure this is the place?''

Casey nodded.

"Do they speak English?''

"A little. Lily said I should hand them the letter and smile. This must be her mother. Oh, Mac, isn't she pretty? That's an *ao-dai* she's wearing. She's so tiny. It all looks so normal.'' Tears momentarily blurred Casey's eyes when she said, "From Lily.'' The porcelain doll that was Lily's mother repeated her daughter's name in Vietnamese and smiled. Casey smiled, too, and handed over the letter. The Vietnamese woman bowed low. Casey bowed, so did Mac. Casey leaned closer to the grilled fence. She touched her finger to her lips, said "From Lily,'' then placed them gently on the little woman's cheek. She touched her lips a second time, "For papa-san.''

"Please wait one moment,'' the little Vietnamese said softly. Moments later she was back at the ornate fence offering a small package to Casey.

Tears shimmered in Casey's eyes when she unwrapped a delicate, gold filagree bracelet. "Thank you. I'll tell Lily you are well.''

After more bows of farewell, Mac said, "Okay, Casey

Adams, we have five hours and fifteen minutes left. What shall we do?''

"Why don't we go back to the hotel dining room where it's cool."

"That's about the best idea I've heard today," Mac said. "We can kill two birds with one stone. We can eat, and I can look at you. I've thought about you every day. Even when my head was full of . . . other things, you managed to sneak in. I can't believe we only have a few hours."

"They'll go by so quickly," Casey said sadly. "Our visit will be over just as it's getting started."

He was holding her hand across a linen-draped table. "I've made it my business to find every Bird Dog pilot and every chopper pilot in Vietnam. I've sent word out on the Bamboo Pipeline that you and I are engaged. They'll carry our messages back and forth. It's done all the time. I think we'll be seeing more of each other. Forget this Saigon bit for now. Besides, its too difficult to arrange transportation. We'll meet in other places so we don't waste time. That's if you're willing to give up dry beds and air-conditioning."

Casey laughed. "I'm not going to sleep in that dry bed. And anyway, I'm getting used to the heat and the humidity, something I never thought would happen."

He realized he was holding his breath, waiting for her reply. What she'd said wasn't what he was hoping to hear. Then, a moment later, she said, "Engaged!" and he let his breath out in a soft *swoosh*. Her face turned pink. She lowered her blue eyes, but he could see a small smile start to form at the corners of her mouth.

"Does it upset you? It was the only thing I could think of. Everyone seems willing to promote a romance over here. I can rescind the order," he said, biting down on his lower lip.

"No, no, it's fine. It's rather amusing. I agree." She chuckled warmly.

"Good. Here," he said, withdrawing a small package from his lower front jacket pocket. "I picked this up from a vendor. It's a sort of engagement ring and cost $7.95 American." He was laughing and so was she when he slipped the gaudy, tacky ring on her finger.

"Will it make my finger turn green?"

"Your finger will probably fall off." Mac threw back his head and laughed deeply.

Casey thought the sound was the most wonderful she'd ever heard. She was aware the other diners were watching with amused smiles. Everyone, she thought, loved lovers.

"Tell me everything about yourself—from the day you were born," Mac said huskily.

She told him. Everything. "Your turn." She smiled.

Mac felt something squeeze his heart. Of course she would want to know everything about him. He knew in his gut she wouldn't understand about Alice. Casey would want to believe him, but in the end she'd get up, smile down at him, and say good-bye. In later years, when he thought about her, he'd remember that she walked out on him in a hotel in Saigon. As soon as possible he was going to write to a lawyer he knew in New York City and tell him . . . tell him to file for a divorce. He wasn't going to cheat this girl sitting across from him. He wasn't going to tell any deliberate lies, either. He just wouldn't mention Alice until the paperwork was in order. Bullshit, letters took too long. Later, before it was time to return to the Tan Son Nhut Airbase, he would excuse himself and see if he could get a call through to the States. The decision made, he felt better. He started to talk. For the first time in his life he was telling *everything* about his life to someone, everything that was in his heart.

Casey said softly, "Marriage for me is forever and ever.

I want to have a wonderful life, because I didn't have a wonderful childhood. When and if I get married, I want my children to be loved by me and their father. I want us both to sit by their beds when they're sick. I want both of us to take them on picnics. I want a close, loving family. I don't care if we're poor as long as we have love. A pet, too. A big, shaggy dog who will love and protect the little ones and be protective of us as well. A little house, a charming house I can decorate with a fence around the yard and all kinds of flowers. The impossible dream. Someday," she said wistfully.

It would never work with this man, she thought. He came from a wealthy family with oodles and oodles of money. His servants would live in the kind of house she described. Servants felt the way she did, not rich, powerful people. She was suddenly embarrassed. She raised her eyes defiantly, daring him to make fun of her. The look she saw in his eyes stunned her.

"Jesus, that's all I ever wanted myself," he said. "Two dogs, though. I want a swing on the front porch and a back porch where you can eat on a real picnic table, food you can eat with your fingers. I never gave a crap about that shiny glassware and six rows of forks. Paper napkins are just as good as linen. I want to eat breakfast in the kitchen with those dogs begging for bits of bacon. I want to live on a budget, to plan a vacation for months. I want the whole ball of wax."

"Then why don't you have all that?" Casey asked, her eyes intent.

"Because . . . I hate going up against my father. I hate to see the disappointment in his eyes when he looks at me. You see, I don't like my father. Maybe I hate him, and that makes me feel guilty. I came over here to get myself together, so when I go back I can do what I please, when I please." His voice turned urgent when he asked, "Do you like to walk in the rain? I mean really walk, without an umbrella, or don't you like to get your hair mussed.''

"I love walking in a spring rain. My hair is curly, so it doesn't matter to me. I don't even own an umbrella. Do you like to walk in the leaves in autumn and smell those same leaves burning?''

"Autumn is my favorite time of year. When I was a kid I always wanted to steal a pumpkin and carve it out myself. I think I wanted to be Tom Sawyer and Huckleberry Finn all rolled into one. The cook always bought the pumpkin, and the gardener carved it. I wasn't allowed to light the candle either, and it stayed in the kitchen window, so no one got to see it. I never even got to go trick or treating. Hell, I missed half my life now that I think about it. Listen, we're getting morbid here, let's talk about something else. Us.''

Casey smiled. She didn't mean to give voice to the thought in her mind when she said, ''I thought most men were married at your age.'' The absolute, totally blank look on Mac's face confused her. He was being so open, so confiding. She blinked. Perhaps he had been involved with someone at one time and it hadn't worked out. ''I'm sorry, I shouldn't have said that.''

"No problem,'' Mac said tightly. She looked like a daffodil in her yellow dress. He thought of fresh churned butter, not that he'd ever seen fresh churned butter, but he had read the term and fixed a picture in his mind of a mound of pure yellow, like fresh gold. She was slim, willowy, with tanned legs and arms. She also had goose bumps on her arms from the air-conditioning. She must be freezing, he thought when he realized he, too, was cold. Maybe, like himself, she hadn't wanted to disturb their confiding moments.

"Listen, honey, it's freezing in here. Let's go outside where we have to fight the heat to get our breath.'' He peeled off some bills and handed them to the head waiter who bowed, smiled, and bowed again.

"I'm going to buy a blanket," Mac said, "and we're going to the Zoo where we can sit and look at each other. If I can find some peanuts, I'll buy them, too. Are you game, Casey?"

"This heat feels delicious. Yes, I am game. Another hour in that restaurant and I would have gotten frostbite."

"We have three hours," Mac said, when they got to the Zoo. He spread the blanket under a leafy tree. "I haven't even kissed you. In my dreams I've kissed you a thousand times. In my daydreams I've kissed you two thousand times. I think you're supposed to say something before I make a fool of myself."

Casey looked around. "I don't see anything here that can stop you. I'm certainly willing. If you hadn't brought the matter up, I meant to."

"Ahh, a forward wench. Come here," he said huskily.

She was standing in his arms, staring deeply into his eyes. What she saw there allowed her to close her own eyes and give in to the moment she'd hungered for all these months.

Their lips met and whispered sweetly against each other. Her lips parted to feel his tongue in the warm recesses of her mouth. She felt dizzy, faint, never wanting what she was feeling to stop. She clung to him, pressing herself against the length of him, her arms locking fiercely around his broad shoulders. They swayed, seared together, in the hot, humid air, neither willing to be the first to move. She heard him murmur her name, felt him run his fingers through her hair. She tried to move closer, to melt into him until she thought she couldn't bear it a moment longer. She moved then, stepping away from him, her eyes dreamy and glistening.

When she stumbled, Mac held her in his strong grip,

gently lowering her to the shell-pink blanket on the ground. His eyes, Casey saw, were warm and soft and full of . . . love, or was it lust?

She almost fainted a moment later when Mac reached for both her hands. "I think I'm falling in love with you," he whispered hoarsely.

Casey licked at her dry lips. She felt the same way, but her inexperience with love only allowed her to nod. She didn't trust herself to speak. She wanted to, tried to. Tears gathered in her eyes. She fell against him, crying into his shoulder. She nuzzled, feeling more contented and safe than she'd ever felt in her life. He was cradling her, murmuring soft words she couldn't understand, and it didn't matter. Finally, hiccuping, she said, "I have never felt this way before. I don't want to leave. I don't want to go back. I want to stay here with you." She was blubbering, acting like a sixteen-year-old. She said so, to her own dismay.

Mac held her away from him for the barest second before he brought her close to him. "Would it surprise you to know I feel exactly the same way? We have the rest of our lives. This is just a moment, a slice of time we have to get through until we can leave this place and move into that little house with a front and back porch. What do you think we should call the dogs?"

Casey bolted from his arms. "But that . . . that means . . ."

"What that means is you'll have to marry me, because I have no intention of living in sin behind a picket fence. My God, what would those dogs think?"

"Who cares what they think. You hardly know me," she croaked.

"I know everything I need to know. I found you. That's all that's important to me. Besides," he said lightly, "we're engaged."

Casey wiggled her finger. "I thought it was a joke," she whispered.

"Back there it was. I had to make a joke out of it so you wouldn't see how devastated I was if you'd handed it back to me. I guess you can say I'm a coward."

"We haven't slept together," Casey blurted.

Mac grinned. "A small matter that can be rectified in a moment. Next time."

"Are we sure there will be a next time?" She snuggled against him, content with all she was hearing. God, wait till she told Lily.

"Damn right there will be a next time and a time after that. As often as I can I'll see you."

She sighed happily. "Promise me one thing, Mac."

"I'll promise anything, just tell me what it is you want."

"Just promise me honesty. If you can do that, then we can have a wonderful life together."

At that moment Mac would have promised to gift wrap the moon and sprinkle the package with stars. He promised. He believed implicitly that he wasn't lying. He held her closer, burying his chin in her sweet-smelling hair.

He wanted to take her back to the hotel and make love to her, but the hands on his watch signaled danger. He told her so.

"Next time," she whispered. "I guess I should tell you now that I'm a virgin."

Mac pretended mock alarm. "No!"

Crushed by his response, she said, "Does it make a difference?"

"Not to me, it doesn't. But if you weren't, it wouldn't make a difference either. Before, when I told you I thought I was falling in love with you . . . that wasn't quite true. I fell in love with you in San Francisco. When it comes to women I'm afraid I don't know too much about the way they react to certain things. I guess you could say I was feeling my way, hoping you felt the same. Do you?" he asked boyishly.

"Oh, yes," Casey sighed happily.

"Will you wear the blue dress next time?"

She nodded, burrowing into the crook of his arm.

"Then it's settled," Mac said exuberantly. "We're in love. It's official!"

Casey laughed. "I've never been in love before. It's wonderful!"

"I haven't either!" It was true, he'd never been in love the way he was in love with this beautiful girl. Now, finally, at long last, he had someone to call his own. Someone who loved him, who wanted the same things from life that he wanted. There was no way in hell he was going to even *think* about his wife now.

They snuggled on the blanket, their cheeks brushing. They talked in soft whispers about the future and the remainder of their tours in Southeast Asia.

When it was time to leave Mac couldn't find the words. He held his wrist out so she could see the luminous hands. Her shoulders slumped, as did his. They were like two beaten, tired warriors when they left the Zoo, the soft pink blanket under Mac's arm.

"Do you mind if we stop at the hotel before we head out to Tan Son Nhut? I want to see if I can get a call through to the States."

"Not at all. I have to get my bag anyway."

Fifteen minutes later Mac saw Casey get off the elevator in the hotel lobby. He spoke hurriedly into the receiver. "Listen, Miss, I'm calling from Vietnam, interrupt Stewart. What do you mean, you can't interrupt him? I'm his client, too," he said angrily. He listened a moment. "Okay, then take down this message and repeat it back to me verbatim." He was listening to the tail end of his message when Casey approached him. She winked at him. In his life no girl had ever winked at him. He felt himself grow light-headed. "Tell Stew to call Benny if there's a problem."

Mac grinned sheepishly at Casey. "People—" he'd almost said lawyers—"don't like to accept calls from Asia. I think it's hilarious myself."

"I do, too. It's amazing that you got through at all. Are you ready?"

"No. Are you?"

"No, but we have to leave."

He took her in his arms and kissed her again, a long, lingering kiss that spoke of the future.

At Tan Son Nhut, Casey's windowless, patched-up C-130 set down. She tossed the Mickey Mouse bag into the yawning opening in the back of the plane. With ease Mac lifted her onto the cargo ramp.

The plane's engines wheezed and sputtered. "You didn't tell me what you wanted to call your dog," shouted Mac.

As the hydraulic ramp lifted with a loud whine, and the wind whipped at her hair, Casey yellled at the top of her lungs, "Fred. What are you going to call yours?"

"Gus," Mac bellowed. The ramp slammed shut and the plane taxied off. He waved frantically. Then Mac checked into the Aviation Company's flight operations office. Fifteen minutes later he boarded a Huey helicopter. He was airborne almost instantly.

Even though they were going in separate directions, they were doing what they'd come to do, trying to make a difference. But they'd also found the love that had eluded them all their lives.